WHEN IT RAINS

A Menage A Trois Love Story

KITTY COX

Spotted Horse Productions

Cover Art by Spotted Horse Productions

Edited by Sarah Williams

TRIGGER WARNING: This story is about recovery and contains scenes of domestic violence and animals used as leverage. Also has references to human trafficking and plenty of shelter dogs with rough pasts.

This is a love story, but finding love isn't always easy.

～

The National Domestic Violence Hotline (www. TheHotline.org) is a 24/7 confidential service for survivors, victims and those affected by domestic violence, intimate partner violence and relationship abuse. The Hotline advocates are available at **1-800-799-7233** (SAFE) and through online chatting at www. TheHotline.org

～

If you or someone you know needs help, but are not sure where to turn, the VictimConnect Resource Center (victimconnect.org) has combined a list that can help connect victims, survivors, and their support networks connect with local resources.
1-855-484-2846

DEDICATION

The biggest **Thank you!** *is without a doubt, directed towards my best-friend; as without her constant pushing, this book would not have been possible.*

Kitty Cop

CHAPTER ONE

*T*he rain was still light, but from the color of the clouds, it wouldn't stay that way. Bracing against the impending dampness, Brook got out of her car and rushed to get the nozzle into her gas tank. Naturally, a gust of wind chose that moment to waft under the canopy, ensuring her hair would be a mess by the time she got to work. Trying to hurry, she slid her card through the reader.

It beeped a denial.

She tried again, and again it beeped, scrolling the refusal across the LCD screen. Brook cursed under her breath and leaned back into her car for her purse. She had to have some cash in there. Rummaging frantically, with another car waiting behind her, she found three dollars. That would buy enough gas to get her to work, but probably not enough to get her home. It would have to do. She'd call Owen later and find out why her debit card had been declined. Right now, her biggest concern was running in to pay without getting soaked.

With the needle no longer on empty, but her guts twisting as if they were, she got back on the highway. It wasn't that far to the animal shelter, thankfully, and she only looked slightly frazzled. At least her little delay shouldn't make her too late.

Pulling into the employee and volunteer parking, she noticed the large black truck and groaned before she got out. Great. Not only was she five minutes late, and it was raining, but she had at least one flunky to train who would probably rather be anywhere else. Plus her boss was going to be pissed. This was the ninth time in a row she'd been late. Could her day get any worse?

She barely made it in the door before Marcy saw her. "Brook!" the woman yelled across the lobby.

She hurried over. "Sorry, Marcy. There was a line at the gas pump."

"Mhm. Do you know how many people would love this job? Plenty. And most of them could get here on time." Her boss sighed dramatically. "Remember, I'm doing this as a favor to your husband, but there's a reason we have a schedule. At least you only have one volunteer to train today."

With the flick of a broken nail, Marcy dismissed her. Brook wasn't about to complain. Evidently Owen's donations to the clinic gave her a bit of leeway. He knew how much the animals meant to her, so made a contribution for their anniversary every year. One large enough to have both their faces plastered on the summer newsletter. Brook thought it was sweet. She'd never wanted diamonds or dresses - her entire life had been about the animals -but thinking of her husband reminded her of the declined card that had to be fixed.

She was fumbling with her phone as she pushed into the back. Hopefully Owen would get the text before lunch and take care of everything. Completely distracted, she didn't see the man until her face smashed into his chest, her cell phone jabbing him solidly in the solar plexus. With a rush of air, he stepped back and chuckled. All she could do was look up in shock.

The t-shirt this guy wore had the shelter name on it, stretched tight across his broad muscles. Damn, she missed bodies like that. Never mind that she'd just run into him full force; the new guy was grinning at her like he'd just found some endangered species. For a moment, Brook's mind started peeling off his shirt before she remembered she was supposed to be very happily married - and if she said it enough, she would forget how badly she wanted to feel this guy's pecs.

"Sorry," she mumbled, trying to act like she hadn't noticed he was hot. "I didn't expect anyone to be on the other side."

He crossed his arms over his chest, proving they bulged as much as his pectorals. "Nah, that's cool. I was just trying to figure out where I'm supposed to be." His smile didn't falter at all, but his eyes roamed across her, pausing at the hand holding her phone. Her left hand. The one with the wedding ring on it. The big, impressive wedding ring her *husband* had given her.

"Community service?" she asked. At his nod, she offered her hand - the other one. "Brook Harper, kennel manager. Sorry, I'm late."

His grip was firm and polite. "Ryder. Um, they said I have forty hours. Any idea how much dog shit that is?"

Meeting these court-appointed volunteers was always a little nerve-wracking. She could never be sure if they'd be thankful for the chance to expunge their criminal record or bitter about it. This guy wasn't giving her a lot to go on except his looks. Those, she was trying to ignore. Since she had no clue what he'd done to get here, being sexy wasn't nearly enough to make her drop her guard, but he seemed nice enough.

"Couple tons, at least," she assured him. "Probably one more of cat poop. So, I'm assuming you like animals?"

His eyes flicked away then back, the movement fast enough she wondered if she'd really seen it. "Yeah. Got a weakness for dogs, ya know?"

"Oh, yeah. I think we all do." She crooked her finger, encouraging him to follow, then continued down the hall.

Ryder had to be over six feet tall and was ripped. Brook reminded herself not to look. She didn't want to give this guy the wrong impression, and everything about him screamed "player," from the too-tight shirt to the too-charming smile. Leading him toward the back, she turned a corner and stole another glimpse. Unlike most of their community service volunteers, he was still smiling. There was no grumbling or trying to convince her he shouldn't be here. No complaining about deserving a better job. Nope, he was peeking in every opening for a chance to see one of their rescues. Maybe that meant he wouldn't be too bad.

She paused at a metal door. "These are the intake kennels. Remember, most of these dogs were either strays, abused, or neglected. Many of them are terrified of people."

His smile faded. "Nah, I gotcha."

"They may bite." She looked into his eyes to make her point. They were brown. Perfectly, completely brown, just like milk chocolate. "Pet them at your own risk. These dogs are waiting for the trainer to evaluate them, so lock them in the runs, clean the kennel, then let them back in. I'll help with the first, but it gets loud in there."

"Like music to my ears," he assured her. "Lead on, boss."

She shook her head at his enthusiasm. He probably thought he'd gotten off easy. They all did - at first. Just clean some cages, and his record got wiped. Then again, he'd probably change his tune once he was soaked with water and covered in kennel mess. Volunteering at an animal shelter sounded like fun right up until they realized it meant more poop and fewer puppies.

The door was barely open before the cacophony of noise assaulted them. Deep growls, high-pitched yips, and drawn-out bays; all of the dogs knew as soon as someone was in the kennels, and did their best to beg for attention. It was so loud that Brook didn't even try to speak to her newest trainee. She just gestured toward the supply closet and pulled out the wheelbarrow. A flat shovel, a rough but wide broom, and a roll of garbage bags were stored inside. When she moved to push it, Ryder grabbed the handle, tilting his head for her to lead on. She did, snagging the end of the hose as she passed. Thankfully, the first kennel wasn't far. Her eardrums were already ringing.

It was easy work. Usually, turning on the spray nozzle sent the dog straight to the back, and a lever dropped the partition, making the front half safe to clean. Grabbing the shovel, she demonstrated where the piles went and why they kept a brush - to scrub off the remains. Finally, a blast of water left everything spotless, except the person behind it. Ryder nodded, holding the door for her to leave first, then latched it before grabbing the lever. Lifting a brow, he waited for Brook to nod. Only when she showed it was ok did he let the dog back in. A wistful smile tugged at his mouth as the fearful stray slunk closer, eyes locked on him.

Without prodding, he moved to the next. She watched, making sure he had everything down. When he finished that one perfectly, she pointed at the rest, then tried to yell over the mutts, "I'll be back in ten minutes to check on you!"

He flashed a thumbs-up but didn't slow down. Impressive. She'd see how long he lasted. As soon as he got a splash of crap in the face, he'd probably demand to be reassigned. They all did. The mental image had her laughing to herself as she headed to the next room.

This one was her problem. The dogs didn't bark as loudly because they'd been in the shelter long enough to know it didn't work. Instead, they rushed to the front of their cages, wiggling excitedly. Unfortunately, their cuteness wasn't always enough. Tall Tails operated as both the city pound and rescue, which meant euthanasia happened. Not every dog could be fixed, and there weren't enough owners for most of them. Space was limited. Never mind that a life locked in a concrete box wasn't humane. Brook walked along the rows, her eyes scanning the cards. At the bottom of each was a date in red.

Anyone with a week or less, she marked on her list. They'd run ads for them, hoping to find the dogs a wonderful home, but sadly, there just weren't enough. It seemed there were never enough open hearts willing to take on a hard-luck case. People only wanted the perfect ones, not the broken, ugly, or quirky things like the dogs that had been abandoned here. As she came down the last row, she paused. This one had three days left.

"Hey, Gummy," she crooned, kneeling to see the aged mongrel. He leaned against the chain link front, wiggling his old body, his tongue lolling out of a toothless mouth.

"Maybe we'll get you a home yet. You're such a good boy, aren't ya?"

Without hesitation, she stepped in and knelt to hug the old man. His person had passed away, leaving him neglected and too old to get adopted. Brook kept hoping, but each week, he was ignored. She'd take him home herself if her husband wouldn't lose his mind. But he would. One dog was the maximum their family could support - or so he kept saying. It didn't stop her from wishing.

But eventually, she pried herself away. There were hundreds of dogs and only one of her. She checked on her trainee, gave marketing the list of priority dogs, ordered another pallet of food, then spoke with the trainers. Running a kennel had a lot less to do with petting dogs than she wished, but at least she was helping, and it kept her from feeling useless. Like always, the day went by all too fast. Between tracking the records and arranging adoption ads, before she knew it, her shift was almost over - and Owen still hadn't gotten back to her about her little money problem.

Brook grabbed her phone and dialed her bank. When she tried to check the balance, she ended up transferred to an operator. She explained her problem and was transferred again.

"I'm sorry, Mrs. Harper. That account has been closed."

"That's impossible," Brook insisted. "When?"

"This morning, from our records. Owen Harper filed the forms. He's listed as the primary account holder."

Brook sighed deeply. "Yes. Thank you." Her next call was to her husband.

It rang three times before he picked up. "What!"

"Owen, our bank account was closed."

He grunted on his end of the line. "Yeah, I moved banks. The new one has better interest on savings."

"That's nice," Brook said, trying hard to be calm, "but I'm at work, my car's on empty, and I used the cash I had to get here."

"And?"

She wanted to ring his neck. "And I'd rather not run out of gas before I get to the house!"

"This is why I tell you to keep cash, Brook." He sounded like a parent explaining something simple to a child. "You can always call an Uber."

"No, I can't! Remember, my card isn't working, and I don't have any cash left. Can you stop by the shelter?"

"I'm in the middle of something. I won't get out of the office until nine." He huffed, obviously annoyed. "This is why I didn't want you working. I can't leave, and I hate to think of you stranded there alone."

"I'll be fine," she insisted. "I'll just... I dunno... I can borrow money from someone, or something. I just wish you'd talked to me before you did that. I look like an idiot now. My card was declined at the pump, and I'm borrowing money from people I barely know? If you'd just told me, I could have grabbed a twenty, but I don't have enough gas to get home - and it's embarrassing."

"And next time you'll know better. Look, hun', I gotta go. Client's on his way in. Love ya."

"You, too," she grumbled, hanging up.

With a deep breath, she leaned back in her chair and closed her eyes, trying to think of how she was going to make this work. As she let the air slide from her lungs, a soft tap came at the frame of her open door. She jerked up quickly, finding the new guy standing there, completely soaked. She couldn't be sure if he'd been outside in the storm or just had that much fun in the kennels.

"Everything ok?" he asked. Ryder's smile had disappeared, and that wet shirt convinced her eyes to drop to his chest for a split second.

"Yeah. You get finished?"

He shrugged. "Think so. I have a question, though. Dogs in that room, they get adopted?"

"Sometimes. We're required to keep them all for a week, so their owners have a chance to find them. After that, our trainers evaluate them. The overly aggressive or very ill are euthanized. The lucky ones are cleaned up and put up for adoption. The ones who show potential are given some training, then get the same thing."

His tongue flicked out, moistening his lips. "What about the discarded fighting dogs?"

"Usually bully breeds. All too often, pit bulls." Brook pressed her lips together and shrugged. "It's a toss-up."

"The really mangled ones?"

She shook her head, knowing who he was talking about. "Even if she does pass the behavior analysis, her chances aren't good. Vet's probably going to have to amputate that leg, and that's a lot of money that could be used to save even more lives."

He cleared his throat. "Nah, I gotcha. Still gotta take out the bags, but is there anything else you want me to do?"

She looked at the clock on the wall behind her. The guy's honest concern for the dogs made her feel a bit generous. "No. If you want to get out of here, I'll put you down for the full eight hours." It was only ten minutes early.

Those big brown eyes caught hers. "You sure, Mrs.

Harper? I can carry around some dog food or help with another kennel bank."

She shook her head. "No. Thank you, Ryder. Although, when the next pallet comes in, I might hit you up." She looked at the clock again. "I'm about to head home myself."

"Well, the offer's there." He reached into his pocket and took the last few steps to her desk. "I didn't mean to eavesdrop," he said softly, pressing something to the wood before turning and walking out.

Where his hand had been was a crisp twenty-dollar bill. It took a moment before her brain processed why he'd left it. He'd heard her on the phone with her husband. She grabbed the cash and hurried after him.

"Ryder!" she called, just loud enough to reach him. He paused, barely glancing back, so she jogged to catch up. "You didn't have to do that."

He shrugged. "Came to ask about the dog and heard you say you needed to borrow money for gas." He turned to face her. "Pretty sure working at a rescue doesn't make that much, and you can pay me back later. I'm gonna be around for a bit."

"Thank you, but - "

He stopped her. "It's twenty bucks. Not a big deal. Thinking you might get stuck out in the rain? Hearing another news story about some woman run over on the side of the road? Would rather not." Then he leaned forward, his hands lightly clasping her upper arms. "Not a big deal, Mrs. Harper."

Instinctively, she stepped back. "It's Brook."

"Brook?"

She nodded. "Short for Brooklyn. They don't call me Mrs. Harper around here." She huffed a giggle. "I don't think anyone gets to be a mister or missus in a rescue, except the adopters."

"Yeah? Works for me. And it's beautiful."

He flashed a seductive smile, then just left. Brook couldn't help it; she stood there with her mouth hanging open. Did he just flirt with her? Her! She paused to let that sink in. That man was too pretty to be real, but she could enjoy the compliment - and the view. It wasn't like being married made her blind. Then again, he had loaned her the money to get home, so he might not even mind.

Her husband, however, definitely would.

CHAPTER TWO

*R*yder's money got Brook home safely. The moment she made it inside, the sound of thumping told her Calvin needed out. The mutt wasn't impressed when he saw the rain, but it gave him a little incentive to hurry. Unfortunately, he was so excited to get back in and greet her that he didn't stop to let her clean his feet. Enthusiastically, the dog made laps around her, darting into the living room a few times just for good measure, and leaving muddy paw prints in his wake.

Of course, he aimed right for the cream-colored carpet her husband had picked out, and the dog's muddy trail wasn't subtle. For a moment, she thought about waiting for the mess to dry and then just vacuuming the dirt away, but she knew better. The mud would stain if she didn't clean it now, and with the pale carpet, that wouldn't be a small job. The one thing she didn't do was blame Calvin. How could she be mad that her dog was thrilled to see her? It wasn't his fault it was raining.

When Owen finally got home that night, she was still on her knees, scrubbing away the last of the mud. He paused just inside the front door, gave her a disgusted look, then retreated to his office. With a sigh, Brook went back to cleaning. She wasn't sure if he was simply exhausted or annoyed with the mess her dog had made. She also didn't care.

Half an hour later, he returned to stand over her. "Dinner?"

What he didn't do was ask how she got home or say anything about their last conversation. He hadn't made a single comment about the fact that she was *still* cleaning, let alone offered to help. Combined with the way he'd acted earlier, she couldn't stop the feeling of resentment. Yes, she was in a bad mood, but her husband sure wasn't helping. He had it easy. All he had to do was go to the job he was so proud of and let her handle everything else. Besides, could he not see that she was *busy?*

Brook continued to rub at the last bit of mud, seething on the inside. "Leftovers are in the fridge. I'll get something when I'm done here."

He grumbled under his breath in annoyance. "I put in twelve hours at the office today. I'd hoped that *at least* you could have dinner ready when I got home."

"You know how to work the microwave," she shot back. "Besides, I'm kinda in the middle of cleaning."

"Yeah, the mess *your* dog made. That isn't my problem."

Her fingers tightened on the rag she was using. "Oh, kinda like how me getting home isn't your problem? Or telling me that we're changing banks isn't your problem? Sorry, Owen, I was busy today trying to figure out how to get gas in my car because you went off and started doing things like the Lone Ranger, and now you think I owe you dinner? Oh, but wait! What I do isn't as important as your *job*. Well, fix your own dinner and let me know how it feels."

"I work so you can have this house!"

Brook just looked up at him coldly. "So it's my house? Just mine? Nice to know. Does that mean I get to make the decisions about who lives in it?"

"Ours," he corrected, ignoring the rest. "Brook, why don't you just quit that stupid job already? Then you wouldn't have to worry about things like this."

"Because you don't want any more dogs and I do. This is my compromise." Sponging up the last of the cleaning solution, she tossed the rag into the bucket and rocked back onto her heels. "Now, if you'll let me adopt this sweet dog from the shelter, I might consider it."

His eyes narrowed. "You know I don't like dogs. They're worse than children."

"And I do. Huh, guess that means I'll keep working." She forced herself to her feet, feeling the ache of a long day all the way down her back. "Oh, and I need twenty dollars to pay back the guy at work, cash to make sure this doesn't happen again, and a new debit card to fill my tank."

She grabbed the bucket of dirty water and headed to the kitchen, knowing Owen would follow. Lately, their spats never ended this easily. He always had to get the last word, so when he loomed behind her, she wasn't surprised at all. That he didn't say anything while she rinsed her cleaning supplies meant this was going to be one of those long and loud disagreements.

"What guy at work?" he demanded.

"Ryder. He's one of the community service volunteers. Heard me on the phone with you and loaned me the money. Since I didn't really have any other options, I didn't complain, but I'm technically his boss."

"One of the criminals?"

She wobbled her head from side to side. "Probably. Could be nothing more than a parking ticket, and I don't have access to those files, but yes. He's working there because the court ordered him to. That's why I want to get the money back to him because he won't be around for long."

Owen grabbed her arm, pulling her around to face him. "And then the next one will show up, and another after that, and you have no idea what these *people* have done. Don't that bother you at all?"

"Not really. No."

He snarled under his breath and gave her a little shake. "Brooklyn! For all you know, he could be a rapist who pled out! *This* is why I don't want you there. You should be at home, taking care of our house, not dealing with dog crap and criminals. I make enough that you don't need to put up with the headache of having a job. Besides, I like having you here when I get home. I don't know why you're so against this."

"Owen, our anniversary is on Thursday. That marks six years that we've been married, and yet you still haven't figured out that I'm not some fragile little thing who can't take care of herself?" She sighed. "Look, I know you get worried easily, but I like my job, ok? I like having a purpose of my own. The community service people are minor offenders. More graffiti and less assault cases. They're nothing to worry about."

"But you're my wife," he countered. "Mine! Don't try to make me sound stupid for wanting to take care of you."

She closed her eyes for a moment, trying to keep her

calm, but Calvin heard them. The sound of his nails on the kitchen tile made her jerk her eyes open just as Owen swiped out with a leg, encouraging the dog to go away. He didn't touch the mutt, but she wasn't completely convinced he'd missed intentionally. Calvin got the message, though, and stepped back behind the island. Around the corner, the dog looked up at her, waiting for a command to assure him it was ok to come over.

"Stay," she said, almost absentmindedly, before turning her attention back to Owen. "Look, I'm not trying to make you sound like an idiot, just overprotective, ok? I know you care. I really do. It's just that you care in the wrong places." She leaned back against the counter and crossed her arms. "I mean, didn't it bother you at all that I had no way to get home?"

"You could've called an Uber."

Exasperated, Brook threw up her arms. "No, I couldn't! What part of this is so hard to wrap your mind around? No money. The Uber account was linked to the same card you canceled! I was stuck there, at work, with those same people you *say* you're so worried about, but that didn't bother you at all?"

"I was busy!" His voice was getting louder. "I had an important client on his way, and I can't babysit your ass if you won't just stay home, Brook. I can't be everywhere and do everything. That's why you need to just listen to me more."

"And what about what I want, huh?"

Huffing out her frustration, she pushed away from the counter, intending to walk past him, but Owen wasn't done. His arm snaked out and caught her bicep, clamping down hard. When Brook tried to pull away, his fingers tightened until she was forced to look at him. Each time she tugged, his grip dug into her skin a little harder.

"You're hurting me," she hissed.

"No, you're hurting yourself." He leaned closer, right into her face. "Stop trying to make everything into a fight. Stop thinking you know so much more and just listen to me. You're so stupidly impulsive that you get caught up in the dumbest things, and I'm the only way you'll ever get out." He shook her, inadvertently making sure she could feel every bruise on her muscles. "How many men would've given you a chance, huh? Girls like you? My father said you'd be nothing but trouble, but no, I was convinced you just needed to get it out of your system. You just wanted to play the desperate little slut for a few years, then you'd settle down and act like a proper lady. Don't make me look like a fool, Brooklyn. It'll only happen once."

Finally, she tried pulling down, putting all her strength into it. His hand slipped off her arm, leaving red marks to prove he hadn't simply let go. "I didn't marry your father, Owen. I married you, and I made sure you knew the kind of woman you were getting."

"Everyone can be trained." He stepped even closer, the expression on his face making his words threatening. "If that dog can learn his place, then so can you. Don't you dare think trying to embarrass me will get you what you want."

"No? Well, when you're training me, just remember I also know how to bite." She stood tall, glaring right in his eyes. "I am not your mother. I will *never* be your mother. If what you wanted was an obedient bitch to sit down and shut up, you married the wrong girl." She lifted her chin to make the point. "Oh, and make your own damned dinner. I'm *busy*."

Shoving past him, she headed for the hall. Normally, she would've gone outside with her dog, but that wasn't an option in this weather. So she went for the next best thing: the guest bedroom. Loyally, Calvin trotted along behind her. Each step across the house, she seethed. Her day was getting worse instead of better, and she was so ready for it to be over. Between the debit card that morning, Gummy still not having a home, then the mud on the carpet, and now her husband was back on his kick about her quitting her job? It was all adding up to a pretty miserable day.

Brook thrust open the door and Calvin rushed in, hopping onto the bed with a nervous wag of his tail. Just the sight of him made her feel better. Enough that she refrained from slamming the door behind her, but as soon as it latched, the pressure of angry tears began to push at her eyes. Flopping down onto the mattress, she wrapped her arms around her dog and buried her face in his fur.

"I love you, silly mutt," she mumbled against his neck.

Thrilled with the attention, Calvin rolled onto his back and pawed at the air, coming close to hitting her arm a few times. It didn't matter. There was something about the unconditional love of a dog that could make even the worst day bearable. Just as she was starting to feel a little better, the door creaked softly open. She rolled over with a loud sigh, not surprised at all to see Owen leaning into the room.

"Hey?" he asked, his voice sounding almost apologetic.

"What?"

"Look, I'm sorry. I've just had a lot going on with work lately, and I didn't even think about how you'd end up bearing the brunt of it, ok? I should've opened the new account first so you wouldn't have to deal with those creeps, and I'm sorry."

He was trying. She could see he was trying, but he still didn't quite get it. "Why didn't you talk to me about changing banks?"

The look on his face was complete confusion. "Brook, I handle the finances. It's not something you need to worry about."

"Or my 'pretty little head' might burst?" She scrubbed at her face. "That. Sweetie, that's what bothers me. I'm supposed to be your partner, not your trophy. I don't want you to do this *for* me, but *with* me. I'm mad because you keep shutting me out and acting like I'm a child."

He nodded. "I know. I do know, but I figured you wouldn't want to worry about it. Look, we have just the one account -"

"We have six bank accounts, at least," she corrected. "Yes, it's all shared, but we also aren't living paycheck to paycheck."

"Yeah, but..."

Brook lifted a brow. "But you thought it was worth hurting me over?" She turned her arm to make the point.

"I didn't want you to walk off."

"You bruised me, Owen. I'm not a doll to be thrown around, and what am I going to say when the girls at work ask about this?"

"I know. I'm sorry." He pushed the door open a little further. "I swear it won't happen again, ok? I didn't realize how hard I was holding you, and I wasn't trying to hurt you."

She turned her attention to petting Calvin's head. Stroke by stroke, she tried to ignore the feeble excuses, because Owen *had* known he was hurting her. She'd told him. The problem was that he hadn't cared. He said he was sorry, there was a lot of stress at work, and he was just trying to take care of her. Yeah, and it sounded as empty in her mind as it did coming out of his mouth.

It also sounded like every woman's horror story, but this was *Owen*. He was a bit of a control freak, but not abusive, right? Things had just been tense lately, and they were taking it out on each other. So many little things had been piling up, and today had just tipped them both over the edge. She just had to figure out how to reconnect with the man she'd married and everything should be ok.

But in her experience, when it rained, it poured...

And there was a storm brewing.

CHAPTER THREE

*E*arly the next morning, Ryder pulled his truck into one of the tiny parking spaces and turned it off. Before getting out, he sent off a quick text to his brother. A split second later, he got a reply, reassuring him that Hunter had everything handled on his end. In other words, there was nothing to worry about, so long as he didn't screw this up.

So the moment he entered the shelter, he turned left instead of right and headed for the Executive Director's office. Like always, Marcy sat behind her cheap oak-look desk, staring at her monitor. He tapped lightly at the open door, not surprised at all when the woman's eyes wandered across his body before finally making it up to his face. That was something he was used to. Women either thought of him as a fantasy or a nightmare, and usually, the only way to tell the difference was to wait for the smile.

"Can I help you, Ryder?" she asked.

He took a step inside, watching her face closely. "Yeah, um, I was wondering about adopting a dog."

She didn't smile. "Already?"

Shoving a hand through his hair, he hoped he wasn't making a mess of this. Sadly, Marcy was giving him nothing to go on. She didn't know him so she wouldn't understand, but this wasn't about love at first sight. It was about finally being able to help someone who needed it. Ryder didn't care that the someone was fuzzy with four - possibly three - legs. Sure, he liked the puppy, but he could also be logical about this.

So he went with, "Yeah. One of the dogs that probably won't pass the eval." He took another step into the room. "You know that little bait dog in the intake kennels? Well, my brother and I kinda do a little rescuing on the side, and we think we can help her."

"The blue pit mix?" Marcy asked. "Ryder, her leg is probably broken, and we can't do anything for her legally until the end of the day."

"Yeah, and I was hoping I could take her to the vet the minute her clock runs out." Another step and he was close enough to put a business card on her desk. Hopefully, he wasn't doing something intimidating, but he never could be sure. He just really wanted this woman to approve the adoption. "That's the doctor we use. She's good, and she already knows this is going to be a big thing. It's just that Brook said the dog would probably be put to sleep, you know?"

Marcy picked up the card and read over it. "I can't guarantee she won't have aggression issues. She could be dangerous. Some of the dogs who've been through that don't adjust well to being pets."

"I know." He thought he was going to stop there, but couldn't. "She still deserves a chance, and we can get her training and everything. It's just... It's not her fault she was treated like that, and I want to fix her."

Slowly, Marcy nodded. "Ok. I've got some waivers you'll need to sign, and I'll have to call this vet and check that she's prepared for the type of procedure the dog will need, but I think we can do it. It'll be going through a loophole, unless you have a non-profit?"

"I think so. I'll have my brother email you the paperwork?"

"Perfect." She finally smiled at him, but it was the type that said he should leave. "Come back at the end of the day, and we'll finalize everything."

That was exactly what he wanted to hear. Hunter said things were set up on their end, so this shouldn't be a problem. All that was left was getting Tall Tails to release the dog so they could take care of her. Ryder backed out of the office then turned for the kennels, feeling like a little weight had been lifted from his shoulders. This would make getting arrested worth it, and he was pretty sure he hadn't scared Marcy - not positive, but pretty sure. If he had, she would've just refused him on the spot, right?

By the time he got to the kennels, he'd convinced himself there was nothing to worry about. Then he stepped inside. The dogs met him with their usual ruckus, but he was ready for it. Slipping on a pair of sound-dampening headphones, he pulled up his playlist, cranked the volume, and got down to work. Slowly but surely, the wheelbarrow filled up and the kennels got washed down. Even better, a few of the dogs wagged when they saw him. Brook said this room housed the animals waiting for their owners to find them, but they both knew better. These were the garbage, the pets people no longer wanted or didn't plan for properly. Sure, a few might've run off and gotten lost, but most?

They were just like him. They were what happened

when the idea sounded great, but the reality was too much work. They were the result of years of neglect and abuse. The worst part was that dogs didn't get therapy. They couldn't fake it until they made it. They were just raw honesty, showing their pain behind bared teeth and tucked tails, and yet a gentle word was often all it took to make them feel better. So he gave them as many as he could.

Eventually, he'd moved all the muck from the floors into either a drain or his wheelbarrow. Releasing the last dog back into its run, he made his way out to the compost pile, humming softly to himself until he made it outside. There, he pulled his headphones off, wiped his face on the shoulder of his shirt, and started pushing again. He was lost in his own thoughts as he rounded the side of the building, but the flash of a darting animal made him stop in his tracks.

The dog ran like a puppy, making circles around the grass behind the shelter. The problem was the leash dragging behind it. Knowing how close the street was, Ryder let out a piercing whistle and hurried over, hoping this one would be the friendly kind that would stop for a scratch. The sound made the mongrel turn and prick up its ears, so Ryder tried it again. It worked, convincing the dog to come closer, but just as Ryder's hand closed on the dog's collar, he saw Brook pull herself out of the grass.

"Gummy!" she said, sounding more amused than upset. "You stinker."

"Gummy, huh?" Ryder asked the mutt, getting a wag in return.

Brook made her way over, wiping her hands on her ass with the first few steps. It was hard, but he tried to keep his eyes on the dog, focusing on the white hairs around the old man's muzzle instead of how pretty his boss looked with her hair falling out of her ponytail. After all, she was married.

"Thank you," she said as she reached them. "He's almost fourteen years old, but you wouldn't know it when he gets the zoomies."

"You ok?"

She nodded. "Yeah, just slipped when he bolted after an imaginary rabbit. There's a few bare spots that get slick when muddy."

He sure wasn't about to tell her that some of that mud was right on the side of her hip. She might take that the wrong way. Instead, he just offered over the dog's leash. When her hand closed on it just below his, Brook smiled, but that wasn't enough to make him miss what was on her arm.

"What happened?" he asked, tipping his head at the bruises.

"Oh." She pressed her free hand over it as if trying to hide the marks that peeked out from under her sleeve. "Yeah, I'm a klutz. I mean, Gummy pretty much just proved that, right?"

Not good enough. The way she automatically hid it set off every protective instinct he had. She could try to explain it away all she wanted, but he'd seen enough to know those marks were made by a hand. Five clear lines were bruised from the middle of her upper arm, down toward her elbow. Or it could be the other way around, but nothing else would've left prints like that.

"Did your husband do that?" he growled. Every muscle in his body was tense, ready to pulverize the idiot who'd hurt her like that.

Brook just held up a hand. "Easy there, big guy. Yes, he did, but it's because I was going down." She glanced at the dog and rumpled the hair between its ears. "Seems walking isn't a task I'm well-suited for, so yes, Owen grabbed me, but it wasn't anything bad. He just kept me from breaking my own pride."

"Just..." He closed his mouth and decided to think before he spoke this time. "Sorry. I guess seeing what those dogs have been through is getting to me. Man, do all of them have some kind of sob story?"

Slowly, she nodded. "Every single one. Doesn't matter if it's just being lost for a little too long, it seems that by the time they get here, they're terrified. I think most of them just want to go back home, but sometimes there isn't any home left."

"Even the ones that've been abused," he agreed. "Yeah, I think that's the best part about dogs. They always forgive, no matter what. Sometimes, even when they shouldn't."

"Unconditional loyalty," she agreed.

"Pretty sure they're the only creature on earth that has it."

Her teeth caught on the fullest part of her lip and Brook nodded. "I think that's why I like dogs more than people." She paused and glanced up. "I mean, no offense or anything!"

"None taken, because I agree with you." He chuckled softly. "My dogs don't care if I shaved that morning or smell like a week-long bender. All they want is for me to throw their ball and let them be a part of the family."

She giggled at his description. "How many?" Then she slapped a hand over her mouth. "I meant dogs, not benders!"

"Lots of benders," he teased. "Go on one every chance

I can - which isn't that often. But nah, I have a few dogs. Three, right now."

"I'm so jealous," she moaned. "I have one. I can't even imagine how nice it would be to have my own little pack to hang out with, but my husband is *not* a dog person."

Which only made him hate her husband a little more. "I guess you grew up with dogs, then?"

"Nope." Brook shrugged. "Got my first dog in college, thanks to a roommate who was always willing to break the rules. We snuck it into the dorms - then got kicked out of the dorms because of it. But no, my parents always said dogs were expensive, and we didn't have the money. I had a couple of cats when I was little, but that's about it."

"So what do your folks think about you working at a shelter?"

The smile on her face faded. "I don't honestly know if they have any idea. They don't live close, and ever since I got married, we don't really talk much."

"Sorry," he mumbled, understanding that a little too well. "So I guess your college friend helped you get into this?"

"No. I actually lost touch with her a while back." She paused. "The truth is, Ryder, I work here because the dogs are the only friends I have. I really don't fit in the same circles as the people my husband hangs out with, and I'm perfectly fine with the big, silent, and hairy type." She smiled down at the dog for a split second before realizing what she said. Then, her eyes flicked back up. "I'm so sorry. I don't know why I'm dumping all of this on you. God, I promise I'm not as crazy as that made me sound."

The problem was that it didn't make her sound crazy at all. It made her sound perfect. It also explained why he felt so oddly comfortable talking to her. For the first time in his life, Ryder had just stumbled upon a woman who might be able to understand him. A very married woman, who kept bringing up her husband every time they talked, but that didn't mean they couldn't be friends. Considering the mark on her arm, he had a funny feeling she could use someone who was a lot better at listening than talking.

"I got my first dog when I was twelve," he offered. "My brother and I found this stray, and we made a little door in the back of the shed so she'd have a place to sleep. We weren't supposed to have her, so kept it a secret, but I think she got to hear all of our childhood drama. And she'd just sit there and watch us like she understood each and every word, you know? Man, she was my best friend."

"Yeah. I think the only thing that sucks is that we can't save them all." She petted the dog at her side again. "And speaking of saving, I should probably go run a few ads and see if we can find more homes."

Immediately, he stepped back, out of her way. "Sorry. I didn't mean to keep you."

"No, you're fine. Besides, I think you're the first volunteer who's ever finished a whole kennel." She started walking backwards, giving him the sweetest smile. "So don't work too hard or I'll find something else that needs to be done."

"So long as it's for the dogs, I'm down," he called back.

She grinned. "And come find me in a bit. I have the money you loaned me."

He didn't think it was possible, but her smile grew a little more - and his lips curled to match. Having an excuse to see her again would not be a problem at all. Damn. Why did she have to think the same way he did? Not only was she gorgeous, but for the first time in his life, Ryder had finally found a woman he could *talk* to. Not put on a show, and not pretend to be whatever she wanted; around Brook Harper, just being himself seemed to be all she wanted.

And she was married. Very, very married. No matter what, that was one line he would never cross.

CHAPTER FOUR

*T*wo days later, Owen was still trying to convince Brook to quit her job. It was like the idea had popped into his mind and become an obsession. No matter how many times she tried to tell him she liked working at the shelter, he never seemed to hear. Either that, or he didn't care. She couldn't be sure, but she was getting tired of talking about it.

On the upside, he was giving her a ride to work today, which meant she'd finally be on time. Early, actually, since he still had to drive across town to his office. It was only because he'd asked to take her to dinner that evening. Brook was impressed he'd "remembered" it was their anniversary, but between her hints and his admin's management of his schedule, one of them had gotten through. Granted, an accountant should be better with dates and numbers, but Owen had other priorities, like convincing his wife to stop working.

"I'm telling you," he said, trying to laugh about it, "there's no way you'll make it through a whole day with those animals and be ready to go out. I think Primavera has a dress code, sweetie."

Her eyes were on the bag by her feet. "I'm sorry, Owen. I just thought you'd want to do something over the weekend, not on a Thursday. The surprise was sweet, but if I'd known, I would have asked for the day off."

"Well, no good deed goes unpunished, huh?" He flashed her the charming smile that made her fall in love with him. "I bet if we had a family, you wouldn't need to spend so much time with those dogs."

Her gut clenched. Not this again. "I thought we agreed to wait."

"Maybe I'm changing my mind. If I get this promotion, there's no reason to wait to have kids. We'll be able to afford them just fine."

"Yeah." She picked at a thread in her jeans. "I'm just not sure I'm ready yet."

Even from the corner of her eye, she could see his jaw tense. "Brook, you'd make a beautiful mother. You're so good with those stupid animals, just imagine how you'd be with our children."

Except she couldn't hose down the dirty diapers with a power washer. Or lock them outside when they got too loud. She didn't want to be tied to children. Not yet! "We still need to save for college."

"Don't worry about that, hun. I'll take care of the finances. And just think, if you stay at home to raise our family, we can have dinner together every night." He smiled at the road.

"You think your promotion will mean you get out of the office earlier?" She didn't believe it.

He just laughed. "Well, it might." The car slowed to

turn into the shelter's parking lot. "But we can't stay kids forever, Brook. You're old enough to be a mother."

"I'm only thirty-four."

He didn't respond until the car was stopped. "And I'm thirty-eight. I don't want to be raising kids at seventy. My parents are already asking about grandkids, and what can I tell them? My wife isn't ready? Don't be selfish, sweetheart."

Her mouth twitched in a parody of a smile. "I didn't realize your father decided what I did with my body." Jerking off the seatbelt, she grabbed her bag and got out. "Happy anniversary, Owen. Maybe at dinner, we'll talk about penis enhancements."

His face turned red, but she slammed the door before he could say anything. As she walked into the shelter, her spine was stiff, anger giving it form, but she refused to cave. They'd planned to hold off on starting a family. That had always been what he said, but now that his younger brother was expecting a child, Owen wanted one too. Not like he enjoyed kids. For the last five years, he'd always joked that he was glad they were her responsibility. And if they were, then why did he think he got to choose when she produced one? He might make enough to pay their bills, but money couldn't make her ready to have a baby. Wedding ring or not!

Each step only made her anger simmer. By the time she reached her office, she was ready to rip off anyone's head that said the wrong thing. Happy fucking anniversary, right? With her parents on the other side of the country, the only place she had to escape was the shelter. She'd left all of her childhood friends back home when she got married, and with Owen's crazy schedule, they never really had time to hang out with other couples. The one person she still knew wasn't considered "acceptable" in her husband's opinion. In other words, she was all alone.

Barely in her office, Brook was still putting her things away when a plump teenaged girl swung around the open door frame. "Brook," she called out, "got three pallets of dog food in."

"Thanks, Danielle. See if Tyrone will stack it in the feed room?"

"Nope."

Brook snapped her head around. "What do you mean?"

"Tyrone's off." Danielle grinned. "What about our newest court-appointed volunteer? Then again, you might bring the entire shelter to a halt."

"Huh?"

Danielle giggled. "Even Marcy has been checking him out. Don't tell me you didn't notice! God, he's *so hot*." She meant Ryder.

"And about fifteen years too old for you." Brook flicked her finger back toward the front desk. "Answer the phones or something. I'll take care of the dog food."

The young girl giggled but obeyed. She probably had a crush on him. Brook could remember what that felt like, but it had been a long time. Back when she'd met Owen, he'd made her giddy. Now? The man was just infuriating. The worst part was that he wouldn't even slow down enough to talk about their problems. Every time Brook tried, he blew her off like she was an idiot. With a grumble under her breath about men, she tried to figure out what to do about the dog food. Ryder couldn't be the only person able to lift that much, could he?

Turning on her computer, she pulled up the staff

schedule and saw only a few people who could actually manage to lift one hundred and twenty bags of dog food without hurting themselves. Sadly, the type of person who volunteered at an animal shelter tended to be the young or old. She needed to talk to Marcy about making sure there was a regular on each shift able to handle this stuff.

And today, the only person besides herself actually was Ryder. Heading out of the office, she made the long trip across the building to find him. Like always, he was in the intake kennel. The sound of dogs barking traveled through the metal door, but when she stepped inside, Brook was shocked to find the man completely lost in his job. Sound-muffling headphones were over his ears, and his mouth moved as if he was singing. It made her chuckle a little.

Ryder had to be around her age, but he didn't act like it. Either that, or she acted way too old. It was hard to tell, since only one of them was having a good time - and it wasn't her. Making her way over, she watched him lean down to pet a dog through the fence before shoveling out yet another concrete run. He worked quickly and efficiently. By the time she reached him, he was just starting to spray down the pad.

"Ryder," she yelled, reaching over to tap his shoulder.

He jerked in surprise, spinning toward her. Ducking away from the hose, Brook slipped, hydroplaning on the smooth floor. Knowing she was going down, she relaxed, her mind giving her plenty of time to lament that Owen was right. She'd never make it through a day at work and be ready for dinner without heading home first. That bothered her more than the ground rushing toward her.

Strong hands grabbed her ribs, and the chain-link slammed into her back. But it wasn't the floor. Unaware she'd even closed her eyes, Brook pried them open in shock to find Ryder inches away, pressing into her. He'd dropped the hose, releasing the handle in order to catch her, and it lay dead on the floor. That didn't make the dogs any less noisy, but somehow she was neither wet nor filthy. Her chest heaved with each breath, fear looking so similar to passion. Dear God, Ryder was even sexier up close!

He swallowed then licked his lips. "You ok?" he mouthed, slowly leaning away.

Brook nodded, trying to stay professional. "Thanks."

He just grinned and shook his head, then pointed to the door. She agreed completely. It was impossible to hold a conversation in here, and she most certainly did not need to be that close to him. Not only was Ryder tall, he was twice as solid, and she was too married to be enjoying this.

Once again, he turned into the gentleman, gesturing for her to go first. Brook led him into the hall then leaned back against the wall, checking her shirt for stains. Ryder cleared his throat softly and took a spot on the wall across from her. "Didn't mean to knock you over, Mrs. Harper."

"You didn't," she assured him. "I tried to avoid the hose. Got a big date tonight and wanted to prove I could make it a day without getting covered in something."

His jaw clenched. "Right. Sorry."

She waved it away. "Before I tried to take a header into the dog crap, what I wanted to know was if you'd be willing to help move a few bags of dog food."

"Yeah, sure."

"Like a hundred and twenty?" she added weakly. "You don't have to do it all today, and I'll help tomorrow when I can, but most of the staff shouldn't be lifting too much, and Owen was really worried that I'd end up looking like an embarrassment before I got off work."

He just nodded slowly. "It's fine, Mrs. Harper. The dogs need it."

"Still just Brook."

He swallowed again, his eyes looking up the hall. "No, ma'am. You have a date tonight. I assume it's with your husband?"

"Yeah, we're celebrating our sixth anniversary."

His eyes flicked back, hitting her hard. His face was cold and brutal. So was his voice when he replied, "Congratulations. I think it's safer if you stay Mrs. Harper. I'll take care of the food."

He pushed off from the wall and just walked away. In a split second, Ryder had changed from the sweet dog lover she knew to something very different. The smile he always had for her had vanished, replaced with an air of danger, and now she really wanted to know what exactly he'd done to get court-ordered community service. Maybe Owen was right. Maybe working with criminals was a *bad* idea. Clearly, they weren't all stable.

Before she could change her mind, Brook headed to the front, right to Marcy's office. Her boss sat behind her computer, her eyes moving between adoption applications and whatever was on her screen. At Brook's tap, she groaned and looked up.

"Yeah?"

Brook walked the rest of the way in. "Our community service volunteers? You have their paperwork, right?"

"Mhm."

"Want to let me know what Ryder is in for?"

Marcy's lip curled up on one side, and she leaned back. "You got a thing for him, too, huh?"

"No!" Brook paused when Marcy's lopsided smile changed to a grin. She rolled her eyes, refusing to admit she was anything but a devoted wife. "Look, Mr. Muscles back there just got all weird. I just wanted to make sure I wasn't locked alone with some rapist or something."

"Property damage," Marcy assured her. "Our muscle-bound friend trashed some jerk's car in a fit of rage." She paused, the look on her face making it clear there was more. "Because the jerk was beating the shit out of a dog."

Not what she'd expected. Trashing a car, Brook could believe, but the part about the dog caught her off guard. "Do I want to know how those go together?"

Marcy laughed. "The District Attorney called to make sure I'd agree to him working here. Said there wasn't enough evidence to convict the other guy for animal abuse, but Ryder probably saved the poor dog's life. He used the guy's car as a hostage, basically. Every time the idiot tried to hit the dog, Ryder smashed something on the car. Then, when the police showed up, he admitted it, so the judge gave him a sentence that fit. Why?"

Feeling foolish, Brook shrugged. "I just startled him in the kennels. He didn't do anything, it's just the look on his face, you know? Like he might not be such a nice guy."

"He's fine. I think you're just being paranoid."

"Me too. No more serial killer documentaries before bed, right?" Thanking Marcy again, she left, feeling even more foolish.

Owen must be getting to her. Starting off her morning with an argument about kids wasn't exactly a recipe for a good day at work, and it wasn't like Ryder had done anything. He just insisted on calling her Mrs. Harper. That was polite, not terrifying. So why did she suddenly think he might be dangerous? Was it just because he'd caught her so easily? Was it because standing so close to him had been kinda nice? Could it be because he'd liked it as much as she had?

At least he'd only be around for a few more days. After that, she'd be training the next court-appointed volunteer. Oddly, the thought wasn't reassuring, but it wasn't like she even knew him. Except for the sweet gesture of helping her out every time she needed it, Ryder mostly kept to himself.

CHAPTER FIVE

*B*rook was still at her desk when the vet walked past. Glancing at the calendar, her heart stopped. It was Thursday. For Tall Tails, that wasn't a good day. When the animal shelter first opened, the staff agreed not to euthanize anything on Fridays so they wouldn't have a miserable weekend. Instead, Thursday was the day dogs who couldn't be placed were put to sleep.

Sadly, she couldn't take all of them home. Thousands of animals came through every year, and most of them never got adopted. Brook hated it, but she consoled herself by knowing she could make their time on Earth a little better. Unfortunately, every so often, she still got attached. Her latest was Gummy Bear, the old dog with no teeth. He had nothing going for him except his personality, but that hadn't been enough.

For a long moment, she stared at her hands, her mind whirling. Would it be better to ignore it until he was gone? Should she try to adopt him and then place him on her own? Was there anything she could do to save him?

No.

All she could do was make sure his last moments were happy. It didn't matter if her heart broke; she wasn't the one scheduled to die today. Brook pulled open her bottom drawer and found the bag of treats. He couldn't normally have them because they were a choking hazard for a dog without teeth, but that no longer mattered. If Gummy wanted bacon-flavored chews, he could have them all.

When the vet came to get him, Brook was sitting on the floor of his kennel with the old dog's head in her lap. The two women shared a look as Brook passed over his leash. They didn't need to talk. They both understood. Gummy wagged his tail, eager to meet the new person, but paused to lick Brook's face before following the vet out of the kennel. With his shaggy tail waving behind him, he pranced, thrilled that he'd finally been picked.

One last good day was much better than dying alone, locked in a concrete hell, but that didn't make it hurt any less. When the crash of the metal door echoed through the room, the first tear leaked out. Brook almost managed to regain her composure, until she looked at her lap. Gummy's long hairs clung to her shirt, and her jeans were stained with the filth of the dog run. Owen wouldn't understand. He'd made it clear that he wanted to go out straight after work, not stop back at home to get cleaned up. To him, that mattered more than making some "stupid animal's" last day a bit nicer.

That thought shattered the fragile walls that held in her emotions. Pulling her knees to her chest, Brook cried. Gummy was such a good dog, but everyone looked at him and saw only what was on the outside. That was all that ever mattered. Some cute little mutt that fit in a purse wouldn't stay in the shelter for more than a day, but a loyal friend like Gummy had better be as pretty on the outside as he was inside. It wasn't fair. It was wrong, and what made it even worse was that they didn't just treat the animals like that!

They were all supposed to play their parts. What each person wanted wasn't important, so long as they did everything they were supposed to. Get married to a man who made enough money, have a family, fight about the bills, and drive a fancy car. If she could manage that, the world would think she was successful, but what if she wanted something else? What if she wanted her husband to be a friend as well as the sire of offspring? What if she wanted to make something out of her own life instead of just fulfilling his needs? Maybe even a lover who liked a little spice in the daily grind and didn't think the same ol' thing was good enough. What if her opinions weren't what the world wanted to hear?

It wasn't just losing Gummy that hurt, it was everything. Each year, her marriage got less and less happy. Week after week, she felt more alone. Every day, Owen needed something else to prove she loved him. Over and over, what Brook wanted didn't matter. That was why she wouldn't quit her job at the kennel. It wasn't because she wanted to work here, it was because she wanted to do *something* that mattered, and this mattered - to the dogs. It mattered to Gummy, and it was the least she could do.

She'd been married for six years, and it was nothing like she'd hoped. Back then, she'd had dreams. She'd had friends. Now? She had one old dog who no one else wanted - and was probably already dead - and another at home she barely got to see. It wasn't fair! This wasn't the life she'd signed up for. She didn't even have the comfort of a supportive husband! Oh no. She was the one that should be handing out the comfort. Owen didn't care at all about what Brook dreamed of, so long as his every need was met and she looked like she belonged on his arm.

Deep inside, her heart was breaking, and no one cared. If they didn't see her tears, then they could pretend like everything was just fine. No one wanted to know her. No one gave a shit about what made her happy. The only thing she was good for was hanging on Owen's arm like an accessory. Every executive had his little trophy wife, and she'd been picked, so why wasn't she happy? It wasn't just Gummy, it was everything, and Brook couldn't stop the tears.

Wallowing in self-pity, the only thing she could hear was her heart hammering inside her head, but when a strong arm curled around her, she didn't fight it. She did hide her face, though. Pressing her hands over her streaming mascara, Brook tried to curl against her knees. She didn't want anyone to see her like this, and that thought made her cry even harder.

"What happened, Brook?" Ryder asked, pulling all of her against his chest.

Twisting, she pressed the side of her head into his broad shoulder. "Gummy's gone." The words were a wail.

"Oh, baby," he breathed, rocking her. "I'm so sorry, I had no idea. I gotcha, Brook. You can have my shoulder as long as you need it."

"Gummy's gone. He was too old, and no one wanted Gummy Bear, and now he's gone, and it's all my fault."

"Nah." She felt Ryder's hand slide down the back of her head. "It's not, Brook. You were good to him. You're good to all of them, and they know it. These dogs love you. You do the hardest thing anyone can, and it makes a difference. It's ok, beautiful. At least you loved him enough to cry."

She didn't know how long she wept, but having his arms around her helped. So did the gentle reassurances he handed out so easily. For the first time in years, she felt like it was ok to feel. For just a moment, she didn't have to be a robot, and at least one person understood. But eventually, her eyes ran dry. Hoping it wasn't obvious, she tried to wipe at her face.

"I'm sorry," Brook mumbled between them.

Ryder used the bottom of his shirt to help, revealing some of the most impressive abs she'd ever seen. "Don't be, Mrs. Harper." His voice was tender, as if he understood. "Hey," he whispered, cupping her cheek. "Need me to take you home?"

She shook her head. "I'm ok, Ryder. I just hate this part, you know?"

"Yeah." His thumb wiped at the trail the tears had left. "Me, too, but at least someone loved him enough to cry. I bet a lot of these dogs don't get that."

She looked up at his eyes, finding them waiting. He didn't look through her, he looked *at* her. He looked at her the way she wished someone would, and his hand was still sweetly on her cheek.

"Ryder..."

The corner of his lip lifted. "I don't force myself on women, Mrs. Harper. I just thought you needed a friend."

A weak giggle slipped out. "Pretty sure you wouldn't need to."

"Huh?"

"Force yourself - " She sucked in a breath. "Oh my god, I shouldn't have said -"

His chuckle cut her off. "Promise I didn't take it the wrong way. You're kinda like my boss, remember? I just know how nice it is to have a shoulder. Figured I'd share the wealth, I guess."

Before she could convince herself not to, Brook clutched his arm. "Thanks. My friends don't understand."

"Then you have the wrong friends."

"They're more like my husband's."

"Mm," he grunted. "Then maybe you have the wrong husband." He leaned back onto his heels then stood, offering his hand to help her up. "But that's probably what all the guys tell you."

She looked at him for a moment, then gave in. "No, it's not. Most of them don't bother talking to me. The wives are supposed to be seen and not heard, I guess. Wish someone had told me that before I accepted the ring."

"Hey." He stepped closer, his size pressing her toward the wall. "That's bullshit, ok? That crap needs to stay in the 1950s, and if your old man has a problem with it, I'll remind him that a woman's place is at the top of the pedestal, not scrubbing the base of it."

Her brows rose. Ryder wasn't the kind of person to make a long soliloquy. Most of their conversations had been held in awkward sentences, with a few bad jokes thrown in. She certainly hadn't expected him to drop such a fitting metaphor with ease. But speaking of scrubbing...

"I have to get cleaned up." Her eyes flicked to the open kennel door, but his body was between her and it.

He stepped back immediately. "Yeah. Rumor has it that you've got a hot date."

"And Primavera has a dress code." She made it to the kennel door, then paused. "Thanks, though. I mean it."

"Yeah. Me too."

Her brow wrinkled. "Which part?"

"All of it." He smiled. "Mostly the trusting me part.

You need a shoulder, Mrs. Harper, and you're welcome to mine. Want a drinking buddy, and I'll double down. You seem like the kind of person I'd get along with."

"Bet you say that to all the girls," she teased, turning for the ladies room to clean her face.

His voice caught her before she made it a step. "Nope. Most of them I don't want to say a thing to. That's why I like my dog."

Brook wasn't foolish enough to stop. That sounded a little too much like flirting, and having Ryder flirt with her? Not a good idea. Not today. Things were a lot safer when that man was in a completely different room, and she was headed to one he couldn't come in: the ladies room.

First he'd saved her from falling on her butt, then he gave her a shoulder to cry on just when she needed it the most, and he finished with what sounded almost like flirting? Today was her anniversary, for Christ's sake. She shouldn't be thinking about the hot guy who had to help in the kennels because of some court decision. And yes, Ryder was hot. If she let herself think about it, she couldn't even try to deny that.

Tall, broad, and built like the men on the covers of the books she liked, Ryder was the kind of sexy that made women turn stupid. But she didn't even know his last name! He was just Ryder, the guy who cleaned the kennels and understood how easy it was to love these dogs. The sweet man who would only be around for a week, give or take. He might make for good daydreams, but men like Ryder were dangerous. They were the kind of guys who ruined marriages and broke hearts. The kind she should stay far away from, especially when her heart had a big, gaping hole in it, left by a dog she wasn't supposed to love.

With only half an hour left in the day, Brook stopped by her office long enough to get the bag with her change of clothes. She'd clean off the kennel mess, put on something pretty, and fix her makeup. By the time Owen arrived to pick her up, any traces of her crying on another man's shoulder would be long gone, so she wouldn't have to explain.

At least the animal shelter restrooms were designed for people who'd gotten very dirty. The deep sink was good enough to wash up to her shoulders. Thankfully, she had her hair up, so it wasn't disgusting, and she only smelled a little like dog. Her face, however, was a total loss. Brook put on the dress first, then started from scratch, removing the trails of mascara from her cheeks and putting it back onto her lashes. In twenty minutes, she looked like a lady once more, and Owen wouldn't have a single thing to complain about. She'd transformed herself into the perfect empty shell he wanted - one with no emotions or desires of her own.

Her heels clicked on the floor as she stepped into the hall. It didn't take much to go from shit shoveler to accountant's wife, and hopefully, her husband would get a couple of ideas. Maybe, if she tried hard enough, she could put their marriage back on the right track. It was the only hope she had left, but she wouldn't hold her breath.

CHAPTER SIX

Earlier...

*R*yder grabbed two more bags of dog food and walked through the narrow door. Dumb move, jackass, he thought. He'd probably scared the shit out of that cute little thing. He tossed the dog food onto the stack then went back for more. When he saw her slip in the kennel, he didn't know what else to do. He had to catch her. At least he hadn't tried to kiss her, but glaring at her like that, she probably thought he was some kind of freak.

He kinda was.

Big, strong, and dumb. That was all he was. The only friends he'd ever had were his brother and a few dogs over the years. He couldn't even hold down a girlfriend, so why would someone as smart, pretty, and amazing as Brook want to even talk to him? Never mind her husband. Mr. Harper definitely wouldn't be happy with him anywhere around his wife, but she was the kind of person he could

47

talk to. She understood him. Hell, she understood the dogs, and that was kinda all that mattered.

Over and over, he made the trip between the pallets of dog food and the climate-controlled storage area. At least Brook had asked. He half expected to walk by and see her trying to do this herself. She seemed like that kinda girl, all soft and gentle on the outside, but sharp edges and steel underneath. Figured she'd be married, and married women didn't exactly keep guy friends around, let alone guys that had thoughts like his.

His mind ran in a circle for a couple of hours while he walked back and forth, carrying bag after bag. His arms burned, but he ignored it. So long as he didn't think about it, it didn't matter, right? Just one more trip, he kept telling himself, until eventually, there were no more trips to make. Only then did he look at the clock. Ten after four. Not much longer and he'd be outta here.

Thinking about it, Ryder sighed. If they'd let him move in, he would. Hell, he'd carry as much shit as they needed if he could stay close to the dogs. Stretching his arms, he wandered back to the intake kennels to finish cleaning. Too bad women didn't think that was romantic. The big dumb guy that loved dogs and wanted to spend all of his time with them? Yep, that'd be the start of his next story. He chuckled at himself.

He should probably tell his brother - who would either hate it or make it into something heroic. Then again, the more Ryder thought about it, the better it seemed. If he wasn't so vague, it might work. Maybe some broken man who could only find comfort in the silent companionship of a dog and a pretty little brunette who saved him from his issues. Yeah. And how he could fall in love with her, and all his wounds would fade behind the passion they shared, and she wouldn't care about his dark and terrifying past.

Not bad. Not bad at all. He pulled out his phone, hit the first contact, and sent a text. A moment later, the reply came back. It was just a smiley face. Evidently, his brother thought it had potential, but wasn't there yet. Then again, he hadn't really set up a good plot. Where was the conflict? What were the stakes?

Letting his mind wander, Ryder took the shortcut through the adoptable kennel. The door barely closed behind him when he heard it. Buried under the sounds of excited dogs was a whimper that was all too human. The gasps and muffled sniffles were out of place, and it cut right through him. Ducking around the row of cages, he hit the far alley, his feet moving quickly. Near the end of the row, he saw one door partially open. That was where the sound came from.

That was where *she* was. He knew before he could even see her; something about the sound of the sobbing warned him. When he came around the edge, he found her sitting on the filthy floor, her head in her hands, and no dog in sight. The clothes she'd been trying to keep clean were a total loss, and beneath her hands, he saw the dark smudges of mascara on her cheeks. Ryder didn't even think, he just dropped beside her and pulled Brook Harper against his chest.

"What happened, Brook?" he asked, wrapping his arms around her trembling shoulders.

Another sob came out as she curled up against him. "Gummy's gone."

"Oh, baby," he breathed, rocking her. "I'm so sorry, I had no idea. I gotcha, Brook. You can have my shoulder as long as you need it."

She didn't even try to resist. Twisting, she pressed herself against his neck. "Gummy's gone. He was too old, and no one wanted Gummy Bear, and now he's gone, and it's all my fault."

"Nah." He ran his hand over her hair. "It's not, Brook. You were good to him. You're good to all of them, and they know it. These dogs love you." He rocked her gently. "You do the hardest thing anyone can, and it makes a difference. It's ok, beautiful. At least you loved him enough to cry."

The words were barely out of his mouth before he mentally cursed himself for a fool. The diamond on her wedding ring pressed against him, her hands clenched against her face. He could feel it. That stupid fucking ring on her hand and he could feel it, but he'd still called her beautiful.

Didn't matter. None of it mattered. She needed him, and this was something he could do. While she cried out the pain of her loss, he sat there and held her, making sure she didn't have to be alone. It made it better. It took the edge off the pain. He knew, because too many times, he'd been the one crying. If such a wonderful woman needed someone to cry on, then he'd be a pillar of strength for her.

"I'm sorry," Brook mumbled into his shoulder, reaching her hand up to wipe at her face.

Ryder yanked at the hem of his shirt, pulling it from his pants so he could help. "Don't be, Mrs. Harper." He wiped away the proof of her tears as best he could.

The sound of her name made her look up. Those blue-grey eyes of hers held him like an anchor. For a moment, she said nothing. Ryder let his thumb wipe at the line of tears, but he couldn't look away. He just couldn't. She had him completely trapped, even with that god damned ring on her hand.

"Hey," he breathed, pressing his palm against the softness of her face. "Need me to take you home?"

She shook her head. "I'm ok. I just hate this part, you know?"

"Yeah. Me, too, but at least someone loved him enough to cry. I bet a lot of these dogs don't get that."

She looked up at him, her eyes darting across his face. "Ryder..."

He had a good idea what she was thinking. Yeah, he should probably pull his hand away, but he didn't want to. What he wanted was for her to close her eyes, lean into it, and whisper his name just a bit softer. Instead, she looked at him with a hint of fear.

"I don't force myself on women, Mrs. Harper. I just thought you needed a friend."

"Pretty sure you wouldn't need to."

For a split second, he thought his eyes were about to pop out of his head. That was not at all what he'd expected. "Huh?"

"Force yourself - " She stopped, pressing the back of her wrist over her mouth. "Oh my god, I shouldn't have said -"

God, she looked adorable like that. "Promise I didn't take it the wrong way. You're kinda like my boss, remember? I just know how nice it is to have a shoulder. Figured I'd share the wealth, I guess."

"Thanks. My friends don't understand."

Right about now, he wanted to beat her friends into smithereens. "Then you have the wrong friends."

"They're more like my husband's."

"Then maybe you have the wrong husband." The

words just came out as if they had a life of their own, but he wasn't sorry he'd said it. He was just sorry it was true. He also didn't want to scare her off. "But that's probably what all the guys tell you," he added, trying to make it sound more like a joke instead of his honest opinion.

"No, it's not. Most of them don't bother talking to me. The wives are supposed to be seen and not heard, I guess. Wish someone had told me that before I accepted the ring."

"Hey." He could taste fear on the back of his tongue. Think, you idiot. Say something. "That's bullshit, ok? That crap needs to stay in the 1950s, and if your old man has a problem with it, I'll remind him that a woman's place it at the top of the pedestal, not scrubbing the base of it." God damn it. This was why Hunter wrote the dialogue. Fucking stupid thing to say, dumbass.

Thankfully, she didn't seem to notice. Brook leaned her head back and took a deep breath. "God, I'm a mess. I have to get cleaned up."

He saw her glance over his shoulder and realized he was hovering. That wasn't at all how a good friend acted. He knew better, so stepped back. "Yeah. Rumor has it that you've got a hot date."

"And Primavera has a dress code." She made it to the kennel door, then paused. "Thanks, though. I mean it."

"Yeah. Me too."

A look of confusion crossed her face. "Which part?"

The only good response he could give was silence. Fucking bastard didn't even try to care about his wife's feelings? Didn't matter if the jackass liked dogs. She did! Shouldn't that be enough? Brook was upset, and she'd tried so hard to look nice for her date. Unfortunately, she was standing there, waiting for an answer, and he had a funny feeling that the honest one would cause way too much trouble.

"All of it," he said, then added on some stuff that should sound plausible enough.

The smile she gave him was worth it. It glowed, even if the tears still lingered in her eyes. Before he could wallow in the warmth of it, she left. He watched her until the door swung closed behind her, then decided it was a perfect time for a break. Mainly because he'd better get his head on straight or this was going to get very awkward.

Leaving the kennel, he stretched his legs. Brook Harper was too damned perfect. She could manage to cry and look pretty. None of the red-eyed, snot-running kind of crying. Oh, not for Mrs. Harper. She cried with big wet eyes and a plush, pouty lip that begged a man to kiss them. He needed to be a lot farther away before he did something stupid - like try.

He was barely outside before he grabbed his phone. It only took two presses before it was ringing. His brother picked up immediately. "Nice idea, I think we can work with it," he said as a greeting.

"Fuck the story," Ryder growled, keeping his voice down. "Hunter, I'm fucking this shit up. I told you I couldn't do community service."

"What happened?"

He pressed the key fob, unlocking his truck before he was even across the parking lot. "Her name is Brook Harper. Five foot five or so, brunette, big blue eyes, and these fucking curves."

"Nice," Hunter agreed. "So what's the problem?"

"A ring." Ryder wrenched open the door. "She just cried on my shoulder, man. Like, pressed up against me and wasn't even ashamed. I'm a fucking idiot, and I keep trying to tell her she's beautiful, but she's kinda like my boss here."

"So what made her meltdown?"

Ryder's answer was in a soft breath. "A dog."

For a moment, Hunter said nothing. Ryder heaved himself into the driver's seat, knowing his brother was thinking and slammed the door. The sound of breathing was enough. It grounded him.

"They can't fire you," Hunter finally said. "You just have to take care of the dogs, then come home. You got this, bro. I'm only a phone call away. We got this."

"I know, but I don't want to make any more problems for her. Hell, the last thing we need is anyone figuring out our pseudonym, right? I just needed a break to get my head back on straight."

"Want me to volunteer while you get this done?"

"Nah." Ryder leaned his head back and took a relaxing breath. "Just a few hours, man. This girl just blindsided me today, and you know I'm not good at this alone. All I needed was a breather."

"Well, she's married, so not like you can hit a home run with her. Relax, Ryder. Think of this more like character assessment and let me know all the details when you get home."

He chuckled, knowing his brother had a point. "Yeah, yeah. I'll try to keep the freaking out to a minimum. She just caught me off guard when she started crying on me, but I'm cool. Look, I'm freaking out for nothing. I should probably go. I'll be home in a bit."

"Yeah. Miss ya, man. Too fuckin' quiet."

"Same here. Thanks, Hunter." He ended the call and reached for the door.

He could do this. It would be a lot easier if Brook had

been some hag-faced troll instead of the girl he'd always dreamed of meeting, but it was just a week. Forty hours. It wasn't a big deal, and that puppy had been worth it. If he had to guess, she should be home from the vet by now, lying at Hunter's feet, getting her belly rubbed. She'd make up for all his issues with women - and Hunter's - and let them feel almost normal.

But that was one thing they weren't and probably never would be. No one could understand. Even the therapists didn't. They kept trying to prescribe some drug to dull their minds instead of explaining why they felt so empty when they were apart. Trauma, they said. Time will heal it, they said. But the way it was looking, those bastards all lied. It didn't get better, and people didn't understand. He and Hunter were freaks. They would always be freaks, and not a damned thing could change the past. The only thing they could do was learn to fake it really fuckin' well.

CHAPTER SEVEN

*P*rimavera was beautiful. Everything about the place screamed expensive, which was probably why Owen picked it. Brook sat at the bar sipping a glass of Coke, waiting for her husband to get back from the restroom and trying not to think about Gummy. Evidently, a reservation didn't mean they would have a seat waiting, but she honestly didn't mind the break.

Unfortunately, their date wasn't off to a good start. Owen had been on the phone when he picked her up and barely spared her more than a handful of words since. Something at the office, he said. It supposedly couldn't wait. She understood, but it would've been nice to get at least one night a year without interruptions.

"Scotch," a man ordered, sliding into the seat beside her. The rest of the bar was empty, so when he turned to her, it wasn't a surprise. "Can I buy you a drink, gorgeous?"

With a muffled groan, she turned to face him. "Thanks, but no." Why was it that every man but her own seemed willing to flirt?

"Hm," he said slowly as his brow wrinkled. "Not used to getting turned down quite so fast."

"Not your fault," she assured him. "I'm married."

His expression turned playful and teasing. "Shame." Then his eyes flicked over her shoulder, and Brook was forgotten. "Alison!" he called out. "Hey, lady, how have you been?"

Unable to help herself, Brook turned to see his date. She had no idea what she'd been expecting, but the sight was exactly what she needed. Beautiful, blonde, and wearing a red dress that was slinky in all the right ways, the woman marching toward them was very familiar. Six years ago they'd been inseparable. Now? Brook might never get the chance to see her, but she still thought of the woman sauntering closer as her best friend.

"Alison?" she asked, shock in her voice.

Alison's face lit up, and her pretty red lips parted in a gasp of surprise. "Oh my god! Brooklyn Sanders!"

"Harper," Brook corrected, sliding from her stool to hug her longtime friend. "I didn't know you were still in town!"

"Of course I am." Alison flicked her clutch to the man beside her. "Jonathan MacKeenan, crime and thriller author. Jon, this is my best friend from college. What are the chances of this?"

"Considering I haven't moved in six years? Pretty good," Brook teased. "It's so good to see you, Ali."

Alison just hugged her again. "Yeah, it really is. Did your husband let you out of jail or something?"

"Anniversary dinner."

"Ah." Her tone conveyed her distaste. "So I guess you *are* kinda like a prisoner. Leah and I just got a place in the burbs to make the commute shorter. Call me - we can play whenever you want. You don't even have to tell him."

Owen's voice broke in from behind them. "Tell me what?"

Alison took a deep breath and turned, lifting her chin defiantly. "That I miss my best friend and enjoy hanging out with her."

"I'm sure. If you think my wife wants to - "

"Be friends with a lesbian?" Alison asked bluntly. "Oh. I'm sorry. Was I not supposed to say that?"

"Ali," Brook hissed.

From the look on Owen's face, he was not amused. "I was thinking 'hang out with little girls who have no manners.' Excuse me." He caught his wife's arm, tugging her away from the bar.

"Stop," Brook hissed. "Ali was introducing me to her client."

When his eyes flicked to the man, a tiny crease appeared on either side of his nose. It looked like Owen smelled something bad. Right now, Brook was just hoping he didn't cause an even bigger scene, and for once, her prayers were answered.

"Yeah. Give me a second, sweetie, and let me see if our table is ready."

It was, thankfully. They were seated in the middle of the floor with plenty of space around them. Even better, Alison and her author were on the other side of the room. While Brook could see them, there was no chance of her conversation being overheard. Granted, it was the same old boring stuff Owen always droned on about. Smiling at her husband, she let her mind wander, thinking back to her college days with her best friend. The pair of them had gotten into their fair share of trouble, and it looked like

Alison hadn't bothered changing that much. Brook was a little jealous. Ok, a lot. Alison sounded like she was perfectly comfortable with the woman she'd become. Brook wasn't. Not at all.

But she made it through the appetizer by making generic agreeable noises. Owen was explaining all about his most recent success at the office. She didn't know accounting was a competitive sport, but Owen certainly felt it was. He also acted like she was too stupid to understand, so never offered enough details to make the stories easy to follow. Nope, all he wanted was to have a sounding board, and she'd mastered that in their second year of marriage. By now, she was an old pro.

Eventually, he brought the conversation to her. "So how was your day, sweetie?"

She pulled her attention back to the present. "It's Thursday, Owen. Those are never good."

"Right, the shelter. Have you thought about joining one of the city functions? I'm sure we could get you on the board, and that would give you something better to do."

She took a deep breath to prevent herself from saying something stupid. "I like what I'm doing, but I thought maybe a vacation would be nice."

"Oh?"

"Yeah." She was warming up to the idea as she spoke, imagining a luxurious holiday so they could reconnect. "We could get away, find someplace romantic, and stop fighting about work all the time. Remember when we were dating, how you'd talk about going to Hawaii and spending all day on the beach?"

He chuckled. "Yeah, and imagine the sunburn I'd get. Do you really want to surround yourself with young girls who still look good in a bikini?"

"Uh." Her mouth dropped open. "I thought you liked how I look in a bikini!"

"Well, yeah, but it's not like you're eighteen anymore, sweetie. Let's be honest. Neither am I." He patted his paunch. "Age does this to us."

"I'm barely thirty-four, Owen!"

"And after you get stretch marks?" He paused, chuckling to himself. "Maybe we should go."

Brook took another bite of her entree to keep from yelling. Slowly, she chewed, then swallowed, washing it down with a very healthy gulp of wine. "I'm not ready to have a baby. It won't happen this year." There, she'd put her foot down.

Across the table, her husband's face was tense. "I didn't ask, Brook. We *are* going to start a family. Am I clear?"

"No! This isn't a household chore. This isn't something you get to decide on your own." Her voice was growing louder.

"You're my wife, damn it! Don't you think six years is long enough to wait?"

"I think being a parent is about a lot more than marking an X on a calendar, especially when you keep saying you hate kids. Why now? Why is it suddenly so important?"

"My entire family is moving forward, except us." He slapped his hand on the white tablecloth. "They expect certain things of me. Why can't you see that?"

"Doesn't what I want matter?" she shot back.

The sound of his teeth grinding could be heard across the table. Brook sighed. There went a romantic dinner together. All they did lately was fight. It felt like Owen wanted her to be someone else, and she wasn't ready to give in. He had this image in his mind, and whoever it was, it wasn't her. She knew his parents put a lot of pressure on him, but he was thirty-eight! When would he stop worrying about it?

"I should have known you weren't the type of woman who could handle this life," he grumbled under his breath. "I convinced myself you were smarter than you appear, but maybe I was wrong. Maybe you want to end up some piece of shit trailer trash?" He leaned closer, his eyes narrowed in anger. "Shoveling shit for a living, surrounded by a million dogs, shacked up with some guy that can't stay sober? Sounds a lot like the college life, huh? Still want to be a kid, Brook?"

"I'd rather be happy in a trailer than miserable in a mansion," she shot back. "Maybe a drunk husband would give a damn about the woman he was with instead of treating me like a paper doll to show off."

"Don't you dare take that tone with me."

"Or what?" She leaned back, pushing away her plate. "I said 'I do' not 'I'll serve.' Don't ever think I'm your slave."

"You're my wife!" His voice was loud enough to make people look.

She glanced over at Alison's table. The blonde had her eyes right on them. The romantic dinner had just turned into a public spectacle, and Brook felt her face growing hot. She pushed back some more, needing to escape.

"Excuse me, Owen."

His hand snaked out, grabbing her arm. "Where do you think you're going?"

"Ladies room. Please let go. I just need to calm down. This was supposed to be a date, not a debate. I'll be back."

Slowly, he released his grip. Brook took a calming breath, then stood and walked across the dining area. Eyes followed, burning a hole in her back, and conversations began to hum in her wake. She couldn't get to the bathroom fast enough.

The cold, harsh fluorescent lighting helped. It wasn't romantic. It wasn't pretty. It just clarified every flaw in everything. Owen was an asshole, and she would not just sit down and shut up like he wanted. She didn't have to! Before they got married, she was so close to getting her own degree, but he'd convinced her to wait. He told her she could go back to school later. It hadn't happened, and now she was completely reliant on him.

Her stomach dropped to her toes. He'd also taken all the money. Owen had moved their finances around, and she still didn't have a bank card. He hadn't even bothered to give her the account number. She knew the name of the bank, but that was it. He probably hadn't meant to, but Owen had cut her off from every safety net she could think of. Her parents were across the country, she had no friends, and now she didn't even have her own money.

But staring in the mirror didn't help. The harsh light pointed out the tiny creases around her eyes. She wasn't old - not yet - but she wasn't a stunning college girl, either. If her marriage was falling apart, what would she do? She was almost middle-aged; she couldn't just start over! She could either end up the crazy dog lady or be stuck as her husband's little Barbie doll. Or maybe he was right. Maybe she was just trailer trash who'd tried to rise above her place.

Brook took a deep breath and told herself she was overreacting, but she knew better. She'd gotten complacent. Thinking she loved her husband, she'd just trusted everything he'd done, and he'd been taking advantage of that. Maybe it was time she started doing something about it? If taking care of herself ruined her marriage, then it wasn't a very good one to start with, right? Right! As soon as they got home, she'd make sure at least one thing worked out in her favor - there was no way she was going to have Owen's child. Not with their relationship in such an ugly place.

That was when the ladies' room door swung open. "Brook?" It was Alison.

"I'm in here."

Alison scampered in, rushing to give a hug without asking. "I gave you two minutes to keep your pride, but I couldn't wait any longer. Are you ok?"

For the first time in years, Brook relaxed, letting her head drop onto her friend's shoulder. "No, Ali, I'm not. I can't make him happy. I think my husband hates me."

"Hush, it's ok." She slowly rocked from side to side. "It's not supposed to be all on you. He's gotta do a little trying, too."

"I know." Brook sucked in a breath and leaned back. "I'm sorry to pull you away from your author."

"Jon told me to check on you. Said if I didn't, he would, so I'm checking." Alison grinned, the smile meant to make Brook mimic it. "The last thing I need is to try and control the press if they find out some New York Times best-selling author was hanging out in the wrong bathroom. I mean, that's probably not something they'd let him work off at your rescue, right?"

"Right." The smallest giggle slipped out. "I'm so glad you were here tonight. God, Ali, I've missed you."

"I'm still here. I'll always be here for you, Brook. Don't care if it's a year from now, or twenty. Best friends forever, even if your husband won't let us have play dates. If you ever need me, I'm just a phone call away."

"Yeah." Brook wiped the smudged mascara under her

eyes. "So can I get your number again? I lost it when Owen upgraded my phone."

One deft twist of Alison's fingers opened her clutch, and an elegant business card appeared. "Anytime, ok? I'm worried about you, Brooklyn. I don't want you to ever feel like you're all alone, because if you need me, I'll be there with bells on."

"God, I've missed you, Ali. I've missed you so much."

CHAPTER EIGHT

*D*inner didn't get any better, but at least Brook had eaten most of her meal before it turned into a verbal sparring match. They both skipped dessert, and the ride home was tense. Owen pulled into their drive and stopped, jamming the car into park. He took a long, frustrated breath, turned as if he was going to say something, then changed his mind. Before she could ask what, he got out of the car and slammed the door, storming toward the house.

Brook followed, giving him plenty of space. As she stepped inside, she could hear him throwing something around upstairs. This wasn't going to be one of those cold shoulder types of fights. Nope. Something was going to break.

For a moment, she debated just going to bed, but it was too early for that. Besides, she hadn't done a thing with her dog. At least that was something Owen wouldn't try to get involved with. Kicking off her heels, she decided Calvin needed a little more attention tonight. Partly in honor of Gummy, and partly as an excuse to be anywhere but with her husband. Happy sixth anniversary, right?

She barely opened the door to the study before the excited thump of a tail brought a smile to her face. Springing open the kennel, she hurried Calvin outside. Hearing another crash from above, she followed him through the door. He did his business first - since he was too old to be a silly puppy - then came back for a little more personal attention. Somewhere in the grass, he'd also found his ball.

It was such a simple thing, throwing the ball for her dog, but with each toss, a little tension faded. Every time the mutt wrestled to get it back, it warmed her heart a bit. Dogs were just so honest. All Calvin wanted was her undivided attention, and only for a few moments. He didn't expect the world. He never asked for something she couldn't give. A hug, a scratch between the ears, and someone to throw the ball so he could gladly bring it back - those were the simple joys in life, and she was more than willing to give them.

She kept throwing the ball until Calvin's tongue nearly dragged the ground. The dog deserved unconditional love, and giving it made her as happy as it did him. Why couldn't Owen see that? How could he just ignore how much her pet meant to her? Why did he want to change everything about their life together to please some trumped-up ideal that no one could ever reach? Why didn't he care at all that he was making her miserable? Didn't he love her?

When Calvin couldn't do more than walk across the yard, she called him in. Rubbing her hands in the scruff of his neck, she offered just a bit more affection before releasing him into the house. The crashing had stopped, but Owen was still storming around. Evidently ignoring him wasn't going to cool his temper, so she should probably face it head-on.

When she turned for the stairs, her stomach clenched. Walking up, the dread seeped into her muscles, making her feel so weary. She was sick and tired of all the drama. All the fighting!

At the top, she saw the devastation. Towels. Packages of toilet paper. A box of tampons. Everything from the bathroom had been thrown recklessly into the hall. Cautiously, she stepped in. Why had he destroyed their bathroom? Owen was prone to fits of rage, but this made no sense! Then she saw it.

Tossed into the wastebasket was a small, pink packet. Beside it were the foil inserts. All of them were empty. Her three-month supply of birth control pills was gone. He'd popped out each one and thrown away what was left.

For a moment she couldn't even think; she just stared. He'd thrown away her pills. He said she was going to have his child, and when she said no, he threw away her birth control pills! Each time the thought circled through her mind, she got angrier, until all reason fled before it. With her hands clenched into fists, she screamed across the house.

"What the fuck do you think you're doing?"

Before he could answer, she stormed into their bedroom. The drywall took a beating as she slammed the door open, the knob crashing into it. He had to be in here. This was the only place he'd go. Brook filled her lungs again.

"God damn it, Owen. You *do not own me!*"

He stepped out from behind the half-open closet door, bare-chested, with his pants hanging open. "Shut up, Brook."

"You threw away my pills."

"Flushed them."

"And you think that's going to get you an heir to your throne? Doesn't work like that. I said I'm not going to have your child, and I meant it. If you refuse to let me use the pill, then that means you're not getting a piece for a very long time, I guess."

He slammed the closet door and surged toward her. The look on his face mirrored the way she felt: pissed. Brook turned, expecting him to yell, but he didn't stop. His arm yanked her the rest of the way into the room while his other hand found her throat. The next step shoved her into the wall, his entire body keeping her there.

"You will learn to do what I say!" he screamed, shoving her with each word.

Her head bounced off the wall once, then she pulled, trying to get free. As she slapped at his arms and tried to kick at his legs, Owen's hand moved to her hair, wrenching her head back, but the grip on her throat was too tight, too strong. She couldn't get away! He kept shoving, as if he couldn't remember how to stop, and nothing she tried could break her free. Quickly losing oxygen, the dull pounding against the back of her skull and the strong thumb over her windpipe were doing the trick. She couldn't breathe! In seconds, the only thing she could hear was the rasping of what little breath she could sneak past his fist and the pounding of her heart trying so hard to push the blood past the iron grip around her neck.

When the world started to fade at the edges, she

panicked, but it didn't help. Her screams didn't get past his anger, but they were enough. They were barely enough. From downstairs, somehow, her dog heard and rushed to the aid of his pack.

Calvin burst into the room with his hair up. From the way his lips were raised, she knew he was growling, but he looked so confused. The dog's head wavered between Owen and Brook. She wanted to tell him to leave. He needed to find somewhere safe, but the stupid mutt loved her. He loved her enough to pick sides, and her husband paid her best friend for it with a sharp kick to the ribs. Calvin yipped, but the pain told him who the enemy was. Stalking closer, his eyes were locked on Owen, and the friendly mutt had become a monster.

Owen snarled out a curse and shoved her into the wall, finally releasing her. Brook slumped to the ground, sucking back gulps of air, barely aware that her husband was reaching for something. Too late, her mind put all the pieces together. In the corner of the room were his golf clubs. On the other side was a pissed-off eighty-pound dog. Brook screamed, but it didn't help. Owen swung over his head. The impact was sickening, but it wasn't enough. Calvin cried, then whined, but she couldn't find enough air to make her muscles move. Then there was nothing but silence.

"That," Owen snarled under his breath, "is what will happen every time you try to fuck me over. Do you understand, Brook?"

"Go to hell."

Without a pause, he kicked her right in the gut, forcing out what little air she'd found. "Do you understand!"

"Yes," she gasped, trying to make her lungs work again.

She bobbed her head emphatically, hoping he could see. "Yes."

"Good. Don't you dare forget." Then he kicked her again.

❧

*D*awn was just breaking when Brook woke up. She'd never made it to bed. She'd never even made it out of her clothes from the night before. She'd only made it into a crumpled heap on the floor, but the sound of snoring assured her that Owen didn't really care.

It took a minute to run a full check of her body. Nothing appeared to be broken, but Brook wasn't sure that mattered. It all hurt, and the last thing she could remember was Calvin trying to protect her.

That was what made her get up. Confused and a little scared, she did it silently, her eyes locked on the lump in the bed only a few feet away. Beside him, the digital clock glowed, showing 5:43. His alarm wouldn't go off for about forty-five minutes. She had to hurry.

Scampering back downstairs, she prayed her dog was ok. Owen hated him sleeping in the bedroom, so maybe he'd left him outside? In the back of her mind, she couldn't stop thinking about the golf clubs, but hoped she'd only dreamed that. She had to check first. That was all she could do. She had to look anywhere Calvin could be.

The backyard was empty; so was the kennel in the den. She checked both bathrooms, but the doors were open and there wasn't a dog in sight. With her heart pounding in her chest, she made her way into the garage. It was dark and silent, only a small light from the garage door opener leading her way. She just had to be sure. She had to check everywhere because she couldn't stand not knowing.

Edging around Owen's car, she froze. The tall black garbage can stood with the lid flipped back. Part of a leg and a very still foot could be seen. Brook smothered the wail that wanted out but rushed forward. She had to know!

Inside, she found her dog. His body had been thrown carelessly alongside the kitchen scraps and paper waste. He hadn't even been given the courtesy of a bag to shield him from view. Calvin, her friend for the last four years, was gone. He'd died trying to protect her, and all Brook had done was sit on the ground and cry. She hadn't fought back. She hadn't tried to run. She'd sat there, letting it all play out before her, completely and totally spineless. Tears begged to be released, but she wouldn't cry. She didn't deserve that, because she'd done nothing. She'd just sat there, completely useless.

It would be the last time that ever happened.

She was done. Her husband was abusive, and her dog had paid the price. The least she could do was make sure his death mattered. Flipping the lid closed, she made her way back inside, mentally cataloging the things she'd need so she wouldn't break down. The sight of Owen erased it all. Standing there in wrinkled pajamas that proved he'd just crawled out of bed, her husband's glare was anything but apologetic. He looked ready for round two. Obviously the fight wasn't over.

"I'm going to make this very clear," he said, malice dripping from every word. "You will learn to do what I say, or I will take away something else. If you ever try to fight me again, I'll make sure you regret it more than you do now. You're a beautiful, intelligent, and respectable woman, and I expect you to start acting like it. Is that clear?"

Her head moved back and forth, denying his words even though she knew he meant it. "What more do I have to lose?"

He jerked his chin at her. "Everything. Your parents are too far away and too damned broke to save you. You don't have any friends left. Without me, you'll be alone, starving on the street. Don't push me, Brook. I'll throw your ass out and make you dream of the days when all you had to worry about was being a good wife."

She understood what he was saying, but didn't agree. That didn't mean she was dumb enough to tell him. Right now, he was angry enough to kill her. "Ok," she whispered.

"And you're quitting that damned job. Today!"

She just nodded, biting her lips to keep them from trembling. Deep inside, her mind was spinning. She had nothing. No money, no place to go, and no one to come to her rescue except one friend who she hadn't talked to in years. That meant she needed to be everything he wanted until she could figure out how to get out.

"Good. Now go get dressed. I'll take you to the shelter so you can quit in person, then drop you back here. We need to leave in thirty minutes, and you're embarrassing."

"Can I get my clothes out of the dryer?"

He smiled, hearing obedience in her voice. "Yes, sweetie. Make it quick."

She did. Then she grabbed a hasty shower, using the streaming water to hide her tears. She didn't dare sob, though. Owen had never understood how much she cared for that silly mutt, but she did. Her dog had given his life for her. There was no way she'd ever forget that - or let her husband get away with it.

It wasn't until she stepped out that she saw the mark on her neck. Dark and red, it was starting to change to purple. Makeup might hide it, but if anyone bothered to look, the handprint was obvious. Brook dried her hair, smiling cruelly at her reflection. It was all the proof she'd need.

Owen didn't know it, but he'd just picked a fight with the wrong bitch. Maybe he had a lot of pressure to live up to the standards his family set, but that was not an excuse. It certainly did not give him the right to threaten her or kill her dog. This crossed the line. It went so far across the line that she could barely play her part, but she had to. Right now, she couldn't leave, not until she had a place to go, but this was going to be the start of a new war - and she was damned sure she knew who would win.

First, she had to convince her husband she was compliant. Keeping to the schedule he'd set, she rushed to her closet and found a respectable pair of slacks and a nice polo shirt. Next, she made only the lightest use of her foundation and concealer. A few swipes of mascara made it fit, but she wasn't going to bother with shadow or liner. Her hair went back into a simple ponytail, but it was her choice of shoes that screamed the real defiance. Digging into the back of her closet, Brook pulled out a pair of black, steel-toed work boots. Nice and shiny, they were completely functional - for packing and moving everything she owned.

With ten minutes to spare, she jogged downstairs to let him know she was ready. If Owen wanted her to change her life, she could do that. Brooklyn Sanders had never been a pushover. It wasn't until she was married and took her husband's last name that she'd lost her common sense, but he'd just drawn the battle lines right across her dog's body. Brook Harper might be an idiot, but Mrs. Harper was her title, not her fate. Her husband had no idea that he'd married a woman who had no problem changing the rules.

This war was going to be a very cold one, but she wouldn't stop until she'd won back her freedom.

CHAPTER NINE

*O*wen didn't trust her at all. When they arrived at Tall Tails, he followed her in. She found Marcy easily, but when she stepped into the Executive Director's office, her husband came too. While he hovered, Brook explained that she no longer had time to work at the rescue, so her resignation was effective immediately. Her boss was stunned into silence - something that rarely happened. Owen tried to help by explaining that they were going to be starting a family, but it only made the line on Marcy's forehead deepen.

Confused and bewildered, her boss nodded like she understood, but only barely. From the look on her face, she couldn't quite make the pieces all fit together in a logical manner, but neither could Brook. Owen was the only person who seemed to think any of this made sense. Maybe it did in his warped and twisted mind.

When they turned to leave, Owen's hand clamped down on her arm hard enough to bruise. Marcy's eyes flicked right to it. She evidently knew something wasn't right, even if she had no clue what to do. Right now, Brook just hoped she didn't say a thing. Shooting her boss a look that begged for her understanding, Brook let her husband all but drag her from the room.

Across the lobby, a shadow caught her eyes. Big, tall, and wearing both his black shelter tee and matching black jeans, Ryder leaned against the wall with his arms crossed. His eyes followed her, the look on his face murderous, but she finally understood it. Ryder wasn't dangerous; he was protective.

She pasted on a smile, catching his eye as she was dragged back to the car. When Ryder moved to follow, she shook her head, hoping Owen didn't notice.

Ryder paused, his eyes narrowed, then he took a long breath. "Mrs. Harper?" he called out, making Owen stop in his tracks.

Her husband turned, dragging Brook with him to glare at the man. "She doesn't work here anymore."

"Oh." Ryder pushed himself away from the wall. "Was gonna let you know this is my last day. Any way I can get a picture with you, ma'am?"

"With me?" Her head snapped to Owen, then back. "We were just leaving."

He pulled out his phone and shrugged. "Just a quick one, so I can post it to my friends. Let them know I'm not lying when I said I was working at a shelter and all."

Her eyes flicked to Owen. "Is that ok?" she whispered.

Her husband released her with a tiny push, propelling her toward the man. He didn't have to say a word. His actions made it clear that she'd best make this quick and not draw any extra attention to herself.

Ryder stepped beside her and bent just enough to put his head at the level of hers. Holding his phone up, he angled the screen toward them. That was when she realized what he was doing. He was trying to get a clear shot of her neck! With a charming smile, Brook looked up at his face, effectively baring her throat. The electronic click went off twice in quick succession.

"If you give me your number, I'll send you a copy." Ryder chuckled, his face turned to the ground. "This way I can remember the woman who taught me how to clean up my shit, right?"

"Sure." She recited her number and patted his arm. "Thanks, Ryder. I hope you enjoy your last day."

"Will do, Mrs. Harper. Good luck with whatever you do next."

Her cell phone buzzed in her purse, but Brook didn't bother to check. She didn't want to give Owen an excuse to look at that picture. He had to know that everyone in the room could see the bruises he'd left on her throat, but maybe he honestly thought this was normal? Could he really believe that no one would say a thing? Then again, no one really had.

Without pausing, she marched herself right out of the building she used to love. This was the one job she'd always wanted. Maybe it didn't pay enough to cover her bills, but she'd managed to make a difference to at least a few dogs, and those dogs had repaid her in their own way. Just like Calvin. Just like Gummy.

The thought made her eyes blur with unshed tears, but she didn't have time for that. She'd cry later when her husband wouldn't be able to see. Right now, she had to focus. She had to play the part of the perfectly meek and docile wife. She had to do whatever it took for Owen to forget that she'd ever tried to have a mind of her own. The sooner he believed she was complacent, the sooner she could figure out how the hell to get out of that house!

The drive back home was filled with a list of what Owen expected of her, including a schedule for sex. He understood that her birth control could still be working from the previous dose, so he *kindly* allowed her a week for the hormones to wear off. After that, he expected an enthusiastic attempt to get with child. It was easy to tune him out. The hard part was not rolling her eyes.

It was almost ten a.m. before her husband finally went to work. He took her keys when he did, but not her phone. What he left was a list of her duties for the day. It looked like something out of an old movie: laundry, house cleaning, and a menu for dinner. Evidently, in the six years they'd been married, Owen hadn't figured out that Brook wasn't a gourmet chef, and she couldn't make roast lamb without a trip to the grocery store. It wouldn't just appear in the fridge by magic. The whole thing was just more proof that he'd obviously lost his mind.

She made a lap of the house, trying to just walk off her anxiety. It didn't help. In the garage, under the very same roof, her loyal dog's body was still waiting in the garbage can. For a moment, she wondered if she should bury him, but decided against it. That would only make Owen angrier. What she needed to be doing was finding a way to get out of this hell.

She was trapped on the other side of the country from her family. Not that they had any resources to help. Her parents weren't well-off. Her older sister had an entire brood of children to look after. They weren't the trailer trash Owen raged about, but they were barely a step above it. When Brook had gotten married, her parents hadn't been thrilled with the idea of her moving so far away. Unfortunately, she finally understood why. There was no way for them to help when she needed it most.

But she could help herself. And yes, divorce was at the top of the list, right under escaping. There was no excuse that would make her forgive that man. He'd *killed* her dog. Never mind that he'd physically abused her, what he'd done to Calvin was so much worse. All her excuses had been destroyed with that heinous act. She had no more reasons to try to save her marriage. She just had to figure out how the hell to get out of this house. What she really needed was a friend to help her think. Someone she could bounce ideas off of.

Brook paused. Someone like Alison!

Rushing back to the entryway, she found her purse and began digging. The first time through, she couldn't find it. For a moment, she wondered if Owen had stolen the card from her purse, then she remembered she hadn't put it in the main pocket; she'd slipped it into the coin purse on the front.

Right where she'd left it, the card for Alison Brewer, literary agent, was as pristine as it had been last night. Brook dialed, listening to it ring.

"This is Alison."

The sound of that voice made all the fear, stress, and anxiety manageable. Brook's breath rushed out, her back hit the wall, and she slowly slid to the floor. "Ali?"

"Brook?"

"He killed Calvin. Last night, he was so mad at me that when we got home, he threw all of my birth control in the toilet and killed my dog!"

"Where are you?" Alison's voice was insistent.

"Home. He made me quit the rescue and brought me back. I'm supposed to have the house clean and dinner ready for when he gets off work."

"When?"

"Um." Brook tried to remember how long it took Owen to drive home. "He gets off at five. Well, he's supposed to, and I have a feeling he's not going to work late tonight."

"So about six hours. I'm out of town, so it'll take me a bit to get there, and I'd rather you weren't in the middle of packing if he decides to come home early."

"Huh?" What was her friend talking about?

Alison just laughed gently, the sound meant to be soothing. "Honey, I have a really nice couch. It's not a lot, but I swear to you that I'm not going to smack you around. Besides, I'm not letting you spend another day with that asshole."

"But... What about Leah?"

"Leah loves you, Brook. She's said a million times that she wishes you'd come visit more. I mean, it's been years since we've seen you. Think of this like making up for all that lost time."

"You're going to let me stay with you? But I can't. We've barely talked in years, and you have a job to think about."

Alison shushed her softly. "Doesn't matter how long it's been. Granted, this isn't the best plan, but I'm working with what I have. Now is there any place you can go until I can drive there? Just over two hours, sweetie."

Brook shook her head even though Alison wouldn't be able to see. "No. I don't have any friends but you. Owen made sure of that. I didn't even realize it until last night, but he makes me feel bad for spending time with anyone but him, so I just kinda stopped. I don't know..." Her voice trailed off. "Just a guy from the shelter who was kinda nice."

"Can you call him?"

Brook thought about Ryder sending her the picture. "Yeah. I think I can."

"Ok. Call him and see if there's any way he can help you out. If not, I can find someone, I'm sure. Just need to get you and some clothes out of the house before your husband comes home. Don't worry about the furniture or anything else. Just grab enough to get by, ok? We'll buy anything else. The most important thing, though, is you. Do you understand?"

"Yeah."

"Good," Alison said. "Now call your friend, then text me and let me know. I'm gonna get on the road. If there are *any* problems, then just wait until after lunch to start packing. I don't want that asshole to come home at the wrong time." She paused. "Never liked him, but now I hate that fucker."

"Me too," Brook breathed. "And when you get here, I need you to take me to a few banks. He took the one thing I loved, so I'm gonna take half of what he cares about."

"That's my girl. I'll talk to you in about two hours."

Brook hung up with her long-lost best friend and dialed the number listed beside the picture of her bruised throat. It rang four times before going to voicemail, so she left a message asking Ryder to call if he had a moment and that she hoped she wasn't bothering him. Thirty seconds later, her phone rang.

"Mrs. Harper? This is Ryder from the shelter."

"Hey, um..." She had to swallow around the lump that appeared in her throat. "I know you don't know me very well, but I don't know who else to call."

He chuckled. It sounded almost relieved. "Brook, if this has anything to do with the mark on your neck, I'm more than happy to help, but I'm supposed to be at the shelter until five."

"I'm leaving him."

For a moment, there was nothing but silence on the line. "Give me five minutes, and I'll call you back." The line went dead. He didn't even bother saying goodbye.

She stared at the phone in shock, but he'd said five minutes. If he didn't call back, then that was his way of saying no without needing to actually *say* it. Not like they were friends or anything. Hell, she'd probably spent a grand total of two hours with the guy all week. But she'd spilled her guts, and that shame was trying to turn into anger, so Brook decided a distraction was in order.

She had a backpack filled with all of her bathroom supplies when her pocket began to vibrate. Brook hurried to reach her phone, answering with a clipped, "Hey?"

"Brook? It's Ryder."

"I didn't really think you'd call me back!"

He made a disappointed grumble. "There is no way in hell I wouldn't come help, just had to see if I was gonna be breaking the law again. If you text me your address, I'll be over in a few minutes. Marcy said she'll even keep me on the clock because helping you out sure as hell counts as community service."

"Oh." Somehow she'd been expecting the worst. Hearing that everything was happening? She couldn't believe it. "Ok. I'll do that. Thank you, Ryder! Oh, thank you so much."

"You're welcome. Now hang up and text me your address so I can GPS it."

She did, then she began throwing things together as fast as she could. It wasn't much, but she could get what she needed to make a new life. And she could find the one thing that mattered most - to her husband. His money. She hurried into his office, not even caring if she left a mess in her wake. Yanking open the drawers, she fumbled through files until she found it. A list of their bank accounts and the latest statements. Each one had the account numbers clearly printed at the top. There were more than she expected.

Staring at the stack of papers, Brook realized Owen had been slowly but surely cutting her off from everything. She'd thought it was accidental, but she was wrong. He didn't want a strong and independent wife. He wanted a puppet. He wanted a little trophy to show his father that he could be just like him. Unfortunately, he picked the wrong woman, and now she had help.

Thirty-two minutes after she sent her last text, a dark truck pulled into her drive. A second later, her phone beeped with a message from Ryder. She ran down the stairs to greet him, then paused. Heading up the street was a white cargo van that she'd never seen before. Ryder was waving them toward the house.

"Called some movers to help grab your things. You willing to point out what we should load?"

On impulse, Brook thanked him the only way she could. She wrapped her arms around the big guy's waist and hugged. Patting her back awkwardly, he chuckled.

"Thank you, Ryder. I know you barely know me - "

He gently ran a hand over the back of her hair, soothing her. "Let's just get you out of this house and someplace safe until your friend can pick you up. Marcy said you can hide out at the shelter."

"Yeah. There's just one thing." Closing her eyes, she took a deep breath and admitted her nightmare out loud.

"My dog's body is in the garage, and I don't know what to do with him."

"Nothing," Ryder said softly. "Let's worry about you first, and if I have to, I'll come back for him tonight, ok?"

"But -"

He shrugged. "Unconditional loyalty, remember? He'd do anything to keep you safe, so don't mess it up now. We'll make sure he's taken care of one way or another. I promise."

Overwhelmed with relief, she led the way inside and started pointing out the boxes she'd thrown together. It was nothing but the basics. Sadly, she couldn't risk taking more than that, but it would keep her clothed until she had a new job, a new home, and a new life to start living. With a little help from people who were barely more than strangers, she was going to put her life back on track, and that meant leaving all of the old behind.

Well, it sounded good, at least. Besides, as a single woman, it wasn't like she had to worry about hosting her husband's parties or any of the crap she'd always hated. In a few hours, she'd have no reason to be a very good wife.

Brook grabbed the clothes from her closet and shoved them into a garbage bag. She made sure she got all of the nice ones, too. If Owen had taught her anything, it was that appearances mattered, and maybe a short skirt could make her new life just a bit more interesting. Never mind that her husband had also taught her all about how to secure her finances. If he thought moving it around would keep it out of her reach, he was going to be very shocked. She gave up everything for him: her degree, her family, and her own dreams. The least he could do was make sure she had enough to support her until she was a legally single woman.

When everything was packed into the van and truck, she only had one thing left to do. Brook walked into the kitchen and placed a simple note on the island. She didn't mince words or try to explain anything. Scrawled across the paper in permanent marker were only four words.

I'm not your bitch.

CHAPTER TEN

Earlier...

*W*hen Ryder got to the shelter that morning, something was different. It took a minute to figure it out, but when he walked down the hall toward the kennels, he realized Brook's office was empty. His stomach tensed, feeling like it had dropped to his feet, but maybe she just had a few things to do before she came in. Besides, running late was pretty normal for her.

At least he hoped so. It was his last day at the shelter, and he'd almost convinced himself to ask her if she'd like to hang out later. Not a date. Certainly not that. She was married and he? Well, he had enough issues for the both of them. He just wanted to see her again, just because she liked the dogs as much as he did, but she wasn't here, and he had plenty of work to do.

He was pulling out his things in the intake kennel when Danielle waved him down. He couldn't hear her over the clamor of the dogs, but she had both arms extended fully and was waving like she was directing a plane. Parking his wheelbarrow, Ryder gestured for her to lead the way and followed.

He was barely in the hall before she rounded on him. "Brook quit! I mean, she's quitting! You have to talk her out of it!"

Yeah, that knot was back with a vengeance. "She's quitting?"

Danielle pointed toward the front of the building. "Her and her husband are in with Marcy right now, but that's not the bad part. Ryder, her neck! I think she got mugged."

That knot? Yep, it had grown into a monster, and it was rolling in the bottom of his belly. Ryder didn't need to hear anything else. He didn't even bother answering Danielle. He just pushed past her, heading toward the front. If anyone had hurt Brook, then he'd make them pay - and rip her husband a new one just on principle.

Had it happened on their date the night before? Had someone held them up for her husband's wallet, the car, or Brook's purse? Had it been him? Was she ok? Each thought made him walk a little faster, and he wasn't the only one. On the back side of the rescue, everyone was making their way to see her off. The rumors were flying, everything from her being pregnant to her husband making her quit. He didn't have time to listen; he just wanted to make sure she was ok.

He stepped into the lobby just as she left Marcy's office. Her husband was with her, one hand in a death grip on her upper arm. Ryder dropped his shoulder against the wall and waited for Owen to adjust, to wrap an arm around her, or something - anything less brutal. But he didn't. He also didn't seem to care at all that the world could see the dark mark across the middle of her throat. Ryder wanted to rip the man's head off, but he couldn't. Not here. He'd been warned that any more arrests would send him to jail - alone. That meant he had to plan this just a bit better.

That was when Brook looked at him. The tension in every muscle of her body was visible, but when he saw her eyes, he knew he wasn't wrong. She was afraid. Truly, completely, and totally terrified of anyone making a scene and her husband taking it out on her later.

But Ryder couldn't help himself. "Mrs. Harper?" he called out, and her husband jerked to a stop.

The man was of average height, but he was soft and plump. His gut hung well over his belt, and his hair was starting to vanish. If Ryder had to guess, he was probably a high school sports star, a college fraternity member, and now had some middle management job that he thought made him important. In other words, he was nothing, just like every other waste of flesh on the entire planet.

He also looked like he wasn't pleased to have some strange man talking to his wife. "She doesn't work here anymore."

"Oh." Ryder made a point of ignoring the man and talking right to Brook. "Was gonna let you know this is my last day. Any way I can get a picture with you, ma'am?"

"With me?" Like a timid puppy, her head whipped between her husband and Rider. If she could have backed away, she would have. "We were just leaving."

He pulled out his phone and lifted it so they could both see it. "Just a quick one, so I can post it to my friends. Let them know I'm not lying when I said I was working at a shelter and all."

Her eyes flicked to Owen. "Is that ok?"

Her husband gave her a little push. Ryder was ready to catch her, but this was Brook. She barely even staggered, quickly turning into the elegant woman he'd first met. When she moved to his side, he wanted to say something, but knew better. People like that man were always listening, waiting for their next chance to get revenge for any perceived wrongs. It wasn't Brook's fault, but she was the one that got punished. Unfortunately, he'd left the proof of it right across the base of her throat. Ryder just had to angle the phone the right way, and she'd have all the proof she needed.

Then Brook leaned toward him a bit more, exposing her neck as if she knew. On the screen of his phone, he could see she did. She'd figured out exactly what he was doing, and she was trusting him. Now for the hardest part.

"If you give me your number, I'll send you a copy." Ryder dropped his head to the ground to hide the ironic laugh. "This way I can remember the woman who taught me how to clean up my shit, right?"

She recited her number, but that was all. As she was walking away, he sent her a quick message, just a thanks and the image, but she didn't acknowledge it. Maybe her husband would forget before she even got home. Hopefully, *she* wouldn't.

Then she was gone. All around him, the other volunteers were rambling about what had just happened. Ryder wasn't the only one who'd put a few things together, but most of the others just wanted to gossip. Going out of their way to help her? Wasn't gonna happen. Ryder, however, sent a text to his brother, asking him to see what options they had. Hunter responded, letting him know he was on it, but that was all. Then again, stealing a woman away from her home was typically called kidnapping. Well, unless she asked for help.

Two hours later, his phone began to vibrate. He was in

the last bank of kennels, the farthest from the door, but Ryder ran. There was no way she'd hear him if he tried to answer, and he knew it was her. It had to be. Who else would call? Hunter always texted.

Then it stopped. Darting into the hall, he swiped at the screen, breathing a sigh of relief when he saw the voicemail. He didn't even bother listening to it, just called her back.

"Mrs. Harper? This is Ryder from the shelter."

"Hey, um..." She sounded nervous. "I know you don't know me very well, but I don't know who else to call."

"Brook, if this has anything to do with the mark on your neck, I'm more than happy to help, but I'm supposed to be at the shelter until five."

"I'm leaving him."

His mind spun, running through his options. "Give me five minutes, and I'll call you back." He clicked the button to disconnect as he started jogging toward the front, mashing out a message to his brother, as he went.

"Marcy," he gasped, leaning around her door. "Mrs. Harper just called me, asking if I could pick her up."

"To come back to work?" She sounded both confused and hopeful.

Ryder just shook his head. "To get her away from her husband. He's the one that hurt her, and you have two options - "

The shelter manager cut him off. "Go. If she needs to stay here, that's fine, just get her *out*. I'll keep you on the clock, because helping her sure as hell is community service and you're big enough to make sure that asshole doesn't try to stop you."

That was all he needed. The adrenaline was starting to set in, but doing was Ryder's specialty. His brother handled the pretty words; he took care of the action. Right now, what Brook needed was a whole lot less talk and a hell of a lot more action. In other words, he was the perfect man for the job.

With his keys in hand, he was headed to the parking lot, listening to her phone ring. When she answered, she sounded terrified of what she'd hear. Well, it was about time she realized that not everyone was going to let her down.

"Brook? It's Ryder."

"I didn't really think you'd call me back!"

"There is no way in hell I wouldn't come help, just had to see if I was gonna be breaking the law again." He wrenched open the door of his truck and climbed in. "If you text me your address, I'll be over in a few minutes. Marcy said she'll even keep me on the clock because helping you out sure as hell counts as community service."

"Oh. Ok. I'll do that. Thank you, Ryder! Oh, thank you so much."

"You're welcome. Now hang up and text me your address so I can GPS it." As soon as he heard the phone click, he started the truck, sending off a message to his brother.

Hunter called a small moving company just to make sure she could get this done fast. Ryder barely made it to her house before the moving van pulled in behind him. The thanks he got? Brook let go of all her proper and just wrapped her arms around him. For a moment, he thought she was going to cry, but not this woman. She wasn't that kind of girl. No, she had already started making plans.

Then she told him about her dog. He promised her he'd take care of it, but she didn't need the details. Right now, she was the most important thing, but her dog might just be able to get his own revenge, too.

With the help of the movers, they got all of her stuff out and back to Tall Tails. Marcy had blocked off one of the adoption rooms, where potential owners got to play with the pets. It was out of sight and unlikely to be needed for anything else. She didn't even give Ryder the chance to say a thing, just snatched Brook away from him and hauled her back there, muttering comforting words the whole way. That worked out, though, because he had things to do. There was still a cargo van full of her stuff and nowhere to put it. At least, not until her friend arrived, and he wasn't really sure it would all fit. Brook hadn't exactly packed well, just fast.

Instead, he emptied out the van, moving it all to the back of his truck, and then tried to guess what she'd need most. Anything else, he could take to her as soon as he was off, or rent a storage unit for her, or keep it at his house. Whichever she needed. Then again, while she was waiting, maybe he should just ask.

He was almost to the room when he saw Marcy walk out. She was smiling from ear to ear. "Her friend's here, and she's taking Brook to someplace safe." Then her face began to fall. "But she won't be able to work for us. If her husband found out?"

Ryder just rubbed the woman's arm. "Guess that means Danielle might have a chance to move up now, huh? She seems like she'd be pretty good. And don't worry about Brook. I have a feeling a few of us will take real good care of her."

Marcy's eyes just narrowed. "Don't you go thinking you can just sweep her off her feet, young man."

He shook his head. "No, ma'am. She was just real good

to me, and I don't take well to people picking on anyone smaller than them."

"Lemme guess. Or you'll break their car?" She was referring to the incident that sent him here in the first place.

Ryder just smiled and reached for the door. Opening it softly, he stuck his head in - and froze. The "friend" that had come to rescue Brook looked a hell of a lot like his agent. His agent, who had agreed to keep his identity a secret from the public. His agent, who Brook had called her best friend.

Alison looked up and started to say something, but he shook his head, begging her not to give him away. Not yet. Not until he had some idea of how to explain what it was he did for a living! He'd been hoping to impress Brook, to make her think that he was a nice, successful, and trustworthy kind of person. The type of person she could lean on if she needed a hand. What would she think if she knew the things that went on inside his head?

Thankfully, Alison just shut her mouth just as fast. Oh, she made a few jabs at him, but if she hadn't, it would have looked weird. Alison picked on everyone. Unfortunately, he didn't get a chance to talk to her alone until they started loading Brook's stuff in Alison's car. Under the pretense of working out how to get the rest of her things to her, he pulled his agent aside.

"You know Mrs. Harper?" he asked.

Alison just glared. "I am *not* answering that until you explain to me why the hell you're volunteering at the rescue."

"Uh. Community service. Not a big deal. Just got forty hours for trashing some asshole's car. Look, it's my last day, and then the whole thing gets wiped. Not even a blip on the news, so stop fretting. Why didn't you tell me you knew her?"

"The same reason you didn't tell me you were volunteering. It just never came up," she hissed. "Why?"

He just waved that away. "How do I help?"

Alison sighed before reaching up to grab his shoulders. "You're sweet, Ryder, but you can't. Not right now. She needs to get her head on straight, have some peace and quiet to figure out what comes next, and have a little girl time. I got this."

"Yeah." And he honestly believed her. "But if you need me, you'll let me know?"

"I promise. The two of you will be the first people I call, because she kinda doesn't have anyone else to fall back on." Then she rubbed his arms lightly. "And I won't tell her who you are until you ask me to, ok?"

"Thanks. But if she needs anything - money, muscle, um, anything - we'll help."

Alison nodded. "I know, but answer me one thing. Why? The two of you don't like talking to people, but you dropped everything to pick her up?"

He just ducked his head, feeling like a little boy all over again. "She likes the dogs, Alison. I mean, she loves them, and they love her right back. I *always* trust the dogs."

"Yeah. Don't worry, the dogs are right." She turned him back toward the shelter. "Now go finish your sentence. I'll take care of the damsel for now."

CHAPTER ELEVEN

*W*hen Alison arrived at Tall Tails, Brook was locked into one of the adoption rooms, sorting through her belongings. Marcy had done everything possible to make things easier, but it was still the most embarrassing experience Brook could imagine. Every last person in the building knew she'd been tossed around by her husband. People were looking at her with sad eyes and tip-toeing when they passed. She felt like a pariah.

Even the door opened gently when Marcy escorted Alison in. The pert blonde, however, changed everything. With an enthusiastic squeal, she crossed the room in two steps and hugged Brook tight enough to suffocate. There was nothing at all subtle about Alison.

"We're going to be roomies!" With a giggle, Alison dropped onto the couch, giving Brook back her breath. "Ok, so how much crap do we have to lift into my little car?"

Brook shoved her jumbled clothes back into the bag as

she answered. "A bunch of boxes, some garbage bags of clothes, a backpack, and me."

"We'll figure it out." Alison winked playfully. "And this gives us plenty of reasons to go shopping together. Ok. And you said we need to run past the bank?"

A knock at the door interrupted. "Yeah?" Brook asked.

Ryder stuck his head in - and froze. For a second, his head twitched back and forth. Wrenching his eyes away from Alison, he looked back to Brook. "Were you needing help moving that stuff?"

Alison leaned back and grinned. "Is this who helped get you out of the house?"

"Yeah," Brook mumbled.

Ryder chuckled awkwardly. "I was, um, just..."

"Flirting," Alison clarified. "Which is cool, since my *friend* is newly single..."

"Stop," Brook hissed, smacking Alison's arm lightly. Ryder was shaking his head, looking almost panicked.

Alison looked between both of them, the smile on her face becoming more and more devious with each second. "So, big guy, we would love a few extra muscles to move things. Thank you."

While the tone of her voice was always playful, the honest appreciation was impossible to miss. Ryder seemed to have a little of that old-school type of gentleman thing going on. Those two little words - thank you - were all the reward he required. He helped move Brook's stuff from the back of his truck into Alison's little silver car, promising he could have the rest taken to a storage unit if that was easier. While Brook focused on getting her most important things, Ryder and Alison worked out everything else. Both of them insisted that Brook shouldn't need to worry about it.

Then it was time to go. For the first time that morning, Brook actually realized she was leaving everything behind. It had all happened so fast that she hadn't stopped to let that sink in. Now, she couldn't do anything else. The job she'd loved, the people who'd stepped up even though she barely knew them, and her dog were about to be little more than a memory. Her wonderful dog, who she'd loved so much, was really and truly gone. Her life was changing, and she had no idea if it would be better. All she could do was hope she hadn't ruined everything.

"Thank you, Ryder," she said, hugging the man. "I don't know why you did all of this..."

This time, he actually hugged back. "Because this is how you deserve to be treated. Thanks for letting me."

"Yeah." She rubbed his arm gently, then took her place in the passenger seat.

With the back of the car filled up like she was headed to college, the two girls made their way out of the parking lot and into town. Just one more step on the road to her life. They spent almost two more hours visiting banks before they finally hit the highway and headed north. Brook hadn't been able to get much. Owen had locked her out of every account but one, although she'd gotten a few hundred dollars from that. It didn't feel like nearly enough to start anew.

The trip wasn't far, but if this worked out, it could mean her salvation. To Brook, she was escaping, and that made every mile a little more important. It was also terrifying. Owen wouldn't just give up. It wouldn't take much for him to think of Alison and come looking for his wife. Who knew what would happen then. Maybe he'd just file for divorce? Maybe he'd try to get her to come back "home." Not that he could say anything to make up for what he'd done, but Brook had a sinking feeling this wouldn't be quite so easy.

Somewhere, surrounded by farmland, she turned down the radio and decided to face it head-on. "I'm gonna need a job, and I don't have a car."

"Yep," Alison agreed. "So we'll check out listings at the shelters. Leah and I can carpool on days you need a car or something. We'll work it out."

"And your wife is ok with this?"

"Check my texts." She gestured to her phone laying on the dash. "Told her I was picking you up, but you can read her answer for yourself."

Brook swiped at the screen and navigated her way to the text messages. There, at the top, was the conversation with Leah.

Alison: going to pick up Brook. She's staying with us for a bit. Cool?
Leah: Great! How long is she staying?
Alison: Dunno. Gonna be a while. She's finally leaving dickhead.

"Dickhead?" Brook asked, looking up.

Giggling, Alison shrugged. "Gotta admit, I was kinda right."

"Yep." Then she went back to reading.

Leah: We're gonna have to find something better than the sofa for her.
Alison: so you're ok with this?
Leah: Of course! I know how much you've missed

her. She's always welcome! I figure Brook's family, right?

Alison: exactly.

Those words hit something in her chest. Before she could stop it, her throat pinched closed, and her eyes began to sting. Brook gasped, trying to catch her breath, but it didn't help. It had been four years since she'd really seen these two, but Alison still thought of Brook as the sister she should've had. Never mind that Alison's wife was perfectly fine with it. There hadn't even been a question; they'd just welcomed her right into their life – massive problems and all – with open arms.

The first tear leaked out with a sniff. After that, she was done for. Those few tears turned into a waterfall. Within seconds, her nose joined in. When the first sob burst from her throat, Alison shoved a tissue under her face. Brook took it, and Alison pulled another from the dispenser attached to the sun visor, offering it as well.

"I came prepared," she said soothingly. "Have a purse full of makeup, two packs of tissues, and even baby wipes to remove the evidence. It's just you and me, Brook, so stop trying to be so damned tough. I think you deserve one hell of a good cry."

She gave in. As the tears poured down her cheeks, Brook tried to explain, but the words were broken into gibberish. Somehow Alison still understood. From the murder of her dog to how isolated she'd been, the past six years came tumbling with the tears. Little things began to make sense. All of those quirks she'd ignored. The seduction that had made her feel beautiful. The guilt that had slowly begun to weigh her into submission. As she bawled out the end of her "happily ever after," Brook realized what a prison she'd fallen into.

Owen kept her under control with little things. He'd made a home for them far from her family. He'd convinced her to quit college, giving up her dream to be her own boss. He'd kept her busy with the demands for his career, always promising that once they got ahead, it would be her turn. Slowly, year by year, he'd cut her off from the world, making her reliant on him and him alone.

Then he'd attacked her pride. She was never good enough. She wasn't smart enough. It didn't matter what it was about, she could never quite meet the level of excellence he considered normal. She spent her marriage trying to play catch-up to an ideal that was always out of reach. But it was subtle. The manipulation eroded her confidence. Her husband's affection always came with a caveat, proving that only *he* would be foolish enough to love her. She was broken, damaged goods, and she was lucky he had a weakness for things like that.

It had come upon her so slowly that she didn't even realize she was being abused. It was just her normal life. Sure, she and Owen weren't perfect, but she was his pillar of support. He'd never hurt her, not at first. Maybe her emotions had been bruised, but he'd never really hit her, just a shove here or there. She couldn't blame him. Hell, she'd probably do the same thing if she had that much pressure on her. Besides, no one was perfect. He still loved her. She always knew, because he'd made a point of telling her that over and over.

It had only taken six years for Brook to become a victim. When she was in college, she'd been the strong one - the kind of girl who wouldn't take crap from anyone. With Alison at her side, they'd painted the town a few times over. Sitting huddled in her friend's car, wondering what she was supposed to do next, had never been on her radar. This wasn't how her life was supposed to go! She was supposed to flaunt all the expectations and prove she was a strong woman, capable of taking care of herself.

And Alison listened without judgment. Mile after mile, the girl who had once been her partner in crime proved that not everything turned to shit after a few years. Alison picked up right where they'd left off. Her compassion came with a smile, an uplifting joke, and a whole lot of honest sympathy. When Brook talked about the loss of her dog, her best friend wasn't immune, tearing up right alongside her.

Knowing she wasn't alone – wasn't wrong for feeling like this – was what she really needed. Just like when they'd first met in college, the years apart didn't seem to matter. Alison understood her. Sure, their lives were completely different, but that wasn't important. Deep down, under all the superficial crap, they were kindred souls. That meant Brook didn't have to face this alone. She may have been a pretty crummy friend, but Alison never once blamed her. She just wanted to pick up where they'd left off.

"Hey," Alison said, slowing down to exit the highway. "You mind if I take a few days off to hang out with you?"

Brook shook her head. "I'd kinda like that. It'd also make it easier to do a few things. I mean, it's probably stupid, but I have to get some birth control. Owen trashed what I had left, and I just don't want to... I dunno." She closed her eyes and sighed.

"And I'll hold your hand when you file a police report," Alison promised.

Brook just shook her head. "No report. I just want to

get away, and if I have to go back to court, he'll find me, Ali. No. I'm gone, I'm safe, and it's over."

"Brook!" Alison hissed. "That's not how this works."

"I..." Brook couldn't even finish the sentence. "No, it's over. I'm moving on. I'd really rather no one knows about this. I just want to pretend like I didn't just ruin the last six years of my life, ok?"

For a long moment, Alison said nothing. Finally, "So, birth control, and then I think we'll see a movie. Some stupid chick flick filled with beautiful women, right?"

That finally made the faintest smile touch Brook's lips. "You sure your clients won't mind?"

"Pretty sure, and if they do? They'll get over it. Rose Solace is the only one who has a book ready to shop around. The rest are somewhere in the middle. Besides, it's always better to do the icky things with a friend, right?"

"But..."

Alison waved her off. "When we get home, I'll let the big five know Rose has a book out. If you're nice, I'll let you read one of the published ones. Anyways, give them a few days to drool over it. By the time I check the offers, I should have the publishers fighting each other for the privilege of paying out the best advance. It'll be fine. Besides, Rose Solace won't care. That's one author who keeps telling me to take more time for myself."

The smile proved Alison honestly liked that one. Sure, she'd become a successful enough literary agent that she only had to work with the people she wanted to, but she rarely smiled over anyone quite like that. At least, the only other person Brook could think of to get *that* kind of smile was the one Alison now called her wife.

"Is Rose really hot or something?" A weak giggle

proved Brook was teasing. "Does Leah know you have a crush on one of your clients?"

"Promise, Rose isn't my type." But Alison paused. "Huh."

"What?"

Slowly making her way through the city streets, Alison just shook her head. "Nope. I'm forming a plan. You're gonna have to wait to see how the plot of this one ends."

Brook huffed out, "Bitch."

"Oh yeah," Alison promised. "I'm also a fucking genius."

And that was all Brook got. No matter how many times she asked, Alison wouldn't say another thing about it. Even worse was when Leah refused to give a hint. They did, however, make it very clear that she was not a burden. It only helped so much.

CHAPTER TWELVE

*A*fter Brook left, the shelter was in an uproar. Just the rumor that she'd quit had caused a stir, but when she came back? That all but proved the mark on her neck hadn't been an accident, that she hadn't been mugged. No, the entire shelter now knew that Brook Harper had been abused by her husband, and Ryder could only imagine how hard that must be for her.

Shame was the strongest leash. It's why most victims never tried to escape because at least they knew what to expect from their abuser. Ryder remembered the feeling, and it made his heart go out to her. It also proved just how strong she really was. For Brook to walk in here with her head held high was probably the most impressive thing he'd ever seen, and he might not get the chance to tell her.

That didn't mean the shelter stopped running. Marcy was doing her best to get the staff back to work, but they kept trying to cluster in the hallways to talk about what had just happened. Unfortunately, they didn't know the half of it. They hadn't been to her house or seen Brook finally let down her masks. Ryder had.

He'd also made a promise.

So, as soon as Marcy returned to her office, he walked in and shut the door. The Executive Director glanced up, frowned slightly, then leaned back in her chair. She didn't smile, but today wasn't that kind of day. She also didn't seem upset.

"Please tell me that whatever this is about, it's good news this time?" she asked.

"Not exactly." He dropped into the chair before her desk. "Brook's husband killed her dog last night. I'm willing to bet it was supposed to put her in line, but we didn't have time to do anything with its body."

Slowly, Marcy's hand drifted up to cover her mouth, and the woman let her eyes close. For a moment, she just stayed like that, almost as if she was praying silently.

"Please tell me you know where it is?" Her voice was soft, but it didn't tremble. That in itself, proved just how strong this woman was.

"It's in the garage. I wanted to go back over there and see if I could get it."

"No."

The word came out as her hand reached for the phone. She didn't yell, but the tone made it clear there was no debate on this. While Ryder tried to think of some way to convince her, Marcy's finger was stabbing out a number. When she lifted the receiver to her ear, a cruel smile touched her lips.

"Yes, I'd like to report spousal and animal abuse," she said into the phone. "Uh huh. This is Marcy Tipelton from Tall Tails animal rescue. One of my employees has reason to believe that Owen Harper beat his wife and killed her dog in a domestic violence dispute last night. The animal's body should still be in the garage as proof." She listed off the address then paused for a moment. "Yes, the Executive Director. Uh huh. Correct, felony animal abuse. I don't know what charges you can file for the domestic violence. Yes, I'm sure he'd be willing to make a statement. Oh? Well, considering that we just helped the wife get out of the house, I am sure it wasn't an accident." She paused again. "Thank you. Call me if you need anything else."

Ryder's mouth was hanging open in shock. "You want me to file a report?"

She just met his eyes. "There's no want about this. Ryder, you *will* go on the record. I'll be damned if that asshole is going to get away with this. If that means I have to remove all your hours here to make sure you keep coming back until the cops do something about this, you'd damned well better believe I will."

"No need," he promised. "So far as I'm concerned, you just became my hero. I just hope they get there before that bastard cleans it up, but I have a picture that might help."

Marcy shook her head. "Owen's too stupid to worry about a dead animal. He'd never even think that what he's done is a crime. And it won't do much, but it might just be enough to help Brook get away from him for good."

"What do you mean?"

She tilted her head slowly. "It's animal abuse. The government doesn't consider that to be as serious as we do. In other words, if Brook won't press charges, a cop and an animal control officer will probably go over there tonight, give him a citation, and he'll end up with a slap on the wrist."

He couldn't believe that. "For *killing* a dog?"

"Yep. He won't get arrested, just ticketed. Still, there'll

be a court date, and it will go on his record. Most likely he'll pay a fine, but he might get probation. This is also a known sign of more serious abuse, which is why I'm pushing it." She let out a frustrated sigh. "Abusers always go after the dogs first - well, any pet. They take away whatever she loves, using it to control her. Owen just doesn't know how far Brook will go for the animals. He can't understand that she honestly loves these creatures like her own children, and it might be the only reason she'll be willing to file a report with the police. Most women just want it to go away."

"Yeah." He leaned forward, intending to get up. "I'm gonna do everything I can to make sure she never has to go back there."

"Ryder?" Marcy asked, her tone halting him before he stood.

"Don't try to talk me out of it."

Marcy ignored that. "Why her?"

He huffed, knowing where she was going with this. Marcy had run his background check when he applied for the puppy. She knew more about his personal life than most people, and she hadn't taken it easy on him. Nope, she'd even gone so far as to call his brother.

"She deserves a chance," he replied. "It's not her fault she was treated like that. No different from any of the dogs I've rescued, and you know what? Brook's just as loyal. She's also in just as much need right now, and this time I can do something about it."

"Mm." Marcy nodded, taking that in. "Willing to take some advice?"

"Sure."

"Women like Brook? They don't want to be rescued. They want to rescue themselves. Let her. Give her everything she needs to make that happen, but don't you dare *do* this for her."

That wasn't at all what he'd expected. He'd braced for some wisdom about how she'd need time to get over this, not... that. "What do you mean?"

"You can't make her divorce him, but you can give her every reason to want to. You can't make this easy for her, but you can help her get through it. If you want to rescue Brook Harper, then the best thing you can do is give her someone she can trust. Ryder, she just lost everything, and she's going to want the chance to earn it all back. Earn. If things come too easy for her, she'll bolt, because that's what strays do. They get really nervous when things feel dangerous, and right now, Brook will think anything easy is very dangerous."

He chuckled. "Yeah, but at least she has the loyal companion part handled. I know her best friend. Alison Brewer? She's a Labrador. Always happy, perfectly loyal, and completely devoted."

"Mhm." Marcy crossed her arms and tried, but couldn't stop her devious smile. "Pretty sure she wouldn't mind a Rottweiler to go along with that."

"A rottie?" He thought he knew where she was going with this, but still wanted to hear her say it.

"Big, strong, and protective. Yeah, I guess a mastiff would do too, but you already have the black thing going on today. Look, you have her number. Just give her a few days to settle in, then send her a text making sure she's ok. Offer her a ride somewhere, or tell her about that puppy you took home. Something - anything - to make sure she doesn't think she's alone in all of this. Normal things. That's what will help her."

He nodded, because she was right. He wasn't sure how

she'd known or if she was just that naturally empathic. Then again, she did spend all day dealing with abuse cases. Everything she'd just suggested was the human version of what they did for the dogs. Things like regular schedules, passive attention, and calm voices helped most of the animals at Tall Tails find happiness again. If it worked for them, the same thing should work for Brook, but Ryder had a feeling that getting Brook's trust wouldn't be that simple.

She'd all but told him so the other day. Granted, he was kicking himself for not saving Gummy for her, but she hadn't mentioned the old man was on his last few days. No, she'd just put in the extra effort to make sure those days were the best. She'd sucked it up and *done* something, rather than whining about it. That was how she'd ended up in the grass, by pushing the rules enough to take the dog outside one last time.

And that was the day she'd admitted she was all alone. It was a feeling he could relate to, but he wasn't sure how to fix it except to offer her a friend or two. Allison would be better at that, but Ryder intended to get on the list. See, Brook might be a professional rescuer, but he knew how to save the damsel in distress. It was pretty much the only thing he was good at. This time, however, the stakes were a little higher.

Thanking Marcy for her insight, he left, taking the long way outside the building to get back to his kennels. Sure, the day had been insane, but the dogs still needed a clean place to sleep. He just had one thing to do before he locked himself away for the next few hours. Grabbing his phone, he decided this deserved more than a text.

His brother answered immediately. "Hey, you ok?"

"Allison just picked up her best friend," he said. "Yes,

Brook. Yes, that Allison. They're already gone, but I figured you should know that."

Hunter didn't respond immediately, proving he was just as shocked as his brother. "Ok. This could get complicated."

"Don't think so." Ryder explained what had happened when he saw Allison. "She didn't expose us, but I think we can trust Brook. Look, she's not like most people."

"How can you be sure?"

Ryder paused. That was the hard part. He couldn't know, not really. "It's just this gut feeling I have. I mean, if you'd met her, you'd understand. She reminds me of Penny."

"Oh." The words were barely a breath.

If he had to guess, Hunter had probably just sat up straight. They hadn't talked about Penny in a long time, but that didn't mean they'd forgotten. She'd basically become their standard for honesty and loyalty. No one else had ever come close, and Ryder knew his brother would understand exactly what he was saying.

"So what are we doing, man?" Hunter finally asked.

The problem was that Ryder didn't have an answer. "I'd say call Leah. Allison's going to be busy with Brook for a bit, but Leah will keep us in the loop." He stopped a step before the back door of the shelter. "Hunter? I'm doing this. With or without you, I'm going to take care of her."

"Then I'm in, too. If it means that much to you, then we'll take this as far as we need to."

"She's special," Ryder explained. "I can talk to her."

"Really?" His brother sounded impressed, not shocked.

"Yeah. She doesn't look at me like I'm stupid. I dunno, there's just something about her. I can't stop thinking about her."

"Chemistry," Hunter said, as if that was enough of an answer. "That mysterious, elusive drug that turns men into idiots."

Ryder chuckled, recognizing the line from a book. "Fair enough. But look, she honestly needs a hero. I think we can help her."

"We're not heroes."

"Nah," Ryder agreed. "Doesn't mean we can't put in a damned good effort, though. C'mon, what do we have to lose?"

It took a little too long before Hunter answered. "Everything. Ryder, if we screw this up, we could lose every last thing."

"Yeah. I know. I'm still doing this."

CHAPTER THIRTEEN

*a*t exactly 5:47 that evening, Owen called. Brook punted it to voicemail. He didn't bother to leave a message.

The next morning, he called again at 7:45 before heading to work. Again, he didn't leave a voicemail, but Brook knew his schedule well enough. Then again at lunch, and one more time after he got off work. Brook decided she was just going to block his number if he kept calling, but the next time things were different. The message he left made Brook rethink all of her feeble plans.

"You can't run from me Brook, and calling the cops about your stupid dog isn't going to make me go away. There are only two places you could go. Since your phone is on my account, it isn't hard to find. GPS says you're at an apartment complex in the burbs, which means you're with *her*. I knew you were having an affair. I don't care if most guys think it's a turn-on." The anger in his voice made it almost crack. "I will *not* tolerate my wife screwing around. Not with some man, and certainly not with a dyke! I gave you time to have your tantrum.

Now, I'm going to remind you of that promise you made me."

While she'd been told about the report filed for her dead dog, she had no idea which promise he meant - but it couldn't be good. Did he mean her wedding vows? Was he talking about that threat to make her life even more miserable? Dozens of ideas whipped through her head, but none of them were good. One thing was certain. She needed to get a new phone, and fast.

Leah picked one up on her way home and added Brook to their family plan. Brook's old SIM card was thrown away, and the phone turned off and shoved in a drawer somewhere. It was stupid, but somehow, being included as family felt better than any of the other promises the two women could make. Leah said it was just convenient, but the smile proved that was a weak excuse. The reality was that if the Brewers were loaning her a phone, then Owen had absolutely no rights to it. He couldn't demand records. He couldn't have it tracked without doing something illegal.

In other words, it wasn't just her best friend that was taking care of her. Leah was completely on board with all of this. But that wasn't enough. First, Brook's parents blew up when she called them to give them her new number. They were frantic that she should come home, but none of them had the money to make it happen. Then, over dinner that night, the conversation with Leah and Alison turned serious.

"I'm telling you," Brook said, swirling her food on her plate. "Owen knows where I am. I mean, he used that 'Find My Phone' thing, and said it showed him your apartment."

Leah gently rubbed her arm. "So what are you going to

do? Just keep running every time he threatens you?"

"Yeah." Brook looked between her only two friends. "What other options do I have? I mean, I probably have enough money for a bus ticket to my parents'."

"Not yet. We all know you'd hate it there, and I'll think of something," Alison promised. "Maybe get you enrolled in college again and send you off to live in the dorms?"

Brook groaned. "While yes, I want to finish my degree, I have no interest in living with kids young enough to be mine."

"You're not that old," Leah whispered loud enough for it to carry.

Alison winked at her wife. "But you are."

"Hush!"

"Seriously, though..." Brook said, stopping the couple before they could get out of hand. "I've got about six hundred dollars, if I include credit. Is there any place around here I could lease for that?"

Alison shook her head. "No, sweetie. And certainly not immediately. I know it's not that great to sleep on the couch - "

That wasn't her problem. "Ali, I don't want Owen breaking down your door to find me. If I'm not here, then you won't have to deal with my mistakes, ok? That's all it is. I like your sofa."

"Oh!" Leah chewed quickly, obviously having an idea. "I think one of the ladies at work has a spare room. I could always ask her if she'd mind - "

Brook stopped her. "I'm not interested in being a charity case. I hate it enough that I'm putting you two out, but someone I don't even know?"

"Brook..." Alison groaned. "This isn't charity. This is what friends do."

"Yeah? After I ignored you for how long? Never mind asking some stranger Leah works with? Now *that* would be charity."

Leah waved her hand, pulling the attention to her. "None of that. Ali knew Owen was the reason you didn't call. It's not like he made a secret of how much he hated us, either. Homophobe."

"Idiot," Brook agreed. "But that still doesn't change things."

"Kinda does," Alison assured her. "Not calling me because you're sick of my company is one thing. Not calling me because your husband makes it almost impossible? Not even in the same realm. Besides, Leah isn't any fun to go shopping with."

"I hate shopping!" Leah groaned.

"It's fun when you have money," Brook teased. "Which is something I'm a little short on, with no clue how to fix that. Seriously, what the hell can I do? McDonald's?"

"Always hiring," Alison joked. "Them and Wal-Mart. I just have a funny feeling there might be a few more options in town."

That was when Leah's head jerked up. "Oh!"

"Oh?" Brook asked.

The wives shared a look. Alison smiled. Leah shrugged. Neither of them said a word, leaving Brook to wonder what they were planning this time. From the way they were nodding at each other, it had to be pretty good, and Brook had a funny idea she was going to end up in the middle of it.

"What?" she demanded.

Alison waved her down. "It's nothing. Leah just reminded me of a job opening. I have to check and see if it's still available, but it just might work out."

"Do I even get a hint?"

Reaching over to grab her hand, Alison's face was completely serious. "Only one. It has to do with dogs. Trust me, Brook. I know you well enough to know what you'd truly enjoy doing. Hell, I think I know you better than you know yourself lately."

"Probably." She squeezed Alison's hand back. "And I do trust you. Right now I'm willing to try anything."

Leah made every effort to muffle her giggle, but it didn't work. Alison stuck her tongue out. That was when Brook realized just how that sounded sitting across from two lesbians. The first laugh was little more than a squeak. That sounded silly enough to force out another. Like a chain reaction, the insanity of her ordeal, the stupidity of the joke, the stress of the last few days, and the horror of her own freakish laugh all combined. Brook giggled. Alison joined in, mostly just because Brook couldn't stop. That only made it worse. In seconds, she was laughing hard enough that it brought tears to her eyes.

If asked later, she'd never be able to explain it. Nothing they'd said was really that funny. Her situation certainly wasn't, but maybe she finally felt safe enough to do it. Maybe a laugh was what she needed. It really didn't matter. The only thing that was important was that Brook still could. After everything that had happened, she still remembered how to enjoy something.

～

That night, Brook was almost asleep when she heard Alison tiptoe through the living room. The sliding glass door to the balcony opened softly, then closed, but it wasn't enough to completely cut off the sounds from outside. After barely a minute, she could hear her best friend talking. She had to be on the phone.

"Hey, sorry it's so late." There was a long pause. "Well, yeah, I have a few offers, but that's not why I'm calling. Have I mentioned lately just how wonderful you are? No? Aw, c'mon."

Alison's giggle sounded almost flirtatious, even if it was quiet. "Keep telling yourself that. No, but seriously, I have a question. Remember that thing you were talking about?"

For a moment, her voice got too soft to hear. Cracking open one eye, Brook could see Alison pacing the narrow space. Her face was turned to the ground, but she was bobbing her head like whoever was on the other end had some very valid points.

"I think this might work out, and she's in desperate need of a room. This'll be perfect. Yes, the same. No, it's not like that. Swear. It's all up to you, but she'd be thrilled to work with dogs again." Again, Alison paused. "Uh huh, exactly. I haven't said a thing, but I just had a feeling you'd come around." Then she giggled. "No, she's only read one. I gave it to her earlier. Pretty sure she's more into Regency than contemporary. Yeah."

Brook knew she was the subject; she just wished she could hear the other side. She could never be sure if Alison would tell her everything or think the surprise was a better joke. Not that she'd keep anything important, but Alison had a sick sense of humor. Usually a very accurate one, too, even if Brook spent a lot of time as the brunt of it.

"Ok," Alison went on. "Yeah, I think we can do tomorrow. How about just after lunch? Perfect. Well, let's make sure everyone gets along, then we can talk about all the details. Thanks, sweetie. Yeah. No, I have a funny feeling you'll really like her. She's been my closest friend since I was about eighteen. Oh hush, it hasn't been that long, and don't you dare start counting. Ok. Yeah. See you then. Have a good night, and get something ready to show me. Bye."

The glass door slid open, and Brook didn't bother trying for stealth. "I'm awake."

"Good!" Alison flicked the lock and made her way over, claiming the coffee table as her chair. "You have a job interview tomorrow. Jeans, t-shirt, and sensible shoes. No need to impress with clothes, since the duties will include something you're an expert at - shoveling shit."

"Hey, now."

Alison giggled. "Dogs, Brook. Paid position, with a room and meals. All you have to do is walk the dogs and handle the icky parts."

"Really?" That sounded almost too good to be true.

"Yeah." Alison rubbed her arm. "It's for this reclusive author of mine who makes some amazing books. The house is secluded enough that Owen would never find it, and if he did, there's no way he'd get onto the property. If for no other reason than that, I think it's worth considering."

Brook nodded, agreeing completely. "Where?"

"Like five, maybe ten minutes down the road, just outside town. If things get stupid, it's close enough you could walk. I mean, might be a hike on foot, but you certainly won't be stranded."

"Oh god, thank you." Brook sat up and wrapped her arms around Alison. "I can't thank you enough for everything you've done."

"And I'd do it all over again to get you back. I've missed you. Now, I understand, so don't you dare feel guilty, but I've really missed having a real friend around.

118

It's not the same with Leah. I can't talk to her about, well, her!"

"I swear I'll listen anytime you need it."

"Good." Leaning back, Alison tapped her nose. "Because I have years of kink stored up that I need to tell *someone* about. You have *no* idea how freaky my wife gets!"

"More toys," Brook teased.

Alison just laughed. "Honey, I think we have the market on those things. You know how some couples have the adult drawer? Oh yeah. We have a closet. If you ever end up in need, you just let me know. I probably have one."

"Eww. I am *not* sharing *that* with you. Not happening, Ali."

"Pssh. Not with me. You'd totally be sharing with Leah. I mean, c'mon, who do you think wears the pants in our family?"

Brook didn't hesitate. "Your wife."

"Hey now!" In retaliation, Alison grabbed her ribs, digging her fingers right between the bones. "Take it back."

"Can't make me!"

"I'll tickle you until you give in." She was doing exactly that. "Say it. Say that I'm not the bitch in this family!"

"Ok." Brook gasped, trying to suck air around her squeals. "Ok, I give in. I'll say it! Stop, and I'll say it."

Alison's hands paused. "You'll say what?"

"You are not the bitch. Nor is Leah." Brook finally managed a deep breath. "Damn, Ali, you're anything but a bitch. But your wife still wears the pants."

"Oh! I'll get you for that!" Her fingers resumed the torment, but this time they were both laughing.

CHAPTER FOURTEEN

*T*he next day, just like she'd promised, Alison packed Brook up for her job interview. There were a lot of smiles, a few giggles, but nothing Brook said would get Alison to talk about it until they got there. "Trust me," she insisted, and it seemed that was as much as Brook was going to get.

Then again, as a literary agent, Alison represented some of the best authors in the industry and had connections Brook couldn't dream of. Without those, this chance wouldn't exist. Thirty-four years old and getting divorced was about all she had to put on a resume, and it certainly wouldn't impress anyone. Sure, there was that little bit about working in an animal shelter, but plenty of people had.

Somehow, her best friend had taken all of that, mashed it together, and pulled out a miracle. There was no doubt about it, working for some best-selling author would be a lot nicer than a fast food job. Then there was the part about living somewhere Owen would never find her. The only problem was how little Alison was willing to share about this woman.

Brook had figured one thing out on her own. Rose Solace was pretty good. The first night she stayed at their place, Alison had passed her a book - a rather steamy one - and asked what she thought with a sly smile. After devouring the novel, Brook thought they might just get along - if Rose was anything like her writing style. The woman's specialty was ménage à trois.

Never mind that anyone who could turn two men picking up a girl at a bar into a love story had Brook's complete respect. As a bonus, Rose had a few foster dogs and an extra bedroom. She'd been looking for someone to help with the kennels and keep the mutts entertained when she got lost in her writing. That was one thing Brook knew how to do.

Of course, 'Rose Solace' was a pen name, but what little information she had to go on said that Brook might actually enjoy this job. Well, if she was lucky enough to get it. But Alison's smugness made Brook think she had a pretty good shot.

The car turned down a long, tree-lined drive just outside the city limits, and Alison finally decided to break her silence. "Ok, keep in mind this is my favorite client. Sounds like the job comes with a room in the house and shared meals with the family. There are currently four dogs, but that changes."

"So all I need to do is clean up after the dogs?" Brook asked, staring at the beautiful stone farmstead sprawling at the end of the lane.

Alison nodded. "But I don't want you to feel pressured. If you aren't thrilled with the idea, you're welcome to the couch for as long as you want. I *only* offered this because you insisted it would be best."

"You know I'd feel better keeping Owen away from you."

"Yeah, just like I know you'd be the first one to help me if I ever needed it. Just keep that in mind."

Brook smiled at the truth of that. "I just can't envision you making a break from Leah. She's perfect for you."

"And seven years older than me," Alison pointed out. "You're the only person who didn't think I was crazy when we started dating." She eased the car over the gravel toward the front door. "Just remember, I've known you longer than your ex-husband did. "

"Husband," Brook corrected. "Divorces don't happen overnight, you know."

"Fuck that," Alison told her. "Try it. Call him your ex. Divorce that bastard in your mind right now, and he won't have any more power over you."

Brook couldn't help but huff a weak laugh at her insistence. "Ok! Fine. I'll try."

That devious smile reappeared as she turned off the car, but before Brook could ask, Alison was out, gesturing for her best friend to join her. A few butterflies danced in Brook's stomach, but it wasn't too bad. This woman was a writer with a flair for kink, so it wasn't like she'd judge anyone, right? And this was just about taking care of some dogs. Brook loved dogs.

The ladies didn't even make it to the front door before it creaked open. What stepped out was not the elderly woman Brook expected. Oh no, it was a man. He was tall, broad, and built in a way that made her think more about book covers than authors – and oh so familiar. Brook froze. The man, however, took one look at Alison and his face split into a grin. He didn't seem to recognize Brook at all.

"Hey, girl," he teased Alison, hurrying over to wrap her in a bear hug. "It's been too long."

She poked his pectoral with one finger. "Don't give me that. Where's your brother?"

The man jerked his thumb toward the other side of the house. "Cleaning up the kennels. So is this the potential dog walker?"

He turned his eyes on Brook, and her guts twisted. He was exactly as gorgeous as she remembered, but this had to be a joke. At the shelter, he'd acted like he didn't know Alison, and now he didn't seem to know her? Whatever she was missing was enough to keep Brook's mouth shut.

But her eyes worked just fine, and she didn't need to feel bad for checking him out now. Hell, she knew what lay under that shirt, because he'd used it to wipe the tears from her eyes. The sound of his voice was just as charming as she remembered. Granted, if this was Rose's son, then maybe this job wouldn't be such a good idea. Shit, maybe it was her husband? Was that why he wasn't acknowledging her? Because it would piss off Rose?

"Hunter," Alison said, "I'd like you to meet my best friend, Brooklyn Sanders. Brook, this is Hunter Collins."

Hunter?

"A pleasure." The man's voice was perfectly pitched to add a few extra meanings to that.

Alison smacked his arm. "Stop. This is not *that* kind of interview."

He laughed, but a moment later, Alison squealed as a second man surged behind her, hugging her hard enough to lift her off her feet. With his face pressed beside her hair, it wasn't until he set her back on the ground that

Brook realized he was a perfect copy of the first. Holy fucking shit. One was distracting, but two? Wait. There were two?! This wasn't possible. Any second now, she was going to wake up and find herself on the floor of Owen's bedroom again, because *this* was completely impossible!

"Ryder!" Alison wailed, smacking at his arms. "If I have bruises, I'm making you tell Leah."

"I take better care of my girls than that," he assured her, looking up. His eyes hit Brook, and he paused, tilting his head slightly before turning it to his twin. "I take it you've met?"

"Um." Brook looked between the men. "I guess we haven't yet."

Alison lifted a hand dramatically and stepped over so she wasn't in the middle of their circle. "And now for the big reveal. Brook, Hunter and Ryder are my favorite client. Yes, they're identical twins. No, you aren't losing your mind. Together they make Rose Solace, and I can't even tell you how many best sellers they've produced."

"Just one this year," Ryder explained.

"Still early," Hunter pointed out.

Brook's mouth was hanging open. "Wait." And it wouldn't stay closed. "You both write *romance* novels? Together?" This was not at all what she'd expected.

"Porn," Hunter teased.

"More like erotica." This from Ryder.

"Nah, more like porn. It's manly to write porn. All that love and cuddling shit is for chick lit."

Alison groaned. "And if you can get a word in between them, let me know how. Boys, why don't you at least show her around and see if this might work out?"

Ryder dropped an arm over Alison's shoulder. "I told you, even if she doesn't want the job, we've got a spare room, and you don't. Brook took care of me, now I get to return the favor."

"And she may think you're some creepy perverts."

Unable to do anything else, Brook shrugged. "And when has that ever stopped me? Besides, I read the book. They'd have to be perverts to write that - just like I'm one to read it, right?"

"*The* book?" Hunter asked pointedly.

Alison decided to clarify. "Double Trouble. You know, the bar scene one. It's my favorite, and what I had available to loan her. C'mon, guys, one of you show her around. The other needs to talk to me about what's in the pipeline."

Ryder crooked a finger at Brook. "Kennels are this way. Hunter, you handle the real work."

"Yep. Alison, you know where the office is."

Left alone with Ryder - she was pretty sure it was Ryder - Brook tried to keep her cool. She'd braced herself for living with an older woman, but two men? *These* two men? She needed to reevaluate her questions, and fast. The first one that came to mind was why Ryder hadn't said anything. The next was how to tell the guys apart. All she had to go on right now were their clothes. Hunter had on a pale grey t-shirt while Ryder's was black. She had a funny idea they wouldn't always keep this color scheme.

"Um..." She jogged to his side, the pair of them walking around the house to what looked like a barn in the back. "Should I call you Mr. Collins? I never got your last name at the shelter, and you always used mine."

"Ryder's fine," he assured her. "Besides, I'd like to see you try to figure out how to differentiate which Mr. Collins you mean without using our first names."

"True, but wouldn't that be like a cheat code? Just go

for the default Mr. Collins, instead of praying I put the right name with the right guy?"

"We answer to both." He tossed an understanding smile her way. "If it helps, I'm shorter, he's leaner."

Brook's eyes roamed over his chest before she could stop them. "Not seeing much pudge." Owen was pudgy. Ryder was ripped!

He chuckled, but it sounded almost shy. "I meant size. I've always been broader. Figure he's the brains, I'm the brawn, ya know?"

Awkward. She needed to find something that was a bit safer if she was going to be working for him. "So you both write?"

"Yeah. I do the description and world building. Hunter does characters and dialogue. We trade off on who comes up with the plot and main storyline."

"That's pretty cool."

He grunted. "I guess. So are you honestly ok with this? It's fine if you're not, you know."

Her feet paused. It was only a second, then she forced them to keep going. "I'm fine."

"Yeah." He glanced away. "Just so you know, I was going to offer a room, but Alison beat me to it."

Brook knew she should say something polite, but she couldn't help herself. There was one thing she needed to know, and being alone with Ryder was the best time to ask. "Why didn't you say anything? Back at the shelter, you knew Ali, but you didn't say a single thing."

"Uh..." He gestured to the rock-sided barn and angled his feet that way. "The truth is, our pseudonym is a pretty big deal, ok? Most people would love to sell that story to the press, and it could destroy our career. I just..."

"Didn't trust me," she finished, not at all offended. "Ok, that makes sense."

"Mm." He said nothing for the last few steps, then leaned ahead of her to get the door.

Brook stepped into heaven. The building had once been a barn, but it had been converted into something much more suitable for dogs. The tall ceiling had exposed rafters with massive lights hanging between them. The floor was all rubberized tiles like the type used in public schools, but what once had been stalls were now banks of kennels. Most of them were empty.

"Not a lot of dogs," she pointed out, moving to the first happy face trying to poke through the bars.

Ryder chuckled, trailing in her wake. "Just four right now. We don't have the time to take more than eight, and only if we think we can find homes for them quickly. Most of them are hard-luck cases who would have been euthanized without a bit of TLC, ya know?"

"Yeah."

Her attention was stolen by the scarred mutt trying to claw at the kennel. She knew that face. The poor thing had been slated for euthanasia because of her injuries. She was the one Ryder had asked about just before he loaned her money for gas. Without hesitation, Brook stuck her fingers in far enough that the pup could go crazy licking them.

"You saved her?"

He shrugged. "Yeah. Just didn't seem right knowing she'd been treated like that and not stepping up to help."

The way he said it didn't sound like he was talking about the dog. She looked back and found his eyes waiting. "Thank you."

He almost smiled. "Well, I promise, feeling like a hero

doesn't hurt me much, either. I figure it's a mutual thing, you know?"

She didn't, but that wasn't really the topic she wanted to discuss right now. Mostly because she had no clue what to say. Time to get back to her potential job. "So what would I be doing?"

His hand reached over her shoulder to scratch the puppy's floppy ear. "Think of it like babysitting. They need to get out and play - the entire yard's fenced, but that doesn't mean it's always easy to catch them. They need basic training, the kennels have to be cleaned, and um, feeding, of course."

She noticed his first thought was making sure the dogs got personal time. "Ok. So what about buying food and stuff like that?"

"Oh, huh." He nodded to himself. "I guess we didn't think that far ahead. We've just always taken care of it. Hunter can set up an account at the pet store up the road if you're willing?"

"You know I'm not, like, a trainer, right?"

"Yeah, but I figure you know how to manage this better than we do. Besides, you've had a dog, so you probably know how to teach them to sit and can help us potty train them. We try to get them used to living inside, but a few get worried, like this little girl. They've lived in a kennel or on a chain all their lives, and so much freedom makes them nervous."

"Ever thought about portable kennels so they have a den in the house?"

The smile he flashed her could have lit up the entire building. "Yeah, but when we're on a scene, it's kinda hard to break off without losing our train of thought. Ends up with the poor thing ignored for hours at a time, and that's just not fair. Was kinda hoping you'd be like a dog nanny for us when we're on one of those mad scientist streaks."

Brook laughed and pushed back to her feet. "That doesn't sound much like work, in all honesty. Sounds more like a dream job. What's the catch?"

Crossing his arms over his chest, Ryder turned his back to the kennel and leaned against it. "Tell me, *Miss Sanders*, how many people do you think are willing to move in with two guys who spend all day thinking about sex? The men want to stay far away from us, and the women tend to go two ways. Either they decide crawling in our beds is a good way to earn a bonus, or they're preparing for the sexual harassment lawsuit."

She let her eyes close with an understanding groan. "Right, and I'm going to assume you two aren't broke. Celebrity gold diggers. I gotcha."

"I never got that impression from you, and Alison swears you're not like that. Said you're just looking for a chance to start over."

She nodded, pinching her lips between her teeth. "Still working on figuring out how to do that. Ryder, I was an idiot. Dropped out of college and became a cute little trophy wife. In other words, I have no real work history, no credentials, and my position at the animal shelter was secured by my husband's large donations. Are you sure I'm the right person for this?"

"Gonna freak out if you walk in on us talking shop?"

"Shop?" She wasn't keeping up.

He grinned. "Yeah, sex. Anal, oral, normal. Trying to figure out where all the arms and legs go in a specific position - you know, things like that."

Something about his smirk dared her to answer honestly. Brook shrugged, feeling her mouth curling into a matching smile. "Nope, but I'm betting the part where you act it out is pretty impressive to watch."

The grin stayed, but his eyes narrowed slightly, scanning her face. "Like Twister, I'm telling ya. Hunter and I all wrapped around each other on the office floor."

"Couch is probably more comfortable."

"Bed, actually." A laugh burst out. "So this is the part where I stick my foot all the way up in it and scare you off before you even start. I'm guessing since you were married that you're straight? So how'd you and Alison meet?"

Brook nodded. "Um, Ali and I got assigned to the same dorm in college and became fast friends. Kindred souls, you know? I got the men, she got the women, and between the two of us, we spent a few years painting the town. Over a decade later, and she's still my best friend in the world, even if I don't deserve her. She's the one who helped me sneak a dog into the dorms."

"Nice. Alison has been amazing as both an agent and a friend. Truth is, I still think it's funny that she actually reads our shit." He gestured to the house. "Let me show you what's inside."

She fell in beside him again. "Hey? Does this mean I might get to read a few of your books?"

Ryder glanced down, a hint of color on his cheeks. "Sure, I guess. Hell, Hunter will probably throw them at you and ask for a woman's honest opinion."

"Not you?"

He just shrugged. "Writers tend to leave little bits of their soul in everything, you know? I mean, I know thousands of people read it, but actually talking to someone who has? I guess it's a bit intimidating, wondering how much they're picking up on and how much is pure imagination."

She stopped, forcing him to face her. "I'll make you a deal. You don't try to judge me, and I won't judge you. Whether that's stupid mistakes, past histories, or the kink we most prefer, it doesn't make a person good or bad - it just makes them real."

"Woman like you probably doesn't have much in the way of kinks." He chuckled wryly. "So sure, Ms. Sanders."

"Brook. If you're Ryder, then I'm just Brook. Besides, I'm kinda working for you this time. And so you know, being married for six years didn't mean I was dead. I lived on books like yours. I just never got to do anything about it."

"We'll see what you say after you've read a few. Let me show you where you'll be staying."

CHAPTER FIFTEEN

They barely stepped inside before two dogs assaulted them. One was a German Shepherd mix, and the other looked like some kind of hound. When he bayed, it proved her right. Brook greeted them like long lost friends, unable to wipe the smile off her face.

A laugh made her look up to see Hunter following them. "Sherlock and Einstein." He pointed at the hound last. "I think they like you."

"Told you." Alison wandered in behind him, patting his shoulder before looking down at Brook. "Scared off yet?"

"Nope," Brook assured her. "I think this is exactly what I need to get my life back on track."

"And," Ryder said, "she'll be perfect for the job."

Brook saw Hunter's expression change briefly. Surprise widened his eyes, but it was gone quickly, the seductive smile back before she was sure she'd seen it. He reached down, petted the closest dog, then gestured to the side.

"Your room would be over here. Comes furnished, since I was told you have little more than what you could carry."

He led her up a short hall with four doors, then opened the first one on each side. Peeking in, she saw cool green decor on the right and warm autumn shades on the left. Other than that, both rooms were massive, with a king-sized bed, two large dressers, and enough floor space to stretch out.

"You're welcome to either."

Ryder moved behind her, his hand gently touching the small of her back. "Keep in mind, your color choice could tell us all about your personality."

"So I should pick the warm tones and convince you I'm a ton of fun?" She looked back to find his face hovering over her shoulder.

He met her gaze easily, making no move to step back. "Or the cool ones and make us think you're calm and reliable."

Alison cleared her throat. "Except you haven't even talked about salary and business. Stop flirting, Ryder. She hasn't been single that long."

Brook laughed when he quickly stepped back. Even the thought of a man like that flirting with her was nice. She couldn't be sure if his reaction was from getting caught or because he didn't want his friendly nature to be taken wrong. Considering what they'd already been through? There was a definite feeling of awkwardness - at least on her part.

But what if he *was* flirting? A few times at the shelter, she'd thought he was, but had that been wishful thinking? It wasn't like this was the type of job someone kept for years, so she probably wouldn't turn him down. Granted, that was the same kind of thinking that convinced her getting married and dropping out of college was a great idea. The last thing she needed was to find herself relying on some overbearing man - again - but she missed feeling like she was desirable.

Looking just a bit too smug, Hunter led her back through the house to a large, masculine office. For some reason, when she thought about an author, she imagined either a typewriter or some antiquated computer with one of those big CRT monitors. These guys obviously didn't agree. Two desks faced each other, large flat screens angled in the corners so they could talk easily. Beneath were massive boxes that glowed with LEDs and hummed with fans. Even the keyboards were fancy - which made sense as soon as she thought about it - but half the letters were worn away, the backlighting shining up through heavily used keys.

Alison tapped her arm then pointed to a pair of chairs in the corner. "They made sure peons like us could be comfortable in their man cave."

"Doesn't look much like a man cave." Brook was pleasantly impressed.

Hunter dropped behind the desk closest to her. "Does when we're going head to head in Battlefield. And it sounds like you enjoy the dogs and you're willing to babysit them. The job comes with a room, dinner with the two of us when we're here, free range of the kitchen when we're not."

Ryder made an annoyed noise. "What he's trying to say is to make yourself at home, grocery costs are covered."

"Basically. My brother seems to think you're not going to lose your mind if we talk dirty around you, and Alison says you're not a gold digger."

Brook huffed out a startled laugh. "How did you know Ryder and I talked about that?"

Alison patted her arm. "They do that. You just have to

get used to them. For a while, I was convinced they wore microphones or something, but they keep saying it's all about the body language."

Hunter looked a bit too proud of himself. "Something like that. See, Alison is like a sister to us. If she says you're good, I'm willing to believe her. The job pays fifteen hundred a month."

"But all expenses are covered," Ryder added.

That made Brook lean forward. "Wow, ok. I'm sure you guys know I'm desperate, so I'm not going to say no, but that just made me very happy. Only one problem. I don't have a car."

Hunter waggled his finger between himself and his brother. "We do. Usually, one's always available. I should warn you, though. We're not much more than a step up from college guys."

She looked around the room pointedly. "So by this time tomorrow there should be dirty underwear all over, dishes molding in the sink, and a funky Cheetos smell coming from your rooms? Figure I can ignore the steady stream of women passing through."

Beside her, Alison pressed her hand over her mouth, but Ryder couldn't stop the laugh. Hunter, who seemed to be the ringleader, leaned back in his chair and nodded with a very pleased expression. A little too pleased.

"I didn't believe you, Alison, but you were right. She fits right in." Hunter stood and walked the four steps to pause before her, offering his hand. "Welcome to the family, Brooklyn. I think this might even be a pleasure."

∿

*M*ost of what she'd taken when she left Owen had gone into boxes. Alison arranged for those to be put into storage. For now, all she had to worry about were the things she'd squeezed into her best friend's car. Needless to say, it didn't take much to move her stuff into her new room.

It took longer to straighten up her clothes and hang them in the closet of the green room. Just a motley collection of t-shirts and jeans, a couple of dresses suitable for dating, her one business suit for job interviews, and the stuffed dog she'd carried with her for most of her life. That went on the bed, between the pillows. It was the only pet she had left.

After that, she went exploring. The house was large, but not massive. Four bedrooms, who knew how many baths, and at least three living areas - if she counted the study. The kitchen was nice but not extravagant, and it wasn't like she could spend much time checking out a bathroom. The property, however, was a different story.

Five acres and all of it was beautiful. The trees had been planted in an organized fashion. Smaller yards were fenced off so a few dogs could play without getting out of hand. In the very back, she found a miniature forest with a long, winding trail. The barn was the most interesting. It had been designed to hold at least twenty dogs. Inside was climate-controlled, and each run had access to a smaller area outside. Of course, picking up the poop would be her job, but Brook didn't care. With the cute little rakes and a wheelbarrow she found in a supply room, it would be a breeze.

And both men assured her that the dogs were always welcome inside. On impulse, she found a leash and headed for the scarred-up little pup Ryder had picked up from the shelter. A tag on her kennel called her Amelia. It fit. The daring little girl reminded Brook of the pilot: half adventure, half glamor. From what Brook could remember, the poor thing had been used as a bait dog, but that didn't seem to make her any less fond of people.

With only a slight limp, Amelia trotted beside her, and Brook made a lap through the overly green grass to give the pup time to piddle. Instead, the curious little girl looked at everything. Shrubs were monsters, pots were playthings, and the pebble path that led to the back door was very suspicious. Brook took her time, waiting until the little dog relaxed before trying to move closer, but eventually, she just gave up and lifted Amelia into her arms.

That seemed to be the reassurance the pup needed. Crooning sweetly to keep the little dog calm, Brook stepped into the house, giving the poor thing time to look around. It didn't matter. Amelia shook, trembling in pure fear, but never once did she try to bite. Nope, the little dog who looked like she'd once been used to train others to fight just snuggled closer. Brook's goal was a wire kennel set up in her room. If she could make it that far, maybe the confined space would help Amelia adjust to the strange new sights and smells.

That was when Hunter walked around the corner. He saw what Brook was holding and smiled fondly, but Amelia wasn't as thrilled. She whimpered. A second later, Brook felt something very warm and wet against her ribs, making its way lower. She just laughed, rocking from side to side to distract the dog.

Hunter rubbed at his mouth to hide a grin. "Don't know how to break this to you."

"I know," she assured him. "She just pissed all over me. Just don't want to get it on the floor."

He shrugged. "Laminate. Unfortunately, that's the problem we've had since she came back from the vet. Makes me think they had a building for the dogfights, and when she went inside, that's when they turned the others loose on her."

"Well, I set up a kennel in my room. I thought maybe she could try spending the night with me. Give her enough time to get used to being inside without too much coming at her, you know?"

"Worth a shot. Need help?"

She paused to kiss the little dog's head. "Well, I'm currently trying to decide if she'll be ok while I grab a shower or if I should wait and make sure she settles in."

"Mm." Hunter looked amused. "I suppose I could sit with her and talk sweetly while you have that shower. Gives me a chance to check out how girly your room has become."

With a laugh, she turned to her door. "Sorry to disappoint. I don't really own much, so it's basically the same."

Leading him in, she tilted her head at the far wall, proving her point. Except for the kennel at the foot of the bed and the stuffed dog, nothing had changed. Everything she owned fit in the closet and half of one dresser. Hunter headed straight for the bed, tossing his long body across it casually, then reached for the stuffed toy.

"Dunno, Brook, we may have to talk about your style sense. Once there's plushies in a house, it's all downhill from there."

Giggling at his bad joke, she eased the poor puppy into the crate. A simple packing blanket was draped over most of it, leaving only the front open. As soon as Amelia was back behind the confinement of a kennel, she started to relax. When Brook withdrew, the puppy licked her hand, earning a rub between the ears.

"Looks like she approves." She was trying hard to ignore how very sexy Hunter looked sprawled across the bed. Single for less than a week, and her mind had already decided it was time to move on. Evidently, she really didn't miss her husband that much. "You don't mind watching her for a few minutes?"

His grey tee stretched across his chest, the color complimenting the emerald green comforter. Lying like that, he looked like a man begging to be jumped on, but she knew better. He was just sexy, and if she was going to live with these guys, then she'd have to get over it very fast. She might be in need of a reset, but the two people nice enough to give her a chance weren't really the ones she should consider. If Brook had learned anything, it was that a pretty face was only good to *look* at.

"I've got plenty of time," Hunter promised. "I'm stuck until Ryder finishes with the ballroom scene. Still don't know how he can keep track of which girl is in which dress. He keeps saying the colors are symbolic, but after the third pass through the room, it's just a sea of flowers in my head, you know?"

"Nope," Brook assured him, yanking open a drawer to find clean underwear. "I'm assuming Regency? Or is it medieval?"

"Regency. Our vixen caught the attention of two men, and I think it's going to bite her in the ass."

That made her laugh. She glanced to see if the joke was intentional, but from the look on his face, he still hadn't caught it. Digging for a pair of comfortable shorts and a baggy shirt, she couldn't stop herself. "Punny, Hunter. You write threesomes and make ass jokes?"

"I think you need to read more of our books. You know, not all women are into that."

"But all of them are into threesomes?" She dared to glance over her shoulder.

He was petting the stuffed dog. "I think a lot of women are curious about it. Many find it erotic, even if they'd never try it personally. But see, we write emotions, not smut. That means each relationship we create has to be true to itself and sweet in its own way. Not everyone is happy with serial monogamy, you know."

As he spoke, her brows kept moving higher. "And how is one woman with two men anything at all like 'sweet'?"

"Women are complicated and diverse. You tend to feel about everything. Men? Nah, we're simple. Food, sex, comfort. But the comfort part is different for each of us. Some want to be reassured, some want to show off, and others just want to not be alone. Put two very different men with one complicated and intelligent woman, and you get a relationship that could work if only people could figure out how to be that honest."

"Well, I'll be very honest. I smell like dog pee." She waved the clothes at him. "I'll be quick, and if you happen to have another book, I sure as hell won't complain."

Hunter shifted, getting comfortable. "Pretty sure I can do that. Take your time. Amelia and I have stuff to talk about."

CHAPTER SIXTEEN

*T*he bathroom was impressive, like everything else in this near-mansion. Brook enjoyed every moment of it. This was so different from the suburban home she'd shared with Owen. The best part, though, was the guys. "Rose Solace" was actually kinda fun to hang out with, and hearing about what went into writing a book was intriguing. Their laid-back attitudes let her feel like it was ok to just be herself - like she didn't need to worry about impressing them. It was nice.

With her hair wrapped in a towel, but the rest of her dressed, she made her way back to her room. She was barely through the door when she realized the man sitting hunched before the kennel wasn't the same one she'd left. It wasn't just the color of his shirt, but something about his posture. Hunter was always stretched out and confident. Ryder? He withdrew into himself a bit. There was a shyness about him that he tried very hard to hide.

"How's she doing, Ryder?"

His head snapped around, pleased surprise on his face. "Terrified. I tried to get her to come out, but she's perfectly happy to stay inside the kennel. Traded off with Hunter after hearing *all* about how she peed on ya."

"So you made it through the ball?"

A soft chuckle slipped out as he leaned back, resting his shoulders on the side of her bed. "Mostly. Made it as far as he'd written."

"Cool." She pulled the towel from her hair, then flopped onto the bed to rub the last of the water from it. Lying on her belly, she could see the puppy. "How does that work? I've always wondered how two writers collaborate like that."

"Well, it's different for everyone, but we got into a groove a long time ago. When we start a new book, we spend a couple of days talking it out. It's like making up the story. Then Hunter goes crazy. He sets up the dialogue and characters, leaving scenes in brackets for me to fill in."

"Like, 'they walk through a garden?' That type of thing?"

He nodded. "Pretty much. Could also be a basic description of a person - brunette girl, curvy - that I put into something a bit nicer. Then, when that chapter's done, he moves to the next while I go back and smooth it all out, add fluff to the dialogue tags and put description around the internal thoughts."

She was nodding, her mind on the book she'd read the night before. "It works. I couldn't even tell two people had written it."

"Yep. Although being a partnership made it almost impossible to find an agent. We were unknowns, and everyone worried we'd break up in a year or so."

Made sense. Granted, being not only brothers, but also twins, did mean they wouldn't fall too far apart. "Then you found Ali, huh?"

"Tossed a query at her even though she didn't typically represent smut, but she said she loved stories that bent expectations. When she found out we all live in the same town - which was how we found her - we had a face-to-face, and the rest is history."

"How many?"

His brow furrowed as he tried to follow her question. "Novels?" She nodded, and the crease disappeared. "Forty-two. Twenty-four best sellers. We're giving Danielle Steel a run for her money, even if society isn't quite as accepting of our idea of romance."

"Mm." She tossed the towel into a corner. "So why romance?"

He laughed, dragging a hand over his face. "That's what everyone wants to know. Evidently, we're supposed to write murder mysteries or something."

She gestured at his body. "Couple of big, imposing guys like you? Figured you'd be more into action or drama."

"And romance has both, plus more sex. Problem with other genres is that it's all been done. Romance? Doing the same thing over and over never gets dull. Just think how many stories are about alpha males wooing some timid and plain girl and how she blooms under his love. You think that's not kinda hot for a guy, too?"

"Really?"

He smiled. "Think about it. The story may be from her perspective, but this troubled man steps up and not only takes care of his girl but shows her that the person he can see is something to be proud of? Yeah. I think that's what most men want. Makes us feel like we're doing something right, making her proud of what we love."

That made a lot of sense, actually. Ryder definitely gave off the caregiver vibe. Hunter, not so much, but he was the kind of guy who could make anyone proud of herself. Brook rolled onto her back, staring at the fan spinning lazily above. There was just one thing she was dying to know.

"So you stay single to keep the creative juices flowing?" She glanced at him from the corner of her eyes, watching his reaction.

Ryder shook his head, his eyes on the puppy. "Nope. Stay single because falling in love is easy on paper. Our characters are hot, sexy, and suave. Us? Nah. Hunter and I are nerds. We can put on an act for a bit, but the details? Pair of brothers who still live together, are obsessed with unwanted dogs, and spend all day writing trash? Not the best pick up line. I think Amelia's passed out."

He'd just changed the subject. She knew it, and could see the embarrassed tension in his shoulders, so she let him. "I already fed the rest."

"What about you?" He leaned his head back to look at her. "Had dinner, yet?"

"Nope."

"Wanna?" He pushed himself to his feet, turning back for her answer.

For a moment, Brook's heart fluttered. She was flopped on her back, her hair spread around her, with Ryder looming above. All she had to do was reach out, and she could pull him down on top of her. She could almost imagine the way his muscles would feel beneath her hands, and that scared her. Was she really incapable of living without a man in her life? Yes, he was gorgeous, but she was too old to be thinking like this!

"Yeah," she said, smiling weakly. "I should probably eat once a day."

He offered his hand, and she let him hoist her up. The

expression on his face was guarded, but it made her wonder if he'd been thinking the same thing. Was this as weird for him as it was for her? Could she be projecting her own fantasies onto him? Had he done that intentionally? She was probably just being a desperate idiot. It wasn't like either of the twins would have to work hard to find a woman - one a lot more impressive than her.

Which was good, because Brook didn't have the willpower to say no. It had been so long since she'd gotten any attention from a man that it didn't take much anymore, but damn. As Ryder led her from the room, she couldn't help but notice how very nicely his ass was shaped. It had been far too many years since she'd had her hands on an ass like that, and she definitely missed it. It was begging for a woman to grab it and pull him closer.

Or a man.

From the way he talked, he sounded straight, but her "gay-dar" wasn't exactly perfect. They wrote romance. He'd confirmed her suspicion that neither of the brothers was dating seriously. If he was gay, then it all made perfect sense.

Her mouth started before her mind could clamp it shut. "Hey, Ryder? Remember how you were asking about my preferences? Does that mean I get to do the same?"

He paused, then turned slowly. "I like tall, curvaceous brunettes with blue eyes. Smiles do me in. Intelligence makes me drool like a dog with a bone. And a girl that isn't ashamed of what she likes and is willing to go well outside the boundaries of 'normal'? Yeah. Find me one, and I'll fall in love like any of the guys in my books." He lifted a brow, proving he wasn't ashamed at all. "You?"

She laughed. "I was just wondering if you were straight, since you'd asked me. Wow."

He nodded, crossing his arms. "Yep, I like women, yet I figure you still have a type."

"Um." Did she want to admit that? He'd basically just outlined her, and well... Fuck it. "Over six feet tall, and dark. Italian, Hispanic, Mediterranean, mixed ethnicity, I don't care, just give me dark eyes and hair, with something besides alabaster skin. Muscles are always nice. Then again, that's because size *does* matter, and I don't just mean his arms." She laughed, a little embarrassed. "I like confidence. I like brooding. Haven't figured out which I prefer, since they don't typically come in the same package. I dunno. Does that count?"

"A wordsmith, you are not." He moved to her side, guiding her through the maze of a house. "Maybe we'll have to pick your brain for some of our next work."

"Oh, so I can help with the sex scenes, huh? Trust me, don't squish the boobs into one. Painful."

She said that just as they stepped into the kitchen, and a laugh answered. Holding a hot skillet in his hand, Hunter had heard and was very amused. He was still grinning as he returned the pan to the stove.

"I should have known that a friend of Ali's wouldn't be either shy or demure." He tilted his head to the counter. "Sit. You a vegetarian?"

"Nope."

He nodded, looking devious. "So you like meat?"

The playful innuendo was there, as if he was daring her. "Oh yes," she assured him. "Preferably hot, but cold will do if there's nothing else. Have a fondness for nice thick pieces."

He cleared his throat, but Ryder saved him from answering. "Coffee?"

Brook giggled. "Yes, please. And nope, can't twist that into something perverse."

He flicked his eyes to hers. "Steamy. You see, my brother and I sometimes need a little help to keep it up all night."

"I'm outclassed." She tossed her hands into the air, admitting defeat.

Leaving the stove, Hunter stepped closer, grabbing her waist. "You're also getting double-teamed. Up." As he said the last word, he lifted, dropping her rump on an empty section of counter.

Without thinking, she spread her knees, mostly to prevent kicking him somewhere sensitive. When his hands lingered for a moment, she realized that placed him right between her legs. Once again, she was a little too close to a man who was way too beautiful to not think of naked. That didn't mean she was going to turn stupid, though. Nope. Even with her wits rattled by hormones, they still worked just fine.

"Guess this means I get to watch?" She returned the smug look he'd worn only seconds before.

His hands left her waist but moved to the counter beside her hips as he leaned just a bit closer. "Well, we have to break you in, still. Wouldn't want to scare you off so soon."

"I see." Behind him, Ryder claimed the stove. Brook's tongue flicked out to moisten her upper lip. "I was going to ask which of you handles the meat, but I see it's a team effort."

"Works better like that," Ryder assured her.

Hunter just smiled. "Is there anything we should know you don't care for before we start? Did you need a safe word?"

He was so damned close, and the bastard knew he was having an effect. She leaned back, but that only pushed her breasts against her shirt. Brook tried to ignore it. "I dunno, I'm pretty easy. I'll try anything once."

His eyes flicked down. "Right. Um. Food?"

Maybe the odds weren't as bad as she thought. It seemed she wasn't the only one distracted by the banter. "What's on the menu? Do I get to pick or just sample it all?"

The pan clattered, and Ryder cursed under his breath before clearing his throat. Hunter, however, wasn't ready to give up. "Well, I'd been thinking about something sweet." He smiled. "But I'm starting to like the idea of spicy."

"Looks to me like Ryder's doing all the work."

"And I'm the one having all the fun. I think we all win." Slowly, he leaned back, smiling proudly.

Ryder grumbled again, then shifted his hips before making an obvious adjustment. Brook watched, then turned her eyes to the other brother. "Your turn."

Seeing the dare, he called her bluff, reaching down without turning his back. Brook's eyes dropped, then jerked right back up. Holy shit. If the size of that bulge was any indication, she was never going to look at either guy the same. Blood was trying to rush to her cheeks, but she wasn't the kind of girl to blush. She hadn't even done that in college. Nope, she would not give them the satisfaction. Relaxing her jaw, she ignored it, and the flush faded before it was noticeable.

That didn't mean Hunter missed it. He raked his eyes over her. "Need a new pair of shorts, yet?"

"Nope. These are moisture-wicking. Great for working in messy situations. I assume that after dinner you both will be writing?"

"Or planning the next story," Ryder clarified. "We're currently ahead of schedule and wouldn't want to finish too soon."

She groaned. "Maybe I just need to stay out of the kitchen. You two are such a tease."

They shared a look, then both chuckled. Brook couldn't read what was on their faces, but obviously, they didn't need real sentences to communicate. Probably one of the perks of growing up constantly together. Before she could say anything, Hunter stepped away, joining his brother. As if putting on a show, he headed in to help, the pair moving together perfectly.

Ryder passed him the pan, then turned for a pot. As soon as he finished, Hunter stepped over, giving Ryder back his space, and reached for plates. It was almost choreographed. With her mind stuck in the gutter after the double entendres they'd been trading, she wondered if that was how they got the ideas for their books. They looked so comfortable around each other, not like most men. There was no hesitation about touching, no awkwardness over the spacing. It was almost like they were one, yet so very different.

They might be identical twins, but that didn't mean they were exactly the same. Ryder was broader. Hunter was almost an inch taller. It wasn't just that. Hunter was the obvious leader, but Ryder was the bouncer. It was like seeing two dogs of the same breed. The color and basic features were the same, but after only a few minutes, their personality made them unique. Beautiful, gorgeous, unique creatures that she was going to be spending an awful lot of time around. The best part was that they weren't shocked when she joined in with the crass jokes. They almost seemed relieved.

Yep. She needed to get used to sexual tension. She also needed to remember that she wasn't a college student anymore. She was too old to be acting like this, and these guys were her bosses, even if they were a whole lot of fun.

CHAPTER SEVENTEEN

*H*unter sat before his computer, his eyes on the mostly blank page, but his mind was on her. Brooklyn wasn't quite what he'd expected from Ryder's stories. At the shelter, she sounded confident, in control, and completely professional. In person, she was fun, a little timid, and hiding something. Granted, considering what she'd just been through, he didn't really blame her.

But he certainly hadn't expected the witty comebacks or girlish giggles that came so easily while they'd made dinner. It had been nice. No, nice was the wrong word, but he couldn't think of anything else. Suffice it to say he completely understood why Ryder had called him that day. She was alluring in a way that made him want to break every rule they'd agreed on before she got here. Those shy smiles and sultry eyes? Yeah, she had him wrapped completely around her finger.

The sound of a throat clearing made his head jerk up. Ryder leaned against the wall, staring at Hunter's monitor. "Get stuck?"

"Nah. Just distracted."

His brother's head tilted toward the backyard. "She's out there with Rosa. Just don't tell me you want to get rid of her already."

"Wrong distracted," Hunter assured him. "I like her. I thought having a woman in the house would be hard to get used to, but she isn't. She fits with us."

Ryder huffed, pushing off the wall just to throw himself into his own chair. "I think she's scared. Not quaking in her boots or anything, but I mean, you can still see the mark on her neck if you look, and the day her ex hauled her into the shelter and made her quit? Bro, it was bad. She'd become so meek and pliant. She had to be completely terrified, but I couldn't do anything or she'd be the one paying for it."

"Then she called you to get her out."

For a moment, Ryder just nodded as if thinking that through. "And the woman I helped move out of that house wasn't the same one I saw at work. She was determined, driven, and ashamed, but not of what he'd done to her. I think there's more to our new housemate than she's ready to admit."

Hunter's eyes flicked to the monitor, but the book sprawled across it wasn't what he was thinking about. "You know, Alison said she'd lost touch with Brook. Hadn't heard from her for years and just happened to bump into her at a restaurant." His hands itched to do something, but typing wasn't it. He wanted to strangle her ex. "You know that's how it happens?"

"How what happens?" Ryder asked.

"Abuse. First, she loses any semblance of outside support. Her husband makes her dependent on him, severs ties with everyone she can trust, and praises her for it.

Until then, he'll be charming, charismatic, and shower her with gifts and compliments. It's how he gains control. But once she's vulnerable? He'll start making the demands, and it doesn't take long before the fights change from words to fists."

Ryder dropped both arms onto the desk. "What are you saying?"

"That this has been going on for a very long time. It doesn't happen fast, and she's probably so lost she doesn't even know herself." He shoved his keyboard drawer back and groaned under his breath. "We're going to have to tread lightly with her, but she's staying. After everything she's been through, she deserves to have a happy ending, and if we can make that happen, then we will."

"Hunter." Ryder just shook his head. "You can't just write the future. Doesn't really work like that, bro. There's no delete key in real life."

"Sure there is." Leaning back, Hunter crossed his arms and lifted his chin. "It's called money. We've got it, she needs it. What else are we going to do with it, Ry? Buy another house?"

"I kinda like this one. But she's not going to just *take* our money. She's too proud for that. Never mind that Owen made money into a big deal. Man, you should have seen how she reacted when I loaned her twenty for gas my first day. Woulda thought I'd given her a blank check, and she paid me right back. The next day, she went out of her way to put it in my hand, thank me, and make sure I hadn't been put out."

"So what are we going to do?" Hunter asked.

"We," Ryder told him, dropping his voice, "are going to be nice to her. We're going to let her screw up, not give a damn, and make sure she knows it's ok. We're going to treat her the same way we'd treat one of the dogs that has been kicked until it's ready to bite or run. We're going to give her time, patience, and understanding."

"She's *not* a dog," Hunter insisted.

Ryder nodded. "I know. Doesn't mean it won't work. Just stop and think about it. When things were at their worst, what did you want more than anything else?"

"You."

"You already had me." Ryder took a deep breath. "We've always had each other, but that doesn't mean we didn't want more. Think about it, Hunter. What did you lie in bed wishing for?"

Those days were the last thing he wanted to think about, but he couldn't stop himself. The sound of Ryder sobbing into his pillow came back all too easily, and nothing he'd been able to do had stopped it. He'd tried. He would have taken all of the abuse if he could, but they wanted twins. A perfectly matched set to make the buyers happy. And if the boys tried to run away? The punishment was swift, and usually Ryder was the one who took the brunt of it.

"Someone to make it stop," he whispered.

"Yeah. To protect us. We can do that for her." Ryder's hand closed on Hunter's arm. "We know what she's going through. We're the best people in the world to make this easier on her, and she needs us."

Hunter knew there was truth to that, but only the easiest one. "What if she doesn't want us?"

"Then we can still help her." Ryder chuckled softly, letting go of his brother's arm. "Although I think we're ok on the wanting part. She was smiling at you pretty sweetly over dinner, bro."

"Yeah, but she didn't give me the 'fuck me now' eyes like she did you."

"She did not!"

"Not when you were looking," Hunter clarified. "But when you weren't? Oh yeah. Her eyes were undressing you something fierce. I think your little crush might be a mutual thing. She's got the hots for you."

Ryder just waved him off. "Doesn't work like that, and you know it. Soon as she figures out that I'm a freak? Girls like her don't do things like that."

And yet, Hunter knew his brother was hoping. "So you want me to start warming her up to the idea?"

"No! She's had a shitty week. I'm pretty sure the last thing she's looking for is a piece of ass, ok? Us? After everything she's been through? Nah, man. Let's just be the good guys for once, ok? This isn't like one of our books."

But that was where he was wrong. This was exactly like one of their books. All of Ryder's descriptions were of women like her. From the hidden wounds in her pride to the amazing curve of her hips, Brook was exactly the kind of woman they both fell for. And the heroine never started out knowing what she wanted. The two heroes always had to convince the girl it would be ok. Together, the three of them always overcame the societal expectations and found their own happy endings. It would just take a little longer in real life than it did in a novel.

"You're plotting something," Ryder grumbled, "and I have a feeling it's not in Brook's best interest."

Hunter shook his head. "Nothing like that. I just think that for the first time in my life, I'm willing to take it slow and see where this goes. No expectations. If something happens with her, then it does. If not, then we'll be the heroes in another way."

"And how the hell is that going to work?" Ryder asked. "We're giving her the chance to start a new life. We start screwing her, and she'll ditch us just as fast as every other woman has. You know as well as I do that threesomes aren't something that lasts. They're great in books, but in real life? It's a one-night deal, and I'd kinda like to have Brook around as a friend more than just a damned hole to stick my dick in."

That was not at all what Hunter expected his brother to say. Granted, he should have, but Ryder wasn't exactly the sentimental type. Well, except for the dogs. Alison was the only person who'd managed to stay in their life for more than a few months, so their best friends tended to have four legs. The dogs were the only ones who'd ever listened without judging them.

Alison never asked, which was why they'd gotten so close with her. Every time they got talking about the touchy stuff, she always let them change the subject. Oh, she'd call them on it, but mostly just to let them know she didn't care. A little of it was to assure them that she'd listen if they ever *did* want to talk about it.

And Alison said Brook was a lot like her.

So what if Brooklyn Sanders was the kind of girl to have an open mind? Right now, it still wouldn't matter. She had too many of her own issues to deal with. Their screwed-up pasts weren't even on her radar - nor should they be. Then again, it might give them common ground, some way to prove they weren't going to make her life any worse.

Granted, there was always the chance that she'd fall madly in love with his brother. They'd been working together for a week, and she already seemed more comfortable with Ryder than she was with him. Hunter just had to figure out if he could accept that.

Not like he had any room to talk. He'd never stopped to consider Ryder's feelings when he'd started dating his ex. When she'd asked him to move in with her, he'd considered it, and Ryder had never complained. He'd been perfectly supportive – or had tried. Nothing could quite hide how much the idea of living alone scared his brother, and the time Hunter spent without him? It never felt right – but if Ryder had the chance to find happiness with the woman of his dreams? Hunter wouldn't stand in his way.

"You got quiet, bro," Ryder said.

"Yeah. Just trying to figure out what I'm going to do if you get the girl." His chuckle wasn't as chipper as he'd hoped, but it wouldn't have fooled his twin anyway. "She's perfect for you, though. Hell, she's just perfect."

"Can't do it without you." Taking a deep breath, Ryder turned to his own computer, powering it on. His eyes stayed locked on the monitor. "You know that."

"You have before."

"Not for more than a few hours!" Shoving a hand into his hair, Ryder groaned in the back of his throat. "I always say the stupid shit. That's why you write the dialogue. I can handle the action, but talking? I screw it up!"

"Doesn't look like you're screwing it up. Looks to me like she trusts you. I think she kinda needs that right about now, so you'd better put some effort into getting over this, or she'll be the one hurt because of it."

Ryder's head snapped over. "Huh?"

"How do you think that girl will take it if you blow her off? After everything she's already been through? Right now, the thing she needs most is a friend. Maybe two. If it gets to be more than that? Yeah. It's going to take a little time, and that means you'll have plenty of chances to practice talking to her all by yourself."

"What about you?" Ryder asked.

Hunter shrugged. "I'll be doing the exact same thing, but working on doing instead of just talking. I like her, Ry. I really do, but there's no way in hell I'm going to steal your girl, not when you've just rescued her from the bad guy."

"Our girl," Ryder assured him. "We're a matched set. Can't have one without the other. Kinda the problem."

"Yeah, but right now, I think her problems outrank ours." For a moment, he paused, then tapped at his monitor. "And that's where we went wrong with this book. We've been too focused on the guys' problems. We forgot to give our little heroine any."

"Have any ideas?" Ryder asked.

Hunter was reaching for his keyboard. "Yeah. I finally figured out why she's an old maid. Would rather live alone than put up with some abusive husband or fiancée. I think our little love interest is going to be the kind of woman with a little pride and a whole lot of spine."

"Just like Brook," Ryder agreed.

CHAPTER EIGHTEEN

*D*inner was fun and tasted pretty good. Brook had grown used to prefab meals, so pork chops was a wonderful change. The conversation was even better. Having two dogs sitting beside her, begging, and being allowed to feed them tidbits from her plate? Oh yeah, she could get used to this.

From what she could gather, Sherlock, the German Shepherd mix, was Hunter's buddy. Einstein, the hound-like thing, had a preference for Ryder. Amelia was just a sad case who had no options at the shelter, so Ryder had decided to help her out. Back in the barn was one more. Rosa was a large mastiff mix who knew nothing. She'd been with them for two whole weeks, liked to chase cats, and except for being friendly, knew absolutely nothing about being around people or other animals.

That was why Brook decided to spend a little time with her. Amelia seemed happy enough in her kennel in the bedroom, but Rosa couldn't spend all day in a small run. She was a big dog and needed to do big dog things.

With a couple of tennis balls and a knotted rope in hand, Brook headed outside.

First, she took Rosa to one of the yards. While the mutt galumphed around barking at everything from bugs to trees, Brook cleaned up her kennel. When that was done, she pulled out the filthy mat the dog had been sleeping on and rummaged in the storage room for something better. There, she found an old dog bed. It was little more than worn cloth and crumpled stuffing, but at least it was better than leaving her on bare concrete while the other was cleaned. Hunter knew the dogs would destroy things and said that she shouldn't worry about it, so Brook decided to win over this mutt with kindness.

When that was done, she picked up her arsenal and plopped herself down in the grass. First, she tried throwing the ball as close to the dog as she could. This made Rosa pause. Tracking it until it stopped, she then moseyed over to sniff. Suddenly, with a massive bound, she pounced on it. Brook laughed, praising her for playing.

That was all Rosa needed. A simple "good girl" resulted in a mad dash around the grass. She grumbled and snorted, chewing on the tennis ball as if it was a piece of gum. When it became clear the dog wasn't going to bring it back, Brook held up the other.

"Rosa! Hey, girl. Want this?"

With lips flapping and skin heaving, she galloped over. Unfortunately, the dog couldn't figure out how to get the second ball while the first was in her mouth, but a person had this one, so it had to be better! Completely distracted, she dropped the first ball in a sodden heap, gleefully taking the other on a march around the yard. Brook picked up the first and did it again, but this time, when Rosa dropped the ball, she got praise.

In half an hour, she had the mastiff not only fetching, but bringing it back and letting go on something like a command. The big girl was getting tired - if the length of her tongue was any hint - but she wasn't done. Brook threw the ball again, and her pocket began to vibrate.

Shoving slimy fingers into her shorts, she found her phone. "Yeah?"

"Well?" It was Alison, checking up on her.

Brook giggled. "They're fun, and the dogs are amazing. Already got pissed on, though."

"Please tell me it was the dog and not one of my boys?"

"Yeah, the puppy."

Alison sighed, but in jest. "Ok. So, now that you've been there for most of a day, what do you think?"

Rosa was back, so Brook took the ball and threw it again. "Well, they're drop-dead gorgeous, but you already knew that."

"Mhm."

"Smart, funny, and pretty laid back. What are you looking for here?"

"My best friend," Alison told her. "I'm hoping to hear that person who disappeared after getting married. C'mon, Brooklyn. We both know you're not afraid to speak your mind."

"True, but they're your clients. I just need a couple of months to get on my feet and save enough for a deposit. I'm not going to screw up your big money-maker."

Alison groaned. "No, that's Mrs. Harper. I'm looking for Brook Sanders. Talk to me, girl."

"You're trying to say you stuck me with two hotties and aren't worried at all about the fallout if I jump on one? Hell, both? And then they get pissed at each other, blame you for bringing me here, and you lose a best-selling author?"

"Yeah, pretty much. First, our contract gives me rights they can't just back out of. Legally, I'm covered. Second, those guys are my closest friends, besides you. Third? There's nothing you can do that will come between them, ok? Hunter and Ryder know how to take care of themselves, and there's nothing in the world that can make them hate each other. Oh sure, they'll fight. Hell, I've seen them throw a few punches, but I don't think they could live without each other."

Brook tossed the other ball to the dog, leaning over to grab the first. "Least there's that. They're fun, though. I mean, when Ryder was working at the shelter, we got along great. Now that there's two of them? I've been doing my best to remember they're just friends, but damn."

"Damn?"

Brook giggled. "Ali, the sexual tension they throw off? Holy shit. Cooking dinner had me thinking about running to the special store for toys, if ya know what I mean."

Alison laughed. "Yeah. Hunter's well-known for that. I think it's some defense mechanism. He always tries to cover up his lack of confidence with flirting."

"Lack of confidence? Hunter?"

"Mhm." From the sound of her voice, Alison knew she was dropping a bombshell. "He's confident he can talk a woman out of her clothes. He's not confident she'll think he's worth much."

"I think that's Ryder," Brook corrected.

"Nope, it's both. Ryder's always been the quiet one. Takes a lot to get through his shell. He'd rather just avoid you than try to be chatty."

"Uh." Brook swapped the balls again, but this time

Rosa gave up. The dog just flopped in the grass beside her, so Brook moved closer to pet her belly. "Ali, Ryder's been easier to get to know than Hunter. You sure we're talking about the right guys, or did I get them mixed up?"

"Grey tee was Hunter. I can't remember what Ryder was wearing."

"Black game shirt." Brook knew; she'd been looking at him enough. "Either way, they're really sweet. I got a nice dinner cooked for me, and they both are trying hard to make sure I'm comfortable in the house. It's a little weird, but I keep reminding myself that I've had roommates before."

"So still like the job?"

"Yeah." Brook flopped onto her back to stare at the stars. "Right now I'm lying in the grass with a mastiff. I mean, the house is lovely, the dogs are all sweet, the view is amazing, and it doesn't really feel like work. I have a question though, and you're not required to tell me."

"Shoot."

"How rich are they? I'm getting the feel of comfortable, not excessive. I know you keep saying authors aren't well paid."

Over the phone, the sound of keys clicking could be heard. For a moment Alison was quiet. "Google says Rose Solace's net worth is about thirty-six million. That help?"

"Fuck me," Brook breathed. "Ok, that's a lot more than comfortable. They don't act like rich snobs, though."

"I know." Her best friend sounded proud of herself. "They aren't dicks, Brook. Ryder and Hunter are some of the nice guys. Oh, they're perverts. I mean, you read their stuff! Everything they put out is hot, and I don't just mean the sales. They're sensual, kinky, and very aware of what turns a woman on, but it's not really something they can brag about. No different than Leah and I. Society has expectations, and they most certainly do not fit into that. They can't even admit they're the brains behind Rose Solace or the sales would dry up. Romance authors are supposed to be women, you know."

"I know, and I'm ashamed to say I expected a mature woman."

"Yeah, that's why I wanted to get you there first. If I told you it was a pair of good-looking men who write love scenes? One of whom had already jumped up to help? Pretty sure you wouldn't have been interested. Mrs. Harper never would have asked the same person for two favors, because 'that's just not done.'"

"Right. After Owen, it's so hard to remember that it's ok to just be me. He had so many rules, and they just piled up slowly. Even when I met Ryder at the shelter, I thought he was hot, but kept telling myself not to even look because I was married. Now, I'm living with him and his identical fucking twin! Strange how serious they are about the writing, though. It's a craft, and they want to be masters."

"They are masters," Alison reminded her. "Some of the top sellers in the genre are under their name. That doesn't mean you'll like the job. I just wanted to make sure you know that you can come back at any time. I'm just across town."

"Nah, I'm good, sweetie." Brook giggled. "I'm lying in a country yard, playing with a dog, and able to talk with my bestie without anyone standing over my shoulder. There's no way Owen would ever find me out here."

"Yeah." Alison's voice turned soft. "I'm so glad you left him. Owen hated me. He hated you talking to me."

"Mhm. He kept asking if I was sleeping with you.

Remember when we took that long weekend to go camping? I dunno, like five years ago? When I got back, he lost it, convinced we were having an affair and that there had to be some extra man involved."

"Eww," Alison teased. "I mean, you're cute enough, but a dick? Uh, no." First, she made a puking noise. Then she laughed at her pathetic attempt to be a stereotypical lesbian.

"I know, I know, disgusting things," Brook added with a giggle. "And I'm supposed to add some rant about dildos always being shaped like penises. Unless you prefer baseball bats? Maybe a flower?" They both laughed. "Nope, pretty sure a flower would *not* work. Sorry, Ali, I think you're stuck with dicks."

"I'll deal with it if you keep laughing like that. I haven't heard you sound happy in a long time." Alison took a deep breath, a hum coloring it on the way out. "Girl, I've missed you.

"Me, too. Thanks, Ali. I needed this. I just don't want to screw up."

"You won't." Alison paused for a moment. "Brook, they didn't really have a job. I mean, they kept saying they wished someone could help with the dogs, but Ryder really wanted to do more, so we asked Hunter if he thought this would work."

Brook groaned. "Ali! I hate charity. This whole thing has been hard enough without feeling like I'm a beggar."

"It's not charity. It's putting people together who can help. Look, it was Leah who set this up, ok? When I told her I saw Ryder at the shelter when I came to pick you up? Well, she called them and said you'd be staying with us. She reminded Hunter how they'd been wishing someone could help with their rescues, and mentioned that Ryder'd already been working with you. Anyways, Ryder called me back, saying you made things so easy on him when he was working off his sentence." She paused. "Which he forgot to mention to me, by the way. Anyways, he was adamant that no matter what, they had a room, would love the help, and if your husband tried to touch you, they'd make him pay for it. I guess Leah mentioned something about Owen calling your phone."

From the background, Alison's wife spoke up. "You're not getting me in trouble, are you?"

"Yes, honey. You deserve it."

"Well, just make sure Brook knows that payback's a bitch. Borrowing my phone to call you so I'd just accidentally get your number? I owe her."

Listening to them bicker, Brook was smiling. "She never admitted that."

"Not to you," Alison teased. "She fessed up to me on our first date. Look, you're like the sister I always wanted to have. Those boys are like the brothers. I figure if all of us can get along, then I'm the one winning, and if not, I don't lose a damned thing. Just tell me you're ok with this?"

"I'm ok with this," Brook assured her. "Thank you, Ali. I should have listened to you about Owen, and I promise I won't make that mistake again. If living with some super-hunks is gonna make you happy, then I'll suffer for my best friend."

"Suffer, my ass." Alison sighed, but this time it sounded relieved. "Thanks, Brook. I mean it - you always have a place with me, but I worry about those boys, too. They keep themselves locked away from the world, and I know there's stuff they just won't talk about. They aren't just clients, not after so many years. They're like family."

"My best friend's brothers. Easier to keep my mind above their belts if I think like that." Brook paused. "Nope, never mind. That doesn't really help much. They have some seriously nice chests, too."

"No boobs," Alison teased. "Least they aren't hairy. Ugh. Let's not even talk about back hair. Just don't even understand how you can tolerate the scruff on their face. Like kissing sandpaper."

"Unlike you, I kinda like scruff." Brook shifted over, gathering the drool-soaked toys. "One of us has to, right? Speaking of that, since I'm now living so close to you, when are we going out?"

"Hunting for a date?"

"Nope," Brook assured her. "Just you and I, dinner, maybe some wine. I want to catch up on everything I missed while being a good wife. I just want some time to hang out with you and hear all about everything that's happened. Oh, and maybe hear some of those kinky things you and Leah get up to that you've been just dying to brag about."

"Deal." Alison paused for a moment. "I have a couple of meetings this week in the evenings, but next Friday you're all mine. And I'm buying you dinner, just for bragging rights."

"It's a date," Brook promised. "God, I've missed you."

"Me too, honey. Welcome to the rest of your life. Now stop being a damned prude."

CHAPTER NINETEEN

*B*y the time Brook headed inside, it was getting late. Soft voices coming from the study told her the guys were deep into their writing. Snores from her own bedroom told her Amelia was fast asleep. Brook joined her. Even though it was a new house, she passed out almost immediately. It felt like only minutes later when a whimper woke her, but the light had changed to that soft morning color.

Amelia whined again, then pawed at the kennel door. That pulled Brook the rest of the way from sleep. "You gotta go outside, sweetie?"

The puppy's thumping tail was as good as a yes. Pulling on a pair of shorts, but forgoing a bra in the panic of puppy necessity, Brook wrenched open the kennel and hurried out the back door. She barely remembered a leash. Amelia's feet were just in the grass before the little girl let loose. After that came the wait for the rest of her business. Man, the mornings were still cold.

She was clutching her arms over her chest when the back door opened. One of the guys wandered out holding a big hoodie. His eyes were still half-lidded, his feet bare, and in this state, she couldn't tell which one it was.

She hoped hearing his voice might give her a hint, so greeted him with, "Morning. I hope we didn't wake you."

He shook his head. "Nah. Was waiting for the coffee to finish when I heard the sound of a piddle emergency. Put this on."

"Thanks." She took the jacket gratefully, giving the pup a little more leash.

Doing her best to manage both the dog and dressing, she somehow got both arms into the proper holes. That was when the brother stepped just a bit closer. Gently, he lifted her hair out of the collar.

"It's Hunter," he said softly. "I could see you trying to figure it out. You know it's ok to ask, right?"

Brook sighed but nodded. "Thanks. Last night, I honestly thought I had it."

"Yeah? So what're our tells?"

She shook her head slightly. "Tells?"

"You know, the thing that makes you sure it's me and not him."

"Oh." She looked back at the pup, a nervous giggle slipping out. "You're more outgoing. Ryder tends to notice the details."

"Not bad." He rubbed her shoulder. "Not quite perfect, though. Also doesn't help you at all if we're doing something quiet, like reading or sleeping."

"Yeah, that makes it harder. You know, most twins aren't the same. Close, but not perfect."

The smile he gave her was almost shy. "Yep. Most twins also didn't grow up like we did."

"Oh?"

"Uh." Hunter glanced over to the barn. "Yeah. Got

bounced around a lot. We were adopted from Russia as infants, and well, not really the easiest kids, so we ended up re-homed a few times." He shrugged. "From the time we were nine, it was just us against the world. I guess that's why we have a soft spot for the dogs."

"Oh." Brook shifted closer. "I know it doesn't help, but I'm sorry. Guess that kinda explains why you two read each others' minds, huh?"

"Yeah." This time, his smile was easier. "Ryder's a bit shy, so we'd swap places, you know? The more often it happened, the easier it got to know what he wanted. Kinda goes the same the other way, too. Since no one could tell us apart, we joined forces, I guess."

"Is that why the books?"

He froze, then forced himself to relax. "I guess. Never really thought about it too hard. I mean, we always got the jokes about two is better than one, and I guess it just kinda started from that."

"Really?" Brook jerked as Amelia tugged to follow a leaf in the yard. "You write romance and never thought about why?"

Hunter gestured for her to follow the puppy. "Let's take her back to the kennel. If you're nice, I might even share my coffee."

"So that's a no on the question, huh?"

He chuckled, falling in at her side. "Pretty much. I'll give you the light version. When we were thirteen, we lived in this place that had an entire wall of romance novels. No TV, no consoles, and most certainly no internet, so we read all the books. At least twice. Then we talked about them and tried to make them better."

"Thirteen and already figuring out how to woo the ladies?"

"Yeah." He waved her down. "Least we thought so. Most of that stuff was crap. We watched our latest father figure beat the snot out of his wife and couldn't understand why the women in those stories would think it was sexy. They were old books, you understand. Back when women got raped and then fell in love with the barbarian who'd done that to her. So, all of our guys were sensitive."

"You ever figure out that women like their men to be strong, not cruel?"

She asked that just as they got to the barn. Brook reached for the handle, but Hunter's hand pressed the door closed as he leaned over her shoulder. Standing behind her, the size of his body gave her little room. Then his breath teased the edge of her ear.

His voice came in a rough whisper. "There's a line. It's a very fine line. We need to be strong, but gentle. Demanding, yet understanding." His hand closed on her hip. "Making you nervous increases awareness, but making you afraid does nothing for romance. Let me get that door for you."

The hand on her hip guided her over, while his other pulled the knob. When he stepped back, Hunter watched her closely, waiting for her reaction. Brook fanned at her face dramatically, then scooped up the puppy, carrying Amelia to her kennel. Like a lost puppy himself, Hunter trailed behind.

Setting Amelia inside, a giggle slipped out. Then another as Brook stood to latch the kennel door. "Is every day going to be like this?" she asked, turning to face him.

"Like what?" One of his eyebrows twitched up, proving he knew exactly what she was talking about.

Brook gestured between them. "Every time we're in a

room together, you're flirting. Mostly showing off, but still."

"Want me to stop?" He crossed his arms and leaned back, just like Ryder had the day before.

The similarity made Brook smile. "Nah. I'm just trying to figure out what you're up to. Am I some experiment for your next novel?"

"Kinda. Mostly it's that I have a weakness for pretty brunettes who know how to enjoy life." The dark lashes around his eyes made his stare that much more intense.

She could feel it. Oh damn, could she feel that look, and having a man like him call her a pretty brunette? Yep, that was how she'd ended up married. Everyone wanted to be complimented, but when you'd grown up without them, each offhanded comment hit that much harder. It had taken Brook six years to figure that out.

"OK." She wrenched her eyes away and headed back toward the house, patting Hunter's arm when she passed. "Flirt all you want, be as crass as you like, but do me one favor?"

He fell in beside her. "Sure."

"Lay off the compliments?"

His hand closed on her arm, and he stopped, pulling her around to face him. "Why, Brook?"

She tried to pull away, and Hunter's fingers immediately let go. The whole time, his face was calm, understanding, but insistent. In other words, he was going to make her answer, and she owed it to him. She was living in his house, after all, basically working for little more than charity. She clenched her jaw and sighed, trying to find the right words.

"Owen convinced me to marry him by making me feel special. He said I was beautiful, smart, and amazing. The last time I spoke to Owen? I mean, my ex-husband. Um, he basically said I was the perfect wife: pretty, smart, and respectable. I just needed to be reminded every so often what I was supposed to do." She licked her lips and slowly raised her eyes to his. "Everything that made me fall in love with him became his weapon, and my dog was the one who suffered for it. My *dog!* So, yeah, I'd rather not be pretty, smart, or anything else, if you don't mind."

Hunter stepped back as if burned. "God, I'm sorry."

"Me too. That's when I left. It's why I'm here - because I gave up everything for a man who made me feel beautiful." She huffed out an attempt at a laugh. "Now I'm just trying to remember who I really am. I'm just looking for a chance to start over."

"Yeah." He gently turned her toward the door. "Coffee. And while we drink it, why don't you tell me what else creeps you out."

She didn't say anything until they were in the kitchen, and Hunter didn't ask. He did lead her toward a quiet little breakfast table and made her sit while he got a cup for both of them. Before he joined her, he convinced her to pass over the hoodie - which he tossed onto the counter - leaving her in little more than pajamas. Oddly, she didn't care. Even without a bra, Hunter had suddenly become a perfect gentleman.

"So," he said as he slid into the chair across from her, "You hate compliments. What else do we need to know?"

Slowly, she turned her cup between her palms. "I don't have the money to file for divorce. That's why I needed a job so bad. It shouldn't take long for me to save up enough."

"We can help with that."

"No." She shook her head. "Thanks, but I only left a

few days ago. He made sure I couldn't get my hands on any significant amount of money, which is why I'm working. I want to do it myself this time. The last thing I need is some man taking care of me, because that's how I got myself in this situation to begin with. I appreciate your offer, but I think it's a really bad idea. I just wanted to get someplace safe."

"And now you are," he promised.

The smile she gave him was honest. "Thanks, Hunter. He thinks I'm with Ali, but it won't take long to figure out I'm not. It should keep him from causing problems."

"Hey." He reached over and rubbed her arm. "She told us your ex was a mess. What else, though? If compliments make you upset, what else does?"

Down the hall, a door opened. Evidently, Ryder was awake now. Brook lifted her cup and took a drink, trying to think of what made her feel awkward, but nothing came to mind. It was like a word that stayed just out of reach. She knew things would show up, but for the life of her, she couldn't think of a single example.

"I don't know," she finally said. "I just really have no idea who I'm supposed to be, and I keep thinking I'm doing it wrong."

That was when Ryder staggered into the kitchen. His jeans hung low on his hips, and he hadn't bothered with a shirt. There was something about a barefoot man, half asleep, that made her smile. The twins didn't try to impress, they just did. That made their beauty even more unbelievable. It also made it completely safe. Men like these dated celebrities, not divorcees with drama-filled pasts. That made them safe, right?

Ryder's eyes roamed over them as he headed to the cupboard. "Catch me up."

Hunter didn't hesitate; words just fell from his mouth. "Talked about the carousel, divorce needs to be started, ex is a class one villain, dog paid the price. Compliments itch."

The last made him pause, his head snapping to Brook. "Really? You hate compliments?"

That was freakish enough to make her laugh. "Yeah. Itching is bad?"

"Very," they said in unison.

Ryder made a gesture, indicating that he'd answer in a moment. While he poured his coffee, Hunter slid his chair over to make room. It only took a second before Ryder returned, stirring the cream into his cup. The tinkling of the spoon against ceramic was gentle. He took a long sip, then sat down where she could easily see them both. That was when she realized what they were doing. Their posture, their words, everything this morning was designed to make her feel at ease. It was sweet.

"Itching?" she reminded him.

Ryder nodded. "When we were in fifth grade, this kid was allergic to peanuts. He had a reaction a few times, and he always complained about how much it itched. Then one day, someone pulled a prank and gave him a peanut butter cookie. He took a massive bite and within minutes was in bad shape. We're talking EMTs in the elementary school kinda bad."

"It left an impression," Hunter added.

Ryder nodded at him. "So, a couple of months later, our mom decided she was going to show us off. We got dressed up in these matching little sweaters - "

"Wool."

Ryder tossed his brother a look but kept going. "No shirts under it, just nasty wool things, and man, they itched like crazy. What we didn't know was that it was an interview. Our second family was looking to find someone to take us off their hands."

When he said nothing for a moment, Hunter took over. "They really wanted puppies, not kids. Our job for the next six months was to look perfect at all times. We lived in hell, and half the clothes we wore were uncomfortable."

"They itched," Ryder said, sharing a look with his brother.

Brook noticed the shadow on his jaw, proving he hadn't bothered to shave. It made him look like an adult, but something about that glance exposed the little boy still inside. She also knew these boys were still keeping secrets, but she wasn't offended. She hadn't earned the right to hear them yet.

"How many families did you two have?"

They both shrugged. "Depends on how you count," Hunter admitted. "Around junior high, we realized that if we were too much trouble, we didn't stay long. Can't even count the number of overnights we had before we got returned."

"They can do that?" she asked. "Isn't adoption supposed to be a permanent thing? Or were you fostered?"

"Adopted," Hunter grumbled. "The reality is that there's no law preventing adoptive parents from rehoming their child. It's the dirty little secret of international adoptions, and we got caught in the middle."

"I'm so sorry," she breathed. "That must've been hard."

Ryder made a dismissive face. "By the time we were eighteen, we'd already learned how to take care of ourselves. We'd also figured out that being twins meant we had something going for us, so we used it. As long as we always matched, we could change place as often as we wanted."

Brook waggled her finger between them. "And it doesn't make you crazy to have people confuse you?"

They both shook their heads.

"Even after all that?"

"Nope." Hunter took a sip, then leaned back, cradling his cup in his hands. "We didn't get a shitty childhood because we were twins. We got that because we were assholes. Our first mom warned us that she couldn't handle our attitudes, but we thought we were winning. When she placed us with another family because we were overly aggressive - "

This time Ryder broke in. "We trashed her place a few times because smashing things terrified the woman. Started with the cookie jar, so we kinda asked for it."

"Doesn't make it right!" Brook hissed.

"No," Hunter agreed. "It doesn't, because we were just boys. We also didn't realize that her husband was doing the same thing. We were supposed to have been her salvation, not more fuel for the fires. But we always had each other. They never split us up, so unlike most foreign-born adoptees, we were never lost. We always had a family."

"You ever talk to her? Your first mom?"

Ryder shook his head. "Nah. We got out and never looked back." His eyes found hers, looking all the way through her. "Staring into the abyss doesn't help. We turned our backs on it and just kept heading for the horizon. Eventually, our first book sold, then the third hit the best sellers, and now none of it matters."

His gaze held her, proving his casual tone covered

painful wounds. "You never told Ali any of this, so why me?" she asked, unable to look away.

Ryder took a long breath before answering. "Compliments shouldn't itch, Brook. I'm also not sure I could stop giving them."

He pulled his eyes away as he stood, grabbing her cup with his for a refill. It took a moment before she realized what he meant. When she did, she smiled, glancing up to see Hunter watching her. He was trying to say the words were just his version of the truth, nothing more, and it felt really damned nice. It almost made her feel like there was nothing wrong with her.

"Still want the job?" Hunter asked softly.

"I just don't want to take something the wrong way." She turned her eyes to the wall, reminding her face not to flush. "I thought I was going to be living with a mature woman, not a pair of good-looking men who like to flirt. I don't want to be like one of those other girls."

Hunter nodded in understanding. "Let's go with friends. Just a couple of roommates. No different than living with Alison, right? I'm pretty sure she can't stop flirting with anything that moves."

"Wait. You mean you've been checking out my tits?"

Ryder placed the cup before her. "Thin shirt, no bra? Yeah, of course, we have. Unless you'd rather I lied about it?"

She lifted her cup in salute. "Just like college all over again, but with nicer furniture. I can do that."

The strangest thing was that she could. Something about these two guys made her feel like they were on her side - and not to get anything out of it. Hell, there was probably nothing she could give that these guys didn't already have. But that wasn't it. The truth was she'd never met anyone like them - except her best friend.

Yeah. She could do this. She might even like it. For the first time in years, she felt like she could actually breathe. It might not make sense, but she'd take it.

CHAPTER TWENTY

Their little talk soothed a lot of Brook's fears. It also made her realize just how messed up she'd become. Owen's manipulation had been subtle but effective. She had no idea how long she'd been second-guessing herself, but she was ready to stop. Granted, it wouldn't be that easy. It never was.

But she still had a job to do. It only took a few days to find her routine, and living with the twins was a very comfortable change. Eventually, she went with Hunter to get dog food. They stopped at the local Pet Palace. Like most pet stores, it had a selection of everything she could imagine, and then some. While he went to the front counter to set up an account, she headed to the back. There were two complete aisles of nothing but collars, leashes, and harnesses. Beyond that, she found an assortment of doggy beds.

She'd made her way to the toys when a warm laugh made her look up guiltily. She was clutching a fuzzy thing that looked like a stretched-out duck. In the head was a squeaker - except that the sound it made was more like a quack. At the end of the aisle, Hunter was grinning.

"Amelia or Rosa?"

She had no idea what he was talking about. "Huh?"

He tipped his head to the toy. "Who were you thinking about? The boys don't really like tug toys. Einstein does fetch, but Sherlock prefers to just chew everything up."

"Oh." He meant the duck. "I just thought it was kinda cool. I mean..." She squeezed the head, making the thing grunt. "Hadn't heard one like that."

"You seen the giggle ones?" He took three steps and pulled down something that resembled a happy troll. When he shook it, the noisemaker sounded like a demented child's laugh. "Scared Sherlock enough to make the old man growl." He shook it again.

"Poor guy. So he likes chewies?"

"Yep." Hunter tossed the troll-thing at her. "You should see if Amelia will play with that. Get the duck, too. Now, what would Rosa like?"

She let her eyes roam over the selections. "She loves to fetch. Sucks at it, but she'll run herself into the ground."

"Think she'd like tug?"

Brook could only shrug. "No idea, and I have a funny feeling she'd win."

With a chuckle, he made his way over to the ropes. One after the other, he pulled down three of them in different sizes. After that, he moved to the plushies. "What do you think, a bear for the old man?"

"Sherlock?"

He nodded. "Yeah. He loves killing these things. I just hate the ones filled with those plastic beads. They get everywhere - and when he gets to shaking it?"

She could imagine the spray of beads across the house.

"I bet stuffing is more fun. Then he gets to pull the guts out." She plucked a hedgehog from the rack and handed it to him. "Einstein seems like more of a squirrel kinda guy."

"Definitely." Hunter started rummaging through the hanging toys. "You see anything like that?"

"Um." She flipped past a couple. "Maybe this? I'm not sure if it's a squirrel or a meerkat, but has polyfill."

"Perfect. Now get some for the girls. Can't have them going without."

She paused. "Hunter, how much are you going to spend? These are like five dollars each."

He moved past her, rubbing her back when he reached for something on the other side. "Brook, these dogs deserve to have a few nice things. I thought we could get a bed for Amelia, too. You know, for the kennel in your room."

"Really?" It came out sounding just as thrilled as she felt. "I mean, um..." She sighed and gave up. "Thanks, Hunter. It's been pretty nice to have a dog around."

"Just make sure you pick one that will work when she doesn't need the kennel. Some dogs don't like sleeping on the bed. Gets too hot." He winked. "And before you do that cute little naive thing again, yes, that's where Einstein and Sherlock sleep."

"You're not worried about the sheets?"

"Fuck no. They make more of those, but I can't get another Sherlock." He stepped closer. "Ryder and I actually *like* the dogs. It's kinda why we have them. Now help me find them some toys."

That was all the encouragement she needed. Moving down the row, she picked up a couple more things she thought the mutts would enjoy, then moved to the next aisle. She didn't even notice Hunter was gone until he reappeared with a cart and told her to start filling it. She was happy to comply, grabbing cow hooves by the handfuls and size-appropriate knuckle bones for each of them. By the time they made it back to the dog beds, the cart was almost full.

"Ok," Hunter said, balancing a plaid-covered, memory foam-filled bed above their haul. "What else do we need? Shampoo?"

Brook chewed on her lip. "New collars?"

"Lead the way."

That was back on the other side of the store. She headed right for the cost-efficient nylon options, but Hunter stalled out by the leather collars. While she sorted through brilliant neon colors, he flicked through spikes and hand-tooled designs. Finally, she found something that looked like it would fit the timid little girl.

"What about this one?" She held up a thinner blue adjustable collar.

He countered with black leather and rhinestones. "I think this is a little more her style. Pretty, yet tough, all at once."

"Yeah, but this is eight dollars and how much is that?"

He shrugged. "Do you like it? Does it suit her?"

"Well, yeah, but I bet it's like thirty bucks."

He just lifted an eyebrow. "Brook. Do you like the damned collar?"

"It's just going to get ruined, and who knows if the next rescue will fit into it."

He chuckled. "Right. I've seen how you look at that dog. Are you going to hurry to find her a home? You think she'd fit in some suburban house with a child that squeals and a wife who gets angry every time she piddles on the expensive carpet?"

She couldn't wrap her mind around what he was saying. "You don't think she's adoptable?"

He tossed the collar at her. "I think she's already found someone who loves her to death. I mean, if she's not the dog for you, that's fine, but if you want to keep her? Then keep her."

She ran the sparkly thing through her fingers. It would be just the right size and had plenty of room for Amelia to grow into it. The colors were even perfect. The larger stones were lavender, and there were enough clear crystals to make it almost blinding. But that wasn't why her eyes were stinging. It had nothing to do with the collar, and yet everything.

"I don't understand."

He moved closer, pulling the nylon collar from her fingers, then hung it back where it belonged. "What's the confusing part, sweetie?"

"You're giving me a job, a place to stay, and now you're letting me keep a dog?"

"Yeah, that's pretty much it."

Her eyes shifted from the collar to his face, then back. "So what's the catch?"

"It's a big one." One more step closer, then he hooked a finger under her chin and made her meet his eyes. "I want you to try to stop that. Stop worrying about what someone else will think. Stop being terrified that your opinion is going to be wrong." He smiled, but it was sympathetic. "Opinions can't be wrong. That's not how it works, and all I want is to see my friends feel comfortable enough around me to be themselves."

"It's not that easy."

He tilted his head slightly, denying her words. "It kinda is. Now, that doesn't mean doing it will be easy, but the deal really is that simple. You want to keep the dog, then you have to try to be you. What do ya say?"

"And that's it? Amelia's mine?"

"Yep. If you want her, but she comes with the collar."

Brook took a deep breath, but it didn't feel heavy. Nope, this one felt like it took the weight of the world right off her shoulders. "Then my dog gets to look like a princess." She dropped the collar on top of the bed and closed the last step between them, wrapping her arms around his waist. "Thank you."

"Yeah," he breathed, hugging her back. "Now *that* is a good girl."

It took a second before his words sank in. When they did, she slapped at his chest playfully. It was very, very solid. "I am not a dog."

"Nope, but I have a funny feeling that positive reinforcement works just as well on you as it does them."

"Hunter!"

He caught her shoulders and turned her toward the front. "Time to check out. Think you can find your way back here next time without me?"

"Of course."

He chuckled. "And think you can remember to buy toys for the dogs?"

"Definitely. What I will not promise is to spend this much money!"

And it was quite a bit of money. Including the dog food, the total came to just over five hundred dollars. Thankfully, the store had one of the teenage boys help bring the six bags of kibble out to Hunter's SUV while they hauled out the rest. The toys went in the back seat. The bed took up the floorboard. The collar, however, Brook fished out and set in the passenger seat. She'd just made her way around back to help with the food when one of the boys groaned, sounding annoyed.

"Can't believe that creep's back."

Hunter looked up. "Who?"

The teenager pointed to a man reading the signs taped next to the door. "Him. Showed up yesterday asking about animal rescues in the area. We gave him a list, thinking he wanted to adopt or something, but then he started quizzing us about which ones were hiring."

Brook leaned a bit farther - and froze. Something about that man was just a little too familiar. It took her a second to place him, but when she did, her guts clenched in fear.

"Hunter?"

"Yeah, babe?"

"We need to go."

He peeked around the side. "What's up?"

Her answer was a whisper. "I know that guy."

She expected him to look shocked, but that wasn't what she got. Hunter's jaw tensed, and he turned to glare at the man. The hand she could see was clenched in a fist. "Get in the truck."

"What if - "

He didn't let her finish. "Just get in the truck, Brook." Then he slammed the door at the back. "Thanks, Brian. I'll see you next week?"

The kid looked confused. "I thought Brook was going to be taking over."

"She is, but I'll probably tag along. Thanks again." He almost turned, but stopped to add, "And it'd be great if you forgot you've ever seen her. Her ex is trying to cause problems."

"Sure, Mr. Collins. Got a crazy ex myself. Drive safe."

He waved, then jogged back across the parking lot, pushing the flatbed cart like it was a scooter.

Hunter didn't waste any time. He hopped into the driver's seat and started the truck, but he didn't pull away. His eyes were locked on the man loitering around the entrance. "Is that Owen?"

"No."

"Are you sure?"

She slipped lower in her seat. "Pretty sure I'd know my husband. No, that's the guy he uses to track down people. Usually whistleblowers or embezzlers, but the guy's a private investigator. I have a funny feeling he's looking for me. Owen knows I'd do anything to work with the dogs, which is why he's asking about shelter jobs."

"Ok. And which car is his?"

She glanced around the parking lot but didn't recognize any, and she certainly wasn't going to sit up for a better view. "I'm not sure."

"Ok. Any clue why this guy would be at a pet store out here?"

She lifted her hands to rub along either side of her nose. "Owen tracked my phone to Ali's place. Used the find phone feature, I think, since it's on his account. Leah got me a new one, but I have a feeling this is the closest pet store to Alison's apartment."

"Yeah," he grumbled. "Do you think he saw you?"

She just shook her head and sank lower.

Hunter reached over and rubbed her knee. "I'm not going to let him hurt you, Brook, but I'd like to see what he's driving."

"Why?"

For a moment she wasn't sure he'd answer. He just breathed, his eyes flicking between the mirrors and the man outside the store. "If you ever go missing, I want to have a place to start looking. I promised you I'm not going to let that man hurt you again. Not now, and not ever." He caught her hand and squeezed gently. "I promised Alison I'd keep you safe. To Ryder and I, that means completely safe, not just some half-assed attempt, ok?"

"Ok," she whispered.

He flicked his eyes over and smiled, but it didn't last long. Movement caught his attention, making Hunter sit straighter. A second later, he pulled at the rearview mirror, angling it for a better view. The look on his face was terrifying, but Brook wasn't worried. That anger wasn't for her.

"Blue SUV, looks like an Escalade. Bastard is seriously compensating for something." He chuckled, then put his own truck into reverse. "Ok. He's gone, sweetie. We're gonna go home, and I need to talk to Alison, to tell her she might be being watched and what this guy is driving. I don't want him sneaking up on her."

"Yeah," she whispered, then cleared her throat, forcing herself to sit back up. "Hunter?"

"Hm?"

"Thank you."

This time, the smile he flashed her was brilliant. "Always. The Collins brothers take care of their friends, and that means you."

CHAPTER TWENTY-ONE

*W*hen they got back, Hunter pulled the truck past the house and right up to the barn. Brook barely had her seatbelt off before the back door opened, making her flinch in place, but it was Ryder. Evidently he'd been waiting for them. She hurried out to help.

"Hey," Hunter said, coming around the other side. "Keep your eyes open for a blue Escalade."

"Sure." Ryder grabbed the first bag of dog food, flexing magnificently. "Why?"

"Looks like Brook's ex has a P.I. sniffing around pet stores in the area. He's asking about rescues around here."

Ryder paused, slowly turning back to his brother. "He's looking for her?"

"Seems like that."

"But she's ok?"

Hunter grabbed his own bag of kibble. "You doing ok, Brook?"

The rhinestone collar was clutched in her hands.

Slowly, she walked it through her fingers, feeling the crystals. "Yep. I'm doing pretty good."

Ryder just looked at her as if assessing every nuance for a hint that she was lying. Slapping his arm, Hunter pushed past him, taking the dog food to the storage room. With one last glance, Ryder followed.

"Go see if that collar fits," Hunter called back. "We'll get the food."

Well, hell. Of course they would. They were giving her a place to stay, feeding her, and now protecting her from the mess she'd made for herself. That meant she'd just been relegated to some delicate damsel in distress, and her behavior lately wasn't exactly helping. Brook took a deep breath and grabbed the bag of toys from the back seat, reminding herself how much she owed these guys. Then she went to find Amelia. Scooping the dog out of her kennel, she carried her inside, walking fast enough no one would notice how misty her eyes had gotten.

Since she'd left Owen, one thing had become very clear. Brook wasn't the same person she used to be. In all of her memories, she'd been strong, tough, and feisty. Now? Just the thought of her husband had her cowering in the truck. When one of the twins told her to do something, it felt like she obeyed without question. Never in all of that did she think about what she wanted. Nope, she'd just gotten used to letting someone else do it for her.

But Amelia made it all worth it. There was something about the unconditional love of a dog that let her forget all of her own mistakes. Back in her room, Brook buckled on the collar - which fit perfectly - then flopped onto the bed with the little dog. It wasn't long before the duck toy had started a game of tug o' war. The first time Amelia growled, Brook laughed, making the little dog cower. A few pets assured her that playing really was allowed, and they were back at it.

That was why she didn't hear Ryder come into the room. She had no idea how long he'd been there, but when Amelia nearly rolled onto the floor, he laughed. Just like the pup had earlier, Brook jumped as if she'd done something wrong. He waved her down.

"She's come a long way in a couple of days. I think you have the touch."

She shrugged, pulling Amelia back onto the center of the bed. "I don't know. I think it's more that I don't make a big deal about her mistakes, but let her know when she's done something right. Most dogs respond pretty well to that."

He tilted his head but refused to look away. "And people. We talked to Alison, told her about Owen's friend making an appearance."

"Good. Thanks."

He took a deep breath. "She filled us in on a few things. How long has it been bad? Was this the first time he hurt you like that?"

"Look, it's not that big a deal - "

"Kinda is."

She flopped back on the bed, slowly rubbing her dog with one hand. "Ryder, I'm not trying to drag you into the mess I made, ok? I just need to get back on my feet and start over."

"Ok."

"And I don't really want to drop my problems on you. You two didn't ask for that."

The bed sank as Ryder lowered himself to the edge. "I

can see that. So now that I'm sticking my nose in your business, what comes next?"

"Huh?" She turned to look at him.

He leaned back, bracing his weight on one arm. The other scratched Amelia's hip. "We're going to keep writing sex-filled, horribly perverse books. When we get the time, we'll bring on another hard-luck case - " He tipped his head to the puppy, " - and spoil it until we can find it a home. What are *your* big plans?"

"I haven't gotten that far. I just need to get enough money to get my own place, then get a real job, and see where that takes me."

Ryder shifted, reclining on his side. The dog still kept a barrier between them. "Why?" He looked right into her eyes when he asked that.

"Why what?"

"Why is that your plan? Why not do it differently?"

Brook sighed. "Because no one is going to do it for me."

"Ah, but you're forgetting something." He gestured to the room. "All expenses paid. All you have to do is something you enjoy anyway, and our pet deposit is pretty cheap. So why not just do this until you figure out what the next big step is going to be?"

"Look." She rubbed at the tension that was starting to settle between her eyes. "I know you and your brother are trying to help me and all, but I don't want to depend on charity - "

Again, he wouldn't let her finish that thought. "We need help with the dogs. We really do. If Ali hadn't asked, we probably would have run an ad in the paper eventually, but the idea of letting someone else move in?" He made a face and shook his head. "Knowing our luck, we'd end up with some prude who couldn't laugh at the dirty jokes."

She chuckled, ducking her head. "Some of them are pretty bad."

"Yeah, but you still don't get upset. I figured a woman like you would be much too mature for our sick sense of humor." He was trying not to smile, but it wasn't working.

"Trust me, I'm very immature. Owen liked to remind me of that on a daily basis."

Ryder nodded but didn't say anything else.

"What?" she asked.

"Owen said." He reached between them, brushing a strand of hair behind her shoulder. "How often do you think that, Brook? How often does Owen still take over your mind and tell you what you should and shouldn't like, how you should or shouldn't act?"

"I guess a lot."

"I guess so, too. Hunter said your personality can change like someone is flicking a switch. One minute he is with this smart, confident, funny woman. The next, she's all worried that she's a problem. That's not the Brook I met at Tall Tails."

She knew he was right. "What am I supposed to do?"

"You're supposed to be you."

"But I don't know who that is!"

He smiled, but it was almost sad. "I know. Trust me, I know. When you've spent a few years trying to fit into a mold someone else forces on you, it's hard to remember when their expectations end and you begin. But I have an idea."

She nodded, begging him to keep going.

"How about the three of us try something new and insane? While we're at home, fuck what anyone else thinks. If I compliment you and you don't like it, then tell me to fuck off. If you have a bad day and decide to cuss me out, I'll tell you that you're being a bitch. If Hunter puts on his arrogant snob routine, we can both put him back in his place. No more worrying about the 'rules' we're supposed to live by. Let's try making up some of our own. What do you think?"

"Really? You honestly think that's going to work out?"

Ryder's lips curled a bit higher. "Sweetie, I think that's how Hunter and I live normally. Weren't we all just talking about your preference for meat the other night?"

"Yeah..." She rolled onto her back, but a little giggle slipped out. "I think that's because I spent a few days with Ali."

"She's a good influence."

Brook gasped. "She's a loud-mouthed pervert!"

"So's my brother."

"Oh?" She turned her head back to him. "And what are you, Mr. Collins?"

"A closet romantic." He paused. "Oh, and a quiet-spoken pervert. Can't leave that part out."

On impulse, Brook snagged the pillow under her head - and whacked him with it. "You tease!"

He grabbed her arm, flinging the pillow onto the floor. At the excitement, Amelia decided it was time to go, abandoning the bed and the silly humans wrestling on it. With the dog out of her way, Brook lunged for the pillow under Ryder's head, but she never made it. He caught her other hand and rolled her onto her back, pressing both her hands above her head. And he just held her there. No matter how hard she squirmed, she couldn't break free. He was just too strong - and it was sexy as hell.

"Yeah," he said softly. "Now what are you going to do?"

"Give up?"

He shook his head, looking down are her. "Trust me, it's better when you take charge."

"And what happened to the romantic part?"

"Right." Slowly, he released his grip, shifting his hands to the mattress. "I just figured that if I said you were beautiful, you might forget all the other amazing points I'd just made."

"Like how there's nothing wrong with acting like a teenager at least once a day?" She didn't move her arms.

"Or how I like the woman who isn't afraid of having fun." With a sigh, he moved back to lie beside her. "When did it become immature to laugh? Why can't people our age have a little plain, simple fun? Do you really want to spend the rest of your life acting like some dowager in a book?"

"No, but I feel like... I dunno, like I'm wrong when I laugh at something as corny as a sex joke."

"And yet it's still funny." This time, when he reached over, the hair he brushed back was by her ear. "We're not supposed to be perfect, Brook. Our flaws make us unique, and that makes them beautiful. Besides, you're twice as impressive when you stop caring about being something you aren't. Alison's best friend is a whole lot more interesting than Owen's wife."

"Yeah. And I think she has better friends, too. Thanks, Ryder."

"For what?"

"I dunno. For taking the time to say that? For noticing that it needed to be said? For carrying the dog food?" She shrugged. "For the job."

With a chuckle, he sat up. "Then thank you back. For giving me a chance at the shelter, treating me like a person instead of a criminal, reminding me why I love the dogs so much and what it was that made me want to write in the first place." He stood, took one step, then scooped something off the floor. It was her pillow. "And I think we have a piddler on the loose."

"Amelia!" she called, scooting herself off the bed. "Damn it. I'm sorry."

He caught her waist before she could blow past him into the hall. "Brook. Stop worrying. You're going to scare her to death, and this is the first time she's been brave enough to try exploring."

"But..."

He widened his eyes in mock horror. "Oh no. We might have to use the mop! Now let's see what your little girl is getting into."

She followed him out of her room, down the hall, and into the living room. There was no sign of the pup. Ryder went to check the laundry area, but Brook headed for the study. The other dogs liked to lounge in there, and maybe Amelia could smell them. She was halfway down the hall when she heard the high-pitched growl.

"Get it." Another round of growling, then, "C'mon, get it. Pull. Yeah, that's a girl. Get it!"

Brook rounded the corner to see her dog latched onto the laces of Hunter's shoe. Amelia was tugging with all her might, but he was still typing. That didn't stop him from cheering her on - or moving his foot to give her a little competition. It was probably the most adorable thing Brook had ever seen in her entire life. She couldn't stop herself from giggling.

Hunter looked up. "Get it, girl." Then he winked. "What can I say? I like corrupting them young."

"Yeah?" She walked over, stepping softly so as not to

scare the dog. "You know what happens when you teach them to play with shoes, right?"

"Nope." He grinned.

In one smooth motion, she leaned over, caught the heel of his foot, and slipped the shoe off. That was all Amelia needed. With the laces still in her needle-sharp teeth, she took off, hauling Hunter's shoe down the hall with her.

Brook laughed. "They learn to steal your shoes."

For a moment, Hunter just sat there with his mouth open. Then he started laughing. Loudly. "You just gave your dog my shoe!"

"Oh, yeah."

That was when Ryder walked in, carrying the mongrel in question. "A squirter and a shoe addict. Seems this one's a true lady."

This time, it was Brook's turn to be caught with nothing at all to say and her mouth hanging open.

CHAPTER TWENTY-TWO

*T*hat night, after Brook had gone to sleep, the twins were supposed to be writing. They weren't. Instead, both of them stared blankly at their screens with their minds on something. Ryder caught himself looking over, hoping for some reason to bring up what he really wanted to talk about. He just wasn't sure if Hunter's focus was on the book or the woman in the other room.

Eventually, Hunter gave in. "She said the guy was one of her husband's friends who tracked down embezzlers or something."

Ryder immediately spun his chair to face his brother. "And you're sure he didn't see her?"

"I got her in the truck as soon as I realized what was going on. Yeah, I'm sure. The kid from the store also agreed he'd forget all about her."

Ryder scrubbed at his mouth. "How can you be sure he won't take a bribe?"

"Because I gave him a hundred-dollar tip for being so helpful, and promised there'd be more if he took care of my girl - and that was before he loaded the food."

Ok, that was a pretty good incentive, and it wasn't likely Owen could out-spend them. Ryder just didn't like that Brook's ex was still looking. It meant he hadn't given up, and men like that? They were the most dangerous, the ones who were likely to *kill* their wife in a fit of rage. They were the kind that wouldn't give in and sign the divorce, but fight it every single step of the way.

"She's going to need a lawyer," he grumbled.

Hunter murmured in agreement. "Want me to call Cessily?"

Cessily Blackburn was one of the best family law attorneys they knew. She'd come highly recommended, and they'd used her to legally divorce themselves from their adoptive parents. She also understood just how ugly things could get. Her own mother had suffered at the hands of her father, then suffered again when there was no evidence to use in her divorce. Needless to say, she'd be the best. For her, it was always personal.

"Touch base with her," Ryder decided. "Brook will want to make her own decisions, but it'd be nice if Cessily is on the list of her options."

"Can do." His brother smiled. "And I see what you mean about her. We had a moment at the pet store."

"A... *moment*?" Ryder asked, hoping for a little more.

"It started with picking collars for the dogs. I saw one that would be perfect for Amelia, and that led to her realizing she's allowed to keep the puppy."

"She really does like that dog," Ryder agreed.

"Yeah, she does. Enough that she got all teary-eyed and gave me a hug in the middle of the store." He paused. "One of those crushing her breasts against me and hanging on tight types of hugs. Now I know why you lost it at the shelter. She's just got this..."

"Vulnerability masked with strength," Ryder finished. "Yeah. She's so soft and gentle, but not fragile."

"The kind of woman who can take care of herself, but shouldn't have to."

They both paused, then met each other's eyes. Ryder pointed at the screen. "That needs to go in there!"

"Making notes!" Hunter assured him, tapping at his keyboard. "But I don't have a spot for it yet. Naomi is still refusing to fall for the guys. I think we made her *too* tough."

"No such thing. Besides, if she was normal, then why would the men be willing to go through all this effort for her?"

Finished, Hunter leaned back. "Because she's beautiful?"

"They're a dime a dozen. Hell, you know that as well as I do. Beautiful women are good for a little fun, some amazing memories, and that's about it. Brilliant women are the ones worth chasing. A beautiful and brilliant woman?"

"Would never talk to us," Hunter finished. "Would be smart enough to demand more. Yeah, I know. We've been over this." He sighed. "But Brook talks to us."

Ryder nodded. "And I think she trusts us."

Hunter scrubbed at his face. "That's the crazy part. After everything her husband put her through? I half-expected her to be scared of men, but she's not. She's scared of her ex, that's for sure, but not all men."

"I dunno," Ryder countered. "I think she's scared of relationships, not people. Well, maybe her ex, but definitely not all men."

"Well, that's going to make my plan harder."

Ryder's eyes narrowed. "What are you planning this time?"

"Just trying to make sure my little brother gets the girl." He glanced up. "And maybe get in on the good deal if I can."

"That's a given," Ryder assured him. "Look, maybe you should be the one trying to date her. You're smart, and you always know what to say."

"And she already has a thing for you." Hunter shook his head. "It's not happening. This time, you're going to have to take a little risk and put yourself out there."

Which was the problem. That was pretty much the *entire* problem. Once Brook realized what kind of a person he was, she'd run - and fast. The things he'd done when he was younger? Those weren't the kinds of things people were ever forgiven for. They were the kinds of things that took up residence in the darkest part of a man's soul and slowly ate away at the rest of it.

"I can't," Ryder breathed. "I can't do that. She's just a friend."

Hunter's palm slammed down on the desk. "Quit that shit. You're fine. I'm fine. We've got everything we ever wanted, so don't even start sliding back in that hole, because I'll be damned if I let you go in there alone."

Ryder lifted a hand, showing his brother he got it. "What I'm saying is that Brook is a lady, and ladies want a lot more than we can give. They want fancy weddings, nice cars, and kids. They want to have their friends over for dinner parties and go visit the family for the holidays. Now just try to imagine all of that with *both* of us."

"Yeah," Hunter agreed. "Which is why I said you need to get the girl."

201

Ryder just grunted under his breath. "Right, so she can get the complete wrong idea when I can't sleep and head over to your place?"

It wasn't fair to say. Ryder knew it was a low blow even as the words were coming out of his mouth, because that was why Hunter's one good relationship had failed. The second time he'd left her house in the middle of the night, only to be found crashing in his brother's bed the next morning, his at-the-time girlfriend had jumped to the worst conclusion. She'd known they had things in their past they didn't want to talk about. The problem was that she automatically assumed it meant they were incestuous.

"Maybe this time we should try telling her?" Hunter asked.

Ryder shook his head. "Not if we want her to stay."

"But Brook isn't like the others," Hunter insisted. "Why do you think you liked her so much when you first met her? She's different, and I think it's because she's been in that hole, too. She knows shit sucks. We need to at least tell her there's something that will come up later."

"Yeah," Ryder agreed, even if he didn't want to. His brother was right. He usually was. "But can we ease into it? I don't just want to start in on some recitation of what the shrink told us and try to make it sound like an excuse."

"Typically, perversions are formed before puberty," Hunter recited. "Yeah, I'm with ya. Not a very good way to impress her, especially not with her having enough shit on her plate. So how do we even bring up the idea of a threesome?"

"Casually?" Ryder suggested. "I dunno, but with the crap we talk about all day long, it's not like there aren't enough options. The problem will be if she thinks we're hitting on her."

"We are!"

Ryder groaned. "And she just got the shit beat out of her by her last man. But hey, let's start talking about two, who I might add are twice as strong as her former old man. Owen was one of those typical 'has been' types."

"How'd he get *her?*"

"No idea," Ryder said. "Because Brook's pretty much proven that she's not in it for the money, and that's about all he had going for him."

"We have more," Hunter teased.

Ryder chuckled because it was true. "And it was a side effect of getting our heads on right. Look, right now, this needs to be all about the damsel in distress. She's the one who needs center stage, and if it takes her a while before she's ready to flirt back? I'm fine with it. Our armor isn't shiny. We're not heroes."

"But we can be," Hunter insisted. "Ry, when that guy scared her today? I was the biggest, baddest knight with the shiniest armor. Hell, in her mind, when I said she could have the dog -"

"Dick move, by the way," Ryder told him. "I wanted to tell her that."

"Yeah, and you didn't. I'm pretty sure she didn't care who it came from, either. What seemed to get her was that she *could* keep the dog. I'll let you tell her it's ok for her to have more than one."

Slowly, Ryder leaned back in his chair. "So Rosa's staying, huh?"

"Bought a few balls and throw toys for her. Oh, and a tug. You should go help Brook play with her, since our little damsel is convinced her beast will throw her around."

"You do know Rosa will eat at least one couch, right?"

Hunter shrugged. "Then Brook can pick out new

furniture. Look, you said we do this just like with the dogs, right? So the first step was getting her safe. We did, and she's here. The second step is teaching her how to play. She's getting there, and she's been joking with us, but that's just the first signs of interest."

"You're trying to say that fucking us is playing?" Ryder scoffed at the idea.

"No, you idiot," Hunter shot back. "The flirting. The laughing and joking. Letting her figure out where the lines are - and that we pretty much don't have any. But also being allowed to have a say. I get the impression that she's spent the last few years being expected to agree to whatever her man says, and so you know, that's us. We're the men she has now."

"Us," Ryder said softly. "Yeah, so we give her more and more power over her own life. We open the cage, Hunter."

"And give her the option to leave or not. No matter what, we will never stop her. We will never make it an ultimatum, tell her there won't be a job for her or anything like that. No matter what. Deal?"

"Definitely."

"And," Hunter went on, "we need to get her keys, make sure she has her own bank, and all of the things to be independent. The easier we make it for her to bolt, the less likely it is that she'll use any of it. Most of all, we don't push her."

"So you're back in the running?" Ryder asked.

Hunter shoved his head into both of his hands. "Fuck. Yeah, I guess so. Look, I'm just saying that if you end up with her, I'm cool with it. If you and her have a good thing going and decide you need some spice in it, I'm down for that, too."

"Same for you," Ryder promised. "I figure the best

thing is to put it out there, once she's ready to date, you know? Let her know we're an option. Either, or both... Whatever. It'll be awkward as fuck, but..."

"Would give us the chance to explain," Hunter admitted. "And we both know that talking always makes things flow a little easier."

"It's hard as fuck, though." Ryder shrugged. "But I'll stammer through something for her."

"Yeah. Me, too," Hunter agreed.

The problem was that Hunter never stammered. He always had the right words ready. They were his weapon. Ryder? He handled the action. He got the job done without fucking around. Then again, sometimes the only action that was needed was standing in the way and having a shoulder ready if she needed it.

And those were things he could do.

CHAPTER TWENTY-THREE

*F*or the next couple of days, things started to fall into a comfortable routine, and the twins proved they weren't like most guys she'd met. Oh, sure, they spent a lot of time talking about women. Most of them were characters in their book. The first time she walked past the office to hear one or the other ranting about tight nipples or parted lips, she giggled. The millionth? She no longer found it odd. Now when they talked about men, she couldn't help but notice. When they started debating body positions, she found a reason to be close.

That was why she was hovering in the living room, picking up coffee mugs from the night before. She could just hear Ryder and Hunter trying to figure out if it was possible for a man to do something while another joined in. When the conversation spun back on itself for the third time, she gave up and carried the cups to the kitchen, rinsing them out before putting them into the dishwasher.

The twins most certainly weren't typical guys. They

didn't have a maid. They didn't ask her to pick up after them, but taking care of the dogs was not a full-time job. The least she could do was pitch in with dishes and laundry. They were letting her live here, so that made it her house too, and she was going to do her fair share. It was also close to lunchtime. Being hungry probably wasn't helping either of their moods.

If she was going to fix something, she might as well make for three. That meant breaking up the fight long enough to find out what sounded good. Brook headed up the hall, amused to think of a debate over sex positions as a fight. Yep, they were definitely still at it. She peeked her head around the wood arch that served as an entrance and waited for one of them to notice her.

"Unless you want to leave the second guy out..." Ryder sounded exasperated. "I'm telling you, shoving her against the wall is hot for one on one, but not two."

"So, what?" Hunter asked. "Throw her on the floor? Really? There has to be something new, and I don't see this girl as the type to be thrown around."

That made Brook giggle, but she smothered it with a hand. Ryder noticed, his head snapping up to look at her. For a moment he said nothing, then a devious smile inched across his mouth.

He held up a finger to his brother, but his eyes were on her. "I need your help."

"Sure." She stepped into the office.

Ryder closed the distance quickly, his eyes locked on her. Without a word of explanation, he wrapped an arm around her back and pushed her into the wall. As their bodies hit, she gasped, her head tilting back. He was right there, every hard, solid line of him pinning her, sliding against her clothes. She'd never had a man take control like this, and it spoke to something basic inside her, sending her fantasies into overdrive. When he bent his head to hers, she almost begged him to kiss her.

"Where would you fit another man?" he asked, his voice deep and velvety.

She bit her lip, glancing over his shoulder at Hunter, thinking about what she'd heard. "She's not the type to be thrown around, huh?" Her gaze came back to Ryder.

A smile touched his lips. "I dunno. Maybe she'd like it more than I thought."

Brook shifted, dipping just low enough for her belly to slide down his pelvis. Ryder closed his eyes and held her tighter, preventing her from writhing too much. That was exactly what she wanted. With his mind on holding her up, he'd forgotten he was supposed to be pressing her into the wall. She also still had one hand free.

Leaning into him, she shoved at his shoulder to push *his* back into the wall, rolling him off her. When Ryder tried to catch her, Brook's hands found his wrists, pinning both by his ears as she leaned into him, hard. This time *she* had *him* pinned. From the way his chest was rising, he didn't seem to mind.

"Maybe your little girl has a mind of her own?" she asked. "Maybe she wants to be the one pinning the man down?"

Ryder's eyes were her only hint. He looked over her shoulder just as a pair of hands caught her hips and soft stubble brushed against her neck. Hunter's voice came from just behind her ear.

"I think that will do very nicely." He moved one hand up to push aside her hair. "I also think my poor brother is now distracted from the scene."

"No," Ryder promised. "Oh no, I have some amazing ideas for it now."

"So I helped?" She lifted her weight off him.

Hunter stopped her. "Still helping. Lean into him. I need to see where your feet are."

Brook looked back over her shoulder. "After I pushed him, or if I was seducing him?"

Hunter jerked his chin up. "Both. I need to see."

"In the name of art, right?"

He smiled. "Something like that. Ry? What would you do after she pinned ya? Just take it?"

Ryder laughed once, hard enough to bounce Brook against his chest. "Depends on her. If she's trying to tease, I'd remind her just how nice I can be. If she's going to be doing the work, fuck yeah." He pushed at one of Brook's hands, pulling her attention back. "What's next? After you got me here, what would you do next?"

"I need to know the character."

He didn't hesitate. "Regency-era lady, the older sister, often overlooked because of her mannish attitude. Intelligent, self-taught, considered to be an old maid and unable to get married. She's tired of the world telling her what she should do and is well aware of what happens between the sexes. Well, between one man and a woman, at least."

She nodded, taking all of that in, amused at how little resistance Ryder was giving to being held at her mercy. "And the man she has pinned?" She leaned a bit closer, easing up on his arms.

"This guy, he prefers actions to words. He's always been good at the first and weak in the second. His older brother is the charmer, the one who always knows what to say."

"And their station?" she asked.

He smiled, realizing she had a decent understanding of the era. "Normally, they wouldn't be considered suitable. Close, but not quite. She's from minor nobility, they're from new money with no titles."

She leaned a bit closer. "And I assume I'm horny?"

Ryder's voice dropped slightly as her chest pressed against his. "Of course. It's a romance."

Brook shifted her leg outside his, her pelvis brushing his thigh. "I'm sure I'd ask what he wanted, trying to push me around like some common whore."

"He'd say he couldn't resist you anymore." Ryder wrenched an arm free to catch the side of her face. "How he just had to taste your lips."

That was when Hunter moved close again, crushing her against his brother. "And the older brother would make sure she knew how beautiful she is."

Brook tried to look at him, but Ryder's hand held her face to his. "Oh damn," she breathed. "That's hot. Right about now, any woman in her right mind would cave."

A hand slid along the side of her body, another pulling her fist away from Ryder's trapped wrist. From behind her, Hunter held her there, his mass keeping her against Ryder as three hands were free to explore, the last one holding her prisoner. Brook groaned and leaned her head back.

"Guys, you have to let me up, or I'm going to need a new set of panties."

They both chuckled. Hunter's grip relaxed, but Ryder's hands found her hips, tugging them against his. Feeling a hard ridge between them, her eyes flicked open. His were waiting, but he didn't say a single word. His erection spoke volumes, even as he let her go. Evidently, she wasn't the only one to find the situation enticing.

"Oh damn," she whispered again.

He smiled, then looked up at his brother. "From here, I can reach anything I want. Add in a full skirt, and someone walking past wouldn't have a clue."

"And I could kiss her easily," Hunter agreed. "The more I leaned her back, the more access you'd have to her breasts."

Brook glared at him. "Are you trying to kill me?"

"No," Hunter promised. "This is a lot easier with a willing partner." He turned her toward him, slowly, so she could step around Ryder's legs. Then he pushed her back, right into his brother's crotch. "Also interesting to see how amiable you become. So willing to move where you're needed."

Behind her, Ryder groaned. "Ok, let me up. Talk about old women with no teeth or something."

"Hurt yet?" Brook teased.

"A bit."

Hunter stepped back, pulling Brook with him. "And you're not even blushing. Nice." He leaned closer, holding her eyes, and mimicked her question. "Hurt yet?"

Impishly, she reached up to put her mouth beside his ear. "No. Just hot, wet, and throbbing, but I'm used to being let down. You?"

"I'm the one that has to write all of this. Maybe we need a better showerhead, now that we have a lady in the house."

"My hand works fine, thanks." She smiled deviously, then flounced from the room just like a character in their Regency-era book. At the doorway, she paused. "Oh, and lunch?"

The twins shared one of their looks, then both smiled.

Hunter nodded, but Ryder turned toward her. "I'll help," he said.

Brook giggled, feeling a bit more than flustered, but unwilling to admit it. "Am I ever going to understand those?"

"Which those?" Ryder asked, his hand finding the soft spot of her back while they walked.

He had a habit of doing that. She just hoped he had no idea how much she liked it. "The looks. I know you two have entire conversations with them."

"Well, so far no one's really tried." He rubbed her back once before stepping toward the fridge. "That one was easy. Make sure you're honestly as ok with this as you seem."

"And?" She turned on the oven to pre-heat.

Proving there was still a bit of "typical guy" left in the brothers, Ryder found a bag of frozen pizza bites. He let his eyes run down her body, then found a second bag. A small, crooked smile played on his face as he carried them over, looking anywhere but at her. Then he dropped them on the counter, moving to stand right before her.

"I think you wouldn't have said a thing about my hard-on if I hadn't. I think you're very good at pretending not to be anything but calm and spunky." He reached up and traced the line of her jaw. "I also think that if I did any more than this, you'd call Alison and be gone by morning."

Her breath caught. She hadn't even thought about it, but he was probably right. "Saying you want to?" she asked, instead.

Ryder shrugged. "I'm a single man. Been a very long time since I've had a..." He swiped a lock of hair from her brow. "Fuck it. I'm not used to having beautiful women

212

pin me to the wall and tease me, Brook. I'm saying you could turn most men into putty in your hands."

"I'm not beautiful."

"Yeah, you are. And fun. No matter how much you try to pretend to be some proper little employee, you're going to eventually realize that we're shitty bosses. I'm just saying that if you grind against me like that again, I'm not sure I'll be able to just stand there and take it."

She giggled nervously, tilting her face from his hand. "I'm sure Hunter would love the show. Plenty to write about."

"Something like that." His tone said she'd missed the mark completely.

She swallowed, then took a breath before she could find her voice. "What then?"

"I'm not going to say because I'm not ready for you to run off with Alison."

She nodded, showing she accepted that, but her mind could only stray so far. "Is that what you mean about leaving bits of your soul behind? I mean, in your work?"

"Yeah." He stepped back just enough to give her space. "The best advice for any writer is to write what you know. If you get too far outside what your mind can understand, the characters become flat, and the story dies. That means we always leave hints about ourselves, but they mean nothing in such small pieces."

She could hear that he was leaving something out. "You sure it means nothing?"

"No," Ryder whispered. "I just don't want you to get scared off. And I shouldn't have done that - I mean, in the other room. It just seemed like a good way to show Hunter what I meant."

"It's ok."

"You sure?"

Thankfully, the oven beeped, announcing that it was ready for their food. She grabbed a pan and started spreading the pizza bites across it. Keeping her back to him made it just a bit easier to answer. "It's been a long time since I had anyone swoon over me, even if it's just roleplaying to find your characters' positions. I never thought it would be so..."

"Erotic?" Ryder offered.

She tossed a smile back at him. "Yeah."

His hands found her hips again. "I like this. I like the woman who isn't afraid to be flirtatious. We don't want to make you feel uncomfortable, but we like the glimpses of Brook that show up when you stop worrying about what we think."

She turned in his arms, to face him. "Ryder, I'm just supposed to walk the dogs."

Those chocolatey eyes of his drifted to the lunch she was making. "Right. And yet you're doing so much more. You cook, you've been helping keep the place clean, and now you're helping us write. I'm pretty sure Alison gave you a talk very similar to the one she gave us. Something about how she loves you like a sister and knows she can trust you to take care of us?"

"Close enough."

He nodded, ducking his head to look right into her eyes. "Yeah. So does this mean we shouldn't ask for your help as the woman in our manwich?" He tried to look serious but couldn't hide the boyish grin.

She slapped his chest playfully. "Ok, Ryder, you win! I'll rub my body against yours anytime you want, but you are *not* allowed to think I'm some slut. It's just been a long time, ok?"

"Me too, Brook. I figure if something like that is steamy enough to get me hot and bothered, that means it's going to be a best seller. That's it. You're just helping us write, and if we ever cross the line, just say so. Deal?" He offered a hand.

She took it. "Deal. Thanks, Ryder. It just confuses me that you talk so easily about this stuff. I'm not used to men saying what they think."

He chuckled, then reached over her shoulder for the pan. "Writers, remember? We have to know what words work or we don't get paid."

"I'm not a writer."

"Nah." He slid the pan onto the top shelf. "You're the Muse. I think you're doing a damned good job."

"Maybe I'll put that on my resume." She winked at him, then leaned over to set the timer.

CHAPTER TWENTY-FOUR

*B*rook thought about that moment for the next day, trying to decide if she really was ok with it. The answer was yes. She enjoyed playing around with them. The problem wasn't that she was offended, it was that she *thought* she should be offended. Too many years living with Owen had her convinced that her wild side was something to be ashamed of.

The guys didn't seem to agree. Nope, they were trying to bring it out. That sex was a common topic made sense. It was what they wrote about. The way they went about it kept the tension light. Oh, she still noticed how gorgeous they were. All too often, she found herself zoning out, her eyes roaming over one of the brothers as her mind started peeling him out of his clothes. She couldn't help it, which meant she couldn't be offended when they noticed and found it amusing.

Her only problem was that she couldn't quite figure them out. They flirted - a lot. Was it just their nature? Were they simply trying out a line from their next book? Was there any seriousness to it?

Ryder was the worst. His glances were too long, the look in his eyes too hungry. The part of her mind that Owen warped told her he thought she was just a cheap piece of ass. The other half, the one she'd left behind in college, said there was nothing wrong with that. Wanting to be seduced by a sweet and beautiful man was perfectly natural, and it wasn't only men who got to enjoy sex. The referee between them kept reminding her that she worked here. This wasn't a vacation; it was a job. She should not mix work with pleasure unless she was ready to find another place to live.

In other words, she'd stop worrying about it. So long as she didn't sleep with either of them, there was nothing wrong with flirting. Hell, maybe she'd talk to them about dating rules. Alison had kinda offered to run around town with her if she needed a wing-girl for picking up guys. She didn't need to bring them back to the house. She could always grab a cab home the next morning, right? And getting laid might just put her hormones back in place!

She was laying in the second dog yard, smiling at the thought, when a shadow fell across her face. Rosa and Amelia were still playing nicely, which meant that had to belong to a human. Lifting a hand to shield the glare of the sun, a smile lit her face. It was Hunter, and she was sure of it.

"Hoarding that grass for yourself?" he asked. "Or are you willing to share?"

"I'll share. It's finally getting warm enough to feel good."

He sat beside her, his eyes on the dogs. "How much longer until you're doing this in a bikini?"

Brook laughed. "Not happening, Hunter. There's no way I'm showing off my flab in front of you two."

His head twitched toward her. "Seriously? Flab? What are you, a size ten?"

"I wish. More like twelve."

"I like twelve." He leaned back onto the grass, his body angled just above her head. "Promise I'm a better pillow than the ground."

She huffed a laugh and sat up. "Yeah, I don't think so."

Those sultry eyes of his watched her. "Why not?"

"You say you like a twelve then try to get me to cuddle up with you? Hunter, one of these days I'm gonna take that all wrong."

He shrugged. "Remind me of the downside again?"

"You mean, besides your dog walker trying to make out with you?" She groaned and leaned back on her hands. "In case you missed the memo, I was married for six years. Engaged for two. Dating for one. That's almost a decade with the same guy - one who thought erotic was using extra lube."

"And?" His eyes waited for something.

She bit her lips together, trying to decide which part of her mind was in control. Did she really want to admit how much the twins got her going? What would happen if she did? Then again, what would happen if she didn't?

"And you two have perfected sensual." She shrugged, hoping he'd just let it go.

Hunter tugged on her arm. "I really am a better pillow than the ground. Get comfortable so you can get this off your chest. Something's going on in that head of yours, and I'm not going away until I know if the problem is me."

She gave in. Maybe "gave" was the wrong word, since the idea of lying on him was pretty damned appealing, but she'd made her token effort. Brook shifted, lying down with her head on his belly, and picked at a piece of grass.

"I don't want to be that desperate girl, you know? When I first got here, Ryder said that most women came in two types. The first was trying to set up a good sexual harassment case. That's certainly not me. The second? She thought that crawling in one of your beds was a great way to get a bonus."

He plucked the blade of grass from her fingers. "Saying you want to get paid more?"

"No!" She tried to grab it back, but he lifted his hand away. Instead, she picked another. "I'm saying that I have a little dignity, but that doesn't mean you and Ryder aren't distracting."

"Mm." He twirled the strand of grass against her arm. "Distracting is a vague word. Clarify. Use language that is easily understood."

"Oh, is this a writing exercise now?"

"Kinda. Just try it."

"I'm trying to figure out what I want. Who I am, I mean." She groaned. "Ok, that's even worse, huh?"

He chuckled, the laugh resonating under her head. "Yeah. Let's start with the look that wipes the smile off your face with no warning."

She knew exactly what he was talking about. "A lady doesn't... That's how Owen liked to start a discussion about my behavior. For six years I tried so hard to be a lady, but I'm not. I'm really not."

"Maybe Owen was wrong about what makes a lady. Ever think of that?"

"He basically quoted what society expects. A lady doesn't flirt with men that aren't her husband, things like that."

"Mm." Reaching over his head, Hunter grabbed a longer blade of grass, then passed it to her. "Studies show that flirting outside a committed relationship increases personal satisfaction within it. Ladies should flirt, but not necessarily follow through."

"And that's the problem." Tilting her head, she looked up at him. "Most of my life, I've just done things. It's like I don't stop to think about it. I keep telling myself to get better, to have a little control, and then I do it one more time. That's what always made Owen so mad. Hell, that's how I ended up with Owen in the first place! And then him? He tried to put me in this narrow box of what was good and not. Can't there be a middle ground?"

"Spontaneity is good," Hunter assured her. "It's something artists try hard to keep. It's how Ryder and I make our stories." His hand moved to rest on her belly, the touch light. "Tempering it doesn't make it go away completely."

Her eyes moved to where they touched, and her next words just fell out. "Sleeping with my boss would be a bad idea."

"You want to sleep with my brother?" His hand didn't move.

She swallowed, hoping he couldn't tell how foolish she felt. "Not exactly. I just miss it. Now that I'm... free, I guess? I miss the rush that comes with dating, the feeling of being desirable. Sometimes I forget that you're just flirts and find myself thinking about..." She laughed.

"What, Brook?"

"I dunno, making a move, I guess. I know that would be a really bad idea, but you two are just so easy to talk to. I dunno." She pressed her hands to her face. "This is weird, Hunter."

"Hey." He pulled her hand down, then lifted her chin.

"Talk to me. Why would that be such a bad idea? You saying you think we'd take advantage of you?"

"No, I'm saying that crawling in bed with one of you would make this entire situation really awkward."

Again, he laughed. "You mean I'd feel left out if you were sleeping with Ryder."

"Or he might, if I just rolled over and started making out with you, yeah. You're kinda like the only friends I have, besides Ali. I'd hate to piss one of you off, and I have a funny feeling that if either of you had to choose, I'd be the one losing out."

"So I'm still in the running, huh?"

His gentle words made her heart pause. "Is it a race?"

"More like gymnastics. Each move is designed to impress, the applause makes us feel good, but the goal is to win the prize. I like you, Brook. I like having a woman around who is relaxed enough to tell me exactly what's on her mind. That stuffy lady you keep thinking you should be? Tell her to get lost."

She sat up again, her mind trying desperately to catch up. This was not the conversation she'd expected. A second later, Hunter did the same, shifting closer to her back. She swallowed, trying to decide if she should tell him to keep his distance. The words just wouldn't come.

He gently brushed her hair behind her shoulder. "Is that the line I shouldn't cross?" he asked, nothing but empathy in his tone.

"I don't know." She laughed softly, then buried her head in her knees before taking a deep breath. "I've only been separated for just under two weeks, and here I am looking for my next guy. I think I've read too many of your books."

"You've only read three."

"Two and a half." She turned her head, her cheek on her knee. "Trust me, a showerhead has nothing on a pair of erotic thieves or business partners. I have no idea how you two do it!"

A devious smile curled his lips. "Blue balls. You should see them. Almost royal, by now."

"Gross!" She pushed him back in the grass, but the tension was gone. On impulse, Brook flopped down on her belly, her chin on his chest. "I'm ok, Hunter. I just haven't been here long enough to know when you two are being serious or playing around. Just don't be shocked if the next time I'm thrown against a wall, I melt like one of your heroines."

He caught a strand of her hair, twining it around her finger. His eyes stayed on that, refusing to meet hers. "It's flattering, you know?" He looked up at her, then back to his hand. "Most women can't tell us apart. Most don't care to try. But you? Yeah, you not only can, but you also make us feel special and don't even need compliments to do it."

"You're amazing authors." She caught his wrist, pulling her hair from his fingers. "And you've mastered sex appeal. Just don't laugh at me when it works, ok?"

Freed from her hair, his hand moved to her back, holding her against his chest. The position was much more than friendly. From the look in his eyes, he knew it.

"It's the little things I miss." His fingers toyed with the hem of her shirt but didn't move higher. "I tried dating and wasn't so good at it, but things like this? It's kinda nice, huh?"

She caught that first part. "You weren't good at dating? I find that very hard to believe."

"Oh, I know seduction. I do it for a living. Dating is different. Spending time with someone while dressed?

Yeah, I screw that up pretty good." His hand fell away. "Never got married. Neither of us. Our shrink says we have commitment issues, but I think she's wrong."

"Why?" Never mind that he'd just admitted so easily that he'd been seeing a counselor.

Beneath her, he shrugged. "We commit to everything we do, completely. That doesn't mean we'll take something crappy just because it's all there is. I'm not going to stay with a woman who nags me to ignore my brother and go shopping with her every night. Finding one who understands that Ryder is not getting cut out of my life? Not so easy."

She nodded, understanding. "It's not worth it. I stopped talking to Ali because Owen hated her, and it was the dumbest thing I ever did. Besides, if a woman truly cared about you, she'd understand that."

"Kinda what I think. Ryder says it's because we've idolized women in our writing and will never find one that meets the expectations."

She shook her head. "Your girls are all flawed. Sometimes drastically. And look how patient you are with me! I keep acting like an idiot, and you both keep letting me get away with it."

He smiled. "Huh, imagine that. Guess that means you can stop worrying about mentally undressing me, huh?"

She gasped and tried to pull away, but he held her against him. Brook didn't struggle too hard. "You weren't supposed to notice."

"But I did. Maybe next time, I'll rip off my shirt before pinning you to the wall."

"Hunter!"

He laughed. "Admit you liked it and I'll let go."

"Maybe I don't want you to," she countered.

His smile only grew. The tip of his tongue teased his lip, then he pushed, rolling her onto her back, and following. Brook sucked in a breath, grabbing his biceps for balance. He loomed right over her, his body posed to be as seductive as possible.

"You forgot the shirt." Her voice was breathless.

"You want it off, you take it off." He leaned just a hair closer. "But I can't promise where that would stop."

Her breath was coming too fast. "Oh damn. I think I need to get laid."

This time, he had to swallow before he found his voice. "Brook, we should probably get up."

"Before the dogs decide to help."

He looked up, checking on them. "They're sleeping."

"Then you still have to move, because you have me pinned."

"Yeah, um." Hunter shifted. "Has anyone told you that you have amazing lips?" He let go and rolled onto his back. "I have a weakness for them. Lips in general. And that soft, parted thing you do?"

Free, she sat up, brushing the grass from her hair. "Brown eyes do me in. Framed by dark lashes? I can't get enough."

He picked at something on her back. "This is pretty fucked up, huh?"

"Or not. Maybe that's the problem?" She looked back at him and smiled. "Oh yeah. I have a date tomorrow night. Maybe getting out and doing fun stuff will get my mind off you and your brother."

"A date?" The words fell from his mouth in shock.

She nodded. "Yep. Which reminds me. I'm assuming you don't want me bringing guys back here, huh?"

The playful expression on his face fell. "Honestly, no.

Doesn't mean we'll tell you not to. It's your home, too, Brook. At least if you're here, we can kick the shit out of some asshole if he tries something stupid."

"Contradict yourself much?"

Hunter shook his head. "Just being honest. I much prefer you undressing me with those eyes, not someone else. Doesn't mean you should become celibate. I promise that was never a condition of you working here."

"And screwing my bosses is a very bad idea." She climbed to her feet and whistled for the dogs. "I like working here too much to mess that up, even if I need to take a trip to find some adult toys."

He groaned, closing his eyes. "Let's call it friends. I really don't want to get sued."

She tapped his foot with hers, smiling. At least the tension wasn't just one-sided. "I'm not going to sue you. Add it to the contract for employment if you want. Promise, Hunter, I'm flattered, not offended. I just know that rebound sex is a very bad way to keep a job."

He didn't open his eyes, but a smile spread across his face. "Then I hope you get it out of your system tomorrow. Finish that book tonight, Brook. It's one of my favorites."

CHAPTER TWENTY-FIVE

*H*unter and Ryder had no problem with her going out for the evening - not exactly. Ryder even offered to feed the dogs for her. Brook assured him she'd handle it before she left, but he pointed out that she'd need to get dressed and Amelia still couldn't be trusted not to piddle on everything, including people. After nine days with the guys, she was starting to figure out when they were being polite and when they were serious. This was one of those serious offers, so she accepted.

The last time Brook and Alison had been out together was five years ago. Before that, they always tried to have a fancy girl's night at least once a year. That all stopped when Owen decided Alison was a bad influence. Ok, so it was more that he was embarrassed his wife enjoyed having a night out with a lesbian, but Brook didn't want to think about that. Knowing she'd let him push her around hurt enough. Admitting that she'd ignored her best friend because her husband was ashamed of Alison's sexual preference? It made her hate herself a little.

So she'd make it up tonight. Maybe she couldn't re-write the past, but she could pay for it. Digging through her closet, Brook found the best dress she owned. Black, it barely came to the middle of her thighs. The neckline was plunging and curved to accentuate her cleavage, but the best part was the back. The straps were swept together behind her shoulders, leaving it open to her hips without looking trashy. Good for a night on the town or a fancy date - it was perfect.

She styled her hair, leaving it loose to hide the knot of straps. For makeup, she went with sultry, adding enough to both her eyes and lips to remind herself that she could still be sexy. For too many years, Owen had pointed out every flaw, and her ego still was a bit bruised. Alison knew that, so she was also the best person to list the good points.

Five minutes to seven, Brook slipped on her heels and headed into the living room to wait for her date. When she saw both guys sprawled in chairs, reading a little too casually, she knew they had an ulterior motive. She also had no intention of beating around the bush.

"What?" she demanded.

Hunter's eyes lifted over the top of his book. "That's a very nice dress."

"Thanks." She turned, giving them a view all the way around. "What do you think my chances are?"

Ryder dropped his book beside him. "His place or yours?"

"Going to The Glasshouse and have a promise for dessert. Don't have plans after that." She smiled. It was her turn to be devious. "So? Think my date will be drooling?"

The boys shared a look. Ryder shrugged, but Hunter shook his head. Brook waited. Eventually, Ryder answered.

"I think that if he doesn't take you back to his place, he's probably married and trying to hide it. How'd you meet?"

Headlights drifted across the front window, announcing her best friend pulling into the drive. "College. And yep, she's married, *and* her wife knows we're going out." Brook wiggled her fingers. "Write a good sex scene, boys. Make sure you enjoy peeling off the dress. Don't waste the sensuality of it. I'll tell Alison you're on a roll."

Hunter groaned, but he was laughing around it. Ryder just tilted his head a bit, watching her cross the room. "Well played. You look nice, Brooklyn, I hope you have a good night."

She bit her lip and nodded. "Thanks. I mean, for *everything*. I'll see you in the morning if you aren't still up."

"We'll be up," Hunter promised. "Stop in and make sure we know you made it back safe."

"It's Alison!"

He shrugged. "And a waiter, bartender, and quite a few other men who think like we do. Go have a good time."

She did, but didn't overlook what he said. Men who think like they do. That one comment had her smiling wistfully as she climbed into the front seat. Alison looked her over, making a scene of it.

"Shit, Brook. You were cute in college, but a few extra years made a woman out of you. Damn. Those are some curves. Remind me again why you're straight?"

"Because you're married." She playfully slapped her best friend's shoulder. "Thanks. That's just what I needed to hear."

Alison eased the car back down the narrow drive. "From the smile on your face, I'm not the only one full of compliments."

"Nope, that's the strange thing. They were in the living room reading." She paused for that to sink in. "Not writing, Ali, *reading*, and both of them at the same time. They also made sure to say I looked nice."

"Because you do."

"Yeah, but not just a 'you clean up well' kind of nice. And Hunter told me to interrupt them when I get back so they know I made it home safe."

"Aww." Alison tossed her a smile before pulling onto the main road. "That's cute."

"I know! That's like boyfriend level of cute. It certainly didn't come across as big brotherly."

"Thirty-nine, never been married – either of them. They date, if you can call it that, but never long-term." Alison chewed at her lip. "Hunter said things always go wrong when women try to make a guy choose her over his brother. Said he almost lost Ryder once and isn't willing to risk it."

"He told me something about the same. You know what happened?"

"Nope." Alison reached over and activated her phone's GPS for directions. "Neither will talk about it, and that's the closest I've ever gotten to a hint. I mean, most twins are close, but those two? Like two parts of a whole. They don't do anything alone."

"Hence the books," Brook joked. "What's that phrase about writing what you specialize in?"

"Write what you know," Alison corrected. "Wouldn't shock me with those two. But how serious can a threesome get? I mean, eventually, someone's going to get left out."

For a moment, Brook thought about that. "I've read

three of their books now. Four if you count the one you gave me. They always end the same."

"Yep. They always find a way to make love work." Alison shrugged. "You think that's their big secret?"

"I dunno. Ryder said something about how an author always leaves a bit of his soul sprinkled in his work. Maybe that's the part they keep dangling out there, but no one notices because Rose Solace has to be a woman. The strangest thing is how they've both flirted with me all week, but kept backing off. Maybe that's why?"

"Could you do it?" Alison looked at her. "Living with two men. Could you make it work?"

"Hell, I couldn't make living with *one* work. I mean, I played around in college. Probably tried most things in bed, but it was always experimental. Oh, but speaking of them." She turned in her seat. "Since you kinda dropped that doozy about them making up a job for me? Yeah. I've taken over laundry and most of the house cleaning. Figure I'm a professional housewife, right?"

"They notice?"

"Yeah. And last night, all three of us made dinner. It was fun. I mean, I understand how they write now. They make a plan, then everyone just handles the thing that needs to be done. My point is that I just wanted to say thank you. I honestly feel comfortable. Sexually frustrated as hell, but I trust the guys."

"Good." Alison began slowing, their destination just ahead. "That means you have time to decide what you want to do with your life. Any ideas yet?"

"Think I could be a literary agent?"

"You'd need to intern, and that's a year, at least. How's your grammar?"

"Could be better," Brook admitted. "I just like reading

the books and watching the process from behind the scenes. It's a lot different than I expected. I was thinking about maybe finishing my degree by going into English or something."

"Thought about editing? Less selling, more of what you're talking about."

Brook waggled her head back and forth. "I'd have to move to find a big publishing house. Literary agents aren't *all* clustered into New York and California, but the publishers are."

"So you have been listening!" Alison found a parking spot, then turned. "There's always freelance editing. With the rise of self-publishing, it's gotten to be a real business. Some agencies keep someone on staff, too."

"Yeah?"

"Yep and Bishop Literary has been contracting. If you decide to go that way, I could probably set you up. What happened to the veterinary thing?"

"Uh, I'm thirty-four and not wanting to spend the rest of my life drowning in student loans? Plus, that would be about six more years of school. Yeah. I think I want to do something with a bit less debt to profit ratio." She opened the door and stepped out, dragging Alison along with her even though the conversation barely paused.

"Ok. So agent and editor. We have two options. Cooking?"

"Not something I love. Most domestic things I've already burned out on."

"Hm." Alison twisted her mouth to the side, thinking hard. "Thought of running a boarding kennel for dogs? You've always loved them."

"Would rather do a rescue, but the pay is crap. I don't

want to rely on a rich husband to make it through life, ya know?"

"Wanna write a book?" Alison grinned, scurrying forward to get the door. "I happen to know this amazing agent."

"Who is booked!"

"And would make room for her best friend. Stay out of romance, though. Don't want to ruin my best author's chances."

"I know!" Brook bumped her shoulder as they headed to the front desk. "Science fiction. I can talk Hunter into pretending he's me, and I can pretend to be them."

Alison's eyes bugged out. "Uh..."

Before she could continue, a young man stepped up. "Table for two, ladies?"

"Yes," Brook assured him.

His eyes drifted over her subtly before shifting to Alison. "No dates tonight?"

Alison just held up her hand. "Married, hun. Tonight is girl's night. Get to spend time with my single friend."

"Well, if you'll follow me." His eyes darted back to Brook before he led them through the packed restaurant.

Alison swept ahead of her, and Brook slapped her rump. "I don't need your help."

"Oh yeah, you do." Alison put a little extra sway in her hips. "Trust me, girlfriend, you need a lot of my help, and I'm more than willing to give it."

Brook bit her tongue until they were seated and had a bottle of wine before them. Alison poured while Brook looked at the menu. It had been far too long. She hadn't realized how much she missed the company of someone who was just a friend. The kind of friend she could tell anything, who would never judge her. It was even more liberating than walking away from her abusive husband and twice as comfortable.

"Ali, you really think I should write a book?"

"Sure. If you want to work in the industry, I think trying to do it will teach you more than anything else. You'll understand how the author can overlook such obvious mistakes, how the reader finds meanings that weren't intended to be there, and so much more. I also think you're in an amazing position to kick-start your career, and your idea about the Collins boys isn't that bad. I mean, legalities and everything aside, but it would make *my* life easier."

"Huh?"

Alison lifted a finger, pausing her while the waiter came back for their order. Only after he'd left did she continue in a hushed tone. "The press has been begging Rose to do an interview. She's been sitting at the top of the charts, but trying to get them to admit they're the brains? Yeah. Impossible. It's never going to happen, but an interview with a major network? That could send sales through the roof."

"Think they'd go for it?"

Alison shrugged. "Probably not, but I think it's worth having their agent bring it up one day. You'd have to be coached, and you'd need to read everything they've ever written. After that? Shit. Maybe your calling in life could be to act as the face of Rose Solace?"

"Truth?" Brook dropped her elbows on the table and leaned closer. "Ali, I like them. I mean both of them, in a fun to hang out with and stir up things kinda way. Oh, I think they're sexy as hell, but they didn't have to give me a job. Ryder didn't have to come help me move. I owe them so much. If this can help at all, then I'm willing to do it. Besides, I'm good in front of a camera."

Alison laughed. "Oh, it's a very bad idea, but it would solve so many of my problems. I dunno, let's give it a month. Maybe a year. Just remember how great Owen was when you first met him and let's think about this, but it's not a completely bad idea."

"Deal," Brook said, knowing her best friend was only half serious, then decided to change the subject. "So, how are things with you and Leah? She still out of town too much?"

"Always." Alison slowly turned her glass in her hand. "Any day she's out on business is a day too much, but all together it's only about two weeks a year. Thing is, we've been married for almost four years, now. Together for almost seven."

"I know. You've got an anniversary in a few more weeks."

Alison nodded. "Yeah. We're also talking about having a baby."

Brook whooped loud enough to turn heads. Ignoring every manner she'd ever been taught, she surged out of her chair to rush around and hug her best friend's neck. "That's wonderful. I get to be Aunty Brook? Oh, it has to be so confusing. You going to adopt? In vitro? Which one of you gets to have the first?"

"Whoa..." Alison was smiling broadly. "Thank you. You're the first person who didn't start with all the problems. Um. Leah's worried she's too old, so she wants me to do it. She's terrified that being over forty would mean a baby with birth defects."

"And what do you want?"

She glanced down, her cheeks flushing. "I want to do

it, so it works out. Um, and we're either going to do in vitro or some variant. Probably start trying this summer."

"Well, congratulations. I'm proud of you, Ali. You two are going to be amazing moms, and I'll babysit anytime you want."

"I'm going to hold you to that. Now tell me how things are going with my boys."

She had to take a drink of her wine. This was the part she really needed. "I like them."

"You said that."

"They're good friends, but..." She took another sip, then placed the glass far enough away that it wouldn't turn into a crutch. "Jesus Christ, Ali, I can't stop reading into everything they do. They're sensual and flirtatious, and I can't tell if they're serious half the time."

"And if they are?" Alison smiled slyly.

Brook had to rub at her eyes. "Well, then it's going to get really awkward, because I can't pick a favorite. Pretty sure climbing in both of their beds would not be a great way to keep this job."

"Advice?"

"Please!" Brook begged.

Alison lifted her glass in a toast. "Sleep with the first one to make a move. Pretty sure I can get you another job if you need it. Hell, if I get pregnant, we'll just get a three-bedroom place and move you in as the nanny until you're done with college, or whatever. Just don't try to be Mrs. Harper. The Brook Sanders I knew in school wouldn't turn down a man that looks like candy."

Brook giggled. "I also never worked for one, either."

"True. Honey, if you don't want to, then don't. But if you do? Well, you can't keep living your life pretending to be something you aren't. I know. I tried. Stop worrying so much about what is right and wrong. I mean, why did you leave Owen?"

"Because he killed Calvin."

Alison shook her head. "No, that was the inciting incident, as shitty as it may have been. Why were you ready to leave him?"

Brook's eyes dropped to the table, and she had to blink twice to keep the tears away. "Because I lost myself somewhere and I'm tired of feeling adrift."

"Yeah." Alison grabbed her hand. "When I was coming out of the closet, you took care of me. You told me to try what I wanted until I knew who I was. Remember that?"

"Yeah." She squeezed her best friend's fingers.

Alison smiled. "I'm paying you back. For the next year, be as stupid as you want, and I'll be right here for you. I'm gonna have a baby, Brook. The woman I love and I are going to have a real family because *you* told me it's ok to be myself. That it didn't matter if anyone else approved. Now it's your turn, and I'm going to be right here the whole way, ready to catch any time you need it."

CHAPTER TWENTY-SIX

*A*fter dinner, they'd found a quiet little ice cream shop to keep the conversation going. Oh, it wasn't like their glory days, when they would've hit a bar and ended up calling a cab to drag them home. Nope, this was a little better. This felt right.

They talked about decorating the nursery and the complications of finding a sperm donor. Alison admitted she was nervous - about everything. Leah was thrilled, and they already had a slew of names picked out, but she was positive they'd forget something. Brook assured her that it didn't matter. They were having a baby, and everything was going to end up a mess of half-chewed crayons and dirty diapers. That seemed to be exactly what Alison needed to hear.

It was almost two a.m. when Brook snuck into the dark house. One light leaked into the hall from the office, but everything else was dark. Remembering her promise, she headed that way. Halfway there, she paused, hearing her name.

"Like Brook." It was Ryder. "Beautiful and confident,

237

but unwilling to show any of her weaknesses. I just think you went the wrong way with Naomi, here. This doesn't sound like something she'd say."

"So what would she say?" Hunter asked.

Ryder chuckled softly. "She'd tell him to fuck off as her eyes begged him to keep going. But if he tried, she'd probably deck him."

"And that's the problem. Can't push too hard or it all folds. How do you seduce a woman like that?"

"Slowly."

Hunter grumbled in disagreement. "No. You offer a weakness. You show her yours before you ask to see hers. Damn. I can't stop thinking about that fucking dress she was wearing."

"Did you see the back?"

"Oh yeah. And the legs. I could spend a lot of time between those legs."

Ryder sighed. "Me too. She's fucking perfect. Why did we let her move in? Damn, bro. Yesterday I walked into the kitchen to see her bent over the sink, and I damned near grabbed her hips without thinking. No way I can live with a woman like that running around the house in those little tank tops and shorts and not die from blood loss."

Brook was slowly walking closer, but paused when Hunter laughed. "I know. Even worse when she gets me hard, then doesn't even try to hide that she saw me adjust my junk. I keep thinking we should just fuck her for a bit, and accept that it won't work out."

Her stomach tensed. So she'd been right. Everything seemed to be fine so long as she didn't take them too seriously. Unfortunately, it sounded like she wasn't the only one wondering about the what-ifs. She just had to decide if this job was better than the fling. It wasn't exactly the type of thing someone stuck with, right? Still. She needed the money, and no matter what Alison said, getting laid wasn't that important. Was it?

Ryder sighed deeply. "Kinda nice to have her around, though."

"I know," Hunter agreed. "Guess that's what makes her so perfect, huh? She's so god-damned hot, but I actually want to talk to her. It's been almost two weeks, and I was so jealous when she said she was going out."

"No shit." Ryder dropped his voice. "If some guy had shown up at the door, I would have broken his face. I really like this one, Hunter."

"Yeah. See where it goes? No harm, no foul?"

"What if she ends up in my bed?"

Hunter made a noise, thinking about that. "I dunno, man. I'm willing to try the 'just friends' thing - if you are."

"I'd probably fail, but yeah. You end up catching the prize, I won't hate ya."

"Yeah. I mean, just so it's clear."

Brook heard the sounds of gentle slapping. She didn't know if they were hugging or some other boyish gesture, but they seemed to be sealing the deal in some way. She retreated up the hall to give herself enough room to let her steps ring out.

Ryder was still talking. "My brother always comes first. Nothing gets between us, and if a woman can't understand that, then she's not worth keeping, right?"

"Right," Hunter agreed.

Brook stepped loudly, her heels clicking on the laminate flooring. She knew she'd been heard when the dog tags clinked together. A second later, Einstein trotted toward her. She bent to pet him but kept going. When she turned into the office, she paused.

Sherlock was sprawled across the floor, his tail thumping on the rug. Hunter sat behind his desk with his feet propped on the top. In the corner of the room, Ryder was shirtless. His loose jeans hung a little too low, and he was pulling himself up toward a bar braced in the corner, doing chin-ups. Every single muscle in his upper body flexed. She almost dropped her purse.

"Oh, damn."

With a chuckle – and a please smirk – he lowered himself back to the floor. "Have a good date?"

"Yeah. I haven't had a girl's night in five years. Had a lot to catch up on. How were things here?" She looked at Hunter.

"Stuck. Our heroine is being complicated."

"I see." She leaned against the frame of the arch. "Can I help?"

His eyes slid along her body. "The first brother's made a little progress, but only enough to be considered a friend. The other one, she barely knows. She's strong-willed and intelligent, so how do I throw her into a romantic situation with guy number two?"

"Um." She chewed at her lip, then smiled. "Compliments. A man doesn't tell a woman she looks nice unless he's thinking that way. That puts the ball back into her court. If he compliments her on something he shouldn't – I mean, you're still doing the Regency, right?"

"Yep."

"So let him admit she was better at something. I mean, better than him. If she hadn't seen the business deal, he would have lost his fortune. She knew the Lord was going to change his vote. I don't know, but something like that. Let him compliment her for being something other than a stupid but pretty trinket."

He nodded but didn't reach for the keyboard. Instead, he tilted his head, his eyes locked on her. "You're brilliant." His voice was gentle and sultry. "I would have been stuck here all night if it wasn't for you. I think you can create this stuff better than I can."

"Yeah." She ducked her head, watching him through her lashes. "Like that. I think you're a little dangerous, Hunter."

"I don't have to be."

She chuckled once under her breath. "I like this job, and I really enjoy living here. The dogs are great, and you both are absolutely wonderful. I don't think you understand." She looked over at Ryder, who was watching her silently. "I don't want to cause problems." She turned back to Hunter, trying not to admit she'd overheard their conversation. "I'm flattered, but I'm certainly not immune to either of your charms. I'd rather not mess up a good thing."

Ryder lifted his chin, jerking it at her. "Which good thing?"

"Alison told me how close you are."

He nodded, those chocolate eyes locked on hers. "You didn't answer the question."

"Because it's *all* a good thing. You, him, the dogs, the house, and even getting paid to be your housewife. This is all I'm good for, and it's not like I could find another job like this. I feel like I'm at home, and I've kinda been alone for way too long. I don't want to screw up a good thing."

She turned, striding toward her room. That conversation had just taken a turn she hadn't expected, and she didn't want to lose the life she was just getting used to. If she'd learned anything about herself, it was that before getting married, she'd always made the wrong choice. She did what sounded fun at the time, then all too often regretted it. Then, she'd had Owen to make all of her decisions for her. Now, she just wanted a safety net - and preferably one with people she honestly liked being around. She wanted someplace she could call home, where she had friends who accepted her even if she screwed up, and to get that, she had to make sacrifices.

Getting involved with Hunter or Ryder would not be a sacrifice. Nope, it would be amazing - until her life imploded on itself. They had no interest in commitment. They weren't looking for anything long-term. If she caved, she'd end up very happy in one of their beds for a few nights, then sleeping on Alison's couch while looking for the millionth chance to get her life right, and Brook was tired of being the screw up her husband always said she was.

Stepping into her room, she kicked off her shoes and tossed her clutch on the bed, then sighed. She would not give in to the charm of Hunter or the sensuality of Ryder. Nope. It was late. She'd just crawl in bed and lose herself in another of their books, turning each of the male love interests into one of them. If she happened to rub one off before passing out, no one needed to know.

"Hey?" Ryder's voice made her jump in place. She hadn't closed her damned door.

She licked her lips before answering, but wasn't ready to face him. "Yeah?"

"He wasn't trying to piss you off."

"That isn't the problem." She took a breath, then turned. "Ryder, I told him how to convince a spunky girl, and he turned it around on me. It was pretty blatant."

"Yeah." He took a step closer. "He meant it, though."

"Makes it worse."

He huffed a laugh. "Worse?"

"Look, you two are very good-looking men." She gestured to his bare chest. "Distractingly so. That you keep flirting, even if it's just screwing around? You think I'm immune to that?"

"Wasn't sure. You do quite a bit of flirting back, Brook."

"Kinda my point. I like this job. I love the dogs. Hell, I love everything about this, and you two are great. A little too great. I just know how I am, and I need this job."

"How are you?" He took another step.

She sighed and let her eyes close. "Weak, impulsive, indecisive."

"Brave, considerate, and adaptable." His hand closed on her hip.

Her eyes flicked open to find his chest only inches away. "Ryder..."

"I could go on." His voice dropped to a sensual rumble. "Playful, adventurous, loyal. It's the loyal part that gets to me. Every little favor gets paid back tenfold. Then there's the way your eyes light up when someone says something nice. Doesn't take much, and you damned near glow inside. Not what I expected from someone who hates compliments."

She pressed her hand to his chest, hoping to gain some distance. Instead, her fingers slid over the flat plane of his muscle. "I'm not going to cause problems between you and Hunter."

"I know."

"We're just roommates."

He nodded.

Brook traced the line of his pectoral. "Ryder, this is not at all appropriate. I am not trying to get a piece of your fortune. I just kinda like having friends that I don't have to act stuffy around."

"Yeah." His other hand brushed the side of her face. "Pretty nice, isn't it? Why haven't you told me to get out?"

"I dunno."

He bent closer. "I think you do."

"Don't," she breathed before his lips got too close. "God, you're fucking sexy."

A smile flickered across his mouth. "Then I won't. Do I need to leave?"

"No. I'm sorry. I probably overreacted, but..." She looked up, expecting to end with a laugh to soften the words, but he didn't give her the chance.

Ryder's mouth found hers, his fingers sliding into her hair as the hand on her hip tightened, pulling her closer. Brook moaned, leaning into him. He tasted like coffee and felt so solid against her, like an anchor she had to cling to. His strength was the only thing keeping her from believing she was insane, but she shouldn't be doing this. Even as his tongue twined around hers, years of acting like a lady screamed that she most definitely should *not* be kissing her boss!

"I can't," she breathed, pulling away.

He made no move to stop her. "Why not, Brook?"

"You're my boss."

He moved a step closer. "More like roommates, I thought."

With a groan, she shoved a hand deep into her hair. "Because it's not fair to Hunter, ok? He's been so sweet to me, going out of his way to make me feel like I actually matter."

Oddly, Ryder didn't look offended at all. "So he's the one you have a thing for?"

244

"No!" Again, she groaned. "Look, you've been just as great, but that's the thing. I'm not going to choose between you, ok? I'm certainly not going to put either of you in a position to get pissed off at the other. I know how I'd feel if someone did that to me." She paused, taking a deep breath. "Besides, the last thing I want to do is screw this up. I can't."

From the doorway behind her came Hunter's voice. "No, Brook, you're not screwing this up."

She spun to face him, feeling her face growing hotter. "How long have you been there?"

He lifted one shoulder in a weak shrug and walked in. "Exactly long enough to hear that you most certainly are not screwing this up." Using one finger, he waved it between the two of them, pointing out how close they were standing. "He kisses you; you like it. I walk in, and you don't try to deny it. Brook, that's called honesty, and it's all we've ever wanted. Besides, I've never seen my brother willing to make the first move."

With that - and a knowing smile on his lips - Hunter walked out, leaving the door wide open behind him. "Let her think about it, Ryder."

A boyish smile played on Ryder's luscious lips. "Yeah. He's a good guy, Brook. Give him a chance."

When the door closed behind him, she was completely and totally confused. Before her brain could engage, she rushed over and followed them into the hall. The two of them stood at the far end with their heads together, talking softly enough that she couldn't hear.

"Think about what?" she demanded.

Their heads snapped up, but it was Hunter who answered. Walking toward her slowly, he said, "Whether or not you're interested in making this living arrangement a whole lot more... comfortable... for all of us."

From the tone of his voice, she had a pretty good idea of what he meant, but she just couldn't wrap her mind around one thing. "All?"

He didn't answer until he reached her, one hand coming to rest on the side of her hip. "Him, you, and me. All of us. Think of this as three friends, and you'll get a whole lot of benefits." His hand was slowly sliding around to her back, pulling her closer. "All you have to do is say yes." Then he leaned closer, his mouth just inches away. "I promise we won't hurt you."

That was when she felt another hand carefully sweep her hair aside. "Say yes, Brook," Ryder whispered against her neck.

Alison's promise was cheering in the back of her mind as she breathed, "Yes." It was loud enough to drown out the voice warning her that this was going to be a very big mistake. At least it'd be worth it. One night with these two men? It would be so worth it.

CHAPTER TWENTY-SEVEN

*T*hat one little word was all it took. Ryder spun her to face him, and his mouth caught hers as his body pushed her back. Together, the three of them were heading into her bedroom. She didn't even try to fight it. Oh no, Brook clung to him, her fingers digging into the cords of muscle behind his shoulders. His hand moved to her ribs, sliding higher up the smooth fabric. Just as she began to lose herself in the feeling, her knees hit the bed. One man lowered her down, holding her easily. Another reached for her calf, lifting it. Warmth caressed just inside her knee as Hunter kissed his way higher.

She moaned.

"You're in control," Ryder assured her. "You say how far this goes."

Hunter kissed the flesh of her thigh, and Brook's knees relaxed. "I don't..." She swallowed as Hunter kissed just a bit higher. "I can't..."

"Shh," Ryder whispered softly. "It's ok." He leaned back, giving her space, but she grabbed him.

"I can't think with you both touching me!"

Once again, Hunter chuckled, then pressed his mouth even higher, just at the hem of her dress. "Then I must be doing something right. Do you want us to stop, Brook?"

"Oh fuck no." She lifted herself high enough to kiss Ryder. "I'm not that stupid."

"Good." Ryder leaned across her, his body holding her down. His other hand grabbed the edge of her dress and slid it higher. "Because I'm going to have all of you, at least once."

And Hunter pressed his tongue across the satin between her legs. Brook's back lifted from the bed. Ryder's mouth caught her groan, offering one back. She couldn't think. There was too much going on. All she could do was feel. Ryder made love to her mouth, his hands caressing every curve of her body while Hunter eased her panties over her hips. Someone touched her, sliding a finger through her folds and she tilted her pelvis into it. A tongue took the invitation. Every time she reacted, they found another sweet spot. When her hands fisted in the bedding over her head, Ryder sucked at the material over her breast, teasing the hard nipple beneath.

"God," she whimpered.

For a moment, she swore she got a divine answer. With every inch of her stimulated more than she could ever remember, she knew this wouldn't take long. Heat rushed through her as her entire body was worshipped, and exploded in a rush over the lips sucking at her clit. Brook cried out in pleasure, her voice hoarse with intensity, then collapsed.

"I'm sorry," she panted. Then again. "I'm sorry."

Hunter grabbed her hands, pulling her up. "Come here, sweetie."

With his help, she staggered to her feet, aware that she was a hot mess. She felt delirious, and she hadn't even made it out of her dress. The look on Hunter's face said he wasn't anywhere near done. With his arm around her waist, he led her back, guiding her toward the hall. Behind her, a hand lowered the zipper over her hips - Ryder, and he seemed to be following.

"Mine or yours?" he asked.

Hunter's eyes never left her. "Mine. Table on the left."

"Damn, her ass is nice."

"Speak for yourself," Brook said, her hands finding Hunter's waist.

She followed the fabric to a button and eased that open, earning a pleased sound. With each step, her hands moved lower, releasing the next until they stepped into a massive room. Everything was blue - deep, dark, midnight blue. With the last button free, she pawed at his shirt, sliding it higher, but he resisted until they were at the bed. Only then did he release her long enough to wrench it off, throwing it haphazardly to the corner. Free, he grabbed both sides of her face, kissing her hard.

Brook could taste herself on him but ignored it. His fingers knotted in her hair, all of Hunter's control vanishing as fast as hers had earlier. It made her feel powerful, knowing she could unravel this handsome man so easily. With a devious smile curling her lip, she pushed gently, sending his ass down to the bed. Before he could struggle, she moved closer, kissing a line down his chest while her hands worked his pants lower.

He tried to help, refusing to release her hair with one hand, his other shoving at the cloth binding around his ankle. Her mouth moved over his washboard abs, enjoying the creases between them, and lower, until she found a thin line of hair. Her tongue played with that, eliciting another groan from the man, then she pushed him back so she could reach her prize.

Hard, thick, and impressive, his dick begged for her attention with a large drop glistening at the top. Brook lapped at it, and this time the moan came from behind her. She dared to look, finding Ryder closing the drawer to the bedside table, a small packet in his hand. He smiled, then lifted his eyes to Hunter, making a show of opening the condom.

"Go ahead, baby. Finish him. I was enjoying the show."

Her eyes dropped. Ryder's jeans were partially open, the head of his cock trying to get free. *Nice*, she thought before turning back to Hunter. She licked at him again, and he stretched back, crossing his arms behind his head as if daring her. The next time she licked, she grabbed him at the base, then slid her lips over the engorged flesh.

His hips twitched. Slowly, she gave him up, then took him all over again, deeper, until he pressed against the back of her tongue. His hand reclaimed her hair. The next time she slid him into her mouth, she kept going, swallowing as much as she could take at this angle, and was rewarded with a muffled curse. As her lips made their way higher, Ryder's hands released the clasp behind her neck, freeing her dress.

He guided the material down, moving in time with her mouth on his brother's dick. When it reached her waist, he kissed, his lips teasing the curve of her back, moving down in the wake of her clothes. She sucked and licked at Hunter, dragging this out as long as she could, and Ryder repaid her with caresses that moved ever lower. His tongue trailed over her seam, teasing her ass before sliding into her opening. Brook moaned, sucking Hunter in deeper.

Then Ryder was gone, and all she had was the dick before her. Able to focus, she doubled her efforts, teasing Hunter the way he'd tormented her. With each stroke, he twitched, his hips lifting him farther into her mouth, and she took it. When her hand followed up his shaft, he damned near growled. This time, when she took him into her mouth, hot flesh slid between her legs, gliding over her slick skin until it teased that cluster of nerves as he tested her wetness. Brook gasped, sucking air around the dick in her mouth.

"Just fuck her," Hunter begged.

Ryder obeyed. Hunter's dick was barely out of her mouth before Ryder's pierced her, stretching her tight. He was bigger than she expected! A groan slipped out as she dove onto Hunter again, letting the thrusts behind her slide her mouth over the man before her. She moaned and whimpered, gasping when he found a good spot but gave in to their control. Ryder's fingers bit down on the flesh of her hips, and Hunter's clutched at her head, guiding her until he couldn't take any more.

"Brook," Hunter gasped.

She took as much of him as she could, feeling his flesh against the back of her throat. He throbbed against her tongue as Ryder drove her toward her own orgasm. She barely remembered to pop Hunter's cock from her lips and swallow before she groaned from the pleasure.

"Oh fuck," Ryder growled, tensing deep inside her. "Oh fuck, she's tight."

He thrust, moving inside her with determination, building the pressure until she didn't think she could take any more. That was when Hunter's hands found her breasts, teasing and pinching her nipples as she rocked before him. It was too much. Her entire body was stimulated and couldn't take it. One more hard thrust and she was done for, clenching her jaw against the scream that wanted to escape just as Ryder buried himself, groaning deep in the back of his throat. She could feel him pulsing in completion.

Spent, she collapsed against Hunter's stomach. He laughed softly, a lazy hand moving to pet her hair away from her face as he held her. "Hey, beautiful," he whispered. "You gotta make it to the bed before you pass out."

Ryder slid out of her, but his hands stayed, guiding her to the soft mattress. Brook didn't even complain. Her knees felt like jello, and she had a stupid smile plastered on her face. With one more moan, she rolled toward the pillows, not shocked at all when Hunter moved to join her. This was his room, after all. Ryder took a few steps, then was back. One glance told her why. The condom was gone. When he dropped down beside her, she was only a little shocked.

"Just promise me one thing?" She looked between the guys.

"Hmm?" Hunter asked, turning to see her better.

She traced the line of his abs, leaning back into Ryder. "We have to do that once more before you decide I won't work out."

Ryder's arm wrapped around her waist. "I think you work out just fine."

Hunter leaned closer to brush his lips over hers. "And here I was thinking I deserved to get a turn. I'm not done with you, yet, but I'll let you sleep this one off, first."

"Not what you said earlier." She yawned, relaxing into the pillows. "You said fuck me for a bit, then admit it didn't work out."

She didn't even have to open her eyes to know they were looking at each other across her body. She could feel it in the way the mattress shifted. Behind her, Ryder sighed a little too deeply. Before her, Hunter slid his fingers down the side of her face, brushing away the wild hair.

"Brook, were you spying on us?"

"No, I was coming to tell you I made it home safely like you asked." She giggled, finally opening her eyes. "I may have paused when I heard my name. It's ok, Hunter. I knew this job was too good to last."

Ryder shifted lower so his mouth was beside her shoulder. "What part did you start with? Us agreeing that whoever managed to snag you was a lucky man? Or did you get the part about how it's not the same having a woman alone?"

"Huh?" She turned to see him better.

Ryder tugged her closer, demanding her attention. "I've tried having lovers. Doesn't work. Oh, it's a lot less complicated, but without Hunter? It just never lasts. Brook, the part you missed was us complaining because you'd probably be scared of this idea." He gestured to all of them in the bed. "Gross, perverts, and all that. We were trying to decide what to do with our dream girl if she insisted on choosing just one of us."

"So if I can keep this casual, I'm not going to lose my two new friends?"

"Something like that," Ryder agreed.

Hunter turned her face back to him. "Just don't ever try to play us against each other. I *will* send you packing if you even think about it."

"Wouldn't happen," Brook promised. "I put aside my best friend once because my husband didn't want me to hang out with her. I regret it more than anything in my life. I would never do that to someone else." She yawned again. "I also am not lying naked in your bed because I want some bonus. I just think you're really fucking sexy."

In her ear, Ryder laughed softly. "Just him, huh?"

"Nope, you too. You kinda look an awful lot alike, so figured you'd know I meant both." She yawned one more time, then groaned. "Damn, my room seems a lot farther away after getting fucked stupid. I think I'm getting old."

"No, just out of practice. Close your eyes." She wasn't sure which one said that, but it was the last excuse she needed.

Just as sleep began to take control, she felt an arm slide under her neck and another around her waist. Brook smiled. She could get used to this. Oh, it wouldn't work out, but it was nice while it lasted. It had been too long since she'd been anything but a desperate housewife, and she'd forgotten how good it felt to be a little wild. Maybe this was ok. She might be screwing up her job, but it was one more step to finding herself again. After seven years of trying to be what everyone wanted, she deserved to make herself happy, and if the world didn't like it, the world could fuck right the hell off. What wasn't to like about being pinned between two absolutely perfect men?

Besides, she still had one bridge left that she hadn't burned. Alison would be ok with this. She had to be.

CHAPTER TWENTY-EIGHT

*I*n the light of morning - or early afternoon, according to the clock - last night wasn't such a good idea. Brook sat up, alone in the bed, and just sighed. She was a fucking idiot. What the hell had she been thinking to sleep with not just one of them, but both? Even worse, she couldn't just pull a walk of shame and disappear. Nope, she lived here.

When she crawled out of bed, she realized something else. Her dress wasn't on the floor. Oh no, someone had cleaned up, and she hadn't even stirred. That meant the jaunt to her room was going to be in the buff. Well, unless she stole a shirt. Hunter had to have a tee in one of these drawers, right?

It was the third one she tried, and the shirt was large enough to brush her thighs. Steeling herself against the coming awkwardness, Brook opened the door and walked quickly to her room. At least the mess there hadn't been touched. That would have been more than she could handle.

Before anyone realized she was awake, she found a set

of clothes and rushed across the hall to the bathroom. A hot shower made everything a little better. When that was done, she found a pair of jeans and walked straight outside to care for the dogs. In the office, she could hear the clatter of a keyboard, so someone was writing. Hopefully, it was both of them.

In the barn, Amelia was climbing the fence to get attention. Rosa, however, had her face buried in a bowl of food. Evidently, one of the guys had beat her out here. That was just a little more guilt on her shoulders. God, she was an idiot.

Brook mollified herself by putting a leash on Amelia and heading toward the far end of the property. She needed to think, and her little girl needed to stretch her legs. Before she knew it, she'd reached the miniature forest - it was probably no more than an acre of trees - and turned down the trail that wound through it. As soon as she was far enough in, she dropped to sit against a large trunk, calling the puppy closer.

"At least you have a good excuse," she told the dog. "I just do stupid things for no reason. I mean, growing up, my parents tried to make me this perfect little lady. Mom wanted me to follow in her footsteps. She had been a smart girl, made good grades, and did all the right things. Hence I wasn't allowed to do a single thing that might raise eyebrows, you know?" She ruffled the dog's ears. "So when I got to college, it was time to make up for all of it. Thank god I was assigned to a room with Alison."

Amelia was watching her intently, twisting her head with every word. The talking made Brook feel better, so she kept going.

"Yeah. Ali never thought I was a slut. That semester, we got an apartment together. I'm pretty sure we tried everything just so we could say we did. That's how she figured out she wasn't just weird, she really was a lesbian. Me? I never figured it out, but I did meet Owen." She rubbed the puppy's ears. "He made me feel so beautiful. He kept saying I was perfect, and that he'd spent his whole life looking for me. The high I got from that? It was better than anything else. For the first time in my life, I felt like someone could see the real me, but I was wrong.

"I was so happy when he asked me to stay here with him and get married. He promised that I didn't need a degree. I'd be helping him. By the time I took his last name, he'd convinced me that all I wanted was to host dinner parties and impress his friends. I mean, that's what I was raised to do, after all. Keep up with the Joneses, act right, and your life will turn out right. That kinda thing. We spent our second anniversary arguing about how it was normal to have sex once a month. That's when he started calling me a slut."

Amelia's head lifted, and her tail started to wag. A second later, Brook heard leaves crunch under someone's foot. A sigh slipped out as she dropped her head to her knees.

"Got space for another?" It was Ryder.

Brook shrugged. "Sure. Why are you out here?"

He slowly lowered himself beside her, then pointed. Following his finger, she saw Einstein with his leg hiked against a tree. "Friend of mine offered to lend an ear, and they are some massive things."

"His ears are cute."

"I know. Full disclosure, I heard the part about your ex calling you a slut."

She sighed and leaned her head back, the bark tugging

at her hair. "You know, mornings after are a lot better when I can just high-tail it home, but I kinda live here."

"Yeah." He stretched one leg out and patted his thigh, encouraging Amelia to come closer. "I'd do it again."

"Huh?" She looked over. That was not what she'd expected him to say.

Ryder smiled shyly. "I like you, Brook. Usually, the women I get along with and the ones that turn me on come in two very different bodies. Look at Alison. I can talk to her for hours, but there's no way I'd end up sleeping with her."

"She says dicks are disgusting."

He chuckled, his eyes following his dog. "Yeah, and I know as well as you that she's mostly joking. Don't take this the wrong way, but, um, the kind of woman who'll usually tolerate us? It's a novelty thing."

"And it's not for you?"

His eyes dropped to his hands. "No."

Was it for her? Did she just jump in bed with them because she couldn't say no? What the hell did she expect to happen? That was her problem. She acted first and thought later. They were gorgeous and sweet, smart and funny. On their own, she'd be daydreaming about a boyfriend, but both? This was just a recipe for disaster, and Brook was an expert in screwing up a good thing.

She let out a bit more leash so the puppy could reach the next tree over. "Ryder, I'm not sure I'm any different. I came out here to decide if I want to call Alison and beg for a spot on her couch or face the shame of trying to live in the same house as you two."

He took a deep breath and, as he let it out, words came with it. "It's not the same without him, ok? I've tried dating and doing the whole one-man one-woman thing, and it just doesn't work. It doesn't feel right if he's not a part of something." The air ran out, and he looked over at her, those dark eyes begging her not to judge him too harshly. "We're freaks."

"Me too."

"Nah." He reached over to push her hair away from her face. "You're beautiful. I tried not to kiss you. So many times, I succeeded, but not last night. I figured you'd slap me, but it would have been worth it. Then that?" He smiled at the ground. "Hunter and I had just agreed that the race was on. If you only wanted one of us, then we'd figure out how to deal with it."

"It's not going to work." She smiled wistfully at the happy puppy.

Ryder pulled the leash from her hands and tossed it into the leaves. "She'll stay with Einstein. And it never works, but I'd kinda like to try."

"A threesome?"

He laughed weakly. "Um, I think that was last night. I meant more like a relationship. You know - me, you, him. What's the worst that happens? You call Alison?"

Brook tossed her eyes at the sky with a muffled groan. "How would that even work?"

"Would you rather we kept our hands to ourselves?"

"No, just..." She looked over at him, surprised to find his eyes waiting. "Bear with me, ok? My mind's spinning and I'm trying to find my balance. How would that work, Ryder? A relationship? I mean, what would you even expect?"

His eyes flicked between hers, trying to find something. Giving up, he huffed out a tense breath and lifted a hand. It was shaking. "This is why Hunter does the dialogue. I'm nervous as fuck right now."

She nodded. "Me too. I think my stomach's one big knot."

"C'mere." He scooted closer, then tugged her between his legs, so her back was to his chest. "How would it work? I guess kinda like it has been, but you'd be ok with things like this?"

Leaning back, she rested her head against his shoulder. "Cuddling?"

He bent until his mouth brushed the side of her throat. "Maybe kissing?"

The touch made sparks flare up her spine. "I think Hunter might feel left out."

His lips caressed her jaw. "He won't when it's his turn. I don't know how to make it work, Brook, but I think being platonic unless all three of us are together is a very bad idea. That, and I don't want to keep my hands off you."

She turned, shifting sideways so she could see his face. "And you wouldn't be jealous if I ended up fucking your brother on the sofa while you're writing a scene?"

"Not really, no. And if I walked in on it, I might just join in."

Air slid quickly into her lungs. "What does your brother think?"

"That you trust me more than him. That's why I'm out here. He's convinced he intimidates you, but he hoped you wouldn't leave. I hope you won't. We've never..." His lips flickered into a smile, but it vanished as his cheeks turned slightly darker. "We don't date, Brook, because we don't have a clue, but we know what we dream of."

That was when she realized what he meant. The books. Over and over, they'd written stories about threesomes turning into love, not just sex. That was the part of Ryder's soul he'd left behind: the dream of finding a woman who could *love* both of them. In each novel, they'd crafted the men to need the other. The heroes always had some driving force that made them feel empty without their partner, and they always thought they were broken because of it. That was why Ryder's face was filled with fear. He was terrified she'd think he was ruined.

Brook reached up to cup his face, twisting to see every nuance of his expression. "Which one is your favorite? Which story got it right?"

He leaned into her touch. "The one we didn't publish, *Shattered*."

"Can I read it?"

He shook his head. "I'd rather you didn't. Not yet." He rolled his head away from her hand. "Fuck, I should have said *Perfect Forgery*."

"Hey." She turned, shifting onto her knees to face him completely. "Let me read that one, then?"

"Yeah, it's published. Why?"

"So I can know what's in your soul. So I can understand what you want, and him."

His eyes narrowed, and his body tensed like he was ready to bolt. "You. We want to share you, seduce you, and see you be completely comfortable with that. We want to find a woman who can laugh with us, but doesn't try to pull us apart when that feeling turns into something sexier. We want someone who understands that Hunter and I have to stay together. Most of all, we don't want you to go, not yet. Hopefully not ever."

"This isn't a simple love story, Ryder." She gestured at the land around them. "Outside of here, what do you think will happen? Couples do things together. Threesomes? How would a trip to the grocery store work? What do you think people will say?"

He grabbed her thighs and pulled her onto his lap to straddle him. "That the Collins brothers are being used by some pretty woman? That we're perverse? I don't care."

"That I'm a slut?" she shot back.

Ryder leaned back, but his hands moved up to her waist. "Ten years, three men - if you include us. That's pretty much the opposite of a slut, wouldn't you say?"

"Two in one night!"

"And you were amazing." He chuckled softly, letting his thumbs trace lines over her hip bones. "I'm also not about to tell anyone what we do. It's not their business. How many of those self-righteous women read our books because it's the best they can get? How many of those men are so ashamed of their performance that they lash out to hide it? Take a wild guess how many people are into BDSM or dress up as furries. They use shame to hide their own desires."

"You sound so sure of it."

He nodded. "I write romance, Brook. I write the things people want to do, but are too scared to try. Do you think that the millions of people reading our smut are doing nothing but missionary? If they are, don't you think they close their eyes and try to imagine they're somewhere else at least once? There's no shame in doing what *you* want to, and I was kinda hoping this might be it."

She laughed, leaning over to press her face into his neck. "Ryder, rebounds never work."

He kissed her neck as his arms wrapped around her body. "Maybe not, but so far this is the longest relationship I've ever had."

"A week?"

He shook his head. "Almost a whole day. You think we should find those dogs?"

"You've never..."

Again, he shook his head. "No, not like this. I've taken women out on dates by myself, but by the next morning it's always over, and it's always empty. I've never found one I could be honest with - about all of this - but I'd really like to try. We've met a few women at bars or other places, but the next morning, it's *always* over." He lifted one shoulder to shrug. "Usually with a whole lot of regret. I'm not getting that from you. Guilt, yeah, but not regret."

"Hard to regret the chance to have two very sexy men, you know."

"Mm." He pulled her closer. "So does that mean you'll give us a chance to sweep you off your feet?"

She giggled. "I think that was last night. But sure. Let's see how bad I can screw this up." She tried to rise, but he pulled her back against him.

"Kiss me first, Brook. Just once?"

"The dogs are running all over the grounds."

He nodded. "I know, but Einstein will come. Just once, alone. I want to try."

It was impossible to resist the pleading in his eyes. She didn't bother to say a word, just leaned closer and found his mouth. Beneath her, Ryder gave in completely, his hands clinging to her like she might be his salvation. One kiss turned into two, then more, their mouths tasting every inch of exposed skin. It was just like she'd imagined.

Thirty minutes later, the dogs found them in the same place.

CHAPTER TWENTY-NINE

*R*yder took Amelia and Einstein, promising to put them up and let Rosa out. When she offered to stay, he shook his head and reminded her that Hunter was still waiting to hear something. Walking into the house alone made her feel nervous all over again. Hunter was right: he intimidated her more than Ryder.

The keyboard was still going, the tapping frantic. Brook headed toward it, refusing to let herself wimp out. She had nothing to be ashamed of. They'd come on to her; it wasn't like she'd tried to take advantage of them. If Ryder was right - and she could only assume he was - Hunter was feeling the same way, so she didn't need to be ashamed. There was no reason for her palms to be so clammy. Knowing that only helped so much, though. At the doorway, she stopped, unable to think of a single thing to say.

Hunter's back was toward her, his face pointed at the monitor. "She left, didn't she?" He sighed, but before she could answer, kept going. "I should've kept my damned hands to myself. I knew - "

"I didn't leave."

He spun around, his mouth open on a word that never came. For a moment, neither of them spoke. Brook took a breath, trying to think of what to say, but she just didn't know what came next. You were great in bed? This is weird? Ryder says we should become one big happy orgy?

She decided to pick up where they'd left off the night before. "You figure out Naomi?"

He huffed, the sound almost a laugh, and his eyes darted back to the screen. "I think so. Brother number two fell back on arrogance because he doesn't really know anything else. Naomi could see right through him. When his attempts to impress her fell flat, she took pity on the guy and kissed him."

Brook giggled. "Did he try the compliment?"

"Yeah, but she was too smart for that. That's the problem with amazing women. The ones worth chasing aren't the ones that are easy to catch. The guy thinks he's doing everything right, is pretty sure he's getting the signals he wants, and then the next morning everything is just kinda weird, and it's back to square one."

"Ever think that maybe Naomi is worried she's nothing more than a party favor? Maybe she thinks those brothers are pretty decent people, but is terrified she's going to piss them off?"

He chuckled. "No. I mean, after the two guys keep laying it all out there? I figure she's just not really looking for something as bizarre as what they want."

"Mm. And what would they tell her if they just wanted a chance to rip apart her virtue for their own entertainment? Then where would she be? Ruined, desperate, with nowhere left to turn? Maybe she's only got one bridge she hasn't burned, but she's terrified that crossing it too many times will make it weak? The problem isn't what they're saying - it's letting her know that they *mean* what they are saying."

Hunter licked his lips slowly, then took a breath. His eyes darted to the monitor again before he pushed himself to his feet and walked right to her. One hand caught the side of her face, the other her hand.

"I mean it. When I say you're a friend, it's nothing but the truth, and we don't make friends that well. When I said I was ok with being just friends, that's only half true." He shrugged. "I feel like a god damned high school boy, but knowing what comes next is Ryder's job."

"Yeah, he's pretty good at that. You? I figure you just know the right thing to say at the right time."

His thumb swept over her cheek. "Not really. What do you want, sweetie? You woke up this morning and were out of the house before I had a chance to say anything. What's going on in that pretty little head of yours?"

She squeezed his fingers, feeling more confident after her talk with Ryder. "I was terrified I'd made a really big mistake. Figured that in the light of day, all those things you said would be forgotten. I knew the dogs were probably hungry and miserable, so took Amelia for a walk after I saw Ryder had already fed them. She and I had a talk, and then Ryder showed up."

"And?"

She tilted her head, a little smile on her lips. "Are your wonder twin powers failing?"

"Miserably. Can't really say I've ever talked to a woman the next morning." He took a breath but let it out just as fast. "Can't really say I ever wanted to, in all honesty."

"But?" She leaned into his hand, making him look at her.

"Last night, when you were with Alison? It was so damned empty in the house. I went to grab a coffee and stopped by the living room, just to remember that you were out. You've been spoiling me, and I mean it. Sometimes you get me going, and I can't stop thinking about all the things I could do to you." He paused. "We could do. But I'd rather have Brook the dog walker than no Brook."

She kissed his wrist, then stepped back to lean against the wall. A little distance wouldn't hurt. "Ok. So I'll ask you the same thing I asked your brother. What exactly do you want from this? What are you going to do when something gets weird?"

"This," he gestured to the house, "is already weird. You know how many women we bring home?" He held up his hand, his fist making a zero. "Their place, a hotel, or anything but our home."

"And yet you keep condoms beside the bed?"

He laughed. "Yeah, in the drawer where I keep my wallet, so I always remember to refill."

She nodded, accepting that, and decided to try the simple truth. "I was going to. Leave, I mean. I thought I should, but I didn't."

"Why?"

"Because I screwed both of my bosses?"

He wouldn't let her off that easy. "Why *not*, Brook?"

She looked to the ceiling, hoping for an easy answer. "Because I don't want to fuck up a good thing."

"Is this still a good thing?"

Her throat got tight. It didn't make any sense. He'd asked a simple question, so why was her body doing this to her? She was supposed to be snarky and in control, not sniveling. That didn't stop her eyes from burning. These guys were just so gentle, so understanding. She'd expected them to act so differently this morning, but they were as awkward and terrified as she was.

"Yeah," she managed to whisper. "I don't think I've fucked it up, yet."

"Oh, sweetie," he breathed, closing the distance. "Talk to me, baby. What's wrong? Did we go too far?"

She pressed her head into his shoulder, breathing in the scent of him. "No. I dunno, Hunter. This is stupid, I just..."

"What?"

"I don't know what I'm supposed to be doing."

He leaned back and ducked his head. "Don't go, Brook. Please, sweetie, just give us a chance to prove this can work, ok?"

"Ok."

A wrinkle appeared on his forehead. "Really?"

She nodded, finally feeling the tension drain away. "Why not, right? I mean, it's not like you suddenly became different guys than you were a day ago."

His shoulders dropped. It was subtle, but she saw it. His words proved why. "I'll keep my hands to myself."

She bit her lower lip. "I'd rather you didn't."

A dozen expressions flowed over his face, and he tried to hide none of them. "What do you want, Brook? Me? Him? Just a pair of horny friends that come with a few benefits?"

"I, uh..." She pushed her hair back with both hands, away from her face. "Do you think it would work? The three of us like some couple from your books?"

He chuckled softly. "Trio or thruple - although I hate that term - and I have no idea. All I know is that from the moment you arrived, I knew you were the woman I'd been writing about. You look just like I thought she would, but you're so much better in person."

"That's no pressure," she teased.

"Brook." He caught her arm. "You're better because you're you. You're real, with all the mistakes that real people have, and not a single one of them bothers me. That's what I mean. You aren't just some two-dimensional character designed to let the reader step into her shoes." He glanced away. "You slept curled up to my chest all night."

"I woke up alone."

"Yeah," he said softly. "I fed the dogs so you could sleep a little longer."

"Oh, I thought that was Ryder."

"He helped. That's when we talked about this. I mean us, I guess."

"Yeah. So what do you want?" she asked. "How does this even work? What happens when someone gets jealous? What happens when someone gets to be more than 'just friends?' What the hell would you do if I fall madly in love with your brother?"

Hunter smiled. "First, he's behind you. Second?" He turned, looking right at his screen. "One is always first. Who says life can't mimic art?"

Ryder let out a heavy breath. "Not gonna happen."

"Might." Hunter shrugged. "I mean, even if it's just kink? Using her example, say you two end up the perfectly happy little couple? Can't see you getting all weird about me."

"Never," Ryder swore.

Hunter looked at Brook. "I think the bigger question is what happens when you decide you're tired of entertaining both of us."

She looked from one man to the other, actually thinking that through. It was possible. They were very different. Maybe one of them would start to annoy her or become controlling. Not that it would matter. Ryder's explanation had been pretty clear. They were a packaged deal. Could she accept that? If she couldn't, it wouldn't be any different than giving up now.

"All or nothing. I get it." She nodded again, but this time to herself. "If one of you drives me crazy, there's nothing that will convince the other to leave half his soul behind. I'm not that special."

Hunter shrugged. "You're pretty special, Brook, but he's my twin brother. We've been through too much to let anything tear us apart."

"I know," she assured him, then pointed at the screen. "Just tell Naomi that talking about it usually sorts out all the weird shit."

"Still weird," Hunter reminded her.

Brook pushed herself away from the wall and leaned toward Hunter. "Life is weird, but I can see you're trying." Then she took pity on the guy and kissed him, the same way Naomi did in their book. She knew it was what he wanted; that was why he'd written it. It was her way of telling him not to give up.

For a moment, Hunter froze, then his arm wrapped around her back as he leaned into her. Gently, he caught her lower lip in his teeth, but she sucked it away, her tongue daring his to follow. He couldn't, a smile ruining the moment, but he didn't pull back too far.

"You're really gonna stay?"

She nodded. "I figure this weirdness is a hell of a lot of fun. Besides, I didn't get to finish my book last night."

"My book," he reminded her. "You know, there's a chair in the corner."

"Your brother going to work out again?"

Ryder moved behind her. "I could. Or if he finishes this damned scene, he might." Then he kissed her neck gently. "So where do we go from here?"

Hunter slipped a kiss on her mouth then stepped back, dropping into his chair. "Brook needs to go shopping, I think."

"I do?"

He nodded, pulling open the top drawer to his right. "Yep. Call Alison, tell her you'll meet her wherever, and talk this over." Then he tossed a set of keys and a credit card toward the corner.

Brook looked at them, then back to him. "What are you doing, Hunter?"

"Alison loves shopping. Leah hates it. I have a funny feeling that you're wishing for a little advice from someone who isn't trying to sleep with you, and she's it."

"And the credit card?"

He leaned back, kicking his feet onto the desk. There was the arrogance he fell back on. "Going shopping isn't any fun if you can't buy things."

"I didn't sleep with you for your money!"

She turned, but Ryder caught her shoulders. "We know. We also saw how empty your room is. Your sole possession in life is a stuffed dog."

"And I like dresses," Hunter added. "You said you have *one*. Let us spoil you a bit, Brook?"

"No." She pointed at the credit card. "Guys, *that* is weird. This? It's just kinky. Paying me?"

Swiveling his chair, Hunter grabbed the card, holding it up. "I'm not paying you for sucking my dick, sweetie. I'm being overbearing and controlling. In order to get you in another dress, I'll give you free rein to buy anything else you desire - you just have to get one dress of your choice."

"Why?"

He smiled deviously. "Because you taste really good, and jeans are such a hassle to get off in a hurry."

Her breath fell out in a rush, sounding like, "Oh."

His arm stretched closer. "And decide if you need to pick up more condoms." He flicked the card again.

She snatched it. "I got an IUD the day after I left. They did the whole screening thing, too."

The twins shared a look, then both of them smiled.

Brook wasn't quite ready to give in. "So what if Alison says to run for the hills?" She lifted the card.

"You'd still bring back my car," Hunter answered. "Knowing you, the card, too."

"And the massive bill I'm going to run up?"

He stood, closing the distance in a single step. "Go shopping, Brook. Buy something that makes you happy and talk all of this out with Alison. Get a dress if you want, or don't. There are no strings. I just want to do something nice for you because I get the feeling that Owen never did. I suck at dating. We don't do it. I just want to spoil you a little, because it makes *me* feel good."

As he talked, she sucked her lower lip into her mouth and nodded. Then she looked at Ryder. "You're ok with this?"

"I'm pissed I didn't think of it," he admitted. "It's the same account, and you know he's right. There's a reason you call Alison late at night while you're out with the dogs."

"You knew?"

Ryder smiled, nodding slowly. "Wondered who you

were talking to when I went to see if Rosa had knocked you out. Heard giggling and figured it out."

She tapped their credit card against her fingers, trying to think of another reason to say no, but got nothing. She didn't need to buy anything, though. She could just take the card and window shop. Besides, she really did want to talk to Alison. Right about now, she could use her best friend's advice.

"Ok. While I'm gone, you two get at least one more chapter written." She snatched the keys and turned for the door, but a hand stopped her.

It was Hunter. "Just have fun, Brook?"

"Yeah." She reached up to kiss his cheek. "Just be gentle with Naomi. She's an old maid who expected to live the rest of her life alone. To stumble into two sweet men? It's a little overwhelming."

He nodded. "Don't worry, the story has a happy ending. Might not be a typical one, but it'll be very happy. I just have to figure out how to get there."

"Me, too." She left before she could change her mind.

CHAPTER THIRTY

*T*he idea of shopping thrilled Alison. When Brook offered to meet her there, her best friend didn't suspect a thing. The guys had loaned Brook their trucks before, but usually, it was to pick up supplies for the dogs. She'd never asked to use one for something like this - playing around. It felt a little weird, but also really nice.

She was sitting at the entrance to the mall, on one of those metal mesh benches, when her phone vibrated. It was Alison saying she'd just found a spot. Brook texted back, letting her know where she was, but her guts were dancing. She tried to remind herself that Alison encouraged this. She was supposed to be finding herself, after all, but what if this was too much? Would her friend be disgusted? Would Brook be willing to bail if Alison suggested it? She just didn't know and couldn't stop worrying.

"Hey, girlfriend!" Alison called, jogging across the street.

Like Brook, she wore just a t-shirt and jeans. She also had her phone in her hand. That was why, when it buzzed,

274

Brook saw Alison look at it, confusion on her face. As Alison reached her, she held up the phone, displaying the text on it.

"Want to explain this?" she asked. The text was short and sweet.

Hunter: Make sure Brook actually buys something? And lunch is on us, she has a card.

Brook groaned, dragging her hand across her face. "Good, Hunter. Make this easy on me."

"Inside. Talk while we walk, and I think story time is coming."

"Oh yeah," Brook agreed.

When Alison hauled her to her feet, Brook didn't resist. She said nothing as they moved through the doors, aware of how many people were within hearing distance. Once they were inside, she moved over, finding a little personal space. Alison just waited, her eyes saying she expected answers.

Finally, Brook gave in. "When I got home last night, the guys wanted me to let them know I made it safely, right?"

"Uh huh," Alison mumbled.

Brook kept walking, her eyes on the stores beside her. "One thing kinda led to another..."

"With who?"

Her feet stopped. "Yes."

Alison grabbed her shoulders and shook her, but was grinning. "Which one did you sleep with, Brook?"

Tingles flowed across her skin as her heart fluttered. Make or break time. Brook licked her lips. "Both, Ali. Ryder followed me into my room, then kissed me, and

Hunter was right there. I didn't mean to, it just kinda happened, you know? Hunter started kissing my neck, Ryder kinda had me distracted, and it just got out of hand."

"And?"

"What do you mean, '*and?*' I had sex with both of them!" she hissed, leaning closer so her voice wouldn't carry. "I mean, well, not full-on sex, but close enough!"

Alison was still grinning. "Were they any good? Did you take turns or just go for the gold?"

"It..." She paused. "I just... I mean, they..."

"Right." Alison dragged the word out then grabbed Brook's arm. "I know that's not your first little orgy, sister, so stop freaking out. In fact, I believe I was in the room at least once. So why is it some big problem now?"

"I'm not some college floozie, anymore. I can't just screw any guy that catches my eye."

"Why not?"

Brook sighed, shifting the subject. "They don't want a one-time thing."

"So that's a pretty good reason not to screw just *any* guy." Alison giggled, then pulled her into a store. "Also explains the thing about shopping. I love this place."

"Ali! Will you take this seriously?"

"Nope."

Before she could say anything else, Alison slipped around a rack of clothes, heading deeper into the department. Begrudgingly, Brook followed. She wanted advice. She wanted someone to tell her what to do! She didn't want to buy clothes with some guy's credit card - or guys'.

"Ali, I'm serious," she whispered, finally catching up.

Alison pulled a cute shirt from the rack and held it up.

"I can see that. I'm trying to say you shouldn't be. Look, what would you do if Hunter asked you on a date?"

"He's my boss!"

"Ahh..." She put the shirt back and found a smaller size, then held it up to Brook. "But it's not like a real job. It's a live-in thing, playing with dogs. How many times does that end up in a relationship? Nannies and married men, and all that stuff you see on TV? So, stop worrying about that part. There's really only one thing that matters. Do you like them?"

"Yeah."

"Both of them? In a get naked and writhe around together kinda way?"

Brook giggled but nodded. "Yeah, kinda why it happened."

"And you want to do it again, huh?"

"Maybe. I mean, is that wrong? They're gorgeous! And it only gets better when the clothes come off. Never mind that when I'm around them, I'm usually laughing, and they try so hard to be sweet all the time."

Alison pressed the shirt into Brook's hands. "Sounds to me like you have a crush, girlfriend."

"I have since you dropped me off. Hell, since Ryder showed up at the shelter, in all honesty. But that's the thing - "

A raised hand cut her off. "Lemme guess. You can't decide which you like more. They're so different, but yet so similar. They both make you feel special and satisfy different needs. Sound about right?"

"Yeah."

She turned to the rack behind her, flipping through the offerings. "It also sounds like the plot of their books. Now, have you read the one about the lonely brothers warped by the tragedy in their past, desperately seeking a woman to make them feel complete but unable to find her?"

Brook shook her head. "No, the ones they've let me read are all happy endings."

"Yeah, I couldn't publish that one. It broke the first rule of romance - no happily ever after. The prose was great, the plot was tragic, but it's always made me wonder if that's just what they expect." Alison shrugged, her hands still flicking through the hangers.

Ryder's comment drifted through her mind, crashing into what Alison had just said. It took a moment before the pieces locked into place, but when they did, she knew. "*Shattered*."

"Yep. Twin brothers, caught up in human trafficking when their adoptive parents couldn't deal with them, who learned all about sex by being sold to the highest bidder. Always forced to work as a pair to satisfy the perversions of their clients, they become unable to love alone. Broken, they eventually find happiness in one-night stands and the company of each other."

Brook felt her knees tremble as all the blood in her body crashed to the floor. "Oh shit. Ali, I need to sit down."

"What?" Her best friend's attention was immediately on her. "Why? What's going on, Brook?"

Still clutching the shirt, Alison found a short bench meant for trying on shoes. Brook almost fell onto it, breathing hard, her mind whirling. The pieces of his soul. Ryder always had this look in his eye when he said that. When she'd asked to read *Shattered*, he'd seemed honestly afraid. At that moment, with those few facts, she knew that book wasn't just any story, it was their history. It explained what Ryder had tried to tell her: the reason he didn't date alone.

"What were the character's names? Ali?"

"You look ready to faint over some book? Holy shit, Brook, are you pregnant? Can I adopt the baby?"

Alison's teasing was the balm she needed. Brook managed a weak laugh but shook her head. "Not pregnant, sorry. Ryder said something about that book. What were the character's names?"

"Um, like Harmon and Richard? I think. Probably one of their few contemporary novels, and pretty dark."

Brook's head bobbled in affirmation. "I think it's a history."

Without a word, Alison plopped down beside her, her mouth open in shock. "Harmon is Hunter. Richard is Ryder. Oh fuck. You really think..."

"Yeah," Brook whispered. "That's what I've been trying to tell you. This morning, I couldn't really do a walk of shame, so took the puppy out. Ryder caught up with me in the woods, and um, he said he can't have a relationship without his brother. That he's broken."

Alison grabbed her hand. "You need to read it, Brook."

"No."

"I'm serious. If you're going to date the brothers, you need to read this damned book. Some of the things they talk about... Brook, they were just boys. In the book, they're fourteen when they're sold for sex. The first time is pretty graphic." She swallowed, looking up with big eyes. "If you're right, Hunter did the talking, but when it came time to perform, he couldn't, so Ryder took charge. They shared it. They shared everything, including the tears. God, they were just boys!"

Brook smoothed the shirt still in her hand, looking at

the beautiful fabric. "My boys, Ali. They said they know it won't work, but want to try a relationship. I thought it was just a kink thing, you know? I mean, it's what they write about, but then that's not how they act."

"If that story's true, they're going to have some serious issues, hun'. I mean, the big kind of serious."

"I know. But don't we all? Hunter said they'd seen a therapist, but she was wrong. Holy hell, this all makes so much sense."

"So what are you going to do?"

For a moment, Brook said nothing. She just let her mind go, thinking it through. She'd spent her whole life being impulsive because the only person she could hurt was herself, but this? This was different. The brothers had let her in. It wasn't much, but they'd given her the tools to break them all over again. They never brought women home. They didn't take credit for their books; a pseudonym got that. They weren't frivolous with their money; they hoarded it because it kept them safe. They were so cautious about so much, including the image they gave, but they were letting her in - and she knew how hard that was.

Taking a deep breath, she looked at her best friend, praying she wasn't a fool. "I'm going to buy a dress. No, a few dresses. Really pretty ones."

"A dress?"

"Yeah. My boyfriends want to buy me pretty things, and I'm going to let them." She nodded, mostly to herself. "I'm dating both of the Collins brothers, and it's going to be a horrible mess, but if they're willing to try, then I'd be a fool not to. Am I stupid?"

Alison just shook her head, a tiny smirk on her lips. "Nope. You're probably crazy, but that's why I love you, girlfriend. It'll never work, you just don't know what you want, and you're so desperate you'll accept anyone that will take you... Is that what you expected me to say?"

"Kinda," Brook admitted.

Alison pressed her head against Brook's shoulder, hugging her with one arm. "Well, that's what 'they' told me about Leah, so they're wrong. Kinda nice to be the normal one for a while, though. I mean, being a lesbian is nothing compared to polyamory."

"Fuck off." Brook bumped her gently.

Alison laughed, climbing to her feet. Then she pulled Brook up with her. "I knew you'd hit it off with Hunter. Ryder's usually too quiet for your tastes, but he proved me wrong, coming out of his shell so fast. Since you've got both? Let's spend some of their millions, ok?"

"Right. Millions. I have hot, sexy, *and* rich boyfriends." That was going to be hard to get used to, but for the first time since she'd arrived at the mall, Brook wasn't ashamed of what she'd done. Knowing they needed her made it feel less dirty and more... possible.

Alison could see it. "Yep, and you're going to need some sexy clothes, girl. C'mon, and I'm sending them pics."

This time, when she hit the clothing racks, she didn't feel guilty about spending their money. She was touched. The boys were trying to do something nice to hide their own fears. She'd been trying to avoid it to hide hers, but they'd put the ball in her court. The least she could do was appreciate it - and buy a few things that would knock their socks off. She and Alison started with dresses, made their way through casual wear, and - of course - ended up in lingerie. Oh yeah, Hunter and Ryder were definitely going to get their money's worth.

CHAPTER THIRTY-ONE

*B*y the time they checked out - spending *only* four hundred dollars - Brook's fears were long gone. Each dress, shirt, or pair of shoes she tried on came with words of wisdom from her best friend. The one that made the biggest impact? "What do you really have to lose?"

It was true. Her perfect marriage had fallen into shambles. Studies showed rebound relationships rarely worked out. That meant no matter who she dated, it was doomed, so she might as well have fun. Ryder and Hunter were definitely fun, sexy, sweet, and so different from what she was used to. Brook decided this was just a phase to reset her brain and was no one's business but her own. It was the world giving her a little bit of good karma, with a touch of the wild side she'd almost lost. And if it happened to work out? Well, it probably wouldn't, but she could at least dream.

When she'd told her parents Owen had abused her, they were mortified. When she said she was moving in with Alison, they told her she should come home where she would be safe. The problem was that she didn't want to be safe. She wanted to be independent. She wanted to try, possibly fail, but always move forward. Her parents, however, thought moderation was a much better option.

By the time she was eighteen, Brook knew her parents wouldn't be happy about her decisions. By twenty-five, she'd stopped caring. Now that she was thirty-four, she knew she would never meet their definition of "normal." Brook had other plans. Hopefully, her family would love her no matter what, but if they didn't? She always had Alison and Leah. She still had people who wouldn't give up on her just because she didn't fit into the box everyone considered successful.

And to pay her best friend back, she agreed to head over to Alison's apartment to look over potential sperm donors. Alison and Leah had a folder filled with candidates. They'd narrowed down their choices to fifteen, but they were having trouble deciding how to pick the best genetic option for their child. From the way Alison talked, the thought of making the wrong decision had her more nervous than anything she'd done before. When Brook offered to help, her best friend nearly wept in relief.

She sent a text to Ryder, since Hunter had been getting pictures during their shopping trip. Mostly, Brook wanted to make sure it would be ok since someone would have to let the dogs out. His response was adorable.

Ryder: Alison's shopping for a baby daddy?! Of course you should help! Tell her and Leah congrats from us.
Brooklyn: Will do. Thanks, hun.
Ryder: Welcome. Any hint on if you're gonna come home for dinner?

Brooklyn: If not dinner, definitely have to finish my book while one of you works out. ;-) Have to show off the clothes Ali didn't get pics of.
Ryder: :-D That could lead places.
Brooklyn: I'm counting on it.

With a silly smile on her face, she followed her best friend back to her apartment. Alison lived in a nice complex, but it wasn't gated. That made it easy to get in and easier to find a parking space. Heading toward Alison's door, Brook pulled out her phone to check the last reply from Ryder when someone called her name. The screen was open, her fingers on the keys as she looked up and saw a man climbing out of a car she knew too well.

It took a moment before her mind caught up. He was tall, blonde, and angry. That was what she noticed first. A moment later, the face registered: Owen. Without thinking, Brook tapped at her phone.

Brooklyn: Owen's here. At Ali's.

Her phone buzzed almost immediately, but she ignored it, shoving it into a back pocket. Behind her, she heard Alison, but her eyes were locked on her husband as he stormed toward her. He'd found her. He'd known she would go to Alison's, but she thought he'd given up by now. God, she was an idiot.

"What do you want, Owen?" she called out.

He looked over, most likely at Alison, then back. "Came to take you home."

"I am home."

Anger twisted his face. "No. You live with me, and you go where I say, you hear me?"

Oh yeah, she did, and he didn't have the right to control her anymore. "You killed my dog! You think I'm going to do anything you want? Alison? If he doesn't leave, call the cops."

Then she turned, intending to walk into the apartment, but Owen wasn't done. He surged forward, grabbing her arm. With a single pull, he yanked her around hard enough that she staggered. A yelp slipped out as she hit the ground and his foot pulled back to deliver a solid kick. A second later, Alison was on him, trying desperately to pull him away. Brook couldn't make out the words, but Ali was yelling.

The world dissolved into chaos.

Owen shoved, pushing Alison away, but her best friend was like a pit bull. She came back harder. Brook helped, kicking at him from the ground. When her foot hit his shin, Owen snapped. He grabbed her leg and pulled, simultaneously swinging out at Alison haphazardly. Flesh connected, and the sound of a woman's cry split the air.

"Get out of here!" Brook screamed at her best friend.

Leah heard the commotion and came tearing out of their apartment. "Someone call 911!" she yelled, rushing toward them. "Owen Harper, if you hit anyone else, I'll beat you with this damned bat!"

For a moment, everything stopped. Owen wasn't used to women who fought back. He always said he didn't like violence, but that wasn't true. He didn't like when people stood up for themselves. While he'd never actually hit Brook, he'd pushed, pulled, and yanked her around. Never too hard, at least not until the night he'd strangled her until she was nearly unconscious. Then he'd kicked her when she was down. So long as she did what he wanted, it never got worse, but when Calvin, her dog, stood between them, he proved that it could.

For years, she'd made excuses, thinking their fights were pretty normal. Now, she knew they weren't. Still, she'd never told anyone what happened, thinking it was her impulsive behavior that caused the problems. He had to do it, to keep her from hurting herself, making a fool of herself, or embarrassing him. That was what he said, and she'd learned to believe it - until his idea of protecting her cost her dog his life. That was when she couldn't lie to herself anymore. That was when she realized how dangerous her husband really was.

And now he was looking at her best friend's wife with the same cold stare. Slowly, Owen lifted his hands and stood. Brook scrambled backwards, looking over at Alison, but her best friend was watching Owen. It was a standoff, or so she thought. Hopefully, someone had called the cops.

Then Owen smiled. It wasn't much, just the corner of his lip twisting up, and he lunged - at Leah. Before Brook could even reach her feet, he grabbed the bat, wrenching it from Leah's hands, and swung. With a grunt, the air flew from Leah's mouth as the bat slammed into her ribs. Alison screamed, rushing to her wife, and Brook went for Owen.

One hand caught the bat, holding it between them. He pulled, trying to get it away, but she was desperate. He wouldn't hurt Leah like he had Calvin. She wouldn't let him! Even if he beat her instead, it would be better. In the distance, she heard tires squealing and hoped it was the police. Dear god, hopefully someone had called the police!

"I'll fucking kill you, bitch," Owen snarled, jerking at the bat again.

Brook said nothing, trying to get another hand on it. If

she held it with both, he couldn't hit her. He wouldn't be able to pull it free. Each time he tugged, she felt the smooth wood slip a little more, but he kept twisting, turning, and all she could think of was hanging on.

Then something strong yanked Owen to the ground as hands pulled her back. "Get inside." It was Hunter!

"I knew it!" Owen yelled. "I knew you were sneaking up here to see a man!"

Brook rounded on him. "Fuck you, Owen. You killed Calvin! I came here so you wouldn't kill *me*, you bastard. You don't own me. You can't make me go back there."

"I'm your husband."

"Not for long," Ryder growled, pulling him farther away. "Keep struggling asshole, and I'll break your fucking neck. Trust me, I've done it before."

Hunter stepped in front of her. "Brook, you need to go inside. Make sure Alison and Leah are ok."

She caught his hand, hovering behind him. "What are you going to do?"

Hunter's jaw was set. Across from her, Ryder held Owen's arms behind his back. The twins looked ready to kill, and for the first time, Owen looked scared. He kept trying to act tough, but there was something in his eyes. He wasn't used to anyone fighting back.

"It's ok, Brook," Ryder said. "Just need you girls inside right now."

"Please?" Hunter asked, looking down at her fondly. "Ryder and I will be fine. Go check on the girls while we wait for the cops."

She met his eyes and nodded. "He's being arrested?"

"Promise."

Rushing over, she helped Alison with Leah. The three of them somehow managed to make it up the stairs. Brook felt like her neck was going to snap with as many times as she looked back, but the boys didn't move. Ryder had Owen, and nothing he could do would break free. Hunter stood guard with his phone to his ear, keeping his body between their retreat and the crazy man who'd just tried to assault them all.

The women were barely inside before Alison went for the medicine cabinet. Brook, however, headed to the window. In those few steps, Ryder had thrown Owen to the ground, and the twins stood over him. It was hard to tell who was taller, but even Hunter was broader than Owen. Ryder, even more so.

It felt like they stood like that for an eternity. The clock said it was just under four minutes. That was when the police showed up with their lights flashing. Brook watched while Hunter lifted his phone then gestured to the man on the ground, and finally pointed back upstairs. The cop - a woman - nodded in understanding before making her way over to handcuff Owen.

The whole thing felt like a dream as Brook's husband was secured and moved into the back of a patrol car. After that, the pair of officers moved to talk to the twins. That was when Ali passed over a glass of water and two little pills, gesturing that Brook should take them. The problem was that she didn't want to take her eyes off what was happening outside.

"It's just Advil," Ali insisted. "And when that's done, we're all probably going to give statements. Brook, did he hit you?"

"I don't know," she admitted. "He threw me to the ground, and he yanked me around, but I don't know what else. I think I got kicked."

"Well he hit me," Leah grumbled, "and I'm definitely pressing charges."

Brook almost looked back, but movement stopped her. The twins and the two officers were all heading upstairs. Another car had pulled into the apartment complex, and it seemed like this had just become a very big deal. In the pit of Brook's stomach, she felt bad about making a scene, but she knew that voice sounded a lot like her husband. It was nothing more than his way of controlling her. This time, she was ignoring it.

Brook hurried to the door to let them all in. Ryder hurried forward. "Who's hurt?"

"Leah," she told him. "He hit her with the bat."

She expected him to run over. He didn't. Ryder cupped her face between his hands and looked down. "Are you ok? Did he hurt you?"

"I'm fine," she promised. "Leah's the bad-ass this time."

Behind him, the female police officer asked, "This time?"

Brook stepped back to look at her. "I recently left my husband because he tried to choke me, kicked me until I was unconscious, and killed my dog when he tried to make it stop."

She gestured inside. "May I come in? This is my partner, Officer Ross, and I'm Officer Baker. We just need to get a statement and see if anyone is pressing charges."

"Yes!" Leah said from the couch. "To both. I want that asshole to go to jail."

The woman nodded as Hunter guided them all inside and closed the door. "I can definitely make that happen," she said professionally. "Unfortunately, I can't promise how long he'll stay there."

"Then I hope you can at least have an officer drive by here tonight and make sure everything's ok?" Hunter asked. "Unless you girls want to come back to our place for the night?"

Leah just waved him off. "We all know it's not us he's after. Just make sure he can't get his hands on Brook."

The officer took the closest chair. "I have a feeling this is going to be a very interesting story."

"Yeah," Ali agreed. "Interesting is my best friend's middle name."

CHAPTER THIRTY-TWO

*T*wo hours later, the police finally left. Somewhere in the middle, Owen had been taken away. Then, all that was left was to make sure everyone was really as ok as they'd assured the police. Mostly Leah, whose ribs had already turned a very vivid shade of purple, but that was just one more piece of proof that would help Brook get free of this nightmare.

The worst part was that she kept dragging everyone else into it with her. She hated it, and Ryder could see the look on her face. When she sighed and reached up to try and scrub the worry away, he moved to the cushion beside her.

"We're not going to let him hurt you. Not now, not ever," he said softly.

She just leaned forward until her head pressed into his chest. "I know. I just hate being so weak. I'm supposed to be strong and independent, not some damsel in distress!"

His strong arms wrapped around her, pulling her against his chest. "I know, baby. I'm so sorry. So, so sorry."

His hand slid over her hair. "But there's nothing wrong with letting the people who care about you help."

Her body tensed at those words. "Ryder..."

Hunter reached over and rubbed her shoulder. "Don't start freaking out. Remember Alison's talk about this big happy family? Well, it's the only one Ryder and I have, so you're just going to have to accept that you're included."

She wasn't positive that was what Ryder had meant, but it made her feel a bit better. Love was just too big of a word to use for whatever it was they were doing. Caring wasn't much better – and implied things – but she understood. She did trust them. She felt safe with them like she did with Ali and Leah. She also really did need a little help right now.

Then Alison's giggle broke the tension. "Oh! Leah, guess what?"

"You spent all our money shopping and left it in the car?" she guessed.

Alison groaned. "No. Well, yes, but no."

"Ok, then what?"

"Brook's screwing both Collins brothers."

Sitting between the brothers in question, Brook groaned and flopped against the back of the sofa. "Why do I love you, Ali? Why?"

Leah laughed, grabbing her ribs. "Told you. I *told* you they were into that. No, you said. Authors often write about things based just on imagination, you said. But I was right. Admit it, Ali."

"You were right, and my bestie is making up for lost time."

Hunter stood, a sigh sliding out as he found his feet. "I have a feeling this conversation's going to take a while, so food?"

With a chuckle, Ryder wrapped his arms around Brook, then guided her against him. "Yeah, something delivered."

Brook tried to resist, feeling like every eye was on her, but Ryder didn't seem to care. When she looked up, Hunter was smiling, but it was Leah's expression that made her relax. They'd never really been *friends*. She was Alison's wife, and Brook had always liked her, but they'd never had the time to get to know each other. Right now, that didn't matter. Leah had rushed outside with a baseball bat to fight off her ex-husband, and hearing that Brook was sleeping with not just one of Alison's clients, but two? Leah smiled at her fondly, not a hint of judgment on her face, just relief.

Then she turned to her wife. "I couldn't think of anyone more perfect for them. Now, why can't we find a man like that?"

"Because you're looking in the wrong place?" Hunter asked as he tapped at the screen of his phone. "Sushi in fifteen, but Brook told us you two are shopping for a baby daddy."

Alison tossed a pillow at him. "Fuck off, Hunter. It's not funny. Can't do it without one, you know, but it's hard. I mean, all we have to go on is a profile. Basic statistics, like height, weight, education, and such. Nothing in these papers..." She walked across the room and pulled out a binder. "I mean, look. It's all just the facts. Even worse, some of them want visitation rights and shit."

Leah shook her head. "Not happening. It's hard enough to find a genetic donor for your child, but when some stranger thinks that gives him the right to raise the kid?"

"I know," Alison agreed. "I took out anyone who

insisted on parental rights. A few checked the box for might want them, so I figured we could see what happens there, but there are just too many loopholes."

Brook leaned forward for the binder. "So what other options are there?"

"Find a man on our own is one," Leah said. "But that's a lot of medical for most people to deal with. The tests and such."

"And going through a lab makes it a little safer," Alison admitted, "but it's still kinda scary."

Brook nodded. "Ok, then what exactly are you looking for in a sperm donor?"

Leah sighed. "We want our baby to be smart, beautiful, but most of all healthy - mentally and physically. If I could customize him? Um..."

"We'd want someone like Hunter or Ryder," Alison blurted out. "Handsome, smart, considerate, and artistic."

Hunter eased himself back down beside Brook. "Ok," he said softly.

Ryder nodded. "We'll do it."

Brook's head whipped between them. "Just like that? Guys, they don't want fathers, they want sperm."

"I know," Hunter assured her, leaning over to kiss the top of her head. "But it's Alison and Leah. Ryder told me you were going to help her find a baby daddy, and we were talking about it when you sent the text that Owen was here."

Ryder patted her knee. "I don't have the first clue how to raise a kid, but they'd make perfect moms. The kind we always wanted. *They* deserve a baby, or a few babies."

Brook nodded, agreeing completely, but looked at Hunter. "Why? I mean, it's a big decision, isn't it?"

"Not really," Hunter said. "Alison's like a sister, and this is the kind of thing you do for family, right? I know we wouldn't screw her over and try to take the child or make problems for Leah with the adoption. I can't trust anyone else to do it but us." He turned, looking at the ladies across from him. "I'd just want to buy some presents and stuff. Don't even care if the kid never knows that I'm more than a family friend."

Neither Leah nor Alison said a word, but tears were welling up in Ali's eyes. Their fingers were laced together, holding tight enough to turn the skin white. Alison stared at the twins; Leah stared at Alison.

"You need to think about it," Brook told them.

Alison just shook her head. Softly, Leah laughed, hugging her wife tightly. "No, we don't." She kissed Alison's cheek. "Our criteria has been someone like them. We wanted to find someone we could trust, and Hunter's right. Most of these guys could take the baby away from me."

"It's not that easy, though," Brook insisted. "Ryder, you'd have to go in dozens of times and jack off into a bottle."

He shrugged. "Send me naked pics."

"Give Alison a roofie," Hunter teased. "Knock her out, roll her over -"

"Eww," Alison squealed playfully. "No! I do not want your dicks! That's Brook's job."

"Kidding," Hunter promised. "Just kidding, Ali. Seriously, though, think about it. We'll do it. Only one downside."

"Twins," Ryder said, sounding a little too smug. When Ali's eyes got big, he lifted a hand. "I'm mostly joking. Identical twins are usually a fluke."

But Leah looked thrilled. "I could handle twins."

"Think about it," Brook said again. "No big decisions after all that drama I just made."

"He made!" Alison insisted. "You did not ask that cocksucker to show up here." Then she gestured to the guys. "And why the hell are you here, anyways?"

Ryder chuckled. "Got a text that said Owen was here. Don't know much about her ex, but know his name and there's no way I'm leaving her to deal with him alone."

"That asshole," Hunter added, flicking a hand toward the parking lot. "Even after you three got inside, he kept saying he'd take his wife home."

Alison wiped at her eyes. "Have you filed, yet?"

Brook shook her head. "No. I need a little more money for the attorney fees and court costs. That's why I wanted to get a job so bad."

"Tomorrow," Hunter said.

"I can't afford it yet!"

Leaning around her, the twins shared one of those looks. Ryder nodded, and Hunter lifted her chin, making her look at him. "We'll make it happen, Brook."

"I'm not taking your money!"

He smiled. "It's a loan. I just have one condition."

"Ok?"

"You take one of us - any of the four of us - with you to go talk to the attorney. I do not want that bastard to have a chance to get his hands on you. Leah, Alison, or us, I don't care."

"Ali can't keep babysitting me! She has clients to take care of." She looked at her best friend.

"Hey." Alison leaned closer. "I get vacation time. I'll make it happen, girlfriend. Hunter's right. Your ex is *stalking* you."

That was when Ryder leaned back, kicking his feet

onto the low coffee table. "I figure it's just a little people watching, which helps us write."

"Which means we both need it," Hunter pointed out.

"So we'll both go," Ryder decided. "I mean, Leah's got work and Alison has doctor's appointments that are going to suck up that vacation time."

Leah nodded. "True, but so will both of you."

Brook just closed her eyes and sighed. "That sounds great. Sounds amazing. I've known you two less than a month, and you're going to not only pay me for doing nothing all day, but loan me money for a divorce, and then babysit me each time I have to talk to the attorney? What happens if this..." She gestured between the three of them. "Blows up in a drama-filled mess?"

Ryder pointed at Alison. "We have one thing in common: our agent is your best friend. In case you missed it, we're talking about having a baby together." He smiled. "Which is just cool. But I'm thinking that worst case? We can put aside our dumb-asses long enough to make sure our baby momma's best friend doesn't get dumped in some creek in the middle of nowhere."

Brook sighed. "Ok. I just know this is going to be a mess, but ok. I need the help, and I know you're right. I'm just..." She bit her tongue on the end of that.

With a groan, Leah lumbered off the sofa, gesturing for Alison to join her. "Help me in the kitchen, sweetheart."

Alison followed, tossing Brook a sympathetic smile, but her words were teasing. "I wanted to listen to the gossip. I'm living vicariously, now that I'm gonna be a mommy."

"Ali!" Leah warned. "You let those three act like adults for at least five minutes or no supper."

"No fair."

As they playfully bickered, Brook waited. Leah had seen her stop mid-sentence. It didn't take a rocket scientist to figure out why. On either side of her, the guys shifted, getting comfortable while each of them found a way to look at her easily.

"You're just what?" Hunter asked.

Ryder grunted at him. "Back off, man. She's been through so much in a very short time. In twenty-four hours, we've totally fucked up her world."

Hunter scoffed. "Fucked up?"

"Yeah," Ryder hissed, leaning across Brook to face his brother. "This is fucked up. I don't care if it sells, it's crazy."

"You saying you want me to back off?"

"No!" Brook snapped. "Hunter, stop. Ryder, please?"

Ryder lifted his hands, showing he was done. On her other side, Hunter bit his lips together, looking like he had a lot more to say. Brook reached over and found his hand, clasping it between hers.

"I'm trying, ok? We all know this isn't something that should work. Oh, last night was great, but one night of amazing sex doesn't mean we're all in love. I like you." She turned to Ryder. "And you. I just know that it takes months to get a divorce final, and it's a lot of money. In a few weeks, we could all hate each other. Maybe the way I squeeze the toothpaste convinces you two to drive me away. I mean..." She looked back to Hunter. "It's been a day. One day."

Behind her, Ryder swept her hair away from her neck. A moment later, his lips found the soft spot beneath her ear. "Do you want this to work, Brook?"

She swallowed, trying to find the answer in her own mind. When she glanced back, he nodded, able to see it on her face. Hunter squeezed her fingers tighter, but Ryder shifted, putting more space between them.

"I don't know," she told him.

"It's ok," Ryder said.

"It's not," Hunter told them. "Ry, listen to her. We'll prove it, and she's giving us the chance. It doesn't matter what anyone else thinks is right. The only thing that's going to make or break the three of us is *us*. It doesn't matter if Alison approves, or Leah, or anyone else. I don't give a shit what anyone thinks they know about us. I just know that we can make this work. We've been making this work, and I'm the one who was against letting her move in!"

"What?" Brook asked, shocked at that revelation.

Hunter nodded weakly. "I said it would be a bad idea. Before I knew you, I mean. I said it was too risky, and if you found out our secrets... If Alison knew..."

"But she doesn't care!"

"I know that now, but stop a minute and think about it from our point of view."

Brook looked back at Ryder. "She read the book, you know." Then to Hunter. "*Shattered*. Ali told me about it. Well, Ryder told me the name. She said she'd suspected since the day she read it."

His fingers went limp in her hand. "That's the book that made her agree to represent us. She couldn't sell it."

"I know," Brook assured him. "It didn't have a happy ending."

Ryder's voice was barely a whisper. "Did she give you a copy?"

She licked her lips, begging for a little moisture in a nervously dry mouth. "She offered. She said I should." Slowly, she looked back at him. "I said no, Ryder."

Hunter's fingers tightened again, then slipped between hers. "See, Brook? That's what I mean. You would have seen right through that piece of trash we wrote. You could've read it and never said a thing, but you didn't."

"Why not?" Ryder asked.

"Because that's not how I want to hear about your life."

He reached up, gently touching her forearm. "Why won't this work, Brook?"

"Rebounds never work," she whispered.

The pads of his fingers trailed over her skin. "Do you want it to?"

"I don't know. I'm not even officially divorced; how can I think about something working or not until I have my own shit together? I mean, what will happen when someone finds out?"

"No," he said gently, stopping her. "I don't care what 'they' think. I don't care what 'they' like. I'm asking what you want. You, Brooklyn."

"It's impossible."

From around the corner, Alison spoke up. "Tell Mrs. Harper to fuck off and die already, Brook. Stop avoiding the question. Do you want to live happily ever after, or not?"

"I thought you were giving us a little privacy!"

Alison grinned and lifted her eyebrows mockingly. "You, my dear, don't need privacy. You need a god-damned push. Sometimes it's ok to dream. Try it - just once - and answer the damned question." She nodded her head once, as if giving a command, then disappeared again.

Brook turned to Hunter. "I'm kinda scared of this."

"Does it hurt?" he asked gently.

She huffed a laugh. "It could."

"We'll be gentle," Ryder promised.

She shook her head. "Not like that." She closed her eyes and took a long breath. "Guys, I thought my life was perfect. I had everything I was supposed to want, and I was sure I had to be broken because it wasn't making me happy. But I was in love, so it would all end up ok - and then it didn't. Realizing that Owen was just a lie that I'd convinced myself to believe? That broke my heart. When my dog died? It shattered it."

"I know," Ryder whispered, still stroking her arm.

Slowly, she lifted her lids, but her eyes stayed locked on the coffee table. "If having one man break my heart hurts that bad, how much worse would it be with two?"

Hunter hooked a finger beneath her chin and slowly turned her face toward him. "It's either broken, or it's not. The number of pieces doesn't determine the pain, sweetie, but rather the distance of the fall. The more we love, the more we hurt. I can't promise that I won't break your heart, but I can swear that if that happens, mine will be hurting just as much."

She ducked her head with a soft chuckle. "That's why you write the dialogue. You're so full of smooth-talking bullshit."

"It's not bullshit," Ryder insisted. "Ok, he does find the pretty words, but it's not bullshit. I've never felt like that." He gestured toward where he'd confronted Owen. "I've never been so worried about someone before. I've never wanted to hurt another man so bad over a woman, and I did. If Hunter hadn't been there? I would have beaten his face into next week. I kept thinking that I'd make him pay for messing with my girl." He shifted closer. "My girl, Brook. Our girl. If you don't want that, please tell me now, so we can all just walk away."

"I'm gonna fuck it up."

"No," Hunter whispered, kissing the side of her head. "I promised you a happy ending."

"I want to try, but I'm gonna fuck this up," she insisted, turning to him.

Hunter shrugged. "Then we'll make a few edits and figure out where things went wrong. I write romance, not erotica."

She couldn't help but laugh. "You're a dork. You know that, right?"

"Your dork?"

She sighed and leaned into his chest. "Yes, Hunter. You're my dork. I dunno what Ryder is yet, but he's mine too. I want to try this fucked-up thing that's completely impossible, but I always did like fantasy."

"And," Ryder said, flopping over to put his head in Brook's lap, "now we have to talk about making babies. I figure I get to go first since I'm the youngest. You can have the second kid, Hunter. I mean, that's like checking off the bucket list, right? Make a million bucks, find the perfect girl, knock up another? All that's left is swimming with sharks and falling in love."

"Nah," Hunter laughed. "Sharks aren't on mine. Dolphins. Figure you can be the brave one."

"You mean you want me to fall in love first, huh?" Ryder looked up at Brook, his expression overly content. "I'm willing to try."

"Me, too," Hunter whispered in her ear, just as the doorbell rang. "And that should be dinner. Ali, Leah, it's safe!"

As Hunter extracted himself to get the door, Alison scurried back into the room. "Please tell me you're still a couple?"

"Trio," Brook corrected, running her fingers through Ryder's hair. "When there's three, it's called a trio or thruple, and Hunter hates thruple. But yeah. I'm trying really hard to forget Mrs. Harper ever existed."

Allison nodded, smiling at her proudly. "Good. I'm tired of being the 'freak' of the family. You were always better at it."

Brook nodded, smiling as she did so. That was exactly what she'd needed to hear, because the truth was that she did want this to work. She wanted it so bad, but she was still waiting for the other shoe to drop.

CHAPTER THIRTY-THREE

*A*s soon as they got home, Hunter set to work. He didn't breathe a word of his plan, but his twin knew. Ryder always did. At least he assumed that was why Ryder was so willing to help Brook with the mutts and then give her a book to finish reading. Hunter, however, had been scouring his contacts. When Brook asked if they'd mind her sitting in the corner to read, both of them swore that was fine. It was more than fine. In fact, it felt pretty nice to have her there. More so after what she'd been through earlier.

But things between the three of them were still a little tense. Since he'd woken up that morning, there'd been too much asking. Gone was the assumed acceptance of everything, and it wasn't just her. He was doing it, and so was his brother. Little things, like if she wanted help with the dogs. Two days ago, Ryder would have just gone out without asking. Now, his brother was terrified she wouldn't want him around.

Not like he was any better. Struggling to get his mind on Naomi and her story, Hunter stared at the screen, writing line after line, just to delete them and start over. Hoping for inspiration, he found himself looking over at Brook. Stretched out on the couch in the corner, she was so peaceful. Those dark lashes of hers fluttered as her eyes flew across the page and half-formed expressions teased her face. He kept wanting to ask if she was enjoying it - that was his book, after all - but he wouldn't. She needed the escape, and that was what their stories were meant to provide.

For a few hours, he wanted to give people their dream, a place to forget the drudgery of life and live every second to the fullest. He'd never expected the drama to become real. He was an author. A boring man who lived huddled before a computer. These sorts of things happened to young and lively college students. That he'd written a bestseller was supposed to be the most thrilling thing in his life. Now?

Now he had a woman, and that changed everything. Brook made everything into something thrilling. It didn't matter if they were talking about what to have for the next meal or tossing innuendos at each other, she made him feel important and special. Like he mattered. That was all anyone really wanted.

It was what the guys wanted in his book, too. That was what they'd never told Naomi. That was how he could finally break through her walls. Smiling at his screen, Hunter's hands began to fly across the keyboard. Bits of conversation and half-worded descriptions appeared, waiting for his brother to turn the thoughts into magic. Everything else in the room faded as his mind got lost in Regency England, watching the sexual tension build between his trio. Their happy ending was in sight. He finally understood exactly how to make it happen, and it would be perfect. Absolutely perfect, he just had to -

"She's asleep," Ryder whispered, breaking into his brother's thoughts.

Hunter looked up, realized what he meant, then glanced over. Brook's book lay against her chest, covering her breasts modestly. Her lips were soft and barely parted. Those long lashes lay against her cheek, but her hands were still clenched on the cover.

"You should probably take her to bed." He turned back to his brother. "Before she gets a crick in her neck."

"Which bed?"

Yeah. That was the problem, wasn't it? They lived together. They'd shared one night, but that wasn't an open invite. She'd agreed to try a relationship, but that didn't mean they could assume what she wanted. Dating wasn't the same as treating her like a sex toy - and she certainly wasn't that! She was the final third of them, the compliment they'd been looking for.

The answer was obvious. "Hers."

"Mm." With a deep sigh, Ryder leaned back and turned his chair, so they were face to face. "Hers doesn't have enough room for three, but might be a bit big for one. Kinda not wanting her to wake up abandoned if she has nightmares."

Hunter just pointed at his screen. "I'm gonna be up a bit. Go get Amelia, then see if you can put Brook to bed without waking her."

But Ryder didn't move. "And when you're done?"

"She trusts you. If she wakes up, I'd rather it was you with her. Ry, we have to take this nice and slow, and that means giving her the option to get used to us one at a time."

"So you're going to keep throwing me at her while running away and hiding? Not how it works."

"Not hiding," he assured his brother. "You can cuddle up with her all night, but tomorrow you'll have a few chapters to work on, and I get to take my girl out. I'll get my chance. Besides, I'm not really worried about you stealing her away. Go make sure she's tucked in and sleeping like a baby."

"Yeah." Ryder stood but didn't move. "How about you wake me when you're done and we switch out?"

Hunter gestured to the screen. "We're ahead of schedule with this one. No reason to hammer away at it all night."

"Yeah. There is." Ryder's eyes flicked over to the woman on their couch. "If you want to split this up, then we're going to split the work. Neither of us gets all girl or all work. You know as well as I do that she'll notice."

Hunter glanced over to the clock, surprised to find it was still before midnight. "Want me to wake you at four, or push till five?"

"Four's fine." Ryder tilted his head to the archway that led into the hall. "I'll get the puppy first. Keep an eye on her?"

"Always," Hunter promised.

His brother left with Einstein following loyally. The click of toes on the laminate hall made Brook's eyes flicker. She almost made it back to sleep when the back door opened. The moment it closed, she sucked in a breath and sat up, looking confused.

"Ryder went to get your dog," Hunter explained softly.

"Mm." She rubbed at her eyes. "I fell asleep."

"I noticed." He tried not to smile at her. "Was your book that boring?"

"No!" she gasped. "But the girl just..." She trailed off, her cheeks getting a little brighter. "The sex scene was really good."

"Which one?"

Her blue eyes flicked up to meet his. "The first one, in the stable. I liked how they shared her. I mean, it wasn't one after the other - they weren't both looking for a hole to fill. They were just *with* her. It was almost like..."

"Two bodies, one mind?" he offered when she let the sentence trail off.

"Yes!" Then Brook's mouth snapped shut. "Is that how it is for you?"

For the first time, Hunter finally understood why his brother hated leaving pieces of himself all over their books. He also wasn't sure he was ready to answer that question. Still, she deserved to know.

"Close. My brother and I have some things we still deal with. We didn't exactly have the best childhood, but we learned to work together because of it."

"Yeah," she said softly. "I can imagine. Ali just gave me a brief summary of *Shattered*, but she said the heroes were victims of human trafficking. Any truth?"

Make or break time. Considering that she already knew, there wasn't really much of a choice. "When you're on the inside, it's different. It doesn't feel like trafficking. It feels like surviving."

She nodded. "And I bet you two were very pretty young men. I can imagine it wasn't easy, but that's the thing." She pushed her hair back. "I can only imagine, Hunter. I can never know, and I won't try to presume. I can only imagine, and I know how shitty my own nightmares are. I am glad you're ok, though."

"We're not ok."

He stopped himself from saying anything else, but that left the words hanging between them, and they were heavy. She knew. From the look on her face, she could tell it was just the tip of the iceberg, but she also wasn't scared. She didn't look disgusted. She looked exactly the way he felt when his brother had shown him the picture of her throat.

Brook pushed herself off the couch and came over to wrap her arms around his neck. "You're ok. You may not be good, but you're here, and you really are ok. You have him, and Ryder will never leave you." Then she leaned back and looked in his eyes. "But even if being ok isn't good enough, it's still a lot better than the other options."

"Yeah," he whispered as his hand cupped her jaw. "And you make this better."

"Funny, because that's what I've been telling myself since I got here. Hunter, I'm ok with screwed up. *I'm* screwed up. I tried perfect, and it was screwed up." She paused to tilt her face into his palm. "And I'm sorry for what I said at Ali's."

He knew exactly the part she was talking about. "That you're not sure you want this to work out?"

"Yeah."

On impulse, he shifted to pull her into his lap. Her legs dangled over his thigh, but it let him put his arms around her back. "Brook, I get it. Ryder doesn't, but I know what it's like to want something and not want it at the same time. We wrote a book, and no one can ever know. It sucks, but we wanted it enough to find a solution."

She snuggled against his neck like she was still a bit drowsy. "You know, male romance authors are starting to be accepted. I bet if you -"

"Shh," he breathed. "It's a little more complicated than that."

"Can I ask why?"

He didn't want her to. He wanted to tell her to mind her own business, but that wasn't how relationships worked. Besides, she'd let them so deep into her life and so far had held nothing back. He figured it was worth a try. If nothing else, if this destroyed everything, then at least he'd know this wouldn't work before it hurt too bad.

"Because there are a lot of people who know us. Not the Collins brothers. We actually picked that name from a book we read as kids, and changed it when we got old enough. I mean twins named Hunter and Ryder? We've had enough families, and knew enough people that..."

"That someone would have a story to sell," she realized. "Yeah."

"Brook, the things that happened?" He tilted his head back to look at the ceiling. "It's embarrassing."

"I know. When I had to walk into Tall Tails knowing my throat was bruised? I knew everyone would talk. They'd all see it. I'd spent my life trying to prove I was this one person, but that mark on my neck made it all into a lie. It turned me into nothing but a victim, and I hated it. I hated it more than anything but losing my dog. Maybe even more than what he actually *did* to me. I hated it so bad that I even thought about staying with him just so no one would ever know. Thankfully, that didn't last long, but I still know how it feels."

"Yeah," he breathed. "I think you do understand. I'm so glad you didn't stay. I'm even more glad you called Ryder."

"Me too." She pressed her face a little closer. "Are you really going to help Ali have a baby?"

He chuckled at the change of subject. "If she wants it,

yeah. I mean, she had a few options, but I think it'd be cool. Not like I'm going to have any kids of my own."

She jerked back at that, confusion on her face. "You don't want kids?"

Well, fuck. He hadn't even thought that through. Had he just shoved his head so far up his ass that he wouldn't be able to get it out? "Uh..."

"Honestly," she insisted.

Hunter just sighed. "I really don't. I don't have a clue how to raise one, and I'll be damned if I'm going to end up like those guys who bought their wives a child to make her shut up. No, Brook, I've never seen myself having kids."

"Me either," she agreed. "But everyone seems to think I need to."

"Why?"

She gestured at her waist. "Uterus, hello? I have one, so eventually it's going to take over my mind. One day - which I'll have you know was supposed to be before I was thirty - I'll be ready, and then my clock will start ticking. I'm just scared. I'm just silly. Don't you know that it's an instinct, and I'll regret it if I don't? And what will I do when I'm old if I don't have a family to come make sure my ventilator is working?"

He couldn't stop the grin that was taking over. "Oh, I see. So you're supposed to breed your own nurses. Gotcha. And here I just assumed I'd get rich enough that we could pay someone to do that."

"Cute ones, ok? I think you and Ryder will need some little Swedish girls with big boobs."

"Prefer brunettes," he countered.

Her mouth paused, open but stuck on whatever she'd been about to tease him with next. "Really?"

He nodded. "Curvy, brown hair, and thick lashes. Full

lips. Yeah, basically like you. Why do you think I said it was a bad idea for you to move in? You're gorgeous, and I knew I'd try to seduce you. I just figured you wouldn't be ready, or wouldn't be interested, or would run screaming from this fucked up thing we do."

She nodded, accepting what he was saying a little too easily. "Is it that weird? I mean, most people have some kind of kink."

"Really? And what's yours, little Miss Perfect?"

She flicked both brows up. "Evidently, I'm really into two guys."

"Before you met us."

She paused to think about that before answering. "Experimenting. Back before I got married, I tried it all. Things that were good, I did again. Things that weren't, I checked off my list and moved on. Owen said I just confused passion with excitement."

From behind her, Ryder asked, "So what didn't work for you?" Clearly, he'd returned.

She turned to face him, but leaned back against Hunter's chest. "Well, I'm not bisexual. I'm not really into exhibitionism, either. Seems I get too worried about getting caught and can't get into it."

Ryder nodded. "I have panic attacks if Hunter's not around."

"In the room?" she asked, accepting that much too easily.

Ryder shook his head. "In the house. Close enough to yell at, I think. There's no set distance."

She looked back at Hunter. "Your turn."

"I hate starting it." He shrugged. "Never get off if I'm the one initiating. Faked it a few times, but it doesn't work for me."

"And if she starts it?" Brook asked.

"You mean you?" he countered.

"I actually meant she, as in whoever you dated for a while."

"Oh." Well crap, he hadn't expected her to remember that. "Um..."

"He can get it up," Ryder explained, "but hit or miss on getting off. My job is the action. His is the dialogue."

Hunter watched as Brook *finally* realized what that meant. He knew she'd associated that with their writing and how they produced their books. Now, she finally realized it was so much more. It was their whole life. Ryder made it happen and Hunter smoothed it over.

"Ok," she said, mostly to herself. Then again, "Ok. So how does this work with us?"

"You let me fail," he told her. "Let me try, Brook. Let me be a romantic and sweet talk you all I want, and when I lose my shit - which we both will at some point - just know it has nothing at all to do with you."

She nodded quickly. "Promise. Guys, you both made me feel so safe when I needed it the most, like tonight? That you even showed up?"

"I told you," Hunter whispered against her ear, "I won't let him take you. If he does, I'm coming for you. We won't let you go that easy, not unless you walk out of that door on your own. I swear."

"Thank you," she said, twisting to wrap her arms around him. "I hate being the damsel in distress, but you're both the exact heroes I needed."

Hunter sucked in a breath. "I know how to get the second brother in Naomi's bed!"

Brook giggled, but immediately slipped off his lap. "Then write. I'm tired, but if you're ok with it..." She glanced over to Ryder. "I was thinking about seeing what your room looked like? I mean, if not, that's ok, but I just..."

"I'll move Amelia's kennel," Ryder promised, hurrying out of the room.

Hunter chuckled at his brother's enthusiasm. "So you know, you're always welcome. I also think you just made his day."

"Yeah." She began backing toward the door. "I think that feeling's kinda mutual. Don't stay up too late, Hunter. I might get cold without you."

She flashed a smile and flounced out of the room, leaving Hunter looking after her wistfully. Damn, she was perfect. He sure as shit didn't deserve her, but something about Brook made him want to fix that. He could feel it, like this warmth in the middle of his chest and a smile that refused to go away.

In his books, he had a word for that, but it wasn't one he was ready to use quite yet. Soon, though. Soon, he'd have to admit that he was falling, and harder than he'd ever thought possible. He just wanted to make sure the other two were ready to dive in after him when it happened.

CHAPTER THIRTY-FOUR

*I*t was dark when Brook woke up. She was confused. It wasn't the strange room or the two heavy men in the bed with her. Those things she remembered. It was the voice. The one that sounded scared and was coming from right behind her.

"I'll be anything you want..."

She rolled to the sound to find Hunter. It had to be him, because Ryder had crawled in on the other side when she'd passed out earlier. Her movement, however, made him say something else. This time, she couldn't quite make it out, but he was clearly having a nightmare. Hoping to comfort him, she scooted closer and gently laid her hand on his hip.

That was the wrong thing to do! Immediately, Hunter surged forward, all but jumping out of the bed. He managed three steps before she could even sit up, but Ryder was already in motion. From the other side, he threw off the blankets and hurried around the foot of the bed.

"You're ok. Breathe, Hunter," Ryder said.

"I'm not fucking ok! It's not going to be ok. Jesus, it never ends. It just doesn't stop, and I couldn't make it. Nothing I said was good enough."

"You're in my room," Ryder told his brother. "You're fine. You're ok. It's all over, and you're here, safe, with me."

"What?"

"My room," Ryder said again. "It was a dream. That's all."

"Ah, *fuck!*" Hunter hissed, proving he was actually awake now.

"It's ok," Ryder promised. "I'm right here."

Then, without a word, Ryder wrapped his twin in a tight hug. Hunter didn't try to resist. Instead, he clung to Ryder's bare shoulders, grasping at him desperately. His face was pressed into his brother's neck, and she heard him gasp almost like a sob.

"I couldn't make it stop," Hunter mumbled into his twin's skin.

Brook didn't know what to do. Sitting there on the bed, she was scared to bring attention to herself, worried she was intruding in something she shouldn't be seeing. Watching the guys hold each other, she realized just how little she actually knew about them, and how very far she had to go. She barely knew them. She couldn't help them. This thing they were doing was little more than just a "good time."

"It was Dale," Hunter mumbled. "I couldn't make him go away. He just..."

"I know," Ryder promised. "I gotcha. I'm not letting go. We're in my room and we're ok. We're going to be fine, Hunter."

"Yeah," Hunter managed, then sucked in a shaking breath. "You already - "

"Brook," Ryder said softly. The problem was that it sounded like a warning, not like he was trying to get her attention.

She decided that was her cue to leave. Sliding across the sheets, she decided to use Ryder's side, simply because she didn't want to stand up between them. Without a word, she padded softly across the room, heading for the door. Her boys needed a minute, and she needed to pee. That was all this was. She wouldn't let her feelings be hurt because they weren't ready to share everything. Nope, she wouldn't blame them; she'd just try to be the kind of person she'd always needed.

"Brook," Hunter said as she passed, pulling away from Ryder to look at her.

She smiled at him. "Bathroom. Then I'll be in the study. It's ok."

"I..."

She nodded. "Yeah. I know. It's ok."

But it wasn't. It really wasn't, and she was lying to them. She was also lying to herself. Nothing about what they were doing was normal. She wasn't normal, they weren't normal, and the three of them probably never would be. So far, she'd been able to keep her own issues at bay, but how long would that last? When would *she* be the one waking up from a nightmare where Owen's hand was around her neck, or her poor dog was being beaten to death?

But she really did need to pee. The problem was that the house was too quiet. She could hear the soft murmur of the guys' voices in the bedroom. She could hear one of the dogs - it sounded like Sherlock from the dragging toes

- making his way up the hall. What she couldn't hear was the pain those guys had to be hiding, because they'd kept it locked away.

It was time for that to change. After finishing her business, she left the bathroom and headed right back for the bedroom. Yes, she'd said she'd be in the study, but this had to be done. It had to be dealt with before she allowed herself to get any more involved with them.

When she rounded the corner, she saw the guys in the same place. Now, they were talking. Ryder had one hand on Hunter's arm, but it didn't distract at all from the two men wearing nothing but their briefs. They also didn't seem to care.

"What do I need to know?" she demanded. "I tried to cuddle with you, and I set you off, so what do I need to know?"

"Brook," Hunter said as he turned to her. "It wasn't your fault. I just..."

"He has nightmares," Ryder finished. "Bad ones, that you probably don't want to know about."

She took a deep breath. "But I do. See, that's the thing. If I'm just a piece of ass, then no. Keep your secrets. If we want this thing to work? Someone has to start talking to me. I'm tired of feeling like I'm on the outside." She held up a hand before they could cut her off. "I'm not saying you need to sit down and spill everything. I get it. I promise I do, but locking me out makes me feel like I'm disposable. I want to know that I shouldn't try to soothe him at night, or the easiest way to help him if he wakes up like that again."

Ryder nodded. "If I'm having one, I sometimes swing before I'm awake."

"So how do I help?" she pressed.

He shoved a hand into his sleep-mussed hair. "Talk to me. Tell me I'm at home, or what room I'm in. Remind me that it's ok, but don't get close. Him?"

"I need close," Hunter finished. "I'll try to run away, but don't let me. I've never swung, but I'll try to leave until I know where I am..." He swallowed. "So tell me who you are, where I am, and ground me."

"Ok." She moved close enough to reach out for his hand. "I'm sorry I scared you."

"Oh, Brook, I promise it wasn't you," he breathed, pulling her against him. "I was a little boy, weak and helpless. Someone was about to hurt me, and nothing I could do would stop it. It had nothing at all to do with you."

"Is it better..." She looked up at his face. "Should I sleep in my own bed?"

"No," he promised. "I like you beside me, I really do, and I'm sorry about all of that. I just don't know how to stop it."

"You had a dream," she countered. "I'm not sure you can stop it. Hunter, I don't expect you to be perfect, ok?"

"I do." He leaned closer and kissed her head. "I want to, but it's easier when I'm awake."

She nodded, remembering what he'd said. "When you can be anything I want? What if what I want is to get to know the real you?"

He froze. Not that he'd been moving, but she felt every muscle in his body pause for a moment. "Brook..."

"If you're going to tell me it's messy, then I have news for you. You don't get to dive into my shit and not expect that to work both ways. You - neither of you - treated me like shit after I let my husband beat me and kill my dog."

Ryder spoke up from behind her. "That wasn't your fault."

"And your nightmares are yours?" She countered. "That's not how a relationship works, guys. Just *let* me *in*."

Both men looked over her, meeting each other's eyes. She watched as they came to a decision. Ryder nodded, Hunter tipped his head slightly, then Ryder moved to her side. She braced for them to say it wasn't going to happen, which for her was a deal breaker.

"They started selling us off when we were twelve," Ryder said softly. "We were placed with this family, and the old man figured he could make a few bucks. A pair of identical twins? He figured he'd struck it rich. The only rule was that we couldn't scream."

"Which we broke," Hunter added. "And he beat us until we decided we'd never do it again. His name was Dale."

"Oh my god," she breathed, wrapping her arms around Hunter's waist. "That's enough. I didn't mean that you had to tell me the story. I meant that you had to trust me enough to admit when there's a problem. I don't need you to relive it."

"He raped us," Hunter told her. "Over and over. From behind."

"My brother would pretend to be me," Ryder said. "He told me he was older, so that made him tougher. He would be him one night and me the next, and I knew that ratting him out would make it worse. I got the beatings; he had to deal with...that."

"Hunter," she almost begged. "I'm so sorry I asked."

He nodded. "That's how it started, Brook. It got worse. When we were older, Dale came back. He wanted more."

Ryder took her hand, moving her to the bed. "I had to make a decision. I had to choose between my best friend and my brother. I chose my brother. To get away before he could hurt Hunter again, I let Penny loose. She was a little blue-nose pit bull that we'd hidden in the shed." He lowered them both down to sit on the edge of the bed. "I knew what would happen, but I still did it. I let Penny loose, and the moment Hunter screamed, she went to save him."

"She died for me," Hunter finished. "She attacked that man, and he beat her to death, but we ran. We ran so hard. We were seventeen with nowhere to go, but we had each other. We sacrificed our only friend to stay together, and you need to know that."

She leaned over and hugged Ryder. "I'm so sorry."

"That's why I saved Amelia. I couldn't save Penny."

Tears were stinging Brook's eyes. "But sacrificing is what friends do. It's what you've both done for me." She wiped at her eyes and looked over to Hunter. "It's what I'd do for you."

"Oh, Brook," he whispered, reaching over to cup her face with both hands, even as she still had her arms around Ryder. "And I don't even want you to do that. I'm fine. I'm going to be fine, but you just made it a little better."

Then he kissed her. It was hard, almost desperate. Her arms were crushed between the twins, but she didn't care. He needed this. More than anything else, right now, Hunter needed to take control back. It was one thing she understood, and if he wanted to use her to do it, she'd let him.

When his body pressed her back, Ryder moved. Brook just went with it, hooking a leg around Hunter's waist. Her satin pajamas weren't enough to hide Hunter's growing interest, willing to let him decide how far this would go. He needed her, and this was one thing she knew how to give.

Lost in the passion of his kisses, she forgot about the other man in the room. Right now, it was just Brook and Hunter. His hands moved up to her breasts, teasing them as he pressed his hips into her. She gasped, pulling her mouth away to suck in a breath of air, but he wouldn't give her lips up. His breath slipped into her lungs before he stole it back, the whole time grinding against every inch of her body.

"Clothes," Ryder said.

Brook felt Hunter's lips curl against hers. "Good thing you aren't wearing much." Then he was pushing her shirt higher.

She reached for the waistband of his briefs, struggling to get them off in their tangle of arms and legs. This wasn't sexy or beautiful, but it felt just as good. Maybe better. All the passion she'd dreamed of was in Hunter's fingers, and she was ready to beg for it.

"Bottoms," Ryder reminded his brother.

"Just watching?" Hunter shot back.

"Man, you started this, and I sure as fuck don't want to hear you whining in the morning. Brook, take off your clothes and come over here?"

Tilting her head up, she found Ryder naked and laying against the pillows. The heat in his eyes was scorching, so she decided to obey. Lifting her hips, she slipped off the satin shorts she'd worn to bed and rolled over. On her hands and knees, she crawled toward him. Ryder watched, his eyes sliding across her body like he was deciding which bit to devour first.

But the moment she was close enough, he sat up and

grabbed her, pulling her body into his lap. Her back was to his chest. Her ass was pressing right into his dick - which had been coated with ample lube when she wasn't looking. She made no move at all to resist, well-aware that he had to know what he was doing. The problem was that she didn't.

"Just grind that nice little ass against that," Ryder whispered in her ear. "And enjoy this."

But grinding wasn't all she intended to do. Lifting up just a little, she felt his tip slide down her ass, then she pressed. It had been a long time, a very long one, but she could do this. She wanted this, and the moment she began to lower her ass onto Ryder's dick, his fingers grew soft.

"Oh, fuck," he breathed. "Baby..."

"Just..." She lifted a little and tried again, feeling his girth refusing to enter. "Don't move."

"Relax," Ryder whispered. "Lie back. I got ya. Just relax, and it'll happen."

The moment she stopped trying, she felt her body give in, and he slipped into her ass. There was a gasp, but it wasn't from her. Ryder's arm tightened around her waist, and for a moment, neither of them moved.

"You'd better fuck her fast," Ryder groaned, "because I'm balls-deep in her ass and it's fucking nice."

"Spread," Hunter demanded, moving between both of their legs.

Brook wasn't sure what they were doing, but as Hunter leaned over them both, she figured it out. Holy shit, this was hot. All of her weight was on Ryder. His dick was in her ass, and now Hunter's was slowly sliding into her pussy. She could feel them both. The heat of their bodies surrounded her. Ryder's arm held her in place, and then Hunter began to move.

Their bodies writhed against each other. It wasn't fast or furious, but it was enough. Filled by both, it set every nerve on fire. Hunter kissed her lips, Ryder teased her nipples, and Brook just struggled not to scream out her pleasure. The louder she moaned, the more excited she got, but she knew they were being gentle. The problem was that she wanted to be used. She wanted them to have all of her, every single inch, and in every way they desired.

"More," she begged.

Hunter gave, just like she asked. The rhythm increased, but so did the kisses. This wasn't about getting off. It was more, so much more, and the men were doing their best to prove it. Together, they were all perfect. They fit. Like this, everything felt so damned good, and she never wanted it to end.

But Hunter was too good. As the pressure built, his mouth moved to her throat, his lips making their way to that soft spot just beside her ear. Ryder was already there on the other side, and she felt like her body was going to explode.

Then Hunter whispered softly, "I need you, Brook," and it was all she could take.

Her eyes flew open and she reached for his neck, pulling his lips to hers as he continued to drive her higher. The moment their tongues met, her body lost control and her back arched. Ryder thrust, driving himself deeper, moving in opposition to Hunter, and she realized what she'd missed out on. This. This was amazing and perfect and hers. All hers.

The only problem was that when she came, she couldn't figure out what name to yell, so she just groaned, giving voice to the things they'd made her body do, as it tensed around both of them.

"Jesus," Hunter gasped.

But Ryder only managed a gravely, "Fuck."

And she felt both of them pulsing, spilling, and filling her. Like everything else, they'd even found a way to finish her together. All she could do was lean back and close her eyes, because this was perfect.

Then Ryder chuckled. "You know, you started that, Hunter."

"Fuck yeah, I did, and I'm pretty sure we need to change the sheets."

"Or the room," Ryder agreed. "Now get off us."

When Brook was finally able to roll into the center of the bed, she was smiling. Maybe their relationship was a mess, but it was real, and that made it better than anything else she could imagine. At that moment, she decided that she really did want this to work. Who cared if it wasn't what she was supposed to do. She'd already tried that and hated it.

This? She loved this. She loved everything about this, even... Before her mind could finish that sentence, she stopped it. That was just her afterglow talking. There was no way she could be attached to *two* people that fast. No, she wasn't there yet, but damned if she wasn't getting there a lot faster than she'd ever expected.

CHAPTER THIRTY-FIVE

*T*he next morning, Brook woke to laughter in the other room. She wasn't sure what the guys were doing - probably writing - but she knew her body ached. Not in a bad way, but just like she'd been used. In other words, she needed a very hot shower.

After the fun the night before, they'd all moved to Hunter's bed. She didn't even want to think about the mess they'd made, but that was the housewife in her. The new girlfriend part was more concerned with testing out her boyfriend's bathroom in his fancy house, because she was going to enjoy this for as long as she could.

She was under the steaming hot water when the shower door opened. "Need any help in there?" She wiped the water from her face to find Hunter, naked, peeking his head in.

"Seems there's plenty of room." She tilted her head, encouraging him to join her. "Sorry, I didn't want to walk down the hall."

"And I didn't expect you to." He moved to soak himself and asked, "How do you feel?"

She bit her lip to stop a giggle. "Were you worried about me?"

"Uh..." He stepped out of the water, leaving it for her. "Yeah, um, I kinda got the impression that you don't do that a lot."

"Taking it up the ass?"

He leaned his shoulder against the cold tile wall. "Yeah, that. I was trying to be polite."

"You fucked me while your brother was balls-deep in my ass, and *now* we're going to worry about polite?"

"No, now we're going to worry about how much you hurt." He lifted a brow, making it clear *he* had no problem talking about this. "Believe it or not, I've done a lot of reading about the way women feel the next morning. Kinda falls in my job description."

She gestured to the bottles around the shower. "Any of these conditioner?"

Hunter pointed beside her. "Black one. Brook, you're killing me."

"Yeah," she admitted as she turned her back to him. "I might be walking a little bow-legged, but I'm ok."

"Sore?"

"A little." Filling her hand with the cream, she turned back as she slathered it over her hair. "I think I might pass on a repeat tonight."

"Kinda figured. Look, about last night..."

"It was kinda my idea."

He shook his head. "I meant the bit before the amazing sex. I was going to say Ryder killed him. He kinda did, but Ryder knew you didn't have the story, and he was worried you'd freak out and think he'd murdered someone."

"Oh."

"Yeah." He moved closer. "And I also remember how I felt the next morning. Brook, my brother and I... we weren't just sold to men. Women paid, too. We, um, performed together for them."

Her head snapped up. "And you still, um, like with me?"

"Fuck together, yeah." He nodded, making it clear he knew what she meant. "Our shrink said that fetishes form when we're still just kids, and um, that's kinda stuck with us. It's..."

"Safer," she finished, guessing where he was going.

"Yeah, I guess. Look, I just want that out there. I want to make it clear that we're not going to change. We're pretty fucked up, and we've never done anything like this before, but I like it. I like this so much, and I don't want you to go, but I get it if you do."

She stepped around him to find the water. "Well, I'm kinda not ready to go either. I kinda like this thing we're doing, and I don't just mean the sex. I mean the rest of it, too. I like the jokes and the way you both make me feel like *I* am not a screw up. I like the sex part too. A lot, in all honesty, but the rest of it's actually better."

"Good." His hands found her waist. "Because I really like you. If my brother dumps you, I'm keeping you for myself."

"Nope." She smiled and leaned into him. "It's a packaged deal, Mr. Collins. I demand both."

"God, you're perfect."

Not caring about the water pouring over her, he leaned in, pressing his mouth to hers. For just a moment, she thought that one kiss was about to lead to a whole lot more, but he stepped back too soon. Even though there was a smile on his face, she still groaned with disappointment.

"Next time," he promised. "Gotta let you recover for what I have planned later." Then he reached for the door.

"What's that?" she asked before he could step out.

Hunter reached over for a towel. As he wrapped it around his waist, he smiled, looking almost shy. "Convincing you to spend the night with just me."

"It's a date," she promised.

Then he grabbed another towel, holding it up for her. "Pretty sure you're almost done?"

"I need one for my hair, you know."

"Right." For a moment, he stepped out of sight, then was back with a second towel. "Am I perfect again?"

She turned off the water. "Close enough. I think I'll keep ya."

～

*O*nce she was dry and dressed, Brook decided to get back to work. The twins had been doing half her chores lately, and she was ready to feel useful. Letting the guys know she was headed to the kennel, she headed out the back, not waiting for their reply. One of them had taken Amelia out that morning, and Rosa had to be lonely.

Unfortunately, when she got to the barn, the mastiff wouldn't come in. Brook had to go into her kennel and duck through the half-door to find the big girl in her run. Rosa was on her hind legs, her feet on the chain link fence at the back, and staring intently at the fence line. Brook looked, wondering what the dog saw, but there was nothing. Thankfully, as soon as she touched the big girl,

Rosa forgot all about whatever she wanted to chase and rushed in for her breakfast.

Almost an hour later, the kennels were clean, the dogs were fat and happy, and Brook was still mostly clean. Then again, she'd been picking up crap for most of her life. She had to be an expert by now. Making an impulsive decision, she took Rosa out to the fenced-in dog yard, then went back for her puppy. Amelia was thrilled, hopping around excitedly enough that Brook just picked the little girl up, hooked the leash to her collar, then decided it would be easier to carry her back to the house.

She'd just closed the door behind her when Rosa blew up, growling like she was about to kill something. Remembering that the mastiff wasn't a fan of cats, Brook hurried around the corner, hoping she wasn't about to see some stray torn to pieces. Instead, she followed Rosa's attention to find a woman pointing a camera her way. Brook immediately stepped back.

"Hey, Rose?" the woman yelled at her.

Brook's heart stopped. This had to be one of Owen's private investigators, or maybe one of their flunkies. That meant he knew where they were. If he knew the dog's name, then they'd been watching her for too long. It meant Owen knew where she was, or would any second now.

"How did you find me?" she squeaked.

The woman smiled as she took another picture. "Wasn't hard."

That was when Ryder stepped outside. The back door slammed, and he stormed over, aiming right for the woman. "Get the fuck out of here," he yelled. "I've already called the cops and you're trespassing."

The woman yelped before she started hurrying away.

She wasn't the athletic type, and Ryder could've caught her if he wanted, but he didn't try. Instead, he turned back for Brook, hurrying over to check on her.

"What did she say?"

"She yelled at Rosa, and she knew the dog's name!" Brook couldn't quite find her breath. She also couldn't make her feet move. All she could do was clutch desperately at Amelia. "He knows where I am!"

"Wait." Ryder's hands found her upper arms, and he forced Brook to look at him. "She said Rosa?"

"She said something like, 'Hi, Rosa,' I think."

"Or did she say Rose?"

Brook thought back over it, the words replaying in her mind as her heart remembered how to beat. "I think she said Rose." As the words came out of her mouth, she realized the stranger hadn't been talking to the dog at all. "Fuck! Fuck, fuck, fuck!"

"What?" Ryder insisted.

"She said, 'Hey, Rose," and I asked how she found me."

Thankfully, Ryder didn't look upset at all. Nope, he was grinning at her like she'd just done some amazing trick. "Rose Solace. She was looking for me, not you. Thanks for covering."

Brook groaned and turned for the house. "Not funny."

"Kinda is."

"Ryder, I was freaking out. I thought Owen had found me."

"Yeah," he admitted as he moved beside her. "I kinda did too, so the whole Rose thing is a whole lot easier to deal with. Besides, who will she tell?"

"And how did she find you?" Brook insisted. "How could anyone find Rose *here*, of all places?"

The words came out just as they made it inside, and

KITTY COX

Hunter was almost to the door like he'd been headed out. Seeing them, he let out a heavy sigh, grabbed the puppy from Brook's arms, set her on the ground, then turned to smother Brook in a massive hug.

"I heard yelling, looked out, and swore I saw someone by the fence."

"You did," she mumbled against his chest. When he pulled back, she told the story all over again.

Hunter just thrust a hand out to his brother. "Pay up."

"What?" Brook asked, completely lost.

Ryder slapped his twin's hand away. "I bet him that no one would put the pieces together. We've used street names from around here, but we put them all in London or Coventry. We've even put a book in the same town, except in Europe."

"But how *this* house?" Brook insisted.

Hunter gestured at the building around them. "Stone farmhouse? Yeah, we use a few of those. It's the only one on the street. I mean, someone would have to be pretty intense to hunt down all the leads, but I told Ryder we should use random names instead of the ones from around us. He said we should write what we know."

"And she was probably a fifty-year-old housewife," Ryder told him. "Pretty sure I could take her."

"So..." Brook looked back and forth between the two of them. "You're not worried about this? You've spent how many years trying to keep it a secret, and now that you've been caught, you don't care?"

Hunter winked at her. "We've been caught before. Had someone waiting for us at the publishing house when we went in to sign a contract. First time with that one, and they'd made a big media splash about how Rose Solace would be signing with them on whatever date it was.

Anyway, some teenaged girl was there with a notebook begging everyone to sign it, hoping to figure out who was Rose."

"She yelled it at us, and we both looked," Ryder continued. "So she was convinced it was us. I mean, she was right, but we told her our sister's name was Rose, and it never went anywhere. Told her we just worked there."

"Which we kinda did, or were about to," Hunter joked.

"Yeah," Brook insisted, "but I just asked her how she found me."

"Mhm, and who is she going to tell? Her Facebook friends? They'll think she's crazy. Some tabloid? Yeah. The house is owned by two men. When someone comes asking, we'll just tell them you're Ryder's girlfriend who spent the night. It won't last more than a day."

Brook looked between both of them. "So I didn't just screw this up?"

"No more than we already have," Ryder promised.

"Besides," Hunter said, "what's the worst they can do? Assume *you* are Rose Solace? Never mind that you didn't live here just a few weeks ago. I think we're ok on this one."

Finally, Brook could relax. She'd been waiting for the other shoe to drop, and for a moment, she was sure that had been it. Either Owen had found her or she'd destroyed the best thing she'd ever had in her life. The strangest thing was that Owen finding her wasn't the part that scared her the worst.

She'd face down her husband a thousand times if that was what it took to keep these two.

CHAPTER THIRTY-SIX

That evening, Brook was doing dishes when a pair of strong hands landed on either side of her hips, pinning her against the counter. Lips caressed the back of her neck, and she knew it was Ryder. That was his thing, and it made her smile.

"I guess that means you finished the scene, Ryder?" she asked without turning her head.

He leaned closer. "Lucky guess."

"Nope. Face it, I just know you and how you like to be behind me." Finally she glanced back at him. "And I'm ok with that."

"Yeah?" His hands moved to her hips, easily finding the waist of her shorts. "How ok with it are you?"

Brook tilted her hips back. "I take it you've been writing sex scenes?" Her ass found something very hard and solid waiting behind her to grind against.

Ryder sucked in a breath. "And now you're just teasing me."

"Were you?" she insisted, grinding against him a little harder.

He grabbed her hips to stop her movement. "Yes! And it was a really good one."

"Tell me," she said as she slid against him one more time.

"Fuck," he groaned as his fingers clamped down on her. "Do that again, and I'm taking you right here."

"Oh, but I might break the plate." She tossed her best sweet and innocent look at him. "Not my fault you're crowding me."

"No?" One tug moved her shorts down enough for his hand to move over her ass. "Too bad for you I can buy more plates."

Then his hand slipped between her legs, not stopping until he found the hard little knot. He pressed and she forgot all about the dishes. As his finger swirled around her clit, all Brook could think about was staying on her feet.

"Dishes," he reminded her.

"Ry -" She sucked in a breath when he tormented her again.

"That's my girl," he rumbled beside her ear. "Just stand there, because you started this, so now you have to take it."

His hand slid inside her shirt, moving from the waist up until he reached her bra. Pulling down one of the cups, he gave himself access to her breast, but his other hand was keeping her distracted. He stroked, swirled, and pressed, moving with her as her hips twitched, using his body to hold her in place. Just when she couldn't imagine anything better, his fingers found her nipple.

Pinned between Ryder, the counter, and his hands, all she could do was lean her head back and enjoy this. Ryder's shoulder was right there, but he didn't kiss her.

No, he watched her, his eyes drinking in every breath she panted and every moan that slipped through her lips. Like this, she felt like some damsel from his stories. The kind of woman a man couldn't resist. She felt beautiful, desired, and oh so good.

"Ryder," she begged. "Please?"

"What do you want, Brook?"

"You!"

She expected him to smile, but he was too turned on for that. The heat in his eyes was intense, almost enough to hide the darkness, but that would never go away. She also loved it. It was a part of him, and she wouldn't want him any other way. Unfortunately, her words had him pulling his hands away.

"I want to see you this time," he said softly. "Your eyes holding mine."

She nodded, turning to face him. "Just us?"

Ryder stepped back. "Yeah. And I've already abused you enough. I'm definitely not going to crush you into that counter. Come with me, Brook." He reached out his hand, begging for hers.

She didn't hesitate. The moment her hand touched his, their fingers laced together and he started walking. He wasn't going to the bedroom, though. That was too far away, especially now that he had her more than ready to go. Instead, he went to the living room, stopping the moment they were inside to peel off her shirt.

"I am going to have you," he promised. "Not your body, Brook. You."

She looked up to meet his chocolatey gaze. "You already do."

His hands stalled as he reached for the clasp of her bra, trapping her in his arms. "Are you sure?"

"Yeah. You're my hero."

"No, I'm not. I'll never be a hero."

She just grabbed for his shirt. "You're mine, and I intend to enjoy every second I get with you."

His answer didn't come with words. It was his mouth claiming hers, hard. His teeth teased her lip, and when she gasped, his tongue stole the chance. Slowly, while his hands peeled her clothes away, Ryder distracted her with his mouth. Her own hands were just as demanding, making hasty work of his jeans. She barely had them open before Ryder pushed her shorts the rest of the way down her ass, leaving her naked before him.

"You're fucking gorgeous," he growled as he yanked his shirt over his head. "And you're mine."

"Both of yours," she corrected.

That got her a devilish smile. "Exactly." His arm found her back.

Together, they tumbled onto the closest sofa. One of his legs dangled off the side, and he used it for leverage. His other knee pressed under her thigh, spreading her as he leaned just a little closer. The whole time, Brook held his eyes, fighting the urge to close her lids as he slid deep inside her body.

"Look at me," Ryder insisted.

She tried. She tried so hard, but her body demanded her attention. The angle was just right, hitting that sweet spot inside her, and he knew it. Ryder pressed just a little deeper, making her hold him even tighter. Her nails bit into the muscles on his arm, but he didn't care. He wanted her, just like this, and she could see it on his face.

This was passion. It was desire. As he rode her body, wringing every sensation possible from her, she knew this was the type of contact she'd always wanted. It was that elusive thing she'd spent so long searching for. It also felt really good, but every time her lids grew heavy, Ryder demanded she keep looking at him.

Watching his face, seeing the look in his eyes as he thrust, over and over, was the most intimate thing she could imagine. This wasn't just sex. It was more, a connection she couldn't even begin to describe. She felt open, vulnerable, like he could see straight through her, and she loved it. She wanted it.

This was nothing more than two people making love in the middle of their home. It wasn't the kind of thing that would end up in their book, but she didn't care. It was him and her. Just them, and this was ok. For this one moment, she had him all to herself, and it felt so damned good. It felt real. It felt like her entire body couldn't take anymore.

Her legs tightened on his back and her eyes closed when the climax hit. She didn't scream, she just gasped his name, but it was enough. Her body exploded, every inch of her on fire for this one man, and he knew. As she clamped down on him, he buried himself as deep as he could with a groan, and his body sagged against her with one last shudder. For a moment, they both struggled to just breathe.

"Brook?" he asked, lifting only enough to see her face.

She reached between them to press her palm against his cheek. "You are my hero, Ryder. Even if your armor is the tarnished kind. It looks better on you."

～

That night, it was Hunter who went out to help her with the dogs. His excitement was her first hint. The second were the looks he kept giving her while he cleaned the kennels. No one found dog shit that sexy, but somehow he made her feel like the mess around her didn't matter. Then, he did the most surprising thing of all.

"What do you think about letting Rosa sleep inside?" he asked.

She looked over at the monstrous mutt. "Pretty sure we don't have a kennel that big."

Hunter shrugged. "What's the worst she can do?"

"Eat a couch!" Brook shot back. "Hunter, she's a bit destructive."

"Yeah..." He reached down to pet the mastiff's head. "But she has to learn some time, right? I mean, if she eats the living room, you'll have to go shopping with me, but I'm ok with it."

Every fiber in her body wanted to protest. Years of listening to her husband had ingrained in her that the possessions were more important than the pets, but the twins didn't agree. They hoarded their money in so many ways, except when it came to the dogs. For them, the Collins brothers knew no bounds.

Slowly, Brook nodded. "We can lock her in my room, though, ok?"

He lifted his eyes, those dark lashes making his gaze look sultry. "Ryder's writing all night."

Her heart began to beat just a little faster. The question was there, but he'd left it open enough that she wouldn't have to work to back out. Too bad for him, Brook had no interest in sleeping alone. Not anymore.

"So does that mean you're going to spend the night with me and the girls?"

He didn't look away. "You can say no. You know that, right?"

"I actually think I just invited you." Then she chuckled

and leaned forward to press her head against the chain link between them. "It's still a little weird, you know?"

"Trust me, I do."

"Yeah," she continued, "but I like this. Sometimes I feel like I should be guilty, or I have these moments where I get worried that I've crossed a line -"

"Like when you fucked Ryder on the couch earlier?" He smiled to show he wasn't upset.

But Brook thrust her arm out. "Exactly! I'm cheating, right? That's supposed to be bad, and yet you knew. I figured you did, because sounds carry well enough in this house, but still."

"I knew because he told me. He said the scene was hot and that he was going to check if you were busy." Hunter looked down at Rosa beside him. "I also happen to know that he's never done that before. He's never *wanted* to spend time alone with a woman."

"Oh."

Hunter nodded. "Brook, we have issues."

"So do I," she countered.

"No, just..." He glanced up. "Just listen for a second. We have issues. We always have, and probably always will. The things we lived through aren't something we'll ever get over. We've learned how to manage it, and how to accept that this is our life, but we're not going to change. We're not going to suddenly get tired of this. We most definitely aren't about to have a problem with finding a woman who gives a shit about it. And you do. You aren't just in this for the kink. I mean, look at last night!"

She winced at those words. "I shouldn't have pushed. I'm so sorry. It wasn't my place."

"It *is* your place. I want it to be your place, and you pushed when you had to. You made it clear what you needed - and I happen to like that. I need someone who isn't going to let me run all over her, push her around, and try to mold her into some shallow character for me to use and forget. I need you, Brook. So does my brother. The problem is that this is moving so fast. We haven't even taken you out, but you live with us. I just..."

"What?" she asked, terrified of the answer.

"You deserve so much more."

"What?!" She flipped the latch on the gate and stepped in beside him. "Hunter, fuck that. You're honest with me, and I know exactly how hard that is. You both spoil me, you've taken care of me, and you've stood up for me. What more do I need?"

He turned to face her. "To be romanced, seduced, and pampered. You deserve to go out to dinner or a movie. You deserve to call your mother, giddy to tell her about your boyfriend - not try to hide whatever this is. You deserve to have a man you can be proud of."

"I do." She stepped into him. "I have two of them, and my mother spent my childhood teaching me to be Owen's wife. My father made sure I never wanted to rise too high. Fuck them. You two? You accept me just as I am, screwed up marriage and all."

His hand slowly moved to her back, holding her against him. "You know, I've never done this before. Not the sex. I mean this. The talking. The laying it out there. I've never before met a woman who makes me feel so fucking safe with her."

She nodded, feeling the sting in her eyes that meant tears were threatening. "I'm going to take care of you. Both of you. I may not be able to fight off the bad guys, but I like this. I like feeling..." She let that trail off, unable to find the right word.

"Powerful," he offered.

She shook her head. "Important. Not in the grand scheme of things, but to you. You make me feel like you actually want *me*. Not just a woman, not some hole to fuck, but me."

"More than you can ever guess."

There, in the kennel, with Rosa panting beside him, Brook couldn't think of anything else to do. She reached up, pressing her mouth to his, and her arms followed. He didn't care that she was covered in filth. She didn't care that his pants were wet on one side. She just had to touch him, to know that this impossibly wonderful man was real - and hers.

Hunter's arms tensed just before he lifted, then he turned her to the wall. Her back hit and she gasped, which bared her throat. Held there, she wrapped her legs around his waist as his mouth found her neck. She moaned, the sound soft and delicate. Behind Hunter, the dog sighed in annoyance and flopped down on the concrete.

Brook giggled at that, but Hunter didn't stop. His lips kissed a line up to her mouth. With the wall supporting her, one of his hands moved to close on her breast, kneading it until her nipple grew hard. Then his palm slid across it, sending sparks through her spine. She tensed her legs, pulling him closer until she could feel his hardness pressing right into her.

"I want you," she panted. "I want you so bad, Hunter."

"Fuck," he growled, lowering her to the ground. "This is why I voted for dresses."

Too bad for him, Brook had other ideas. With one hand, she pushed at her shorts while she turned to face the wall. "Please?" she asked, daring to look back at him.

Hunter was busy freeing himself from his jeans. He

knew what she wanted and wasn't about to refuse. Brook just hoped her asking would be enough. She couldn't stop thinking about what he'd said last night and how he didn't enjoy it when he had to start, but that was ok. She had no problem with demanding, and from the look of his cock, it seemed Hunter liked that about her.

"This," he warned as he grabbed her hip and pulled it into position, "was not what I meant when I said a date."

"I like to skip ahead." Then she pressed back, feeling him.

It wasn't perfect. They were both half-dressed and clumsy, but she needed this. She needed him. Seeing his desperation to have her erased all of her worries from the night before. Maybe it was foolish, but she did want this to work, and as Hunter pressed against her, she decided she would do anything to make that happen.

Brook shifted back, angling her hips to slide her body onto him, and Hunter gasped. His hands clenched on her hips, but she was doing this. Leaning forward, she slowly gave him up just to thrust back onto him, handling everything. He moved an arm to her waist to hold on but made no move to take over. His other hand reached out for the wall, keeping them steady.

Then Brook began to writhe. He wasn't stopping her, so she fucked him. All he had to do was stand there and take it. She stopped caring how she looked or sounded. All that mattered was getting more, and she was willing to wring it out of his body if she had to. Bucking against him, she set the pace and handled the depth. It was so good. He understood, bending his knees just a bit more for a better angle, and Brook cried out at how good it was.

But the best part of all was that it was him. This was Hunter, and he was letting her take control. Something about that made this even better. Neither of them worried about the scripted kisses or the complicated positions. They just fucked in a purely carnal way, and it was honest. It was frantic. It was also fast.

Before she was ready, the pressure was building, but that wasn't just her. Deep inside her body, she could feel her man swelling, and his groans proved he was struggling to hold on. She just thrust faster, wanting him to come first this time, but she was too close. It was always her. They always made sure it was her, but she wanted to feel him lose control - and it was happening.

Then, just when she thought she couldn't take any more, he came. Hunter growled her name and his arm clamped around her belly. She felt him plunge even deeper, and her body loved it. As he pulsed, she stroked him again and again until her own body shattered around him.

Her knees threatened to buckle, but her man was there. His face was pressed against the back of her neck as she gasped his name, and he was breathing so hard. With an exhausted giggle, she leaned back, reaching for his neck.

"Yeah," she gasped, enjoying the feel of him with her. "That happened."

"Oh yeah, it did," he agreed before slipping out of her body.

She tugged her shorts back into place and turned to see him. "Hunter?"

"Mm?"

"I still want you to spend the night, ok?"

His only answer was to step closer and kiss her, but that was more than enough. It proved this crazy thing was really working.

CHAPTER THIRTY-SEVEN

*T*hat was how they spent the next few days. Bringing Rosa inside was just as bad of an idea as Brook had thought, but most of the damage was to shoes and toys. Granted, that meant another trip to the Pet Palace. This time, she went with Ryder, because Hunter had a doctor's appointment. If anything, the younger brother was worse about spending money than the older. They didn't fill just one cart, but two and a half.

Still, it was worth it when the big girl finally decided that the bed was where she belonged. When Brook woke up to find Hunter spooning the almost two-hundred pound dog, she knew this was the life she'd always wanted. Even better, having Rosa in the house made Amelia even more confident.

Unfortunately, it wasn't all playing with puppies and screwing her boyfriends. Oh, there was plenty of that, but Hunter wouldn't let Brook get out of talking to an attorney. Thankfully, he already had one in mind. After a short phone consultation, a woman named Cessily Blackburn agreed to make a house call. She wouldn't be in the area for a couple more weeks, but she'd go ahead and file the restraining order. When it came time to pay, she just told Brook to pass the phone to Hunter.

And just like that, Brook was on her way to being a single woman. Well, divorced, but still. The only downside was that the courthouse liked to take their time about things, so Cessily warned her that Brook should stay close to home until all of the paperwork was finalized. Considering that home meant more time with the Collins brothers, Brook wasn't about to complain.

It was just after noon the next Monday when all three of their phones went off at the same time. Brook pushed herself off the couch, intending to gets hers from the other room but Hunter waved her down. His brow was furrowed as he looked at the screen, but clearly they'd all gotten the same message.

"Ali's on her way over," he said.

Ryder nodded. "ETA ten minutes. She said to get our dicks out of you and get dressed because it's important."

Brook chuckled. "Yeah, sounds like her."

"Baby stuff?" Ryder asked his brother.

Hunter shrugged. "Man, I don't know. She never does this. She usually emails so it'll go on the calendar."

Brook could only think of one thing, and it made her stomach clench. "What if your blood tests came back with a problem?"

"It was just STDs," Ryder reminded her.

Brook gestured at him, proving that was her point.

Hunter slowly turned his chair to face her. "Unless there's something you need to tell us, I'm pretty sure that's not it. We both were checked like six months ago. Clean. Kinda haven't seen anyone since except you."

"I just had mine when I left Owen," she insisted.

Hunter nodded, watching her face intently. "Then it's not that. Now, we could be shooting blanks."

"True," Ryder agreed. "Not like we've ever had a kid before."

Brook was starting to feel a little better about it when a decadent chime rang through the house. It was so unexpected that she flinched in place, making Hunter grin at her. Ryder, however, just yelled for Ali to come in. Evidently, that was their doorbell.

"Where are you?" Ali asked from the other side of the house.

"Study!" all three of them called back.

Her shoes clicked on the floor as she hurried back. The dogs heard her, and all four of them went to greet their guest, but Ali didn't stop to spoil them. That said more than anything else, until she rounded the corner. From the look on her face, whatever it was she needed to talk about was bad.

"What's wrong?" Brook asked. "Is it about the baby?"

"God, I wish," Ali said as she dropped her purse in the corner and moved to claim the other end of the sofa. "Guys, I just got three calls from two major news outlets and one literary magazine wanting to know, since your identity has been discovered, if you'd be willing to give an interview."

"What?" the twins asked, both leaning forward in shock.

Ali nodded. "So I got online and started digging. The problem was that it didn't take long. There's a picture out there on the Romance Readers Forums of Rose Solace." She turned to Brook and help up her phone. There was a very clear image on it. "And it's you."

It was her. Brook was standing beside the dog barn,

holding Amelia tightly, and looking right into the camera. At the edge of the picture, Rosa was bouncing against the fence in mid-bark. In other words, Brook knew exactly when that picture had been taken.

"Fuck," she hissed.

"Yeah, and it gets worse. That picture's been tweeted and retweeted a few thousand times. There's more in the series, but they're all a few seconds apart. Oh, and it's on Facebook, too. At least three different pages have it right up for public consumption, and I can only guess how many groups. We need a plan, because this time, we can't just ignore it."

"But..." Brook couldn't quite wrap her mind around any of this. "That's me! I'm not an author."

"No, but the initial post was on a thread where people were speculating on this mystery author and posting all sorts of hints. Someone said this was the only town they could find with all of that in the same place." Ali tilted her head, admitting she knew it was true. "And according to whoever took the picture, a..." She glanced at her phone. "Hot4Too, it seems. He or she -"

"She," Brook told her. "The person who took the picture was a woman."

"Well, then *she* says that you confirmed you are Rose. Says she called out your name and you asked how she found you?"

"I thought it was someone Owen sent." Brook groaned and flopped back against the chair. "Can't we just tell them that?"

The look Ali gave her said Brook was an idiot. "Yeah, because some random stranger just happens to be friends with the literary agent of this famous mystery author, and that same random chick just happens to swear it's not her. Oh, that doesn't look hinkey at *all*."

"But it's true!" Brook insisted.

"Brook," Hunter sighed. "It's ok. Ali, what's the plan?"

Alison dimmed the screen of her phone and set it beside her as she turned to face the guys. "The way I see it, we have three options. First, you can ignore it and hope it goes away. It probably won't, and I'm willing to bet that it will only grow until it's a monster none of us can tame. Second, you can come clean and admit that you're men writing together under a pseudonym."

"No," Ryder said.

Ali sighed, proving just how stressed she was about this. "Guys, you've already proven yourselves. No one suspects that you aren't a woman, and there aren't any complaints about misogyny in your books. I really think that -"

"No." This time it was Hunter, and he didn't give her the chance to finish. "Because if we do that, the story won't be about our books. It will be about our childhood."

Ali nodded. "You need to think about it, guys. I can spin that. This is what I do, and I have access to some of the best publicity people in the country. We can take over this narrative and make it useful. We can turn your story into some good."

Brook just reached over and touched Alison's leg. "Could you do it? Could you stand up in front of the entire world and tell everyone about crying in bed because you thought you were broken? Could you look professional and respectable as you listed off the *things* people called you in college? And when someone sold a story about you getting fucked by a man while going down on some girl, could you take it with a smile, knowing that idiot had just gotten rich on your life?"

Alison shook her head. "No. I'd end up screaming at the cameras and destroying my career."

Brook just tipped her head at the guys. "And you think they'd be any better?"

Both of the twins were watching her. Their faces were perfect masks, but they weren't trying to stop her. More than anything else, it proved they trusted her, and this was her mistake to clean up. She'd been the one to say the wrong thing, and they should be livid. They should be throwing her out to fend for herself. They weren't, and that felt oddly good.

"Then we need to consider the third option," Ali said softly. "And it's a bad idea. I can't actually condone this, because I can find a million reasons why we shouldn't even consider it, but it's up to you two." Her eyes moved to the twins. "When I took Brook out to dinner after she moved in? Well, she joked about being Rose so she could make herself useful. If you trust her with your entire collection, you could hire her to be the face of Rose Solace."

"I didn't..." Brook said. "Ali, it was a pipe dream. I wasn't being serious! And that was before I was *dating* them."

"Brook," Hunter said softly.

She just shook her head as she pushed to her feet. "I can't do that to them. I mean, these books aren't going away, and that's not a commitment I can exactly back out of."

"I know," Ali agreed, "but it's the only other option I can think of. Why don't you go take the dogs in the other room and let me talk this over with them, ok?"

"Yeah," she agreed before calling Rosa to follow her. She didn't make it far.

"Just stop," Ryder said, surging out of his chair. "Brook, sit down. Ali, shut up for a minute. Hunter?"

"Nah, I'm with ya," his brother agreed. "Let it play out, and if it goes bad, say she was a fraud. We'd have to set a few things up, but I'm willing to risk it. Worst case, we just change pseudonyms, right?"

"Yeah. We've got enough money stashed that we can try this." Ryder nodded. "I'm down. I mean, she already knows all our deep dark, so why not? If she wanted to, she could sell that, so there's no reason not to. Besides, it's some serious publicity."

"Does it itch at all?" Hunter asked.

Ryder shook his head. "Nah. It's like silk. Feels good."

Ali just raised her hand. "And can one of you translate that for us non-twins in the room?"

Ryder actually chuckled, flashing Brook a smile so calm she wanted to see it on him every day. "We're going with Brook. She's got enough dirt on us already that she could just sell the story if she wanted to."

"And," Hunter added, "we're not exactly worried about some crazy breakup. I have a feeling that the same rules apply with this as with her divorce. The best friend of our best friend. We're all going to be tied together no matter what."

"And we trust her," Ryder said softly, his eyes on Brook. "We haven't told you everything, but it's more than we've said to anyone else, and you didn't even tell Ali."

She nodded. "There are some lines that should never be crossed. I think most women understand that, but not a lot of men have had to face it." Without looking, she ran her fingers through Rosa's hair, the feeling of the dog beside her like an anchor. "Guys, this is a bad idea. We've only been together a few weeks."

With a smile, Ali relaxed into the chair. "So we test it out. Let's give it a trial run. If this changes things with you three, we'll call you a fraud, say you had a mental break after the abuse your husband inflicted, and it'll be out of the news in a few days. Granted, it will suck for you, Brook, but then there's the upside. If it works?"

Hunter and Ryder shared a look. "If it works," Hunter said, "this will be the biggest break of our careers."

"Yeah." Alison was smiling. "So think about it. I'm putting off the journalists by saying I have to get in touch with you, and you're a very reclusive author. We've got time. Think it over, but if you want to do this, she needs to know every single book inside and out."

"I can do it," Brook promised.

"*Think* about it," Ali insisted.

Brook scoffed. "Oh, like you and Leah thought about that baby thing?"

"Exactly! Because for the last three years, we've been trying to figure out how to get a child, and we always kept saying we wanted a sperm donor half as good as our guys. So yes, Brook, just like that. We thought about it for *years*. You've been fucking them for a couple of weeks."

"Sometimes," Ryder said soft enough to make everyone in the room fall silent, "we meet someone and we just know it's right. Just like we bump into a stranger and know they're dangerous, it works the other way, too. I knew she was important when she ran into me at the shelter that first day. I just never imagined how important."

"He said she was perfect," Hunter agreed. "He could describe everything about how she looked, but when I asked about her, all he could say to make me understand, was that he could talk to her. That he trusted her. And I do too."

"Guys," Brook insisted.

Hunter shook his head. "I told you, Brook. I need you. We need you. It took one day to break us. One single day, and we both knew it without a doubt. Why isn't two weeks enough for us to be sure of this?"

"Because you barely know me," she insisted. "What if I go crazy?"

"Are you?" Hunter asked with a devious smile.

She scoffed. "Not intentionally!"

"Exactly. And I do know you. I know that you giggle when the dogs lick your face. I know that you hum as you clean the house. I know the way you sound, taste, and feel. I also know that you may get tired of dating us, but you'd still be the *perfect* person for this job. I know you, Brook, and I'm not worried at all."

With a heavy sigh, she dropped back onto the sofa. Rosa was right there, shoving her head in her person's lap to reassure her, and Amelia jumped onto the couch to press into her side. The problem was that she had nothing at all to say to that. Brook knew this was a huge risk for the guys. To her, it wouldn't make a lot of difference, but this wasn't her hard work they were talking about. It was theirs, and they were trusting it all to her.

Beside her, Alison nodded to herself before pushing to her feet. "Ok," she said. "I'll get some contracts and a non-disclosure agreement made up. I won't give it to you until the weekend, though. Brook, start reading, and fast. Boys? *Think* about this. Nothing is set in stone, and my best friend won't care if we change the plan. I'll even break it to her myself. Am I clear?"

"We're not changing our minds," Ryder promised, "but we understand. Sorry, Ali, but family trusts each other."

She walked over to him and wrapped her arms around his waist. "I just don't want this to screw up all three of you finally being happy. Let me be the bad guy, ok? It's my job."

"And Brook's is to take care of us," Hunter told her, stepping in to squish Alison between them. "It's going to be fine. We'll make sure of it."

CHAPTER THIRTY-EIGHT

*A*fter that, Brook got to work. Granted, it didn't feel like real work, because all she had to do was read steamy book after steamy book. Still, she had to pay attention. A lot of it, and to even the most insignificant things. That made her read slower, but it also let her appreciate the twins' writing skills a little more.

All of the details mattered. Whether that was the weather on a certain day or the color of a girl's dress, every single scene was set up to convey an emotion - and it worked. The beauty of their writing was in the things they didn't need to say because the setting showed it perfectly. Then there were the women.

Each and every girl she read could've been her. Sure, some were blonde and some had raven hair, but she was always sensible, sensitive, and a little bit wild underneath. Even more important, every story had a dog - sometimes more than one - and they were usually important to how things worked out in the end.

Three days after they hatched this plan, she was on

their seventh book. The day was too nice to lock herself inside, so Brook took the dogs outside to play. Armed with a canvas lawn chair and a bucket of toys, she was determined to enjoy the beautiful weather and still keep her promise. The dogs, however, didn't agree.

Rosa was adamant that her toys belonged in Brook's lap. Amelia was busy chasing Einstein, who bayed at the top of his lungs every time the puppy bit him. Sherlock? He was lying beside her, panting heavily. Every time Brook turned a page, she threw one of the toys, which sent Rosa scurrying. That made Einstein want to beat her. Amelia took off after them, limping every so often to prove that her leg still wasn't perfectly healed.

"Hey?"

The word was too short and said from right behind her, giving Brook no hint which twin it was. With a sigh, she lowered her book and twisted - then froze. That was Ryder, and he didn't have a shirt on. Holy shit, did he look good like that. Like he was just about to walk over and make her beg for his attention like Josephine in this book she was reading.

Rein it in, she told herself before calling back, "Yeah?"

"They distracting you?" He tipped his head to the dogs.

She smiled. "Not as much as your lack of shirt."

That earned her a smile. Without looking, Ryder flicked open the latch on the gate and strode into the yard. The dogs immediately rushed over, thrilled to have a new play toy, but his eyes were on Brook. All over her, to be more precise.

"Don't even think it," she warned. "I have to finish this one and start the next before dinner."

"Think what?" he asked a little too innocently as he reached her side.

Brook groaned. "Ryder! You know I have to read these. Hell, it was your idea."

"Yeah, it was." He leaned over her chair to plant a quick kiss on her lips. "And we still have until the weekend to see if you feel confident enough to do this. You deserve a break."

"Which means you're horny, right?" She lifted a brow, making it clear she knew exactly how this worked.

He reached up to scratch at his hair. "Usually, but I honestly didn't come out to molest you this time. I was wondering if the mutts were in your way." Considering that all four of them were circling him like cats, it was a reasonable question. Just one problem.

"I happen to like those mutts, thank you very much, and what's with the shirt?"

He glanced down as if he'd just realized something. "What? I don't have a shirt!" She was just about to throw her book at him when Ryder grinned, proving he was giving her shit. "That's actually kinda why I'm out here. I spilled coffee on it, went to throw it in the wash, and saw you." Then he shrugged. "Didn't think you'd mind."

"Oh, trust me," she promised, "I don't."

But Ryder just bobbed his head. "Hey, um..." The look on his face was almost apologetic. "So this thing, I mean, with you being Rose? Um, well, she's kinda a big deal. Like, a lot of journalists have been trying to get us to talk to them. I mean her." He made a gesture as if wishing he could erase that. "You know what I mean."

"Yeah. I'd heard of Rose before I met you." She twisted so her legs were off the side and she could face him better.

He seemed nervous about something, and that was making her the same. "Why?"

Ryder sighed. "Let us be your bodyguards?"

Not where she'd expected this to go. "Uh, ok? You think I'm going to need bodyguards?"

"Yeah," Ryder mumbled as he lowered himself to the ground by her feet. "Brook, your husband will see this. If you do an interview, some screen grab of it will be put somewhere, and he *will* see it."

It felt like all of her internal organs were suddenly being crushed in a vice. She looked up and met his eyes. "Shit."

"Yeah. Hunter and I didn't think about it until today. That means there's a couple of problems."

"Yeah," she breathed. "Like him trying to take half."

Ryder waved that off. "Of all the things to worry about, that's not even on the list. I'm sure Cessily can come up with something, but -"

"How do you know her?" Brook interrupted. It suddenly seemed very important, mostly because this whole thing was going to be a serious strain on their relationship. "She acts like she's pretty close to you two."

Again, he sighed, but this time he was also rubbing at his face. "She handled our legal separation from the people who adopted us. We hadn't seen them since we were kids, but they could've tried to claim a slice of the fame, you know?" Then he chuckled. "And when that was done, we kinda, um..."

"Celebrated?" she asked.

Ryder shrugged. "Yeah. Cess was too busy to date, but she's a friend. I mean, the case took a while, so we got to know her, and yeah, it kinda went there."

"Cool." She couldn't think of anything better to say.

Oddly, Brook wasn't upset. She wasn't even jealous. Granted, she had no idea what Cessily looked like, but she was a smart, driven woman, and that seemed to be what the Collins brothers liked more than anything else. And it wasn't like Brook thought they were virgins when she'd met them. Mostly, she just liked how easily he admitted to having slept with the woman. There were no excuses - not really - but he didn't try to deny it, either. The way he said it felt kinda like he trusted her, and she liked that.

"I guess that means I don't have to hide this thing between us from her then, huh?" she asked.

The corner of his lip curled up. "Nope, she's already figured it out. Said it's about time we found a girl who isn't a closeted prude. She also told Hunter not to fuck it up because you seem nice. So I'm pretty sure she can figure out a way to deal with your husband trying to get his hands on our books."

"Does she know about those?"

"Yep." He glanced over to the dogs. "*Up Schidt Creek?* Yeah, um, she was kinda inspirational."

"And blonde," Brook realized, having finished that book the night before. "More interested in her own aspirations than spending time in a relationship?"

"Exactly." He chuckled. "Brook, seriously, it was a very long time ago. Your husband, on the other hand?"

"Owen," she reminded him. "And I prefer using his name to keep reminding myself that I was dumb enough to marry that man. Yes, Ryder, you two can play bodyguards. If for no other reason than it'll let you be close enough to help me with the book stuff!"

"Oh. I hadn't thought of that."

She winked playfully. "See, I'm inventive, too. Honestly, though, what can Owen do? I mean, except trying to force me to pay half of these book royalties I don't have?" Then she finally figured it out. "Ah, fuck. He can say I never wrote the books!"

"You can say you did, though. You can claim he wouldn't have approved, which is why you're just now coming forward. That your husband was abusive - which only helps your case against him - and that you were terrified he'd beat you if he found out because they're *naughty*."

"But the money?" she asked. "How do I even explain that away?"

Ryder leaned back on his hands, careful not to squish a dog. "You knew you'd had some best sellers, but you wrote because you loved the escape. Sitting at work, you could forget for a moment that another dog wouldn't find a home, or that at the end of the day you'd have to go back to the man who made you feel bad about yourself. So instead, you wrote, and you had your best friend from college put it someplace safe for when you retired. It was supposed to be just something for a rainy day, and you honestly had no idea about the money."

"Oh," she agreed. "That's good. But that won't stand up in court."

He waved her down. "Let Cessily worry about court. You worry about the interviews and just brace for Owen trying to grab his fifteen minutes of fame. He'll call up Entertainment Tonight or something and say it can't be you, so lay down all the foreshadowing first. Then, when you drop your story, it'll make so much sense that the public will gobble it up."

She leaned over her knees, a little too aware of how easily he was taking this. "Ryder, is that how it is for you?

Did you escape into the books, make a trust fund, and set yourself up for a fallback story?"

"Kinda. We didn't have the fallback story. That's just the basics of writing a book. The rest? Yeah, pretty much. Hunter and I were staying in this crappy apartment, working as stockers for this distribution center. It was a while ago. Anyway, yeah, we didn't realize how much we were making until Ali called and said the royalty payments were rejected because we'd capped out our IRA. We needed to open another."

"Whoa," Brook breathed. "That must've been nice."

He nodded. "And when she told us the publishing house was sitting on a check for a couple hundred grand, yeah, we quit. And then we started writing full time, which is nicer. See, that's the funny thing about the whole book industry. All of these overnight success stories? Everyone forgets that it takes about ten years to get there."

"Well, my way is a lot faster. I just jumped on some dicks and *bam,* I'm the face of Rose." She crooked her finger, encouraging him to scoot closer. "Are you two honestly ok with this idea, Ry?"

He moved close enough to grab her hands. "Yeah, we actually are."

"But what if we, I dunno - if this thing we're doing ends."

"Break up?" he asked. "Because yes, I think this is very much a girlfriend type of situation."

She groaned. "That sounds so high school."

"And yet it works. Look, if you dump us, then you do. We'll go find some slut to bang at a bar and then dream up another book so we can drown our sorrows. You'll find some respectable man, fall in love, and get married. I can't exactly see a way this works out where we can't get over the pain and figure out how to talk to you again. And, from everything I know about you, I can't see you turning down a damned good job just because your new boyfriend sucks in the sack."

She pretended to kick at his leg. "Asshole."

"It's true. One dick can't compete with two. But honestly, we're talking about two different hats. Rose and girlfriend. Sure, they're connected, but only in the most superficial way. You're still beautiful, intelligent, and would definitely get paid for doing all of these public appearances."

"Wait," Brook gasped. "What? Paid?"

"Jobs pay people, baby. Promoting an author is a job. Alison gets a cut of our royalties because of it. That's how the real world works, so yes, you'll get paid for having to stand in front of people or cameras and do things. Who knows, maybe you can even do one of those college graduation speech things. Tell all the aspiring youngsters to go forth and fuck while they still can."

"You," she hissed. "Ryder, you're so bad."

"Yeah, but I think you like it." He looked up, doing that thing where his lashes made his eyes look even more amazing. "This is going to work, Brook. It's going to be fine. All I ask is that you keep us close."

She leaned forward just a bit more. "Well, I figure a woman like Rose Solace would definitely have a pair of sexy men flanking her everywhere. Just do me one little favor?"

"Anything."

"Suits," she told him. "Matching."

A slow smile began to grow on his lips. "Sure, but I'm tying you up with my tie when we get home."

"Deal. I'm gonna be a better Rose than either of you could ever imagine."

"I dunno, we have some pretty vivid imaginations."

"On stage!" she hissed.

He just chuckled. "Ah, yeah, you're probably right about *that* part."

CHAPTER THIRTY-NINE

*L*uckily, Brook's attorney was able to make it into town before any decisions were final. It was Friday night, and the twins offered to make dinner while the ladies discussed the legalities of basically everything. That made Brook nervous enough. The idea of the Collins brothers putting on a show made her wonder who they were trying to impress.

It only got worse when Cessily finally showed up. Again, that overly pompous doorbell went off, but this time, Hunter hurried over to answer it. Brook leaned out of the formal dining room where she'd arranged all of her important paperwork in time to see a drop-dead gorgeous blonde waltz through the entry with a *very* friendly smile on her lips.

She wore a knee-length black skirt, a bright green, yellow, and white striped shirt, and a professional black suit jacket over it all, complete with a green pocket square in the pocket. Her heels were tall, making her legs look amazing. Everything about this woman screamed beautiful and powerful, and it was a little intimidating.

"Hunter!" she cooed before leaning in to kiss his cheek. "And where's your better half?"

"Cooking," he told her.

Cessily's brow furrowed. "I thought we were talking about her divorce."

He chuckled. "Ah, you mean *that* better half."

She grumbled and rolled her eyes. "Fair point. I was referring to Brook Sanders, my new client."

"Um, hi," Brook said as she stepped the rest of the way around the corner. "Cessily, I presume? Or is it Ms. Blackburn?"

"Cessily," she said, offering Brook her hand. "Wow, you are exactly their type." Then she looked at Hunter. "How the hell did you manage this?"

"Ryder, actually." He gestured toward the dining room. "And we're in the middle of dinner, if you'd like to stay?"

The smile she gave him spoke of many years together. "I never could turn down your cooking. Just don't hurry. There's a few things I need to talk to Miss Sanders about in private."

"Promise I'll knock first," Hunter teased before heading into the kitchen.

Brook just gestured a little farther down the hall to the main entrance to the dining room. "Brook's fine, and how long have you known them?"

"The twins? They were actually my first client." She smiled fondly as she pulled out a chair and set her briefcase on the table. "That case took almost three years, but they never doubted me. Probably because they couldn't afford to hire anyone else back then. Still, it's been almost fifteen years now."

Brook reclaimed her seat where she had all her documents laid out. "So, friends?"

Cessily flashed her a smile. "Full disclosure, I can't talk to you about the work I do for them without their consent. I also handle a little more than just family law. It happens to be something I'm passionate about, but I also practice general law, specialize in litigation, and have a pretty decent client base for corporate stuff. Now, on the phone, Ryder said you're about to become Rose and were worried?"

She nodded. "If my husband thinks I suddenly have millions of dollars from book royalties, he's going to demand them."

Cessily slid a paper over to her. "Then you're going to need to fill this out. And this..." a second paper moved closer, "is a non-disclosure agreement. It's basic stuff, but will work for now. I'll also want a copy of your contract with the twins and their agent, and we'll have the judge seal those records. Your husband's attorney will know, but your husband won't be able to get any of that in court. Once the judge sees that you've been hired to play the part of an author, and don't exactly have any royalties yourself, well, that whole problem will vanish."

"Just..." Brook snapped her fingers. "Like that?"

"What you're doing is not illegal. Your job requires you to keep the secret. The court cannot disclose that secret for you, and since this proves that you acknowledge you aren't actually the author, but only a person playing the public image of said author, yeah, poof."

That seemed way too easy to Brook. She was expecting some sort of legal nightmare and hoops to jump through. Granted, Owen would still try to bring it up and make an ordeal out of it, but this wasn't exactly the type of thing that had a jury. It was a divorce. Probably an ugly one, but still, just a divorce and division of assets.

"Are we getting the restraining order?" Brook asked.

"Mm." Cessily began digging a little deeper. "I have a report of animal abuse, domestic assault, and documentation to support an unreported claim of abuse when you moved out." She showed Brook a printed copy of that picture Ryder had taken with the bruise on her throat. "So, I'm pushing for a temporary restraining order until your court date, and have a request for a three-year one after that. We probably won't get it, but they usually give us either six months or a year. The judge will give you something. They always do."

"And that's it?" Brook asked. "Just wait for the right day, and then this is all over?"

"Not exactly." Cessily gestured to Brook's papers. "How much of that do you want to keep?"

"Nothing. I don't want *anything* of his."

"Not so fast." She offered a sympathetic smile. "Your husband is going to try to stick you with half the debt. I think we need to claim half the assets with the intention of giving them up if he agrees to let you walk away. Now, most women in your situation, I'd have different advice for, but you already have a place to stay, an income, and no need for a car or other expenses. That's a pretty big luxury."

"I know," Brook admitted. "They've taken good care of me."

"Sounds like you've done the same for them. Look, what you've been through is awful, and I'm not going to lie to you about it, but you were lucky. You got out fast. I was told he killed your dog, and I'm so sorry about that, but he didn't kill you. However, that doesn't mean he'll be happier once you're legally divorced. Some men become even more violent."

"Why?" Brook asked. "He got what he wanted!"

"No, honey, he didn't. What he wanted was a punching bag. He wanted someone to make him feel big and strong, to fall down every time he had a bad day, and to handle all the bullshit he thought was beneath him. You just took his toy away, and now there's a very good chance he's going to start acting like a three-year-old in the sandbox. There's going to be a tantrum. What I need you to do is let me handle it, ok?"

Brook nodded quickly, showing she had no problem with that.

"Good," Cessily said. "And since we're going to get to be very good friends, I want to make one thing clear. I am friends with your boyfriends, nothing more."

Brook could feel her cheeks getting warmer. "I didn't..."

"No, but I also didn't miss the look you gave me. My job is to notice things, Brook. I'm very good at it, so believe me when I tell you that Hunter and Ryder are *just* my friends. I happen to be married to my job, and I certainly don't have time for a boyfriend right now, let alone two of them." She leaned closer. "I also think you deserve them. I just hope you realize how lucky you are."

"I do," Brook admitted, feeling a little embarrassed about this whole talk. "Trust me, they're my heroes."

Cessily flashed her a confused look just as the doorbell rang again. Brook had no idea who it could be this time, but she didn't care. One of the guys would get it. What she wanted to know was why calling the twins her heroes shocked Cessily as much as it had.

"What?" she asked.

The pretty blonde attorney shook her head slightly. "This is really none of my business."

"I'd kinda like to know before I screw up their lives."

Glancing back to the door, Cessily sucked in a deep breath. "They're not heroes, Brook. They're not villains, either. Ryder said you used to work at an animal rescue, so think of them as pit bulls who've just been pulled out of the fighting ring. They're torn apart, bloody, and ready to kill. If you can make it through all of that, they'll be the most loyal companions ever, but you might get bit in order to get there." She lowered her voice at the sound of people talking in the other room. "Don't get bit. Trust them, but not blindly, ok? I love those guys. I really do, and I still don't want to see you having to start all over again."

Brook opened her mouth to insist that the guys would never hurt her, but that was when Ali walked into the room with Leah right behind her. Brook's best friend was holding up a handful of papers with a massive grin on her face, but she stopped as soon as she saw Cessily.

"Miss Blackburn?" Ali asked, proving they knew each other.

"Cessily," she said with a very professional smile. "And the two Mrs. Brewers. How have you been?"

"Good. Is there a problem?"

Brook spoke up. "My divorce."

"Oh!" Alison's smile returned immediately. "Well, good. Glad to see that's finally happening."

Ryder poked his head in from the other side, through the door that led to the kitchen. "Who's staying for dinner?"

Everyone looked around the room, a slight feeling of discomfort tangible in the air. With a groan, Ryder pushed the door the rest of the way open and stepped through. He didn't stop until he was behind Brook with his hands on her shoulders.

"Ali and Leah are here for contracts. Cessily is here for Brook's divorce. Brook is here because she lives here. Cess? If we feed you, will you glance over those contracts for Brook?" He looked at Alison. "No bitching. Don't care what your agency says."

"I'm not fucking my best friend over, Ryder," Alison shot back.

"You? No," he agreed. "Your company, however, is more interested in protecting us than her."

"Wait." Cessily looked between Alison and Brook. "Best friend?"

Brook dropped her elbows on the table and shoved her face into her hands, hoping to rub all of this away. "Ali and I were college roommates. I met Ryder when he did community service at the shelter where I used to work. I had no idea they knew each other because my husband basically isolated me."

"Ah." She reached out, clearly asking to see the contract. "And what are we agreeing to?"

"This is a temporary agreement," Alison said. "Says that Brook will represent the author known as Rose Solace and present herself as the creator of those works with no intention of compensation for the creation of the work. While on trial, she will be paid a flat fee for one performance, with the understanding that a second agreement would need to be negotiated for any subsequent appearances."

Cessily's brows went up. "And who set the price?"

Alison chuckled. "The twins."

"Yeah, no, this is fine," Cessily agreed, handing it back. "It's actually really good."

The guys were just making their way into the room as she said that, and Hunter smiled proudly before he began setting out plates in front of each woman. "Work off the table, ladies. This is a real dinner."

"And it's a celebration," Ryder told them. "Rose is about to go public, Brook is about to be single, and we have a girlfriend."

"Aww," Leah teased. "Well, I'll just add a little more to that. All the tests are good, with what you had before on file, so we're just waiting for my wife to ovulate. You could be baby daddies in as little as a month!"

Cessily's head whipped around to look at the guys. "And who wrote the contract for *that?*"

"No contract," Ryder said. "Because we're not parents, just sperm donors. We waived all rights."

"And if they sue you because the kid inherits something genetically?"

Ryder lifted a brow at her. "Lay off. It's fine. There's a standard agreement which covers that, and we have you to shut it down if anything gets stupid. Let us be happy, Cess. I know it's not your style, but people do it sometimes."

Her mouth opened, paused, snapped closed, then Cessily nodded her head. "Sorry, Ry. Just doing my job."

"I know, and thank you. Now stop." He held up a finger then headed back to the kitchen.

Hunter, however, was claiming the chair beside Cessily, leaving the one at the head of the table for Ryder. "So, I'm pretty convinced Brook has this whole thing down."

"Figured," Alison said. "She always was good at book reports in college. She even had this Fourteenth-Century French Literature class, and it was misery, but *she* of all people made an A."

"Oh my god," Brook gasped. "I'd forgotten all about that."

"Mhm." Alison paused when Ryder came back in with

the last dish. "So can I tell you all my news now?"

"Yes," Hunter said. "Spill it."

"We have been formally invited to be the keynote speaker at the INKed Literary Awareness Celebration." She looked back and forth between the people at the table as if expecting some kind of reaction. When she got nothing, Ali huffed. "Guys, this is big! This is where the big five publishing houses get together and try to outshine and out-brag each other. Putting Rose up there? The news will be all over it! It's the perfect breakout for her."

"When?" Brook asked. "Because I have to read all their books at least once. I have to be prepared for the questions, and I can't do that if I haven't even read them!"

"It's in three weeks," Alison assured her. "You've got time, and we all know you can do this. You've seen them write. You have the perfect story. This is going to be amazing, Brook."

Cessily just reached over for the dish closest to her. "And legally speaking, it's a complete nightmare, but I'll make sure everyone's covered."

Hunter was smiling at all of them. "I think it's all going to work out. This is going to be a good year, ladies, which is why we're celebrating early."

Brook, however, no longer felt hungry. All she could think about were the millions of ways to blow this, and what it would mean for her guys. Three weeks didn't seem like nearly enough time.

As if he was reading her mind, Ryder said, "You're going to be amazing, Brook. Better than we could ever be."

"I hope you're right," she breathed. "God, Ryder, I really hope you're right."

"Have I been wrong yet?"

Thankfully, he hadn't.

CHAPTER FORTY

*A*fter dinner, Brook signed contract after contract. Some were with Cessily, others with Ali. They were for her divorce, her new job, and just about everything else she needed. By the time they were done, she was starting to like Cessily. Sure, the woman was a bit of a pessimist, but she wouldn't let Brook sign a single thing without reading it first. Clearly, she took her job seriously.

It was five days later when Brook had to run down to the courthouse for the temporary restraining order. Cessily met her there, but Ryder was adamant that he be at her side. It didn't take long. With all of the documentation Cessily had, the judge was more than willing to keep Owen far away from her. The only downside was that the restraining order was only in place until their court date, which was three months away.

But after that, Brook's life fell into a very nice routine. Every day, one of the guys had to run somewhere - usually the medical center to jack off in a cup for Ali - which gave her time to read in peace. The dogs were starting to get comfortable in the house. Rosa, however, proved she was a bed hog. Amelia had attached herself to Brook's side, but it was cute, even if she made going to the bathroom into a spectator sport.

Then there were the nights. Gone was any semblance of a normal schedule. The twins wrote until the early hours of the morning, slept in when they could, and got up early when they couldn't. In between the words slowly filling up their manuscript, they found ways to spoil her. The couch in the corner now had a soft throw across the arm. A Kindle reader had replaced the stack of books she'd been trying to carry around. And there was no jealousy.

It didn't matter who she was with, the other just accepted it. Sometimes one of the guys would let her lay on him while she read. That usually ended up in a make out session. A few times, the other twin joined in, but it seemed they no longer felt they *had* to both be with her to make it work. They still didn't like to be too far apart, but Brook didn't blame them. Lucky for them, she was a homebody.

But one week before the big Literary Awareness gala, Hunter gave her the bad news. The event was black tie - and she had nothing at all that would work. Her nicest dress was the one she'd worn out to dinner with Ali, and that was more cocktail and less formal wear. Hunter, however, seemed thrilled when she admitted it.

That was how she ended up here, in a boutique store, locked in a dressing room with an entire rack of dresses, with a middle-aged sales clerk offering suggestions about what to try next. She'd already vetoed anything white. After all, it seemed ludicrous for Rose to present herself as pure in any form. Black was worse, since that made her look like she should be at a funeral. Hunter said no to anything pink.

The last dress she'd tried on had been beautiful, and really worked with her body type. The problem was the color. That shade of green did not go well with her brown hair and almost-but-not-quite olive skin. Even Hunter had shaken his head when she stepped out to show him. This one, however, was a shimmery thing that couldn't decide if it was red or purple.

The top was strapless with an intricate design across it in an almost metallic style. She couldn't tell if it was supposed to be flowers or paisleys, but it looked good. The skirt was long and full, with a diagonal slit that came up to the middle of her thigh. When she had it on, Brook knew it was the one. The only problem? It was a little too close to pink.

"Hunter?" she called out. "Does maroon count as pink? Or like a dark magenta?"

He chuckled. "Let me see."

Opening the door, she stepped out and made her way to the circle of mirrors at the end where Hunter was waiting. She didn't need to see herself to know she looked good. Hell, she felt beautiful in this dress. She felt like she was on cloud nine, like she could conquer the world. She also felt a whole lot like some reclusive author who wrote steamy ménage books while living them out in real life.

Which would kind of explain her reluctance to *leave* home.

But when she twirled in front of the mirrors, Hunter didn't say a thing. "Is it ok?" she asked.

He just pushed himself from his chair and walked toward her, refusing to stop until his hands landed on her hips. "Wow," he breathed. "This is definitely your dress."

"Not too pink?"

"No. It's lipstick colored, which works in so many ways. Damn, you look beautiful."

She had no clue what lipstick he was talking about, but her teeth clamped on her lower lip and she glanced down to check. "I'm going to need new shoes, too."

"Uh huh. And some earrings, I think. Long ones, because that neckline is too amazing to detract from with a necklace." His hands moved along her ribs. "Is it comfortable? Not too tight or loose? The fabric isn't too stiff? You're going to be standing up there talking for a long time, you know."

"No, it's great." Then she thought about it. "But I'd better get some very comfortable shoes."

"Oh yeah." He turned to the clerk. "We'll take it."

The woman nodded. "Yes, sir. That one's thirty-five."

Brook's head snapped around to look at her, but she wasn't foolish enough to ask. There was no way this dress cost thirty-five dollars. There had to be at least a few more zeros on that, but the question was if it was hundreds or thousands. Considering she'd never paid more than eight hundred dollars for a dress in her life - and that was the one she got married in - she had no way to be sure. Naturally, there wasn't a tag.

"Yeah," she whispered. "Let me get out of this so we can wrap it in bubble wrap until the big day."

Hunter chuckled. "Tell yourself it's a present and stop worrying."

"A present," she repeated as she stepped back, heading for the dressing room. "A present that's worth more than I make in a month."

Hunter just smiled like he knew something she didn't. Bastard. He probably did, but she was used to that. He also really liked spoiling her, and the truth was that she kinda did too. She still wasn't sure how to take it, but it was fun to just let one of her boyfriends drop his credit card and handle everything for her.

In fact, it kinda felt right. It felt like what she'd imagined a husband would be like back when she'd agreed to be Owen's wife. Not that she was ready to even think about anything like that, but living with these two was just so easy. It was natural. Maybe Ryder was right. If a person could give off creepy vibes on the first meeting, maybe the opposite was true, too. Maybe the only reason people hesitated was because society insisted that only bad things happened. Maybe, just maybe, if more people dared to trust, then more people would be happier?

She wasn't sure, but she was more than willing to try. If for no other reason than the amazing sex, but the surprising part was that she and the guys had a lot more going for them than just that. They wrote books; she loved to read books. They were impulsive and passionate. She liked to organize and manage things. They put their all into everything. She liked to think it all through first.

Then there were the big ones. They all loved the dogs, books, and hiding away from the rest of the world. They had the same hobbies, liked a lot of the same shows, and generally had the same taste in everything - even food! Somehow, she really had managed to find the perfect boyfriend - or two.

She had the dress halfway off when Hunter's voice came through the door. "Hey, I think we should make Ryder wait to see it."

"Oh?" Brook asked.

Hunter didn't get the chance to answer before the saleswoman cleared her throat pointedly. "Sir, there's a seating area for a reason. You could disturb the other women changing."

He scoffed. "There are no other women, we're the only people in the store, and I'm buying a three-thousand-dollar dress that you're about to get the commission on. I think you can pretend like I'm sitting over there."

Well, that answered her question about how many zeros were on the tag. It didn't, however, keep the saleswoman from huffing like an old school teacher. Brook wasn't brave enough to say anything while halfway undressed, so she just listened.

"And," Hunter continued, "it would be great if you found some very comfortable shoes in a size... What size do you wear, Brook?"

"Eight."

"That one," Hunter finished. "Something beautiful that will match the dress, but that she'll be able to stand in for a few hours. Long earrings, too. Preferably sparkly."

The woman huffed again, clearly not impressed with Hunter's attitude, but she'd have to be an idiot to risk the kind of commission she'd get from this sale. After a few seconds of silence, Brook was convinced she'd gone, but then the dressing room door opened. As she pressed her arms over her chest to cover herself, Hunter stepped into the small room with a smile on his face.

"Hey," he whispered.

"What are you doing in here?"

He motioned for her to turn. "Helping. I want to see how to get this off, because I plan to have a repeat performance."

She turned her back to him. "A very long zipper. I'm going to need a strapless bra, too. I kinda don't have one anymore."

"Bustier?" he asked.

She rolled her eyes. "Function before seduction, ok? The last thing I need are my boobs popping out while on camera. *Not* how we want this debut to go."

"Would fit with the books," he teased as he helped her shimmy out of the dress. "But you really do look beautiful in this."

She flashed him a smile before stepping over the mass of fabric by her feet. "So are you both going to wear tuxes?"

"Of course. It's a black-tie event." He leaned a little closer, hovering just by her ear. "And yes, we own them. We also know how to tie our bow ties."

Even the idea of Hunter and Ryder in matching tuxedos made her insides clench in anticipation. No, she shouldn't think of them as arm candy, but that was exactly what everyone else would see. Casting a glance back at him, she reached for her own clothes.

"Do I get a pregame show?"

"Brook," he whispered as he stepped closer, all but forcing her to turn toward him. "If you're not careful, you're going to get a show right here." Another step and her back hit the wall. "But I'm trying really hard to contain my excitement and act like a gentleman."

"You're buying me a dress. I think that counts. It's a really expensive one."

He smiled as he bent his head, his eyes falling to her lips. "You deserve to be spoiled. You deserve everything you've ever dreamed of. This is what I can do, and I love it when you just let me without fighting me."

She nodded, understanding what he meant, but being so close made her heart beat just a little too fast. "Yeah, but you know I don't want you for your money, right?"

"Why *do* you want me?" he asked.

She looked up to meet his perfect brown eyes. "Because you make me happy. You make me feel like I'm important and amazing." Then she smiled. "And because you're so incredibly sexy that we should probably add a new set of panties to the shopping list."

"Oh, Brook," he groaned. "Not nice. Not even playing fair."

"Maybe we should shop quickly, and then spend a couple of hours destroying the bed I made this morning."

"You," he breathed, "are perfect."

He kissed her hard, but he never once put his hands on her. They both knew that wouldn't end the way they wanted. There'd be no way they'd prevent themselves from taking the next step, then the one after that, and she wanted this dress enough that she was more than willing to wait.

"The only reason," Hunter whispered, "that I'm not going to take you right here is because you said you're not into exhibitionism, and I really prefer it when you get off. A lot."

And that. Yep, there was that point, too, and a little piece of her heart melted at the fact he'd remembered. God, could this guy get any better?

CHAPTER FORTY-ONE

The day of the INKed Literary Awareness Celebration, Brook started getting ready early. She knew the exact look she wanted, and it would take at least an hour to do her hair. Probably another to get her face just right. Everything she needed was laid out on either the bed or her dresser, but there was one little problem.

Thunder rumbled again, making the mirror shake with the force of it. Yes, it was raining, and not just a little bit. For some reason, she hadn't even considered the weather when planning for this, and now, she was convinced her hair was going to fall into a limp, dead heap before she even got on the stage. Then again, that was why she was doing this early. If things went badly, she had a few options for elegant up-dos.

In the other room, the guys were getting ready. They hadn't planned it like this for any reason besides that was where their clothes were. Then again, it gave her time to go over her speech. While Brook painted her eyes and lips, she repeated the words that would convince the world she was someone she wasn't. The words that would serve as a shield for the men she cared so much about, adding one more layer between them and the horrors they'd survived.

Thirty minutes before they had to leave, she slipped off her robe and reached for the dress. It was probably the nicest thing she'd ever owned, but that was getting to be a very tough list. Ryder and Hunter had given her so much. Most importantly was the safety to remember who she really was and the reassurance to actually embrace that person.

And the dogs.

In less than a month, Rosa had grown comfortable as a house dog. Oh, she was big, but her activity level came in bursts. Mostly, all she wanted to do was follow Brook around and lie beside her, almost as if she was scared her person would vanish one day and never return. Amelia was a typical puppy. She made everyone laugh, and had learned to love the sound instead of fear it.

Brook figured the mongrels were pretty good metaphors for her life. Then again, that was what dogs were for, right? To work as a mirror so people could see the simpler sides of themselves. But if this was the type of person Brook had become, she was ok with it. She really was comfortable in this house, and all she wanted was to make her guys happy.

But one single thing was missing from this relationship. She'd told herself it was still too soon to fall for them. She wasn't even divorced yet, after all. There was no reason she should start thinking about who would spill those three heavy words first, and yet she knew they were there, hanging just above all their heads.

She loved them. Both of them. That was why she would play the part of Rose. It wasn't to keep them locked to her - although that had its own appeal. The simple truth was that they needed someone to do it, and she honestly cared about them enough to risk everything for them.

For the last few days, the media had been tossing up minor culture pieces about the mysterious Rose Solace finally making a public appearance. For those who hadn't seen the picture, speculation ranged on her being a gay man to a very old woman. Questions abounded about her reasons for staying out of the spotlight. No one ever guessed that maybe some people just didn't want fame. Oh no, to them, fame was the ultimate goal, not another weight to hang around their necks and complicate their lives.

But she had a plan. Ryder had basically given her the idea, but she'd taken it and run. Now, she just had to pull it off successfully, and she wasn't really sure that was possible. Still, there was no reason that what had happened to all of them shouldn't have a higher purpose.

She was mostly in her dress when a soft tap came at her bedroom door. "Brook?" Yeah, that had to be Ryder.

"Come in," she called back.

He stepped in the door and paused. Slowly, a smile began to curl his lips, but she couldn't miss the rest of him, either. Ryder filled out a tux like a cover model. From the perfectly tied bow at his throat to the glint of his cufflinks, he looked like he belonged on the red carpet and not beside her. Even better, she knew he was only half of her matched set.

"Zip me?" she asked, turning her back toward him.

He sighed as he moved closer. "No wonder Hunter wanted me to see this. Damn, you look good."

His fingers found her spine, sliding against her skin as he moved the zipper higher. His mouth, however, hovered just behind her ear, the last traces of his breath teasing her neck.

"Take this off me later?" she begged.

"Brook, I'm going to take you in this dress, take it off you, and then take you all over again," he promised. "The only hard part will be waiting."

Slowly, she turned to face him. "Trust me, I understand. You look amazing, Ryder."

"Saying I clean up nice?" he teased.

She reached up to trace the line of buttons down his chest. "Nope. I'm saying you're always gorgeous. Damn, you make a tuxedo look good. How'd I get so lucky again?"

With a chuckle, he caught her hand, halting it. "You trusted me. The big, scary-looking guy looming around the shelter, and you kept trusting me."

"Damn, that was a good call on my part."

She tilted her head up, hoping for a kiss, but he shook his head. "That lipstick? I think you're going to have to wait, because it's too perfect to mess up."

Groaning, she gave in. He was right, of course. It was pigmented enough to stain, and glossy enough to smear. Still, she had a couple more things to do, and it was almost time to leave. Snagging her shoes, she sat on the edge of her bed to put them on.

"So who's driving?" she asked. "And please tell me that I'm not going to get soaked before we get inside?"

A perfectly magenta umbrella peeked around the frame of the door. A step later, Hunter followed with a smile. "We got you covered, Rose."

"Hunter," she groaned at the sound of *that* name.

"What?" He shrugged. "For the next few hours, you are Rose, and unless you want people tracking you down, you'd best get used to it."

"And someone's going to recognize me and drop my real name," she reminded him. "So I think you can still use it while we're alone."

He nodded, accepting that. "You nervous?"

"Yes!" she hissed.

"Mm," Ryder murmured. "Hate public speaking?"

"No, actually. It's more that Rose is yours, and I feel like I'm stealing her."

He just lifted a brow. "I'd kinda like to think that you're ours, too. I figure that means you're perfect. Two men for you, two women for us." Then he offered his arm. "Shall we?"

After checking the last buckle, Brook stood and accepted. "Let's. Ryder can keep me on my feet, and Hunter can make sure I only get wet when he wants me to."

"Oh," he groaned. "Bad, Brook. So bad."

"And yet, still funny," she pointed out.

Because of the weather, the dogs would get to stay inside. Amelia and Einstein were in their kennels. Rosa and Sherlock were allowed to stay out, but they insisted on walking the three of them to the door first. When they reached it, Hunter proudly pulled it open - after telling the dogs to stay - and Ryder escorted her out onto the porch. There, waiting only a few steps away, was a very large, very black limousine.

"Seriously?" she asked.

"Photo op," Hunter said as he popped open the umbrella that matched Brook's dress. "You're rich, Rose. Enjoy it."

What she was enjoying most was the way his tux flexed around his upraised arm. "Yep, this could get to be fun," she teased as Ryder led her toward the back.

Thankfully, the driver wasn't waiting by the door or anything. The rain was pouring down, and just as Ryder opened the door for her, a flash of lightning turned the world bright for a split second. The thunder that followed made her duck into the car just a little faster. Then, it was a mess of getting everyone inside and closing the umbrella again.

In other words, it felt a lot like prom night back in high school. They weren't actually the kind of fancy and respectable people who did this on a regular basis. Brook giggled when Hunter dropped onto the seat beside his brother and rubbed the water from his hair. Ryder groaned and tried to push him far enough away that he wouldn't get soaked.

"Have everything?" Hunter asked. "Purse, phone, notes for your speech?"

She lifted her clutch. "Checked and double-checked."

His eyes flicked over her shoulder. "We're good, Don. And the closer you can get us to the entrance, the better."

In the driver's seat, an older man chuckled. "They have an awning set up for the press. You and Miss Solace should be fine."

Brook leaned closer to Ryder. "Does he know?"

"Nope." He bumped her arm lightly. "He knows we've used his company before, but probably hasn't read a single book."

"Bet his wife has," she teased.

Ryder winked playfully. "Probably!"

Thankfully, the drive didn't take too long. The Literacy Celebration was only about an hour away, in the next town over. Still, she watched through blurry raindrops as the sun grew darker and the grey sky changed to black. She'd been to events like this before. They were the sort of thing her husband used to love: a reason to look important. She'd always hated them, which usually ended with Owen pointing out that she was barely more than trailer trash.

This time would be different. This time, she was going to have fun. *This time,* it was her job and responsibility to be a mix between the perfect lady and the inner slut every woman wished she could embrace. In other words, she just had to be herself, leave a trail of breadcrumbs to convince people she was just shy, and make sure to mention the title of their newest book as often as she could.

It was true night outside when Don pulled the limo up before a fancy blue awning. On either side of a narrow aisle, trapped behind velvet ropes, dozens of people with cameras turned toward the car. The moment the doors opened, the flashes started going off. Chuckling to himself, Hunter stepped out, turned back to the car, and opened the umbrella for her.

Ryder came next, moving to the other side to offer a hand. Only then, with her fingers lightly cradled in Ryder's, did Brook slide to the end of the seat and do her best to step out elegantly. It wasn't easy to get out of a car without looking like an idiot, but the sound of so many shutters clicking convinced her it was worth trying. The moment she took Ryder's arm, the questions began.

"Are you an author?"

"Will you be getting an award tonight?"

"Which book do you have in the running?"

"Gentlemen," Hunter said as soon as they were under the awning and out of the rain. "Miss Solace will answer all of your questions tonight. Please." He gestured for Ryder to keep moving as he fell in on Brook's other side, wielding the closed umbrella like a cane.

It looked good on him. The kind of good that usually

required a top hat to pull off, but Hunter was doing it. Ryder, on her other side, was a little more stoic but just as handsome. Ducking her head, Brook couldn't stop the smile, but she didn't say a thing. They had to wait. The good part always came at the end, after all.

This was just the hook. Next would be the rising action, and when she finally got on that stage and started talking, well, that was the climax. She intended to save the resolution for when they got home - because she remembered what they'd said about using those expensive bow ties on her. Talk about a setup for one hell of a series.

See, thinking like an author was easy. Almost natural. She had this.

CHAPTER FORTY-TWO

*T*hey had a table right at the front. That meant there was less distance for Brook to travel alone when they finally called her name to give her speech. Ryder still didn't like it. He wanted to stand up there with her, holding her hand, and make sure she knew she didn't have to do this alone. Granted, public speaking freaked him out. Her? She looked like she was made for this.

As Brook moved behind the microphone, the crowd around them fell silent. At the back, against the walls, every press outlet had sent someone to record this. Most wouldn't use it, and if they did, it would be little more than a brief mention with a still image, but they were still here. For over a decade, Rose Solace had been climbing up the charts and avoiding the tabloids. Today would change all of that, and journalists always wanted to be there first.

Then, before Ryder was really ready, Brook began to speak. "Good evening," she said, proving her voice was as amazing as the rest of her. "For those wondering, yes, I am Rose Solace. What you don't seem to realize is that I'm not important. Not at all. I'm just the one with too many words. The important things about me are all between the pages of those books. Like all authors, I create fantasies using truths that we all know. I take you from where you started, in a place you never wanted to be, and show you that not all the options have to be bad. My only job is to let my readers escape for a moment, and finally get the chance to catch their breath.

"But," she continued, "only for a moment. I create stories we all know too well, and then I embellish. I take the mundane and lift it up to the amazing. I know your wishes and give them to you, because they're my wishes too. I'm not important, and I'm not the master of these stories. You are. Each and every person who reads my books. You're the ones that give them life. I can only give them words."

"Miss Solace," a reporter called out. "Why are you only now revealing yourself?"

She smiled, the look so sweet and gentle. "Because I filed for divorce. You see, there's one universal truth that almost everyone tries to deny. Humans are sexual creatures. Oh, we try to put limits on ourselves and use morality as a constraint, but the vast majority of our lives are ruled by smut. We date because of it, we fall in love because of it, and we have children and grandchildren because of it. We dress nicer, act proper, and push for a little more success all because we want to be the one chosen by the other we want so badly. But when it comes right down to it, it's all just the simple act of wanting to be wanted. In other words, smut."

"Do you honestly think that poorly of your own books?" a woman called out.

"No," Brook told her. "In case you missed it, I was actually saying the opposite. I think that highly of my books. I'm also very well-aware of the fact that in public, we all like to pretend that such things are dirty. And yet, do you have kids?"

The woman tensed but slowly nodded.

"Smut," Brook teased. "We all know how babies are born, and because this is going to be on YouTube later, I'm not about to clarify for the masses. Ma'am, what I'm saying is that my stories are about people who finally stop caring about what others think and accept that each and every one of us are unique. That our uniqueness makes us all the same in a way, and that none of it matters at all."

"How does your upcoming divorce affect this?" the woman asked.

Right on command, Brook bit her lips together and glanced down at her notes. Slowly, she took a deep breath. "The types of things I write are over the top. They're impossible, because it's more than any person could ever hope for. It's simplified, giving everything an easy answer. That's why we like books. They're also about love and sex." She chuckled softly. "Quite a bit of sex, if I'm honest, because that's how we connect to our spouses. The less connection we get, the more we want. And yet, my relationship was not the kind where such things were talked about. No, my husband expected me to be prim and proper, a perfect lady, if you will."

"Damn," Hunter breathed. "She's good."

"Yeah, she is," Ryder agreed. "Look at her working the responses. She's putting Chekhov's gun on the mantle, and if Owen ever tries anything, it'll be right within her reach to finish the story with."

Hunter rolled his eyes. "You're a literary nerd, you know that, right?"

Ryder sighed. "She's making sure all the bits are where she needs them. Happy?"

"Much."

Brook was still going. "I wrote at work. I wrote when I was home alone. I snuck in a few words here or there. At first, I never thought they'd ever get read. It was no different than how I wrote poetry in high school and just threw it away. Granted, my poetry is pretty bad. Still, I knew my husband would never approve of his proper little wife doing something so *dirty,* so there was no way I could take the credit for this."

"What would've happened if he found out?" a man asked. "You're already getting divorced, or so you say."

Brook's eyes moved across the room, shifting from person to person. Some she held for a moment, others got a small nod. Just when it began to feel uncomfortable, she took a deep breath.

"He killed my dog."

That was it. It was all she said, but from the sudden stillness in the room, it said enough. Ryder could see her breathing harder, and he knew this had to be painful for her, but she just stood there before all of those cameras and took it, proving exactly how strong she was.

"I am smaller than him, weaker than him, and he made sure that the only money I had access to was only what he gave me. Me!" she said, thumping her hand on the podium. "I couldn't figure out how to run away until my dog was the one to pay the price for my inaction. I kept thinking that if we worked it out, went to counseling, or tried just a little harder, we could make our marriage work. You see," she told the room, "I didn't want to be one of *those* women. I didn't want to act like my marriage doesn't matter, because it did. It was my entire world... Until it wasn't.

"The changes were slow and subtle. My adoring boyfriend became my perfect fiancé. Then, somewhere in the middle, he was a tired husband, working a little too hard to take care of his family. I can't even tell you when that turned into a controlling one, but it did, and my job was to help. My duty was to be obedient. Everyone's expectation was that if *I* didn't try just one more time, then I was the one who ruined it all. Let me make this very clear. It takes two.

"And before any of you assume that my books were the cause, let me assure you that you have it backwards. These books were where I ran away to when things got bad. That means they were bad first. They were the daydream that reminded me I should try again. The hope that somewhere in my husband was a man who'd fall so hard that we'd have a happily ever after. The problem was that I had almost married two different men. One was sweet, charming, and amazing. The other was dark, brooding, and dangerous."

"Fuck," Hunter breathed, daring a glance over at his brother. "Did you know she was going to say that?"

Ryder shook his head. "I'm pretty sure she's off script."

"And good at it!"

"So," Brook told the room, "where did I get my ideas? Real life. Why did I write? Because we all just want to be loved, and I'm not any different. Why have I hidden away from the publicity I could've had? Because fame comes with a price, and it was one I'd hoped to avoid."

She paused, waiting for another question, but the room wasn't quite sure what to make of Rose Solace. She was too proud, too sweet, and too different from what they were used to. In other words, she was perfect, and looking at her up there, Ryder knew he'd never find anyone else that could come close.

"Hunter?" he whispered, leaning closer to his twin. "Has it been long enough?"

"Oh yeah. I've just been waiting on you."

He nodded. "Think she feels the same way?"

"I think we've all been avoiding those words until this was over, but yeah. I think we're on the exact same page."

"Mm." Ryder just had one more concern. "You think this is going to actually work?"

Hunter turned to face him. "I don't even care. Even if it doesn't, we're still going to take care of her, so we're definitely doing this."

"Equal parts?"

"Mhm. I mean, we still have things to figure out, but I'm good if you are."

"I'm so good," Ryder breathed. "I'm fucking head over heels for her like some stupid teenager."

"Yeah." Hunter slapped his shoulder lightly. "Feels kinda nice, huh?"

"Really nice. Almost like the perfect ending."

"Nah, this story is far from over. Besides, Naomi isn't quite there yet."

The guys shared a grin, but at the same time, one of the reporters had finally gotten enough courage to ask one more question. "Miss Solace? The men who escorted you here today. Are you in a relationship with them? And if so, how long has it been going on?"

Brook's eyes jumped to their table. This was not something they'd discussed. It wasn't one of the many things they'd come to an agreement on regarding how much was safe to put out there. She was going to have to tackle this on her own, but Ryder shrugged, letting her know he didn't care either way. Hunter just smiled.

"Those are my friends who agreed to serve as my protection tonight. You see, I get a little anxious in public. My agent introduced us, and we've been getting closer over the last month or so - since I've been separated. It's pretty rare to find the kind of people you can trust completely, but I've been very lucky. My agent is my best friend. Those gentlemen are running a very close second. And," she added, pitching her voice like she was telling a secret, "they are kinda cute."

The crowd chuckled, but she'd just opened the door. "Rose, are you in a polyamorous relationship?"

"If I was, I bet that would mean that *Thou Shall Covet* would end up as my best book yet, huh? Almost like I had real-life experience. I mean, they say we should write what we know, but I think I did pretty good winging this so far."

"So you are dating them?" someone else asked.

A devious smile was on Brook's face. "I didn't say that, now did I? And remind me again what business it is of yours? No, all I'm saying is that however we love, whoever we love, the whole point is that we all want it, and we shouldn't ever be ashamed of that. Thank you, ladies and gentlemen, but my feet are killing me, and..." She waved at her throat as if fanning herself. "I'm starting to get a little anxious up here."

And that was it. The emcee hurried up to thank her and ask the crowd for applause, and then the next person moved to talk about whatever they would. Ryder and his brother both hurried to their feet, but Brook waved them down. As elegantly as a princess, she made her way to the empty chair between them - hers - and sank into it.

"You ok?" Ryder asked.

Hunter reached over, wrapping his hand around her wrist. "Was it too much?"

"I'm fine," she insisted. "I just figured that if I was hitting all the high points, I should add in a little social anxiety in case I need to use it later."

Both of them stared at her. "Later?" Hunter finally asked.

The smile Brook gave him was almost beaming. "That was kinda fun."

"All you," Ryder promised. "To me, that looked like some kind of inhumane torture."

"No," she assured him. "It's easy when you're the one with all the power in the room. I think I could get used to this."

"Plan on it," Hunter said, leaning forward to meet his brother's eyes. Their plan was definitely a go.

CHAPTER FORTY-THREE

The rest of the event was just boring. It was nothing but other authors talking about the beauty of literacy - which Brook agreed with - but in the most polite and uninspiring way possible. Not that it was their fault. Authors weren't the kind of people who enjoyed the limelight. Not even the Collins brothers. They preferred to spend day after day in their study, lost in a dream of their creation.

Eventually the event ended. Of course, they couldn't get out that easy. A few people wanted to talk to her. Some were from publishing houses like Penguin, who she told to contact her agent and politely handed over Ali's card. Others were journalists wanting just a little more of a story. Brook did her best, but she refused to give out anything else.

It seemed that all those years with Owen had been useful, though. That was where she'd learned how to handle this formal crap. Her time at the shelter had given her experience in public relations and marketing. Not that running ads for a dog in need was on the same level as dealing with a pseudonym worth millions, but the books weren't slated to be put to sleep at the end of the week. In Brook's opinion, *this* was easy.

An hour later, the twins finally managed to get her out the door. The rain had mostly stopped. It was just sprinkling now, but the lightning in the distance promised there was still more to come. Deciding it wasn't worth waiting for Don to pull the limo around, Hunter popped open the umbrella, handed it over to Brook, then slipped an arm around her back. Ryder moved into place on her other side, and all three of them were quiet.

Mostly, they were just letting the success of Rose's first outing wash over them. It really did feel pretty good. She'd actually done this, and after watching all the other authors out there, she knew she'd done a better job than all of them. This whole being the face of Rose thing was something she was actually *good* at. Almost like it was her calling.

For a moment, she thought about grabbing her phone to text Ali because she wanted to brag about how well everything had gone, but they'd already agreed to let her see the news first. That way, she'd be able to look at it with an open mind and handle any bombshells before they went off. Brook knew a little too well that even the most perfect thing could still blow up in her face.

But she was in a great mood. Happy, and the kind that went all the way to her bones. Never mind that she'd basically hinted to the world that yes, she was banging both of those hot twins she was running around with. And whether they knew it or not, the looks on their faces had been the best confirmation of that rumor anyone could ask for.

"You know," she finally said when she saw the limo up

ahead. "I think I'm going to go home and jump in bed."

"Oh, no," Hunter said. "More like get thrown."

"After I get to put my hands on that dress," Ryder reminded her.

She was giggling when Don jumped out of his car, clearly intending to get the door for her. "Miss Sola-" His voice faltered as his eyes went big.

She spun, following his gaze. Thankfully, the twins were faster. That was the only reason the crowbar in her husband's hand didn't do more than make her stagger when it slammed into her face. The handle of the umbrella bent, taking much of the force, and Brook made no effort to hold onto it. Fire radiated out from her jaw, her mind immediately convinced it was broken as her eyes filled with tears from the intensity of the pain. Shoving both hands to the wound, her purse fell to the ground and the umbrella floated away as she staggered back.

Hunter was wrestling with Owen to get the crowbar away from him. Behind her, she could hear Don telling someone there was an attack in progress and trying desperately to explain where they were. Then there was Ryder. He handled the action, and from the look on his face, he was about to prove it. Surging around his brother, he met Owen with a fist to the gut, but not a single sound. Owen gasped, releasing the crowbar, which Hunter immediately kicked off to the side. That wasn't enough for Ryder. Rage had taken over his face, and he wasn't even close to done.

Grabbing the back of Owen's shirt, he shoved the man forward, right into the side of the limo. Then again. The third time, Owen was smart enough to get his arms up, but that just sent Ryder in for more.

"That's enough!" Hunter yelled.

"He keeps coming back," Ryder snarled. "They never stop until they're dead. They don't know how. I have to make him stop, because he will never hurt her again."

Each phrase came with a plunge of Ryder's fists into Owen's body, never missing its intended mark, while Owen slowly slid down the side of the limo. His back, his side, and a few to his face. It didn't matter. None of it mattered. All Brook could hear was the anguish in Ryder's voice. The fear that was driving him. It was one thing she'd never known how to stop, and this time she didn't want to. Her entire face hurt, and for just a moment, she wanted someone else to deal with her issues so she didn't have to.

"Stop and I won't tell," Owen begged.

Ryder's fist paused. "Excuse me?" he asked, but the warning was clear.

"I won't tell them that she's never written a book. I won't point out that Rose Solace's first release was when..." He paused to cough. "She was still in college."

"Kill him," Hunter growled, as if it was an order. "Then he *can't* tell."

"Sirs?" Don, the driver, whimpered. "The cops are on the way."

"Get in the fucking car," Hunter ordered.

"Rose," Don begged, ignoring them to move around to the back. "Miss Rose, come here, sweetie. The cops are coming."

She ignored him. "Owen," she said, proving her jaw still worked even if it hurt like hell. "I warned you." She wiped at the wetness, trying not to think about what was happening to her dress. "I am *not* your bitch! I'm theirs."

Ryder just chuckled, and it was not a friendly sound. "Beg, little man. Beg loud and you might live through the night."

Owen begged. He begged for Brook to save him, for Hunter to stop his brother - even if he didn't know their names - and for the driver to do something. Unfortunately, that wasn't what Ryder had meant. Just as he clenched his fist to exact his revenge, the parking lot lit up with red and blue lights.

That was the only thing that saved Owen. Hunter, however, finally looked up, his eyes landing on Brook's jaw. "Shit," he breathed, reaching for his pocket square. "Baby?"

"It's not broken," she promised.

He didn't care. Without asking, he moved closer, pressing the fancy silk against her skin making it hurt even worse. When she pulled in a breath between her teeth, his palm found the back of her neck, holding her into the pressure.

"That's going to need some sutures," he warned her. "Brook, I know it hurts, but the pressure will stop the bleeding."

"I just wanted *one* good night!" she hissed around him to Owen. "Just one, where you didn't manage to fuck everything up and make me feel like shit."

"You're screwing them," he shot back.

Her eyes narrowed, and she didn't care about anything except how angry he made her. Always, every time she tried to do anything, he beat her down, tore her apart, and made her hate herself. For too long, she'd turned that inward, but not this time. For once, she finally knew exactly whose fault all of this was.

"Yes!" she yelled, the pain in her face only making her angrier. "Yes, I'm fucking them, and there's not a damned thing you can do to stop it. You can't beat me to make it stop. You can't take me away, because they will come find me. They *love* me, Owen. You never did. You loved *you* more than anything else in the world, but these two? They love me - and I love them right back."

"Brook," Hunter breathed.

Owen didn't even notice. "Slut," he spit at her.

Ryder didn't care at all about the cops pulling up around them. He just thrust his fist into the man's face one more time. "You wish," he snarled.

"Sir!" a police officer yelled. "Step away from the man on the ground."

"He assaulted my girlfriend," Ryder called back. "I'm unarmed, but he hit her with a crowbar!"

"Ryder?" Brook begged, looking through the overly bright lights. The police were barely even silhouettes like this, but she could still identify the stance. Guns had been drawn, and they were pointed right at Ryder. "Please, Ry? I need you to let him go this time."

Slowly, much too slowly, Ryder released Owen and showed his open hands - with blood covering the backs of his knuckles - as he stood. When he looked at Brook, his eyes begged her to understand, and she did. He'd only lost it to protect her. He would never hurt her. He wasn't anything like Owen.

"Hands behind your head!" an officer yelled. "Both of you!"

Owen tried. He was still on the ground, yet he struggled to lift his battered arms up and lace his fingers behind his neck. Ryder just sighed, turned his back to the cops and did the same like he knew exactly what was expected. Hunter and Brook were a few paces away from the car, but no one was yelling at them. The problem was that she was sick of being the victim.

"This is going to be ok," she told Ryder.

He didn't say a thing as the police hurried closer. There were at least eight of them, and far too many guns for Brook's taste. It may have been different if they hadn't been pointed at her boyfriend.

"Ma'am?" one of them asked, a woman. "Please step away from the car. Sir, I assume you're the boyfriend? This way."

"That's my boyfriend too." Brook pointed at Ryder. "He was just protecting me."

"Yes, ma'am. We just have to secure the scene. Sir?" She looked at Hunter. "Sir, Officer Brandt over there will take your statement."

"I'm not leaving Brook."

"It's ok, Hunter," she promised. "This time, it's ok. They just want to make sure they know what happened so Ryder doesn't get charged."

He nodded. "But I'm not letting you out of my sight."

"We're fine," she promised. "We're going to be just fine."

But they weren't. All of this would get into the news. Someone would put the pieces together, and the cops were about to get all of their names. Brook's heart was racing on the inside, but on the outside, she was doing her best to keep control.

"I'm nervous," she told the cop as she used Hunter's handkerchief to dab at the laceration from Owen's crowbar. "What happens now?"

"Who hit you?" the woman asked. "And do you need a paramedic?"

"No, I'm ok. It was my soon-to-be ex-husband. The man on the ground. His name is Owen Harper, and there's a restraining order that's supposed to keep him away from me until the divorce is final."

"And your name?"

Brook took a deep breath. "Brook Harper, but I've been using my maiden name, Sanders."

"Uh huh." She tipped her head toward Hunter. "And him?"

"Hunter Collins. The carbon copy at the back of the car is his twin brother Ryder Collins. They were here to protect me tonight. We were all afraid Owen might try something, or one of the fans."

Confusion crossed the officer's face. "Fans?"

Brook just bobbed her head. "I finally decided to do an interview, thinking my husband couldn't stop me. It was a big book thing, and we thought all the security here would make it ok."

And recognition hit. "You're the famous Rose Solace?" the policewoman asked.

"Yeah," Brook breathed, hoping this wasn't a mistake.

The woman began to smile. "And the twins are your boyfriends?"

This time, she didn't try to stop the sigh. "Yeah."

"I *love* your books," the woman admitted. "*Perfect Forgery*'s my favorite." Then she sucked in a breath. "Oh my god, is Owen Harper the villain?"

The villain in that story was the woman's ex-husband. When it had been written, the Collins brothers didn't even know Brook existed, but right now, Brook didn't care. For the rest of the night, she was Rose Solace, and what she said would be the truth - in her own way. Or at least everyone would accept it as the truth.

"Yeah. That was when things first started getting bad. He didn't know I was writing, and now that it's out there? He wants to punish me for it. He's been stalking me, and he's already been arrested for it once. There's another report about how he killed my dog." She reached up to make sure her eyes weren't tearing up. "Calvin tried to save me because Owen had gone from yelling to hitting. Ryder, the guy at the back of the car, filed that report on my behalf."

"And the Collins brothers?" the cop asked, her voice sounding more like she was gossiping than interviewing.

Brook decided to go with it. "Believe it or not, I just met them about two months ago. Kinda makes me wonder if the universe has some kind of pattern, you know? I mean, they're *perfect* aren't they?"

"And you're really dating both of them?"

Brook tried to smile, but a sharp pain stopped it. "You read *Double Trouble*? Yeah, just like that."

"Well, Mrs. Solace, I think I know all I need to. Wait right here, and I'll explain this to the rest of the guys. Sounds to me like this whole thing counts as self-defense."

At that moment, Brook didn't care that she'd got her name wrong, or her title. She just really hoped that all of this would work out. Ryder didn't deserve to suffer for protecting her, and yet this was the only thing she could do. It felt cheap and shallow to use their fame like this, but the female police officer was clearly a devoted fan, and if their books could explain how complicated relationship issues worked, then who was Brook to deny it.

In minutes, Ryder was free, had been apologized to, and Hunter was escorted back over. Owen, however, wasn't getting off that easy. He'd requested a paramedic, but two cops were hovering right along beside him. This time, the woman who loved Rose's books promised he was going to spend a very long time in jail, and the officer promised to make a recommendation to the judge for a very high bail.

The biggest problem was that she'd heard all of that before. When Owen had attacked her outside Ali's apartment; they'd said he was going away, and it hadn't worked. Owen had money, he had connections, and worst of all, he had his own twisted reasons to keep coming after her. The policewoman, however, assured her that breaking a restraining order changed things. It would make it a *lot* harder for him to get out of jail, but she did recommend that Brook consider taking her own security measures to stay safe.

On impulse, Brook reached over and hugged her. "Thank you. All I've wanted is to get away from him, so anything you can do is huge. Is there any way I can repay you?"

"It's my job," she said before leaning back with a grin. "But I also won't complain if you name your next heroine April."

"Done!" Brook promised. "I mean, Naomi's coming out next, but the one after that will be an April. I swear."

"And I'm going to hold you to that, Ms. Sanders."

"Please," Hunter begged. "Can we do anything to keep this from becoming a PR nightmare?"

"I have no intention of putting in this report anywhere that Ms. Sanders is an author. I don't think it applies to the charges, but it sounds like you're going to have your hands full, from what I heard on the news. You deserve this, Rose. Knowing what you've been through to get it? You deserve to finally enjoy your success."

Yes, Brook thought. *Yes, they really did.* It didn't matter which one of them was Rose Solace, they all deserved to finally have a little happiness.

CHAPTER FORTY-FOUR

Since they'd rented the limo for the entire night, Don was more than willing to take them to the emergency room in it. Thankfully, Brook didn't really need sutures. She did, however, get the gash closed with skin glue and told to treat it gently for the next five days. She also got a tetanus shot. When it was time to leave, Ryder didn't even bother asking about her health insurance. He just passed over his credit card.

That was definitely something she would have trouble getting used to, but she liked it. She liked how they just took care of her. She loved how protective Ryder had been, how worried Hunter had gotten over a little blood on her face. It made her feel protected, like she was untouchable with them around.

It was everything she'd ever wanted.

But she also couldn't forget how she'd lost her temper and yelled at Owen. She'd screamed that they loved her right there in the open. Not just that she loved them - which was true - but that *they* felt something for her. They'd never said it, but time and time again they'd proven it to her. She didn't really need the words. Owen had been more than happy to say how much he loved her right before treating her like dirt. If she had to choose, Brook would prefer the actions to empty words.

She just wasn't sure if she had gone too far, if she'd put words in their mouths that they didn't feel. And if she had? Would it scare them away? It felt like everyone had warned her away from dating them, that they had issues, and all the potential downsides. She hadn't seen it. If anything, they were better than even the men in their books. But if she crossed the line, would they cut her loose and never look back?

Those thoughts spun through her mind on the ride home. Not what would happen to Owen or if he'd come after her again. No, her greatest fear was that something would go wrong with this relationship, the one between her and the Collins brothers, because she couldn't imagine living happily ever after without them.

They were almost home when Hunter's phone began to vibrate in his pocket. Confused, he pulled it out, glanced at the screen, and immediately swiped to answer it with a clipped, "Hey?"

On the other end was a woman's voice. Brook could hear that, but she was talking fast enough that the words were all a jumble. It had to be Alison. Hunter's next words confirmed it.

"Almost home, because we had to take a stop at the ER. Yes, everyone's fine, but Owen came after her." He paused. "I promise. Brook has a cut on her face, but she didn't even get stitches." He paused again. "No, we didn't get to see. What's the overall impression?"

Don turned into their drive while Hunter nodded thoughtfully at his phone. Brook glanced over at Ryder, who just shrugged. When the car finally stopped, Alison was still going strong so Hunter just opened the door and stepped out, offering his free hand to Brook.

"Well, that's a good thing, right? I mean, sure, the evangelicals are going to hate us, but we write sex. Nah, I'm ok with that. Yeah, Brook was amazing, Ali. Absolutely amazing, and I'm going to make damned sure that her husband can't come near her again. Fucking bastard lays another hand on her and he won't walk away next time." He looked over and met Ryder's eyes. "Yeah, pretty sure we can afford a self-defense case."

"Ryder," Brook breathed.

He grabbed her shoulders and turned her toward the door calling back, "Thanks, Don. Have a good night!"

"You too, sirs. Ma'am. I'm glad everything worked out." But he didn't leave until they made it all the way to the front door.

"Ryder," she tried again, "I don't want either of you getting arrested for that piece of shit, ok?"

"No deal," he told her while Hunter continued to tell Alison all about what had happened. "I don't know how to make this any more clear to you, but you are worth fighting for. You're worth going to jail for. Brook..." He stepped inside and closed the door behind him, turning to face her. "There's nothing in this world that matters more to me than you."

Behind him, Hunter immediately said, "Ali, gotta go. Big talk time. Yeah. Night, sweetie."

That made Ryder smile, but Brook couldn't quite make his words fit into place. "You mean besides him, right? Because I get that."

"No," Hunter said, tossing his phone at the couch as he came closer. "I don't know about him, but to me? I couldn't choose. It used to be the two of us against the world. Now it's the three of us."

Ryder shot a quick glance at his brother. "I know you can hold your own. I just... you know?"

"Nah, I get ya," Hunter agreed, doing that thing where they only had half a conversation.

Brook partially lifted her hand. "I'm kinda in the dark still."

"Brook," Ryder tried again, reaching up to take her hands in his. "What I'm trying to say is that I never thought this would happen. My whole life, I've honestly believed that the only person who could care about me is my brother. Then you ran right into me, and I realized just how wrong I was." His fingers squeezed hers gently. "I'm in love with you, Brook Sanders. Wildly, madly, passionately in love with you."

"Really?" Hunter groaned. "That's straight from *Paradise Found*."

"It was a good line," Ryder shot back.

Brook, however, couldn't stop the stupid smile on her face. "Are you being serious?" she asked. "Or are you just fucking with me again?"

Hunter was the one who answered. "Serious. Completely serious. I mean, yes, he stole the amazing love line from a book, but it was a pretty good one."

Ryder shrugged. "I don't write the dialogue. I do love you."

"Brook," Hunter said, moving closer. "I do, too. I can give you beautiful words if you want, but it's honestly that simple. I never got hit upside the head with it. Falling for you was more like eroding, slowly but surely dissolving my resistance until every reason I had to keep you away was just gone, and I never realized it had vanished right before my eyes."

"Asshole," Ryder grumbled under his breath.

"Yeah," Brook said, looking between both of them. "I kinda knew. I mean, I guess I hoped, but that's what this feels like, you know? Like the way love is supposed to be in a romance novel." She met both of their eyes, one after the other. "And yes, I'm in love. I mean, I don't have any idea how to say it without telling one of you before the other, but I love you both, I really do. I don't want to choose, and I don't want either of you to ever have to. I just... I like this. I want to keep doing *this*."

"Thank god," Hunter breathed before turning away.

Brook's mouth just fell open as she looked to Ryder for an explanation. "And, I guess that's it?"

"No," he promised. "Um, we were kinda waiting until tonight was done. I mean, for the whole love talk, to make sure this thing with Rose wouldn't make you hate us, or any of the millions of other things I've been dreading." He closed his eyes and let his head drop to his chest. "And Owen wasn't even on my list of ways tonight could go wrong. I'm so sorry."

"Yeah, me too. Ryder, I liked being Rose. I kinda felt like I was good at it. I mean, this is what I've spent my life learning how to do. Not all at once, but piece by piece; it's all the things I'm comfortable with jammed together. I can do this, and if it helps you two sell books, then I'm more than happy to be Rose for as long as you need me."

From right behind her, Hunter said, "Forever and almost always?"

When she turned, she saw him standing there, clutching something behind his back. Dressed in his tuxedo, looking amazingly nervous, there was one place her mind immediately jumped, but she wasn't ready for a proposal yet. She wasn't even divorced!

"Hunter?" she asked, trying to figure out how the hell she was going to ask them to wait.

He swallowed, his eyes looking over her shoulder to meet her brothers. "Still want this?"

"I do," Ryder agreed.

"Guys," she tried, but Hunter pulled his arm out before she could finish.

And in his hand was a stack of papers. Five, maybe six sheets, all printed on very fancy letterhead, covered in paragraphs and words. "Brook, we want you to be Rose Solace for as long as you can manage. Regardless of what happens with our relationship, we still want you to represent us. We respect you and admire you, and I can't think of a more beautiful woman to be the face of my dreams and fantasies."

The air rushed out of her lungs in relief, and a giggle followed. "You..."

"Please?" he asked.

"Yes!" she agreed. "Yes, guys, I will be Rose. I will do my best, to be the best Rose I can." She giggled again. "Oh my god. I thought you were going to propose, and I'm not even divorced!"

Ryder's hand found her waist and he pressed a little closer. "That," he whispered in her ear, "isn't as easy." Then he stepped around her so he could see her face. "This is the first step. Most people wouldn't understand what Rose means to us, but I think you do. Signing this contract, Brook, makes you part of us. I'm not saying it's all I want, but this is the first step." He smiled at her so very sweetly. "Finding a way to make you my wife comes next. I don't even know how to make that possible, but I think we all have plenty of time to figure it out."

"Together," Hunter said. "Because we're so much better when it's the three of us."

She couldn't help herself. "A perfect little thruple."

Hunter groaned. "I take it back. She's not Rose! Our Rose would *never* use such a word!"

"I'm kidding," Brook promised, grinning from ear to ear. "I'm just kidding, I promise!"

He held out the paper again, but this time, Ryder reached into the inside pocket of his jacket and pulled out a pen. "Can we make it official?" he asked.

"Yes," Brook told them, taking the contract and the pen. "I will be your Rose, for now and forever after."

"She's not a wordsmith," Ryder told his brother.

"Nah," Hunter agreed, "but she looks really damned good in the dress."

Ryder made a noncommittal noise. "I'm willing to bet she looks better out of it."

"Yeah, but we have to be careful of the cut on her face. The doctor was very clear that she shouldn't stretch it too much. Means no blow jobs."

"I can work with that," Ryder agreed.

"Guys!" Brook hissed. "Unless you want me to write 'blow jobs' on this, you need to stop!"

They shared a look, both wearing identical grins. Brook ignored it, quickly scrawling her name on the last page. Then, she saw the numbers listed right above it. The numbers she should've read before putting her signature on this document. The numbers that outlined exactly what they intended to pay her for playing the part of their pseudonym.

"Thirty-three percent?" she asked, looking back.

"You're going to pay me a third of the royalties of *all* your books?"

Hunter nodded. "We talked about it, and we both feel that the only way for this to be fair is if we treat you exactly like we treat each other. Everything we have is yours, Brook. Every last thing, equally."

She had to press her lips together to keep from gasping. It took a minute, and she nodded to show she'd heard before she finally got control of her voice. "You really are heroes, aren't you?"

"No," Ryder told her, "but we always wanted to be."

"You are," she told him. "You're *my* heroes, and this is the best happy ending you've ever written."

EPILOGUE

*T*he hype from Rose Solace's debut lasted for almost two months. Sales of all books were up, and the offers for *Thou Shall Covet*, Naomi's book, were the best they'd ever had. The manuscript was complete, which, according to Hunter and Ryder, meant they needed to celebrate. With summer just around the corner, that Saturday was just begging for a cookout. The family kind.

The twins had wood burning down to charcoal in the grill out back. The dogs were all running around their fenced yard, except for Sherlock, who was well-mannered enough to stay at Hunter's side. Brook was in the kitchen, mixing up deviled eggs and potato salad. It was the kind of life she'd always dreamed of: comfortable.

Just then, a chorus of voices proved that the company had arrived. Hurrying, Brook gathered up her things and headed down the hall, past the office, and for the door that led onto the covered porch and open area between the dog barn and the fenced yard. The moment she got close to the door, Ryder hurried over to open it, seeing her full hands.

"Table's to the left," he said, looking like he wanted to help but was afraid of destroying her precarious balance.

Alison was there, setting her own dish down, but she saw Brook and scampered over to help. "Deviled eggs?" she asked, sounding thrilled.

Leah cleared her throat. "Can you eat those?"

Brook eased the tray onto the table, but she'd heard. "Ali?"

"You have to wait," she said.

So Brook looked over at Leah. "Really?"

A smile was her only answer.

Brook nodded. "Let me go get some lemonade, then, so we have a non-alcoholic option."

"Thank you," Alison mouthed silently.

But as she passed the grill, Hunter caught her waist, pulling her back against his chest so he could kiss her neck. "Where are you hurrying off to?"

"Drinks," she said, trying to wiggle free.

He turned her toward the cooler. "Right there, and if I'm lucky, you'll be the kind of girl that gets frisky when she's had a few."

"Girl?" Brook asked. "I'm a little old for that, mister."

"No way. Trust me, I've seen you naked. Definitely still a hot young thing." He grinned, but let her go, turning to his brother. "We need meat!"

"Lots of meat," Ryder agreed, moving to get the platter. "Meat for our girls!"

Brook just let them enjoy their bad jokes. She wasn't going to spoil this big reveal, and she needed a moment to get her wits together. Alison was pregnant! Her best friend was about to be a mother, which would make her an unofficial aunt. The moment she made it in the kitchen, she couldn't help herself. She did a foolish happy dance in place, getting it all out where no one could see. Then she grabbed the pitcher of lemonade and hurried back outside.

The best part of this get together was that no one needed to be ashamed. No one had to worry about what anyone else thought. Brook's boyfriends could be as cute and flirtatious as they wanted. Leah could cuddle with Alison and not have to hide it. It was so perfect that Brook felt like her cheeks were burning from the smile that simply would not go away.

And, as soon as she made it back outside, Leah started grinning. "So," she said, making everyone look over. "Alison has news."

Hunter and Ryder turned, looking both nervous and excited. Brook busied herself with pouring two glasses of lemonade so her best friend wouldn't suffer alone. Alison, however, just leaned back in her chair with a devious smirk.

"Well, sales are up. A few of your older novels hit the New York Times bestseller's list again. The news can't decide if this 'mommy porn' you're selling is the most evil and debauched thing ever, or the next best thing. The public, however, adores Rose Solace, and we have a request for her to speak at an event to raise money for domestic abuse victims."

"I'm in," Brook agreed without even thinking.

Ryder nodded. "Donate some signed books for auction, too."

"Fifty?" Ali asked.

"Make it a hundred," Hunter suggested. "Put half up for auction with all proceeds going to a charity. The other half she can sign and hand out at the event."

"I can do that," Alison agreed. "And do we have a status on Owen?"

Brook groaned. "He bonded out, but the judge made it clear that if he comes near me again, he'll be held without bail." She sighed. "Cessily did everything she could, but because he doesn't own a gun and has no criminal record, the court seems convinced it was just the passion of the moment."

"Seriously?" Leah asked.

Brook nodded. "And that's the biggest problem with domestic violence. It's never taken seriously until it's too late, and then everyone asks why she didn't get out sooner. That's why I want to do this event. If we can help someone without a rich and famous romance author waiting to save her? Yeah, I'm all for it."

Alison nodded. "I'll make sure people know that." Then she looked over at the guys. "Should we add child abuse victims to that?"

The men shared a look. Brook couldn't quite describe the expressions they flashed at each other, but she was finally learning how to read them. Hunter wasn't opposed, but Ryder thought they could do more. When Hunter gave in, Ryder turned back to the three women.

"Human trafficking victims," he said, the words coming out a little too heavily.

Leah twitched in her chair hard enough to slosh her drink across her leg. "Holy shit," she breathed.

"Guys," Ali said. "I don't know how I could write that into Rose's backstory."

"Her boyfriends," Hunter said softly. "I think it's time we stop hiding. With Brook keeping us at the edges of the spotlight, I think it's finally time we stop hiding from our own demons."

"Ok," Alison agreed. "But I'm running all of this past

you three first, ok? I'm not going to ever pry, but I don't want this to be more than you're ready for."

"Pry," Hunter told her. "Push. Don't let us keep running away from the things that are too shameful to talk about, but don't judge us for what we did." His eyes flicked to Brook. "She taught us that it's a lot easier to heal if we have someone on our side. Someone who knows and doesn't hate us for it."

"I will never hate you," Ali told them, her hand unconsciously going to her stomach.

Ryder noticed and sucked in a breath. "Ali?"

"Are you pregnant?" Hunter asked, sounding excited.

She nodded, glancing back to Leah. "Ten weeks, so still too early to say anything to most people. We could still lose them."

"Them?" Brook squealed. "Oh my god, Ali, are you having twins?"

"No," Leah groaned. "Worse!"

"Worse?" Hunter and Ryder asked in unison.

Alison just sighed. "Yeah. So, Ryder cursed us." She reached over for her purse and pulled out a postcard-sized picture filled with a black and white pattern. "This," she said, pointing at a pair of dark dots, "is the identical twins. One placenta, shared amniotic sac, and two little heartbeats." She smiled wistfully for a moment, then gestured to the other side. "And that dot there? That's the third one."

"Triplets?" Brook asked in shock.

"Oh yeah," Ali said. "Evidently we're getting this childbearing thing all out of the way at once. I mean..." She glanced over at Leah. "If they all make it. Granted, multiples are more common with in vitro, and the doctors were thrilled that it worked the first time, but *three?*"

"Never mind finding an apartment with enough rooms for all the kids. As infants, sure, but eventually, they're going to need their own rooms, and a yard big enough to play in..."

"Property next door is for sale," Ryder told his brother.

Hunter nodded. "I'll call a realtor tomorrow. Brook, you ok with that?"

"Huh?" she asked. "What am I being ok with?"

Hunter smiled at her. "Buying the mother of our child a house next door. Would make it a lot easier to spoil them."

"I'm in!" Brook agreed.

"Hunter!" Leah gasped. "You can't just *buy* us a house."

"You," he told her, "are about to raise our kids, and that was the deal. We'd donate, you'd be perfect moms. This is our donation."

"We did say we'd spoil them," Ryder added. "You just happen to get some extra benefits along the way. Besides, three babies are going to be a lot of work. Losing a mortgage payment means Ali won't have to pawn us off to another agent."

"He's got a point," Brook said.

Leah didn't care. Shaking her head, she just stood and walked over to Ryder, who was closest, and wrapped her arms around him. "Thank you," she told him. "You don't have to do any of this, but I know that won't stop you."

"No," Ryder agreed, "it won't."

She released him and turned for Hunter. "And you, too. You're a good man, Hunter."

"And you're going to be a great mom," he told her.

Then Leah found Brook and smothered her in a hug tight enough she could barely breathe. "You're the best sister-in-law I could've gotten. No matter what, you're not allowed to disappear again, you hear me?"

"Promise, but I kinda don't plan on going anywhere."

"Yeah, and we didn't plan on having *three* babies. Three! At once!" Leah laughed. "I'm not complaining, not at all, but seriously!"

"Oh, I know." Brook glanced back at the guys. "But you know... sometimes, when it rains, it pours. And that's not always a bad thing."

BOOKS BY KITTY COX

End of Days - Auryn Hadley & Kitty Cox writing as Cerise Cole **(Paranormal RH):** *Completed Series*

Still of the Night

Tainted Love

Enter Sandman

Highway to Hell

Falling For The Bull Riders (Contemporary Poly Romance):

In Process

Just Hold On

Spur It On

Jump Back On

We Ride On

Take Us On

Gamer Girls - co-written w/Auryn Hadley **(Contemporary Romance):** *Completed Series*

Flawed

Challenge Accepted

Virtual Reality

Fragged

Collateral Damage

For The Win

Game Over

Shades of Trouble - (Contemporary Poly Romance): *Completed Series*

Collide

Converge

Combust

Conquer

Ménage Contemporary Romance: *Standalone Book*

When it Rains

ABOUT THE AUTHOR

As you would expect, Kitty Cox has a love of cats, but also dogs, horses, and pretty much any animal. She's always enjoyed a good love story. A chance meeting involving a martini, a margarita, and some laughs with another author convinced her to finally put words to paper - and now she can't seem to stop.

From the sweet and tender idea of second chance romances, to the hot and dirty thrill of stories intended for adult audiences, the wonders of falling in love are where her imagination goes. She likes to blame it on the hot and spicy climate of her home town in Texas. Then again, it could just be a result of growing up on stolen romance novels hidden under her pillow at night.

∼

Merchandise is available from -
Etsy Shop (signed books) - The Book Muse -
www.etsy.com/shop/TheBookMuse

Threadless (clothes, etc) - The Book Muse -
https://thebookmuse.threadless.com/

∼

You can also join the fun on Discord -
https://discord.gg/Auryn-Kitty

Visit our Patreon site
www.patreon.com/Auryn_Kitty

Facebook readers group -
The Literary Army
www.facebook.com/groups/TheLiteraryArmy/

For a complete list of books by Kitty Cox:

My website -
kittycoxauthor.com

Amazon Author Page -
amazon.com/author/kittycox

Books2Read Reading List -
books2read.com/rl/KittyCox

Also visit any of the sites below:

- facebook.com/KittyCoxAuthor
- twitter.com/KittyCoxAuthor
- amazon.com/author/kittycox
- goodreads.com/KittyCox
- bookbub.com/authors/kitty-cox
- patreon.com/Auryn_Kitty

Made in the USA
Middletown, DE
05 July 2022

68461737R00257